TONY GLOVER

Cars Just Want To Be Rust

First published by Boxkite Ltd 2021

Copyright © 2021 by Tony Glover

All rights reserved. No part of this publication may be reproduced, stored or transmitted in any form or by any means, electronic, mechanical, photocopying, recording, scanning, or otherwise without written permission from the publisher. It is illegal to copy this book, post it to a website, or distribute it by any other means without permission.

This novel is entirely a work of fiction. The names, characters and incidents portrayed in it are the work of the author's imagination. Any resemblance to actual persons, living or dead, events or localities is entirely coincidental.

Tony Glover asserts the moral right to be identified as the author of this work.

Third edition

ISBN: 9798491086023

*This book was professionally typeset on Reedsy.
Find out more at reedsy.com*

Contents

Acknowledgement	v
CHAPTER ONE	1
CHAPTER TWO	3
CHAPTER THREE	12
CHAPTER FOUR	19
CHAPTER FIVE	23
CHAPTER SIX	36
CHAPTER SEVEN	44
CHAPTER EIGHT	59
CHAPTER NINE	69
CHAPTER TEN	73
CHAPTER ELEVEN	80
CHAPTER TWELVE	86
CHAPTER THIRTEEN	90
CHAPTER FOURTEEN	92
CHAPTER FIFTEEN	95
CHAPTER SIXTEEN	103
CHAPTER SEVENTEEN	111
CHAPTER EIGHTEEN	117
CHAPTER NINETEEN	121
CHAPTER TWENTY	128
CHAPTER TWENTY ONE	131
CHAPTER TWENTY TWO	141
CHAPTER TWENTY THREE	154

CHAPTER TWENTY FOUR	161
CHAPTER TWENTY FIVE	167
CHAPTER TWENTY SIX	169
CHAPTER TWENTY SEVEN	175
CHAPTER TWENTY EIGHT	184
CHAPTER TWENTY NINE	189
CHAPTER THIRTY	195
CHAPTER THIRTY ONE	198
CHAPTER THIRTY TWO	204
CHAPTER THIRTY THREE	208
CHAPTER THIRTY FOUR	219
CHAPTER THIRTY FIVE	225
CHAPTER THIRTY SIX	228
CHAPTER THIRTY SEVEN	234
CHAPTER THIRTY EIGHT	243
CHAPTER THIRTY NINE	247
CHAPTER FORTY	255
CHAPTER FORTY ONE	264
CHAPTER FORTY TWO	274
CHAPTER FORTY THREE	285
CHAPTER FORTY FOUR	296
CHAPTER FORTY FIVE	306
CHAPTER FORTY SIX	312
CHAPTER FORTY SEVEN	315
CHAPTER FORTY EIGHT	319
CHAPTER FORTY NINE	328
CHAPTER FIFTY	341
Exclusive	347
Reviews	348
Also by Tony Glover	349

Acknowledgement

To Stevie, Rose and Ruby

And with special thanks to Chris Glover,
Fiona Veitch Smith, Eric and Ailsa who gave me ideas.

CHAPTER ONE

West Neuk Farm

The wrench skidded on the nut, shredding skin from his knuckles. Richard hurled it across the floor and sucked blood from the cut.

'You not done yet?'

'This thing's an antique!'

'Cars just want to be rust, son.'

In a moment his father was beside him. They lay, side by side beneath the motor, gazing up at the engine. In another family, a happier one, this might have been a moment of intimacy – a father and son working together, sharing knowledge, laughing at each other's jokes. Richard Kane and his father worked in silence.

After a while Richard slid free, wiping oil and blood on his overalls. The old man's feet poked out from beneath the car. As he leaned against the bench Richard gazed down at the suede shoes, the grey socks and the green cords riding up to reveal his father's bony shins.

The Jag was chocked with wooden blocks stout enough to take the weight should the jack fail. Richard watched, fascinated, as the rear axle hovered an inch or so above the block; the gap between wood and steel opening and closing as the car moved. He crouched, peering beneath the car to watch his father tighten the wrench.

'Is it shifting?'

His father said nothing. He hated "stupid bloody questions." Richard observed the familiar face, the firm set of the jaw. Metal groaned against metal as the Jag shifted; an ounce of steel tilting the balance one way then another. His father paused a moment to wipe his brow. Richard rested his palm on the Jag's cool, sleek paintwork.

Whenever he looked back on those events he could recall no intent, one way or another. Perhaps it was curiosity rather than malice which led him to act as he did. It was as if someone else reached out a hand to nudge the block. Richard seemed to be watching the scene from above. A witness might have seen a dutiful son checking his father's safety. He slid the block to the side, easing it free. His father, leaning on the wrench, grunted as he felt the nut loosen.

'You *have* chocked this, Richard, haven't you?'

'Of course.' Richard smiled. His father grunted as he put all his strength into one last heave. The wrench turned; the nut squealed as it surrendered.

'Got it!' There was a kind of sigh as the car swayed, the smoothness of the movement belying her weight. She slid away, like a ship leaving harbour. The jack sprang clear, clanging against the bench as the car crashed down.

Richard watched blood spread across the garage floor.

CHAPTER TWO

In the gloom of a January dawn they poured through the broken doorway. A light flashed and Clive Lumley appeared at the top of the stairs, pulling a red silk dressing gown over plump shoulders.

'What the fuck are you doing?'

His voice was a roar; his throat thick with the mung of last night's booze and smoke. The banister rattled as Lumley thundered down the stairs, cheeks pink with rage. DS Bryson Prudhoe stood squarely in the hall of Kyloe House, waiting. He pulled the warrant from his pocket, unfolded the paper and dangled it in Lumley's face.

'Suspicion of Class A, Clive. Don't make a fuss, eh? There's a bonny lad!'

The big man froze; his brow creasing as he tried to focus, to make the shapes on the warrant into words. Officers squeezed past him and fanned out through the house.

'Clive?' Greta Lumley appeared at the top of the stairs, her dressing gown flapping like the wings of an exotic bird. 'What's happening, Clive?'

Lumley waved a hand, shooing his wife back into their bedroom. Bryson nodded at Kitty Lockwood, ordering her to follow.

'Stay with her Locky. We don't want anything "going missing".' Clive Lumley shot out a fleshy arm, blocking Kitty's way. Then he saw Bryson Prudhoe's face and thought better of it. Lumley shrugged, allowing Kitty to run up the stairs. She squeezed past as he sank to his haunches, dragging fat fingers through thinning hair.

Kyloe House was a sturdy Georgian mansion, surrounded by woodland. Officers moved from room to room. The search was thorough, almost clinical, yet it produced little. It was conducted in silence, punctuated by a rhythmic *chink chink* as Bryson fidgeted with the column of £2 coins he always carried in his pocket.

After half an hour Bryson held a muttered conference in the kitchen, out of Lumley's hearing.

'What's the griff?'

They avoided his eye. It was not going well. Bryson Prudhoe had hoped to find a large stash of Class A drugs; something that would tie Clive Lumley to the supply. There was nothing. Bryson scratched his cheek and smoothed his walrus moustache.

He climbed the stairs, picking his way past Lumley. Bryson trudged along the gallery towards the master bedroom. Lumley followed, showing more of his usual swagger.

'What's up, Mister P?' Lumley began to whistle. Bryson turned and was about to ask the title when it came to him. U2. *I still haven't found what I'm looking for...*

The floor of the Lumleys' bedroom was a prairie of white carpet; the pile as deep as snow. One wall of the bedroom was a floor-to-ceiling window overlooking the huge garden. In the grey mist a peacock strutted across the dew-soaked lawn.

CHAPTER TWO

Greta Lumley lay on the emperor-sized bed, flicking through a magazine. Her husband sat on the bed to watch as Bryson moved around, lifting clothes and peering into drawers.

'Your girlfriend here's searched them already,' drawled Greta.

Prudhoe glanced at Kitty Lockwood who sat on a chair by the window, her hands in her lap. He raised an eyebrow. Kitty shook her head, just once.

'You get off on this, don't you, Prudhoe?' said Lumley. 'It excites you. Sexually.' He nodded in Kitty's direction. 'You'll have to put more into it pet!' he laughed. 'Never seen a man more in need of a blow job!'

'No?' Kitty smiled. 'You'll see a lot where you're going.'

In the far corner of the room stood a baby grand piano; a vase of red roses on top. Bryson crossed the room and lifted the lid.

'I didn't know you were musical, Clive?' Bryson ran a finger along the keys, picking out a scale. 'Lovely tone...' His fingers marched slowly down the keyboard until they reached a low E. He sounded the note again. His head tilted as he tapped the key for a third time.

Bryson Prudhoe removed the vase of roses and handed them to Kitty Lockwood. He raised the lid of the piano. For a moment he was hidden from view. The strings twanged as he pushed his fingers into the guts of the piano. The sound rumbled on, fading like distant thunder. Then Bryson Prudhoe surfaced. Between his fingertips he dangled a clear plastic bag, stuffed with white powder.

'Bring me an evidence bag, Locky.' He smiled. 'I think we've found the lost chord...'

* * *

The evidence was bagged and tagged and logged. The property was secured and Clive and Greta Lumley were moved into the holding cells at Shaftoe Leazes Station. The interviews would take the best part of the day, so when Bryson released the rank and file officers they hit the canteen for a late breakfast.

Kitty Lockwood didn't join them. She accepted, instead, a lift from Des Tucker who promised to drop her at her "home" station in the village of Belfordham. Ten minutes into the journey and she was already regretting her decision. Tucker was paired with Andy Banforth and they sat side by side in the front of the car. Tucker had a shaved head and shoulders as wide as a tree. He winked at his partner.

'Locky here's promised a two's up on the way, Andy. In return for the lift.' Kitty closed her eyes and shook her head. Tucker slapped his thigh.

'Joke, pet! Don't have time for romance, do we Andy? '

'Don't have time to take a piss, Desmondo,' said Banforth.

Kitty was perched in the back seat of the patrol car, her book on her lap. She turned up her iPod and pushed the earphones deeper into her ears.

They barrelled along the Belfordham road. Des Tucker loved to terrify his passengers. Kitty felt herself flattened against the seat but was determined not to show fear. As they hurtled through the countryside Tucker kept up the flow of filthy stories, glancing in the mirror to gauge the effect they were having.

'Reading Proust again, Locky?'

Kitty knew that Des Tucker was puzzled by her. She rarely

joined in canteen banter and had heard him whisper that she was "a bit up her own arse." After six miles they reached the T-junction where the road to Belfordham met the Roman Road. The track dropped down from the moors and fell away, crossing the river on a bridge of honey-coloured stone. Tucker was keen to finish his story, so they sat at the junction for a moment.

'So there's this bucket in the corner of the room, right?' Tucker said.

His partner nodded, a weary grin on his face.

'And day by day, week by week this bugger's filling it with his own...*whoah!*'

A petrol-blue Citroen C2 flashed past the nose of Tucker's car, clearing it by a whisker. The Citroen rattled down the hill, bounced over the bridge and disappeared among the trees on the far bank.

'I'm not fucking having that!' They lurched onto the main road in pursuit. The engine purr became a roar, Tucker flashing his blues as they picked up speed. The needle climbed steadily around the dial: sixty, seventy-five. Kitty pulled the headphones from her ears and twisted the seatbelt around her wrist.

'What's happening, Des?'

Tucker said nothing, leaning over the steering wheel, willing the car onward.

The Belfordham road was little more than a broad lane. As it climbed out of the valley it ran through dense woodland. The branches met overhead and blocked out the sunlight. Beyond the flashing trees Kitty glimpsed newly-ploughed fields. The car bucked and rolled like a marble rattling down a pipe.

Andy Banforth grabbed the handle above his door. Tucker's

driving scared him. Both men rolled with the car as it took the bends and closed on the Citroen.

'Going for it, isn't he?' Banforth's voice was tight.

'PNC the twat,' said Tucker. 'Bet you we know him!'

Banforth grabbed the Airwave and called the pursuit in, though he couldn't read the plate on the Citroen. They glimpsed the car as it rounded the next bend.

'Get a number?'

'There's an N at the front.'

'Fantastic, Andy! An N. Fucking Hawkeye, they should call you.'

Their BMW leaped forward and they gained a few yards but the blue Citroen recovered, weaving between the edges of the tarmac, turning bends into straight road. In the back seat, Kitty stared at her knees. Every rise in the road bounced her from the seat. Her knuckles whitened as she twisted the seatbelt.

'Maybe if we slowed down, Des...?'

'Maybe what?'

'He might do the same?'

'That doesn't happen on *our* planet, Locky!' Tucker put his foot flat to the floor. He was buzzing; the adrenaline pumping. Kitty could see there was no way he would let the scrote escape.

They dogged the Citroen down three miles of twisting road. On the rim of the valley the lane straightened as it ran across wide, open moorland. Now they could see their quarry and were gaining all the time. A family of grouse tried to cross the road and the Citroen hit one, sending a cloud of feathers into the air. Now Banforth could read the Citroen's plate and he called in the numbers.

'Blue Citroen C2, November, Alpha...' They bucked over a

rise and the BMW left the ground. Kitty glimpsed the speedo over Tucker's shoulder – eighty five. The Citroen was losing ground but wouldn't give in. As they neared the end of the long, straight road it dipped between the trees and slipped out of sight. They heard the scream of tyres then a roar as a ton of metal was torn apart. Tucker stood on the brake and they screeched around the bend.

Shards of fibreglass lay scattered across the road like yellow pik-a-stiks. Tyre tracks snaked through the wreckage, disappearing through a car-shaped hole in the dry stone wall. The Citroen lay on its side in the field, one wheel slowly revolving. A pall of smoke drifted around the car.

'Fucking Ada!' said Tucker. 'Bit of a mess...' He parked by the ditch.

Banforth set hazard warnings around the crash site while Tucker called it in to Shaftoe Leazes.

Kitty picked her way across the newly-ploughed field. The scent of petrol hung in the air above the furrows of chocolate-coloured earth. As she reached the car the door opened and a head appeared. The driver was young: bull-necked with a shock of bright red hair. He heaved himself free and perched on the top of the car, panting. Kitty recognised the face. The driver tumbled from the car and measured his length in the mud. For a moment he lay still. When he pushed himself up his face was caked in thick mud. A dark welt scarred his brow. He glared at Kitty.

'You fucking bitch!' He spat a gobbet of mud at her feet.

'Come on Kevin,' sighed Kitty. 'Let's get you sorted out.'

* * *

Kevin Robb sat in the back of Tucker's car, his head between his knees. He was dazed and bruised, though without any broken bones. Banforth and Tucker were clearing the debris from the road.

'So, Kevin. What's happening?' said Kitty.

'A fucking canoe! I turned the corner and there was a sodding boat in the middle of the road.' The yellow wreckage was the remains of a canoe that Kitty guessed had fallen from a trailer. 'You going to charge me? That was some other twat's fault!'

'That's not my decision.'

'You fucking will, though, won't you. You cunt!'

'Language, Kevin.' Kitty rolled her book into a tube. 'I'd say it's pretty likely you'll be charged, wouldn't you?' Kevin looked away. He scratched his cheek. Flakes of dry mud fell on the seat.

'Why were you driving so fast?'

'I thought...' He shook his head, scrubbing his eyes with his fists. 'Because you fuckers were chasing me!'

'Have you been drinking, Kevin?'

'Course not!'

'Drugs?'

He shook his head and looked away, across the fields.

'It's the only thing, the ONLY thing!' he said, then stopped, wary of giving too much away. He scratched his arm as he watched Tucker and Banforth clear the road, scuffing the yellow fibreglass with the sides of their shoes.

Kitty looked at Kevin's face as he picked away the flakes of mud. They tried to hide it, to lock it inside the box, but it always spilled over. Anger was the only emotion young men felt they could reveal, she knew.

CHAPTER TWO

'Got a girlfriend?'

Kevin turned to look at her. For a moment she thought he was about to lash out.

'What's it to you?'

She shrugged. 'Just making conversation...I wondered if you want me to call anyone?'

Kevin looked at the floor, Kitty tried again.

'Who do you live with?'

'My mam. Up at Peckwinning.'

'What about your dad?'

Seconds ticked by. Nothing.

'That's a nice car,' said Kitty. 'The farm must be doing well, then...'

But Kevin Robb had finished talking for the day. Kitty sat back. Together they watched Tucker and Banforth kick the wreckage of the yellow canoe into the ditch by the side of the road.

CHAPTER THREE

Shaftoe Leazes

'Thing is, when you're dead, you're dead...' Bryson Prudhoe tore his doughnut in two, dunked the stub into his coffee and popped it between his lips. He stared into the distance, his jaws moving in a steady, bovine roll. Licking sugar from his fingers, Bryson dipped the remaining pastry into the cup. A gobbet of strawberry jam slid down his thumb. He licked it off then blushed when he realised Kitty was watching him. 'You're finito, aren't you?' he murmured. 'Gone.'

Kitty Lockwood raised an eyebrow and smiled in her loplsided way. 'That's a little bleak for me, Bryson, this early...'

They sat at their usual corner table in the canteen at Shaftoe Leazes: two outsiders, huddling together for company. The room buzzed with the murmur of afternoon conversation. The melamine table was sticky with spilt sugar; cratered with cup rings.

Bryson dusted sugar from his fingers. 'I've scooped up too many body parts.' He spread his hands on the table. 'When you've had that thing of breaking bad news to families, you know. This is it. There's nothing afterwards. We are fly shit on a window pane. Pardon my French. When you're dead, Locky, you're gone. Rubbed off. Forgotten.'

Bryson's moustache was frosted with sugar. He ran the tip of his tongue along the hairs, picking up stray grains. Kitty was fascinated by the way Bryson ate. It was grisly, yet strangely compelling.

'Life is one long struggle against destruction and decay. Entropy, isn't it? Holding it at bay. Everything falls apart...'

Kitty tried to change the subject. 'The Lumley job went well.'

'Sweet as a nut, wasn't it? In the end.'

Kitty nodded, smiling. She knew how hard Bryson had worked on that case.

'He's made millions out of other people's misery. Now it's his turn.'

'It was lucky. Finding that bag of gear. In the piano!'

She shook her head. Bryson looked down at his hands, spread his fingers wide. He nodded.

'You make your own luck, don't you?'

Sometimes it was difficult to know whether Bryson was joking. Aware that she was looking at him, his neck flushed pink.

'Anyway! Love you and leave you,' he sighed. 'I have a thousand bits of paper that need to be moved around.' Bryson squared his shoulders, pressing his palms on the table, ready to move.

'I'm done too,' said Kitty. She reached for her bag.

'A quiet afternoon then?' She knew that Bryson was curious about how she spent her time away from the job.

'I'm picking up Molly from school. I said we'd take the canoe out. It's warm enough.'

'It must be nice...' murmured Bryson. 'Communing with nature.'

A young woman in uniform appeared at the table. Orla Harrington, a Community Support Officer, tapped her pencil against her lip.

'Kitty? I'm having a bit of do. Friday. A sort of housewarming. At my new flat? If you fancied it? Any time from nine, really...' Orla glanced at Bryson. 'It's just a few mates. You know...'

It was clear the invitation did not extend to Kitty's plump, middle-aged colleague.

'A party? Right...' The prospect of getting hammered with Orla's friends was daunting, but Kitty knew the word in the station was that she was distant, almost unfriendly.

'Thanks, Orla! I'll get a sitter.'

'Coolio!' Orla scribbled Kitty's name on her pad as she walked away. She paused and turned. 'Sorry. Another thing: there's some random old biddy on the phone.' Orla glanced at her pad. 'The name sounded like ...Carole Robb, or something? She sounds pissed off!'

'OK.' Kitty looked at Bryson. 'Sounds like fun...'

Bryson screwed up his eyes at the afternoon sun slanting through the window. He tapped his fingers on the table. 'Guess you won't be needing that yoghurt?'

* * *

'Our Kevin tells me you've given him another producer.'

'That's right Mrs Robb. He needs to produce his documents by the end of the week. Licence. Certificate of insurance.'

'You're going to charge him with something, then?'

Kitty doodled a face on her pad.

'It's not my decision. He may be charged over the accident. How's he feeling?'

'What do you think you're playing at?'

'Kevin exceeded the speed limit down a narrow road for several miles. He didn't stop, even though it was clear we wanted a word. In the end he caused an accident. He was lucky he wasn't killed. He knows the score, Carole.'

'It was an emergency! Have you nothing better to do? This is harassment!'

'He never mentioned an emergency while he was talking to me, Mrs Robb.'

One of Orla Harrington's magazines lay open on the desk. Kitty started to fill in the quiz – 'Rah or Riff Raff?'.

Carole Robb's voice faded to a distant buzz, a wasp trapped in a jar.

Beside 'Hair Colour' Kitty wrote 'reddy brown,' then changed 'reddy' to 'ratty'. She answered 'What is your favourite look?' with 'worried.' 'Eye Colour?' Kitty wrote 'green,' then changed her answer to 'greenish.'

Carole Robb's moan became a rant. Kitty started to doodle black squares in the margin of the page. How did she get here? How was it that she was chained to a desk listening to another deluded mother defending her idiot man child?

Her mum had been so proud when Kitty got a place at York to study psychology; the first Lockwood to go to university. But Heather Lockwood was disappointed when Kitty fell pregnant in her final year and dropped out on the eve of her finals.

Then Kitty chose to follow her into the police force.

'Finish your course! Make something of your life, Katherine!'

'This *is* something, mother.'

Heather shook her head, vexed as ever by her daughter's obstinacy. They were in the kitchen of Heather's house on Cloud Street, folding the laundry. Heather flapped the sheet, shaking out the creases.

'It's no job for a woman.'

'It was good enough for you...'

'You won't fit in, pet! You've been to college.'

Her mother sat on the arm of the chair. 'Kitty, I started at Lumb Lane when I was eighteen. I walked in to the station fresh out of school. You know the first thing I saw?'

'I have no idea, mother.'

'Halfway up the stairs there's a police constable – a woman, your age – bent over the banister, skirt around her waist. She's yelping while the duty sergeant's tattooing her bottom with the date stamp!'

Kitty bit her lip, stifling a giggle. 'He'd be up on a charge now! Things have changed, mum.'

'I doubt it!' Then, softer: 'They're not bad people, pet. Coppers. They're just... different. Hard nosed. They have to be.' Heather Lockwood folded the pillowcase and handed it to her daughter. 'Is that really what you want?'

'It wasn't all ball gowns and cucumber sandwiches at Uni, y'know? If it happens, mother, I'll handle it.'

Her mother shook her head, flapping the creases from a towel. She knew she was wasting her breath. And so Kitty took the job and was spending her Wednesday afternoon listening to Carole Robb.

CHAPTER THREE

'We can't afford a fancy bloody lawyer! This farm barely makes enough to pay the bills!'

'Let me stop you there, Carole. Maybe you should direct this at Kevin.'

Kitty hung up. The silence was beautiful. It was only later that she recalled the remark about legal fees. Then the question she should have asked: if Kevin Robb was struggling to run a broken down hill farm, how could he afford to run a brand new Citroen?

* * *

In her early twenties Kitty gave little thought to death. Like all young people, she believed she was immortal. Having a child changed that. Now she could see the wheel of life turning as one generation replaced another. Heather, then herself, then Molly: like Russian dolls, one inside the next. Now she was the grown up. Now she must protect Molly, as her parents had looked out for her. She was in charge. She was the next in line.

She had not been completely honest when she had joined the force. She had blurred the facts, implying that Molly's father worked away, rather than that they had separated. It was not a huge lie. Heather Lockwood was always there if Kitty needed her.

During her medical the doctor had asked if she had any history of mental illness or depression. 'Nope. No problems.'

Seconds ticked by. He picked up her notes, reading them to himself. Finally, she cracked. Putting a finger to her lips, as if she had just remembered, she blurted out 'I *was* on

Lofepramine, come to think. Just for a couple of weeks.' The doctor waited. Kitty saw the notes trembling in his hands. 'You know? When my dad...'

The doctor nodded. He pencilled something into her file then peered over the rim of his glasses. 'No problems since?' Kitty shook her head.

'Nope. Sound as a pound.' The doctor ticked the box and moved on.

Much of the time around her father's funeral had been a blur. But she had, on two occasions, afterwards, imagined that she saw him. Three days after his death she glimpsed his face at the wheel of a passing car. It was a fleeting impression; her anxious mind fitting his face onto that of a passing stranger.

More disturbing was the time two months after his death. She was driving along a country lane at dusk. The light was fading and a brisk autumn breeze was swirling fallen leaves around the car. She had not been thinking of her father. Anxious to collect Molly from her minder, Kitty was pelting along Belfordham Road. As she passed through the shadow of a Scots Pine she heard her father call her name. It was a whisper, as if he was behind her shoulder.

'Kitty?' She whirled around, only to see an empty seat.

It had not happened since. Now and again she played with the idea, wondering if it were possible to have a conversation with her father. If she was having trouble with money, or with Molly, she asked his opinion. She imagined what he would say if he were there. It was a game, not a delusion.

It was not that she heard voices. It was more that she had a mental ear cocked, listening for them. Just in case.

CHAPTER FOUR

Liverpool

Neon light shimmered on Richard Kane's lean face.

He gazed up at the sign. Slender tubes of pink and lemon yellow had been twisted to form the words, 'Club Zanzibar.' Someone had spent a fortune making the place look so cheap.

For the last hour Richard had wandered the streets, wary of arriving too early. As he climbed the steps the bouncers, two solid cubes of meat and muscle, blocked his way.

'Evening, sir. Are we a member?' The man's voice was loaded with fake courtesy. Richard saw his own pallid face reflected in the bouncer's shades.

'I'm here on business. Just for tonight.'

The doorman looked him up and down then glanced at his colleague.

'No problem, sir. We can give you temporary membership.'

The bouncers moved apart and steered him inside. A greeter with lank blonde hair looked up from her knitting. She slid a stubby pen and blank form across the desk. Richard scribbled 'Simon Clark', the first name that came to mind. As he pushed away the form, he repeated his new name to himself, hoping it would stick. The greeter found her digital camera and framed up on his face. Richard protested, holding up his hand. Nothing should link him to this place. There must be no trail to follow. It was too late. The flash blinded him, a pink stain burned on his retina.

Dubstep thrummed through the walls, bass notes he could feel in his stomach. Richard and the pale girl waited. The printer chattered and his picture emerged, glossy and still damp, his hand a blur in the corner of the frame.

The man in the photo was a ghost: hollow-cheeked and skull white. When all of this was over Richard promised himself a long holiday. Somewhere hot – he deserved it.

The greeter slipped his card into a laminate. 'Simon Clark,' aka Richard Kane, was now a guest member of Club Zanzi. He pushed open the door to the 'VIP Room.'

The interior was as dark as a bruise. Uplighters threw a dim glow across the walls. The punters huddled in booths; needy eyes twitching to appraise each new arrival. Richard wandered through a haze of scent and sweat and leaned against the bar.

A DJ was hunched over her decks, ignoring the half dozen dancers who shuffled around the dance floor. Two women in their thirties were squabbling over a skinny youth who sat between them, a grin on his face. Fingers were pointed, voices raised. The room had an atmosphere of sourness, of desperation. The Zanzi was the kind of club where drinkers washed up at the end of an evening. This was not his sort of place at all.

The barman pushed a glass of cranberry vodka across the zinc. Richard paid and the barman held up his note to check if it was a forgery.

Drink this and go.

CHAPTER FOUR

Richard scanned the room, looking for his 'date'. A couple of tired and tipsy women glanced up, holding his gaze until he looked away. He had no idea what she looked like. He should have carried a folded newspaper or worn a red tie, so the woman would know. When his glass was empty he would leave. The DJ played 'A Love Supreme.' *Boo bam boo bah...*

A woman with tawny blonde hair slid onto the barstool, her leather skirt creaking as she moved; a mist of scent surrounded her. *What was the word for that? French...* At first glance she was in her late twenties. She looked him up and down, eyes flicking from shoes to suit to hair. *Cassolette...* Reaching into her purse the woman pulled out a note, folded it in two, lengthways. She held the note between her fingers to catch the eye of the barman. Her fingers were slender, the nails lacquered; the note a pale wand, strobing as she waved it. There were fine lines around the corners of her eyes. Early thirties, then. Richard held out his hand.

'I'm Richard. Are you looking for me?'

'I thought you might be!' She beamed. 'Champagne?'

Arched eyebrows, another smile. Richard nodded, scolding himself for using his real name. What had he called himself? *Simon Something?* It was gone. There was still a way out of this. He had made no promises, committed himself to nothing. He would slide off the stool, walk out, never see this woman or this place again. Drop his membership card down a grate and vanish into the night. He teetered on the edge. This was no time to quit.

He summoned the barman. 'Champagne. Two glasses.' She raised an eyebrow. He picked up the cue, the inference that he was mean.

'A bottle, then...why not?' She turned back, her smile in

place, her eyes fixed on his. 'So...'

'Tanya.'

'So...Tanya. You look just the way Clive described you.'

Tanya put her finger to her lips and Richard nodded. *No names.* The barman returned with the bottle and filled both glasses. 'Here's to success!' Richard raised his champagne. Tanya did the same. Appraising him over the rim of her glass, Tanya's cool gaze never left his pale, gaunt face.

'To crime,' she smiled.

CHAPTER FIVE

Belfordham – May Bank Holiday

Kitty Lockwood dropped into third gear, dabbing the brake as she reached the edge of town. Sunlight flickered through the avenue of limes, dappling her face and the road ahead. It was the first Saturday in May and the light was dazzling. Kitty scrabbled on the dash, searching for her shades. She opened the window and the 4x4 was filled with the scent of spring leaves and soft, melting tar.

The little town of Belfordham was jammed with Bank Holiday traffic. A tractor rattled up the hill to the mart, trailing a convoy of utility vehicles heading north to the lake. Holiday dads mopped sweat from their brows and growled at the kids in the back seat. Kitty slipped the Intercooler into neutral and waited for a gap in the traffic. She didn't wait long. Drivers were jumpy when they saw a police car; eager to please.

A posse of backpackers ambled along the pavement. The first walkers had appeared in town on Friday. The trickle grew to a flood as the temperature climbed into the twenties. For the shopkeepers of Belfordham, the walkers were the first sign of summer. Twitchers and tourists all brought cash into the town, but the walkers bought maps and newspapers, tins of dubbin and jumbo packs of Elastoplast.

They spent cash on phone cards, hiking socks and hand-carved walking sticks. When the sun went down they dangled sore feet in the river and supped pints of Belfordham Bitter. The sign at the edge of town read 'Belfordham Loves Walkers.' The town certainly loved their money.

The river ran through the centre of the town. A narrow stone bridge, built in the 1830s, spanned the water. Kitty joined the queue of cars. When she was cruising along the lanes Kitty listened to her iPod, but that wasn't such a good idea when she was driving through the town. The taxpayers didn't want to see officers swaying to Afrobeat while on duty. Nothing should distract her from the radio. So she drummed her fingers on the wheel and hummed a tune to herself.

The river was low, the edges lined with sun-bleached stone. The heatwave had caught everyone unawares. Two weeks ago, Kitty had been out in the canoe with Molly. If they tried it now she knew they would rip the skin on the rocks. She glanced over the parapet, glimpsing swatches of weed floating in the current. Salmon circled the pools, fretting as they waited for the rain that would let them upstream to spawn. Not a drop had fallen since the start of April. The dry spell had lasted forty-one days, the longest since 1910.

Kitty passed the Redesdale Hotel where the sun glinted on the BMWs and Discoveries that filled the car park. The hotel terrace was crowded with lunchtime drinkers, sipping Pimms. Kitty eased the car onto the main street. Her white blouse was no longer crisp and the Kevlar jacket pinched beneath her arms. She pushed her shades up the bridge of her nose and lifted the ponytail of brown hair, allowing the breeze to cool her neck.

The patrol car trundled past the playground, the fire station and the church hall. Belfordham was what the Tourist Board called 'a traditional Borders town.' The cobbled square that once held a busy market was now a car park. In the centre of the square stood the War Memorial, a bronze soldier standing guard over a stone that bore the names of the fallen – Carr, Robson, Pearson and Bell – names still common in the dale.

A queue snaked away from the door of the church hall as the women of Belfordham waited for the Saturday jumble sale to open. A figure stood in front of one of the stone houses which lined the square. She waved, trying to catch Kitty's eye. Kitty pulled up and the woman rested her hand on the sill, tucking wisps of her grey hair behind her ears.

'Thanks for coming, pet!' Mary Hetherington's voice was a whisper, yet faces from the jumble sale queue turned to stare, curious about Mary and the lady copper.

'Fancy a nice cup of tea, pet? Kettle's just boiled.'

* * *

Kitty sank into an armchair in the residents' lounge. The chair wheezed like a punctured balloon. A widescreen telly was mounted on one wall. Mary's handmade candles were displayed in the fireplace; dayglo price tags stuck into the wax. For a moment Kitty thought of buying one as a housewarming present for Orla; then she clocked the price.

Mary handed her tea in a china cup with a shortbread finger balanced on the saucer. She sat, raised her eyes to the ceiling and tried to recall the sequence of events.

'They arrived on Thursday and stayed that night. That was no problem.' Mary ran her fingers across her brow.' They both seemed canny, pet! Unusual, you know. For round here, like. Quite...exotic, I suppose. Well-dressed. But they seemed very canny!'

Kitty took out her pad and wrote 'Mary Hetherington' at the top of a clean page.

'They paid in advance – full whack!' said Mary. Kitty nodded, made a note, then started to doodle on her pad: eyes, paisley patterned fish and bonfires of jagged flames.

'Last night we were empty. So when they asked to stay an extra night, well...' Mary rubbed her finger and thumb together. 'Nathan, he called himself, the dark chap, said they were looking for a house around here. So they'd be out all morning.'

'Dark?'

'Sorry, pet?'

'You said, 'the dark chap'?'

Mary Hetherington circled her finger around her face.

'Dark skinned, you know?'

'He was black?'

'No, pet. Not black. What would you say? Mixed race, maybe? Is that the right word?'

Kitty made another note.

'And asthmatic. He used one of those little inhalers, at any rate. Kept puffing on it. Puffing away. And very smart! Dapper. He wore like, like a waistcoat, sort of carry on. With a chain and that. Watch on a chain, sort of thing? Like – I don't know – like very old fashioned. But he was *very* smart! Very clean. Very good looking. And a lovely voice! Low. Deep. Quite had me going, pet!'

'OK, Mary. Lovely. So... Tell me about the woman.'

'Called herself Tanya. She was a bit...flash, you might say. A bit of a ...' Mary mouthed the word 'tart,' then shrugged. The world had gone mad but she was coming to terms with it.

'She was white?'

Mary nodded.

'Tanned, I'd say. But white, yes. Slim. Attractive. Men would like her. Be all over her! But then ... anyway, this Tanya asked if I could cook lunch. Said they were going to look at a house and they'd be back at one. Not something I normally do – lunches. But these days we need all the cash we can get! Anyway, I had nothing in, did I? So I tappy-lappy down the Spar to get some bits and pieces. I left them in the house – the couple – 'getting ready,' they said. So I come back from the shop and they're gone. And that's the last I saw of the buggers!'

'Why d'you think they've done a bunk? Perhaps they've broken down? They could be on their way back...'

'I don't think so, Kitty, pet. They've had all the towels away, you see?'

Kitty nodded.

'All the soaps, too. Complimentary shower caps – which you would expect. Complimentary towelling robes – which you wouldn't. Folk draw the line at that, mostly...'

'Well...' Kitty shrugged. She was about to give Mary a crime number for her insurance company, then go into the usual riff about the Crime Prevention Officer, when Mary held up her hand.

'Plus! New telly on the wall in their room. Plasma Sony. Widescreen job. They unscrewed that and had it away. Plus – the DVD! Even the ruddy Freebox! Had the lot, the sods!'

Kitty looked sympathetic. But Mary hadn't finished. '*Then* there's the float. That's gone west! Four hundred quid in the till, I reckon. Four fifty. I should've banked yesterday, but...'

Kitty scribbled the details. 'Right...'

'So, no pet,' said Mary. 'I don't think the buggers are planning on coming back...'

Kitty flipped to a new page in her notebook. 'Ok Mary. Tell me again. What did they look like...?'

* * *

Nathan Turner – a tall, broad-shouldered man of around thirty five: mother from Liverpool, father from Sudan. A dapper dresser, almost foppish in his attention to detail: waistcoat, fob watch as well as a wristwatch – a Tag Heuer. A bit of a dandy, is Nathan. Physically fit, though asthmatic. Uses an inhaler.

One way or another, Nathan Turner brings misery into the life of everyone he encounters, starting with his mother and ending with the last person he meets on any given day.

Tanya Brown – in her early thirties. White, tanned, dark blonde hair with highlights; around five-seven in height. Tanya is attractive. Looks like she works out; or trained as a dancer, perhaps. She's limber, supple and toned. Men notice Tanya. Women too.

Both wear silver jewellery: rings, watches, studs. Nathan has a nipple ring, Tanya a pierced navel. Both are good looking, both well-dressed. They are fit, they are foxy, they are fun-loving criminals. Nathan and Tanya use different surnames when they are on the road: Tyler, Temperley, Richards, Renwick, Renton.

CHAPTER FIVE

'On the road' is when they are at work: all over Britain and Europe, when the mood takes them. Credit cards, kiting cheques, fraud, theft, dealing in drugs – the usual bag of tricks, plus a couple of their own invention. Nathan likes to keep it fluid, to think on his feet – that's all part of the fun. He keeps an edge on with a steady supply of white powder – cocaine when he can afford it, crystal meth when he can't. Tanya used to join him, but the truth is she doesn't enjoy it. She doesn't like the way it works on Nathan, either. He can get very mean. Very difficult. Vicious, at times.

She wants him to give it up, but Nathan will never do that, so Tanya doesn't waste her breath any more. There were times in the last year when she thought it was changing him. Changing his personality. Sometimes it seems he just doesn't care any more. He's somewhere else, in his head, somewhere beyond her. She doesn't rattle easily, but this is scary.

So, Nathan's weakness is clothes and food and Class A drugs. And Tanya's is falling for Class A losers. Like Nathan Turner.

Off the road, in their downtime, they like to unwind. They have their favourite spots – the Harlequin, the Camel, the Viper Lounge – though they like to drink at the Zanzi. That was where they met. That's where you can usually find them – the Zanzi.

Then again, most of the time, you can't find them at all...

* * *

The champagne bottle was empty.

'So...shall we get to it?' said Tanya. She was smiling, but it was all business. Tanya was bored. She ran her nails through her hair, shook it down. Conversation with this Richard was sticky. Either he was buttoned up or scared of revealing something. That was her guess. He was certainly full of himself. His accent was posh and he seemed straight, like some tweedy country gent. But he looked down his nose when he talked, as if catching the whiff of something unpleasant. And though he was drinking hard, he gave nothing away. It was time to find out what he wanted; time to discover how she and Nathan could bank some points.

Richard flopped onto the back seat of the taxi. She stretched out in the corner, but he followed her, leaning close, pushing his knee against her thigh.

'I'm not what you think,' he slurred, breathing vodka and cranberry over her face.

'Is that so?'

'Don't usually drink, as it happens.' He ran a finger down her forearm. Her skin was warm, the downy hair rising beneath his fingertips. 'Lovely skin.'

'*I* like it...' She pushed herself further into the corner as the cab turned out of Water Street onto New Quay. Slipping his free hand behind her head he pulled her close. Her hair looked soft, but felt brittle between his fingers. She allowed the kiss, her lips parting for a moment; a softness, an anemone, opening then closing. He slumped back and closed his eyes. The cranberry juice puckered his mouth.

Shouldn't drink vodka.

The taxi rumbled through the city night, down Primrose Road and along the river, passing the ferry terminal. Tanya turned to look out of her window, unsheathed her lipstick and

CHAPTER FIVE

repaired the damage. Richard stared at the taxi driver's neck, fixing his gaze on a ripe pimple above the man's collar.

The taxi dropped them near the Liver Building, close to the river. Richard tumbled onto the street, threw a twenty at the driver and slammed the door. A salty breeze chilled his face. He could smell the sea. He stood for a moment, eyes closed, listening to the river. The tide was beating up the Mersey, a steady pulse of water. Then Tanya slipped her hand through the crook of his arm and led him to a doorway. They were standing at the foot of a tall building. To steady himself, Richard grasped the stone facade, his fingertips burrowing into the chisel marks in the granite. He tilted his head to look up. The wall was as flat as the ocean floor, the cold stones disappearing into the darkness.

The door swung open and Tanya steered him into a dark lobby, the air scented with dust and floor polish. *Cardinal Floor Polish*, the name springing from some childhood memory. He saw his mother polishing the tiles, the smiling Cardinal on the lid of the tin. His mother happy: before the accident, before the silence.

Redness, spreading across the floor.

The door crashed shut, the clash echoing up into inky gloom. Tanya's heels click-clacked as they crossed the marble floor to the lift. All the offices were in darkness. Richard swayed as he read the list of tenants: Proctor Financial Services, Thoburn Debt Recovery, McCullock Factoring.

Tanya hit seven. The lift groaned through the darkness. She leaned against the wall and inspected her face in the mirror, touching the corner of her mouth with a fingertip.

The buttons glowed as they passed each floor. Two, three, four...

Richard got horny in lifts. The enforced intimacy in a public space always set him off. It was a Jekyll and Hyde transformation, an aloof City gent morphing into a Bonobo chimp as soon as the door clanged shut. He looked at Tanya's mouth, the jut of her bottom lip, plush with lipstick. Taking her wrist, he pulled her into a kiss. He was getting hard. He eased her into the corner of the lift, grinding his hips against hers. Was there a hint of desire now, or was she just keeping him sweet? He was too pissed to tell. She fended him off with her forearms, breaking the kiss. God, how he hated being drunk! Hated losing control.

The bell dinged. Tanya peeled herself free and strode down the corridor. He leaned against the lift door, watching her walk, the sway of her hips. She opened the door to a service flat. A wedge of yellow light spilled across the floor. Adrenaline kicked in and Richard was wary now, almost sober. His senses were wide open to danger. It was not too late to end this. He could slide the cage door shut, press the button and disappear.

Tanya paused by the door, smiling as she looked back at him.

When they were through the door Tanya flipped the lock and walked along a dark corridor. Richard shivered. This was a set up, he was sure. Some bad monkey would whack him with a pool cue. That would be the way it ended for him, blood pouring through split bone. He followed Tanya down the corridor: turning left, then right, then left again, like a rat in a maze. Tanya opened another door, this one sheathed in steel plate. He followed her inside.

The room was in darkness. A floor to ceiling window overlooked the river. Lights twinkled all the way along the waterfront, to Crosby and Fleetwood and beyond, up to the

CHAPTER FIVE

Cumbrian coast. On the horizon lay the coast of Galloway, a slender necklace of light.

The green glow of the LCD on the sound system was the only light in the room. *Spillane*, by John Zorn, screamed through the speakers; torn sheets of alto sax and drums like thunder. A big man, his frame eased into a leather recliner, gazed out of the window. He turned the remote in the palm of his hand, flipping it over and over, his fingertips dancing over the buttons.

A squall hit the side of the building and the window was spattered with rain. Raindrops rolled down the glass, melding the city lights. Tanya pressed a glass of whisky into Richard's hand.

'I'll be next door,' she said. She walked out, heels clicking.

The big man and Richard were alone. The man sipped his whisky. His finger tapped in time to the music, a silver ring chinking against the crystal. The track ended. They sat in darkness.

At last the man shifted in his seat. He turned and held out his hand. Richard moved a step nearer then hesitated, his pulse thudding in his throat. Would he be pulled down onto a blade, stabbed through the eye? The blade would twist; blood would stream down the blade. Richard blinked and took the man's hand. Placing his thumb on the big man's knuckle, he squeezed.

The man looked him in the eye. 'Welcome,' he said, without a smile. 'I'm Nathan.'

As he sipped his whisky, Richard watched the ice chink against the glass.

'Clive said you wanted a word,' breathed Nathan. His voice was deep, the rhythm gentle – a scouse Barry White. 'A bit of business,' he said; his voice a whisper. He pulled his inhaler from his waistcoat, puffed it between his lips.

'Yes.'

'So....tell me all about it, Mr K.'

'Clive said you might know someone. Someone who could do some work. A type of....' Richard's voice was a croak.

Nathan touched his shirt cuff. He took a tiny jack knife from his waistcoat pocket, opened the blade and chopped a line of coke on the glass table. Richard stared, a rabbit on a lonely road, wide eyed in the glare of the headlamps. Nathan leaned over the table, hoovering the line of powder into each nostril. He licked a fingertip, dabbed the stray grains and rubbed them into his gum. Then Nathan raised an eyebrow.

'I was told you were the man ... If I wanted ...'

In business meetings Richard was so assured. This was business. Why was he stumbling over the words? He had rehearsed this conversation in his head many times. It had never played like this.

Nathan held up a hand.

'It's a delicate subject.' He sighed, leaning back, feeling the coke hit, dove wings fluttering behind his eyes. After a moment Nathan leaned close, laying a finger on Richard's arm. 'Am I right?' Richard nodded. 'You need to lose something?'

Nathan lowered his head, his gaze still fixed on Richard, who nodded.

'I have a plan.'

'I bet you do,' sighed Nathan. His gaze drifted over the dark, freezing water, far below the window. 'Tell me your wife's name?'

Richard gulped whisky, too much to swallow. It burned all the way down to his stomach then flooded back.

CHAPTER FIVE

The wind splattered rain against the window. Nathan pulled his inhaler from his pocket, puffed it once, twice then tucked it away. 'Tell me what you have in mind.'

A foghorn sounded, the moan drifting through the shadows which covered the river.

Where's your bathroom?' Richard mumbled. 'I think I'm going to be sick....'

CHAPTER SIX

In the afternoon Kitty typed up Mary Hetherington's statement, listing the missing goods and the descriptions of Nathan Turner and Tanya Brown. She walked down the corridor to give a copy to Bryson Prudhoe. She found him, his head in his hands, staring at his office wall.

'We need a chat. Close the door. '

She closed it, softly, then sat down.

'It's this Lumley thing,' Bryson sighed.

Everyone knew that Clive Lumley was a major supplier of every drug from coke to ketamine, but building a case against him had been almost impossible. Lumley worked at one removed from his supply chain and ruled his dealers through fear. Bryson had worked on the case for eleven months. The dawn raid had been the culmination of all that intel and surveillance.

'We're going to Crown Court next month. That cocky sod Stafford's leading for the Crown.'

'That's good, isn't it?' said Kitty.

'There's a lot of flap about this case. I had to do a bit of arm twisting. The CPS wanted to drop it. They're still wavering.'

'You caught Clive in possession...'

'Yes.' Bryson scratched his chin. 'He's bleating about that.'

CHAPTER SIX

She could hear the anxiety in Bryson's voice. 'He says the evidence was planted.'

She closed her eyes. When she opened them she could not meet his gaze. She feared what she might see there.

'But I was in the room,' she said.

'So they'll call you. We need to have a little conflab. Just to make sure we're on the same page on this.'

Kitty nodded; a dip of the head.

'I wrote a statement. I don't know there's much to add to that.'

'Clive Lumley can afford a top brief. We need to be prepared.'

'Ok. No problem.'

She wanted to be anywhere else but in Bryson's office.

'Let's fix a time when we know the trial date. Hokey cokey?'

As she left his office, Kitty's smile faded. Something about their chat left her uneasy. She knew Bryson was a decent, honest man, yet something was wrong. She tried to recall what she had said in her statement.

'I saw DS Prudhoe lift the lid of the piano. He searched inside. When he lowered the lid he was holding a small plastic bag, which contained white powder. I took the bag and labelled it...'

That was the truth. Her conscience was clear. She, at least, did not *know* any more than that.

Kitty escaped the office as soon as her shift ended. She showered, changed into a T-shirt, leather jacket and jeans. She drove to town and raced through Sainsbury's, chucking tins into the trolley. Time was running short. By four she had picked up Molly from Jacqui's house and they were rattling down the lane towards their cottage in Cloud Street.

'How was school, kiddo?'

Molly stared through the windscreen, her brown eyes fixed on the road ahead.

'Fine.'

'How did the maths homework go down?'

They covered a quarter of a mile in the silence. Molly yawned.

'Fine.'

'That's good! You were worried about that, weren't you?'

Molly's eyes never left the road. She blinked.

'Well...' Kitty bit her lip. 'That's all good then.' She had never found an interrogation technique that worked on her daughter.

'After we eat, do you fancy taking the canoe up the river? You could take your camera, maybe?'

Her daughter turned away, watching the hedges flash by. She tapped her fingertips against the glass. 'What's for tea?'

* * *

Richard Kane stared through the window, lost in the jagged horizon of the Cumbrian Fells. The peaks were dark claws against the morning sky. His coffee cooled, the Danish pastry lay untouched. The taste of last night's whisky soured his mouth. He rarely touched drink.

He jumped when his mobile thrummed across the table. Richard pounced on the phone and scanned the screen, groaning as he read the caller ID: George Cunliffe. Closing his eyes, he took the call.

'George! Great to hear from you...'

'And it's a relief to hear you, sunshine. At fucking last!'

CHAPTER SIX

Cunliffe's throaty chuckle wheezed to the satellite and back again. 'The Scarlet fucking Pimpernel! Zey seek 'im 'ere...'

A muscle twitched in Richard's cheek.' What can I do for you, George?'

'You're a hard man to find, Dicky.'

'I'm a busy man, George. A very busy man.'

'Where are you?'

'Right now? I'm on the M6, at this very moment.'

'Where are you – exactly?'

'Tebay Services. Westmorland, you know?'

A line of traffic snaked down the M6 towards the Lakes. Richard wished he was amongst them, just another driver, lost in the column of cars. The old man always found the key in his back and turned it, twisting ever tighter. Richard hated George Cunliffe; he reminded him of his dear, departed father.

'Busy making money?' Behind Cunliffe's smile, Richard heard the snap and click of crocodile teeth.

'Doing my best, George. Got a meeting in Leeds shortly. Can we keep this brief?'

'We have a problem, Dicky.'

'Really?' Richard traced the blade of his knife across the table top, wishing it was Cunliffe's throat. *Dicky.*

'I've had a call from Steve Paiton. He's a contractor at Cutler's Wharf.'

'Right..?'

'Seems your cheque is a homing pigeon.'

'As I said George, I'm a bit pushed...'

'It's flown back.'

'Nonsense! Can't have done!' Richard felt giddy, swaying on the edge of a deep pit. For days he had suspected there would be a problem with the bank: he had prayed they would let the cheques go through. But little people always want to cut down tall poppies. Little people lacked vision.

'Paitons...'

'The wholesalers for the sparks, Dicky. Wiring, ducting, switches. Useful stuff to have in a house. *Those* Paitons! And they won't supply any more without payment!'

'So my cheque has...' He couldn't bring himself to say the word, 'bounced.' 'That surprises me, George. That does come as a complete surprise...'

Silence.

Richard prodded the screen of his laptop, as if the answer to his problems lay in there.

'You *specialise* in surprises, Richard! You should have been a magician. A fucking conjuror! Now can you surprise *everyone* by pulling some money out of your FUCKING TOP HAT?'

'Mmm... can you give me just a moment?'

'You know what they call you on site? Tricky Dicky' they're calling you. Tricky Fucking Dicky.'

Cunliffe was an oaf, thought Richard. A jumped-up bricky who managed to push his snout into the trough. Richard hated him. It was a pure hatred, a rich flood of venom that surged through his whole body. Cunliffe ploughed on, his voice scouring Richard's ears like a gravel wash.

'Steve Paiton has been calling you for days, Richard,' Cunliffe growled. 'He left messages but you never called back.'

'Yeah. I've been on the road. It's all been a bit hectic, to tell the truth.' Richard rubbed his brow. The little people always gave him a headache.

'Look, we need to sort this out!' Cunliffe sighed. 'This is the last lap, Dickie! They're beautiful apartments. Finishing touches, now, that's all. Wiring, paint job. Bish, bash, bosh and bring them to market. Six weeks. Two months, at the outside. But presales are dead. Buying off plan is finished. The golden years are long gone, sunshine.'

'Of course, George.' Richard looked up at the Cumbrian Fells. His gaze wandered over the spikes of stone. But there was no salvation to be found up there. This day of reckoning had been coming for weeks. It was ironic that the crisis had arrived just when he had taken steps to sort everything out. In another few weeks he'd have more than enough money. If only he could say that.

'Punters won't buy till they *see* what they're getting. And they can't see what they're getting until you pay the fucking contractors, can they, Richard?'

Cunliffe left a pause between each word, hammering them home. Richard could see his face. George was so like his own father. He was not merely an oaf, he was a pygmy, a midget. He was a coarse, ugly, provincial cretin who *deserved to die*. Cunliffe had no idea just who he was dicking around. He didn't know how close he was to the edge.

Silence. Static. Richard cleared his throat and dabbed the screen of his laptop.

'Well. I do take your point, George.'

'We're losing ten grand a week on this, Dicky. I'm in Liverpool tomorrow. At the Adelphi. Meet me there. Seven o'clock.'

'Absolutely! The Adelphi. Seven.' Richard tapped his screen. The mobile hissed in his ear while he entered the facts.

'So. What do I say to Paitons?'

Richard looked through the window, allowing his gaze to follow the line of the motorway. The road curved between the steep sides of the fells. Cars and trucks drifted towards the horizon, trailing plumes of dust in the hot, dry air.

'I'm seeing a client tomorrow, George. It's Abid Mirza. Remember him? From Leeds? He has a fabric warehouse. Loaded! Abid has a rather large cheque he wants to give us. He's talking about taking the whole third floor at Cutler's Wharf. Just ask Paitons to re-present. And I'll get on to the bank. I'll explain the funds are on the way, blah blah. We just need a month or so to get it all straight. .'

The earth turned. Clouds drifted over the hills, building castles in the blue sky. Why couldn't he be up there, away from the little people? The mental midgets?

Soon...

'Let me pay them, Dicky...'

The cunning old bastard. For a moment, Richard was tempted. But pride, and wariness, held him back him. 'I couldn't let you do that, George!'

If Cunliffe paid the contractors, it was the beginning of the end. Richard would start to lose control. Cutler's Wharf was *his* project, *his* vision. The only reason he had cuffed himself to the old lizard was because Cunliffe had cash. A bead of sweat rolled down his brow.

'You know, Richard...money's no object. It's not a problem for me. I'd sooner put the *gelt* in than lose their goodwill.'

'I've spent my life in banking, George. I know how they work. I'll have a word. This really isn't a problem.'

'So you say.'

'When banks pretend to be angry it's purely synthetic. It's a tactic. They use whatever works.'

'Don't patronise me, Richard.'

'I'm not George. Sincerely. All I'm saying is, with banks it's never personal. It's just business. Let's talk when we meet.

It's a blip. We proceed as planned.'

Without another word, Richard closed his phone. His brow was dripping – a coke sweat. He'd cut down lately but the stuff was still there, in his blood. He could almost see it. When Nathan had offered him a line he couldn't refuse it, though he'd thrown up all over the bathroom. His heart kicked a beat, racing for a second.

He pressed his palms against his eyes, pushing them deeper into the sockets. Stars flashed and he felt his bones turning to soap. A few seconds later the panic passed. It was a bad idea to stop suddenly. He'd have a word. Text his dealer. Get the red-headed kid to drop it off. Just a little bump. Something for the weekend. He deserved it, for fuck's sake!

As he walked across the car park Richard looked up at the Fells. Sheep were grazing the hillside, tiny specks of grey against the green. They didn't have to go through this kind of shit. One fine day the slaughterman arrived and boosh! No idea when it was coming. No money maze. No mental midgets who had to be finessed, soothed and flattered. Sheep had life sorted out, the little woolly bastards!

He turned the key in the Porsche. The motor purred. The sweetness of the morning had gone. He could see George Cunliffe's face: the oily grey hair, the dark trenches beside his mouth. That fleshy nose, mottled with broken veins. Richard balled his hands and screamed, smashing his fists on the leather steering wheel. He slapped the window and pummelled the door until the knuckles were skinned. He sucked blood from the cuts and suddenly he was there again, back there in the garage, looking down at his father. Watching the blood as it oozed across the floor.

CHAPTER SEVEN

Kitty Lockwood spent her morning in the hills, chasing up fine defaulters. It was an endless quest; a Moebius strip of blank looks and missing documents. There was no single moment when the job could be signed off and forgotten. Many of the young men – they were *all* young men – had persuaded their mothers to lie for them. Some mothers will do anything to protect their sons.

Kevin Robb had been charged with careless driving. As Kitty expected, Kevin had failed to produce his documents at the station.

Carole Robb met Kitty at the farm gate. Carole's jaw was set, her raw fingers twisting a tea towel into tight knots. Kitty sensed this might get tricky.

'If it's Kevin you're after pet, you can save your breath!'

'Is that so, Carole?'

'He's popped over the Carter Bar. To fetch a fan belt for the tractor.'

'OK. I'll try to catch him later. Any idea when he'll be back?'

'Nope.'

'Perhaps you could try his mobile?'

'It's on charge.'

CHAPTER SEVEN

'Right...'

Carole put her finger to her lip, as if she had just remembered something. 'It's Friday, isn't it?'

'It is, Carole. Today is Friday. And that means....?'

'He drives over to Jedburgh, Fridays. Stays over, often as not. He's got friends there. Lads he knows from college. I've told him, I don't want him driving back with a skinful.'

'Very wise.' Kitty took out her notebook. 'Perhaps he's staying over with his girlfriend?'

Carole Robb pursed her lips and looked up towards the hillside. She rubbed her hands on the tea towel. 'It's a long time since *that* one was a girl!'

'He's found himself an older woman?' Kitty had no intent other than to keep the conversation ticking, but she knew she had struck a nerve.

'More money than sense, that one...' Carole stopped. She put her fingers to her lips, as if to stop the words from spilling out.

'You don't approve?'

'She twists her little finger and he comes running.'

'You think that's where he might be? Right now? With this girl ... woman?'

'You tell me, pet. He's a grown man. You know what they're like.'

Kitty saw tears well in Carole Robb's eye. She pretended to scratch the details in her notebook. 'This is getting complicated, Carole. He's getting in deeper.'

The older woman touched the corner of her pinny to her eye. 'I've told him. What more can I do?'

'How's he get on with his dad?'

As soon as the words were spoken, Kitty realised her mistake.

She knew that Carole's husband had killed himself. She bit her lip but it was too late to take back the words.

'His dad did away with himself. Money troubles... '

Kitty realised that the whole story had been condensed into those two short sentences. She pretended to write a note.

'I'm very sorry, Mrs Robb.' The woman shrugged.

'Kevin is talking about joining up.'

'Joining...?'

'The Army. No future in any of this, is there?' Carole looked around the yard, shaking her head. 'He wants to work as a driver. If you do him for this careless driving or whatever, they won't have him. Will they?'

Kitty closed her notebook and tucked it into her pocket. 'I don't know, Carole. I'm just the messenger. I'm sorry.'

She watched Carole Robb look away, turning her face towards the hills. Kevin was a boy, not a man, whatever his mother thought. Now she was losing him, one way or another.

'Kevin must be spending a fortune on that car. How can he afford that?' A skylark rose from the hillside, twisting and turning into the sky. Carole had not heard the question, it seemed. Kitty watched the bird rise, feigning injury to distract predators from her young. 'I don't want this to get any worse than it is, Carole. Will you tell him that?'

Kevin's mother glared at Kitty, her eyes glittered, hard as flint. As Kitty trudged back to the car, the only sound was the skylark, singing as it climbed into the clear, blue sky.

* * *

CHAPTER SEVEN

At one, Kitty ticked off the last name on her list, aimed the 4 x 4 down the valley road and headed for home.

The sun beat down. Fields of rape and clover shimmered in the haze. The interior of the car softened in the heat, releasing the scent of oil and warm plastic. Kitty cruised the lanes with her windows open, grateful for the shade when she left open moorland for an avenue of trees. Her head was sore, tender from last night's bottle of Merlot.

Drinking alone, dad. Isn't that one of the signs of alcoholism?

A glass of wine helped her to switch off, to put a full-stop on the day. She yawned and gave in to the temptation to pull over into a sheltered spot for a nap. She would leave the Airwave switched on, so her conscience would be clear. Nothing was happening. Five minutes resting the old rods and cones wouldn't hurt.

She passed through a tiny hamlet called Hott; a handful of stone cottages clustered beside an empty pub. Here the road ran beside the river, winding along the floor of the valley. Sometimes it ran across open country, at others beneath the shade of silver birch and Scots' Pine. This was one of the routes she had taken on the police driving test. She had driven at speed down this lane in full body armour, telling the examiner everything she was doing. She smiled, remembering that when she had seen the sign for deer crossing she had burbled '*Look out for Rudolph,*' the first words that came to mind.

Kitty pulled into a field gateway and switched off the motor. She lowered the visor to shield her eyes. The engine ticked and sighed beneath the bonnet. The scent of melting tar drifted through the open window. In the hedge beside the road, bumble bees hummed over the hawthorn blossom.

She closed her eyes, listening to the air moving through the leaves. Letting herself go, she floated down through the layers. A van passed and the police car rocked gently in the slipstream. The breeze riffled the trees above the car and she was gone.

Ten minutes later she woke with a start. Running the back of her hand across her mouth she pushed herself upright. Her throat was raw, her eyes scratchy. She blinked until the world came into focus. The lane was deserted.

Kitty looked in the mirror and raked her fingers through her hair. That was the moment she saw her. A figure was walking in the road, fifty yards away: a youngish woman, padding up the centre of the dusty road, walking towards her. The woman was slim, with pale skin and a tangle of black hair. She was in her late twenties, perhaps older. She wore a black Levi vest and black denims. Her feet were bare, stained with dust and melted tar. Though this stretch was usually quiet, it was narrow, the road twisting around blind bends. Walking in the middle of the lane was madness.

The woman in black glanced up at the sun, swaying as she shielded her eyes. She strode on, her pace unrelenting, her eyes fixed on the horizon. Her lips moved, as if she was in conversation.

Kitty heard a sound from down the valley, the drone of a car as the driver changed from third gear to fourth; the note rising to a whine as he shifted up to fifth.

She leaned a bare arm on the sill, the hot metal burning her skin. 'Afternoon.'

The woman strode on, muttering under her breath. It seemed Kitty was invisible. As she drew level Kitty was struck by her eyes, a soft, misty green, like fragments of sea glass. But her stare was fixed, the pupils pinpricks. The drone of a distant car grew as it climbed the valley, a harsh growl now,

CHAPTER SEVEN

steel against steel.

'WAIT!' The woman froze, tilting her head, blinking in the hard white sunlight. Kitty cleared her throat, softened her tone. 'Sorry. Would you mind getting into the car?'

The woman turned to look at Kitty. Her eyes focused as she tuned in to the world.

'Sorry?' Her hands were trembling. 'What did you say?'

Kitty softened her voice, trying to seem less threatening. 'It's probably not a good idea to walk in the middle of this road. I know it seems quiet here but...'

The woman whirled around, as if seeing her surroundings for the first time. She passed her fingers across her brow, up and down her skin. 'I'm walking.'

'It's *where* you're walking that concerns me.' The heat made Kitty tetchy. She had woken with a headache and was taking it out on this woman. She tried to smile. 'You might cause an accident.'

'I don't think so,' said the woman. The car was closer now, somewhere around the next bend and approaching fast. Kitty flashed an image of torn limbs scattered on the road, soft flesh bleeding into warm tar.

'*Please* get in the car!'

The woman turned away, her eyes flicking back and forth. The angry drone was almost there. The car roared around the corner. Kitty opened her door and leaped into the road, seizing the woman by her elbow. The car screamed towards them, surfing on air, tyres barely clinging to the tarmac. Kitty slammed the woman against her door and held her, pressing their bodies tight against the metal. She glimpsed the driver, red-faced and wide-eyed as he hunched over the wheel. Though the glimpse was brief, she knew it was Kevin

Robb.

As the Citroen screamed past, Kitty closed her eyes, turning away on instinct, braced for the impact. The roar of the engine surrounded them, filling the air. She pressed her cheek against the face of the stranger. Kevin dabbed the brake, swerved and shot past them, scattering gravel chippings in his wake. Kitty breathed a lungful of dust. Kevin Robb glanced in his mirror, floored the pedal and was gone. The paintwork was dented and mottled with primer, but Kevin had got his precious car back on the road. Now he was testing his toy, pushing it to the limit. Kitty relaxed her grip and turned to see the woman grinning as she watched the car disappear.

* * *

She sat in the passenger seat, looking straight ahead, her eyes focused on the horizon.

'Name?' Kitty waited, her pencil poised.

'Dorian. Dorian Kane.'

'Where do you live, Doreen?'

'It's Dorian.' She said her name slowly, stressing each syllable as if talking to a child. 'It's Greek — I hate it. My father's idea. Next question.'

'Where do you live? ...Dorian.' Dorian Kane turned. For a long while she let her eyes rove over Kitty's face. Kitty was about to repeat the question when she answered.

'West Neuk. The farm.'

'Alone?'

'With my husband. Richard.' In a whisper she added, 'It's a wonderful place to live.'

'I'm sure it is. But that's quite a step from here.'

'*Quite a step?*' Dorian tilted her head, smiling as she mimicked Kitty's accent.

'A step. A fair distance. A long way for an afternoon stroll. You must have walked five or six miles.' She glanced at Dorian's tar-streaked feet. 'In bare feet.'

'I was only walking down the road. I wasn't hurting anyone. Why don't you chase that car instead? Is it because you couldn't catch him..?'

Dorian turned away, suddenly bored. She gazed through the windscreen and narrowed her eyes as she scratched a fingernail across the window glass.

'I know who that was.'

'Really?' For a moment Dorian's smug, knowing smile faltered.

'I'll sort him out later.'

'Have I done something wrong?'

Kitty found it hard to meet those green eyes. She turned to look down the lane. A carrion crow tumbled from a pine, falling upon a dark stain in the road. The bird clawed the roadkill, stabbing with her beak before tearing and swallowing sticky flesh.

'I don't know, Dorian. Have you?'

'Then why stop me?'

'I'd stop anyone walking down the middle of the road. It's a long way to the nearest hospital.'

'Yes...' Dorian smiled. 'Probably "quite a step"...'

Kitty wanted to slap the smile from her face. Her stab vest pricked, she was tired and she needed to go home. She wanted to sink into a warm bath and soak away the memory of this stupid woman. 'I'm the clown who'd scrape you up and take you there! I have other plans for this evening, Dorian.'

A glass of Merlot. A nice juicy murder on the telly.

Kitty was surprised by the way this woman provoked her. For a moment she considered hitting the Airwave, calling in to see if Dorian Kane had any previous form. But she had committed no offence. She was a little zany, a little drunk perhaps, but not a villain. All Kitty wanted was to finish her shift and go home. No-one had died.

'Look. I'll give you a lift home and we'll forget about it.'

Dorian raised her head and lowered it: a half nod, like a sulky child. Kitty turned the key and they rolled onto the road. They bimbled up the valley road in silence. All the while Kitty was aware of the other woman's presence. There was an odd atmosphere in the car; an imminence, a thickening in the air before a storm.

'*Watch her*,' said the voice in Kitty's head. Yet such caution seemed over the top. The woman was eccentric; that was all. She was distressed, not dangerous. 'But this is important,' said the voice.

As they rattled along, Kitty watched her from the corner of her eye. She noticed Dorian's black jeans were *7 for All Mankind*. Belfordham women favoured outdoor kit, fleeces and cords in fawn or lovat. They rarely wore black, except at funerals. The studs in her ears were discreet and expensive, new moons in silver. Her watch was an *Aquaracer*. Kitty recognised it because she lusted after the same model. Bohemian but well-heeled, that was Dorian Kane. She was used to comfort, used to money.

But there was more. Kitty noted the tremor in her hand as she pushed her fingers through her dark hair. Her tongue was stained a shade of plum: red wine. There was no smell of drink, though her speech was over controlled and her tongue and teeth were stained. Her strangeness might be down to mental illness, or drugs, perhaps.

Kitty counted the symptoms, trying to match them to a drug. Ketamine was everywhere in the countryside; it worked on farmers as well as their livestock. But Special K didn't seem the sort of drug a well-spoken, upper class woman would choose. Cocaine was the most likely drug of choice. Kitty had heard of middle-class users cleaning their crack pipes in the dishwasher. With biodegradable tablets, naturally...

'You and your husband have a fight?' The heavy tyres of the 4x4 hummed over the soft tarmac.

'It wasn't his fault.'

Kitty waited for her passenger to continue, but there was only silence. She tried again. 'I used to fight with my boyfriend. We fought all the time!'

Dorian tapped her nails on the window. 'It wasn't my fault, either, I suppose.' She seemed fascinated by the window, as if this was the first time she had seen glass. 'Is a kiss so bad? One kiss?'

'I suppose it depends on who you kiss...' But before Kitty could finish, Dorian had moved on.

'I suppose I like being told what to do,' she said. 'Doesn't everybody?'

'Well, I wouldn't say that...'

'Richard was stressed,' she said. 'It was nothing! Really! But before I had a chance to explain he went postal! So I thought it was a good idea to give him a bit of space?' There it was again: the rising inflection, as if she were asking a question. 'It's not his fault. It's not the boy. It's me.'

'Why do you say that?'

'Sometimes I behave badly.'

Dorian brushed a strand of hair from her face. Kitty waited, but it seemed there would be no more. She tried again.

'My bloke and I used to fight about money, mostly...' Dorian didn't pick that up, so Kitty tried again. 'Is he a sulker? That's the worst...'

Silence.

'So he was jealous?'

'Everyone gets jealous, don't they?'

Kitty chose her words with care. 'I'm sure. Does it ever get physical?'

Dorian stared at the side of Kitty's face. She giggled; a cackle that ran on too long. Hairs rose on Kitty's neck.

'*Of course* it "gets physical"!' Dorian trilled like a love-struck teenager. 'Richard *loves* me!' She glared at Kitty, an incredulous smile on her face. 'Perhaps *you* should "get physical"! You look like you need it!'

Dorian snorted with laughter, shaking her head. 'Richard would never hurt me.' The car entered a tunnel of lime trees and their shadows flickered across Dorian's face. 'Unless I wanted him to.'

* * *

As soon as they reached the house, Kitty realised that she had seen it before. She had driven past the place many times, each time wondering who was lucky enough to live there. West Neuk was a rambling farmhouse clinging to the side of the valley. The walls were thick stacks of sandstone, the edges worn smooth by centuries of wind and rain. Hadrian's Wall ran along a ridge a mile to the north. Over the last two thousand years, stone had been robbed from the Wall to build barns and shielings. Like every other house in the upper valley, West Neuk was built from stones cut by the Romans.

Dorian's home was surrounded by four Scots Pines, standing sentry at the corners of the house. Behind the house the land rose to a ridge, topped by a copse of pine and Sitka spruce. Kitty jumped down from the police car, the door slamming as it was caught by a gust of wind. The wind whipped her hair into her eyes. Dorian trailed behind her as she crossed the gravel turning circle in front of the house.

'What a beautiful view!' Kitty looked up at the surrounding hills. Dorian muttered something that Kitty didn't catch. Conversation with the woman was difficult – she was always a beat behind. Even a simple exchange was mistimed, out of phase, like a transatlantic phone call.

Kitty let the knocker fall on the studded oak door. Dorian hung back, running her bare feet through the gravel.

'It's OK. I can let myself in.' The tremor in her hands had lessened, yet she tugged at the sleeves of her shirt, covering her hands like a child. 'You needn't stay. Really. I'm sure you have lots of wicked people to catch.'

'I'll just let your husband know why you came home in a police car. He might be worried. Might think you've had an accident.'

Dorian closed her eyes and turned away, her face to the breeze. The front door jerked open and Richard Kane was there, his eyes flicking from Dorian to Kitty.

'What's happened?'

'Nothing to worry about, sir.'

'Where the hell have you been?' This was directed at Dorian.

'Mr Kane, is it?' said Kitty, moving between the pair, smiling as she spoke.

Richard Kane was tall; his neck long, his shoulders broad. His eyes were striking: the pupils dark, dilated against a blue grey iris, the colour of the sea. They were quite a pair, Richard and Dorian. That would be how they would be known, Kitty surmised: Richard and Dorian. He was clearly the Alpha male...

Kane's short, dark hair stood up from his head. For a moment he reminded her of Gregory, Molly's father. He had the same build, the same arrogant stare. On some level Kitty recognised that Richard Kane was the type of man she found attractive. Her favourable impression was short lived.

'I found Dorian walking up the road, towards Hott. So I gave her a lift home.'

'You *'found'* her? What do you want? A medal? She wasn't *'lost'!* '

His rudeness almost made Kitty laugh. 'No! I was...'

'Has she done anything wrong?' He glanced at Dorian, glared at Kitty.

'Not as far as I know, sir.'

Kitty shifted into icy formality. She knew better than to raise the temperature with a man who seemed so close to the edge. But Richard Kane seemed to take this as a sign that she feared him. Kitty sensed his move from defence to attack. He stepped forward, looming over her. She found herself looking up into his eyes.

'I was concerned about her, sir,' she said.

His stare was intense, the eyes still. Then he tilted his head, softening his voice as he spoke. 'Concerned about *what*, exactly?'

Dorian Kane gazed down the valley, scuffing the gravel with

her bare feet.

'Mrs Kane was walking in the middle of the road, which is not....'

'Walking in the middle of the road?' He stretched each word, as if he could scarcely believe his ears.

'Her general demeanour...' Kitty began. She felt herself blush. Richard Kane was smirking now. 'She said you'd had a fight.'

'We had a small, domestic disagreement.' Richard glanced at his wife, his voice soft as velvet. 'The sort of difference of opinion most grown ups have. We had a nice lunch. My wife had a little bit to drink. Not illegal, is it?'

'You had guests?'

'I don't think that's any of your business, is it?'

'No. Of course not...'

Kitty held his gaze. He seemed to be smiling, yet his cold eyes bored into her. She fixed her gaze on the bridge of his nose and curled her toes, pushing all her fear into that one, invisible place. A pulse ticked in her neck. Then Richard Kane looked away, shaking his head.

'Are you married?'

'I'm ... I was in a ...' Kitty stopped. She took a breath. 'That's not important.' She had almost broken a cardinal rule, telling him something personal. It seemed he had got beneath her guard and that disturbed her.

'Then I'm sure you understand. It was nothing. I was a little jealous. It was a misunderstanding. People have arguments. They blow over.'

Dorian Kane, her head bowed, slipped between them. As she passed, Richard linked his fingers around her wrist and drew her inside the doorway.

'Thank you. So much.'

Kane steered Dorian into the darkness beyond. Just inside the doorway an ornate fisheye mirror hung on the wall. In the distorted glass Kitty glimpsed the oxblood sheen of terracotta tiles. In the reflection she could see Richard Kane, holding his wife by the wrist.

The door slammed. Kitty stood on the doorstep, her face almost touching the bleached panels of the oak door. A sound came from the hallway beyond – a cry perhaps, or a peal of laughter. Kitty blew air between her lips. She walked to her car, her footsteps crunching the gravel. The wind crackled through the pines, tugging at strands of her hair. To the west, slate-grey cloud gathered above the fells. Towering peaks of cumulus, furling and folding in on themselves. As she closed the door the sound of distant thunder rolled through the hills.

The heatwave was starting to break.

CHAPTER EIGHT

'Get away, will you! That party will be finished before you get there!' Jacqui Speed pushed her friend towards the door.

Kitty's reluctance was genuine. When Jacqui offered to babysit Molly that evening, Kitty had mixed feelings. Part of her hoped that her friend was booked elsewhere, so she could phone Orla and cancel with a clear conscience.

'You've bought the lass a present! And you never know who might be there!' Kitty raised her eyebrows, pointing at the back of Molly's head. 'Got to let the dog see the rabbit, petal,' Jacqui whispered.

'I'm just going along to be polite,' said Kitty. 'A couple of drinks and then I'm out.'

Kitty had known Jacqui since they were in Mrs Clark's A-level English class at the high school. She was bridesmaid when Jacqui married Trevor, her boyfriend since she was fourteen. They had few secrets.

'There's no need to rush back. I'll make up the spare bed. Molly can stay here, can't you, pet?' Molly nodded. Kitty knew that she loved staying at Jacqui's house. When Kitty asked her why, she said the Speeds were a 'proper family.'

Kitty walked through the town to Orla's flat, which lay at

the end of Carlton Terrace, a quiet cul de sac by the railway line. As she neared the door she heard laughter and the steady thud of music coming from the open window. It was a warm evening; the bats diving and swooping between the sycamores along the tracks.

Kitty knocked on the door. It was yanked open by "Desperate" Des Tucker, out of uniform and half out of his head. Tucker bounced around her like a puppy.

'Evening Ossifer. Come to complain about the bloody noise, have you? Do come in, you can take down my particulars.'

Des grabbed Kitty's wrist, pulled her into the hall and planted a wet kiss on her lips. He tasted of beer and peanuts and the kiss lasted for a moment too long.

'Sweet,' he breathed, as he released her.

Des peeled off her coat, grabbed her bottle of wine and steered her into the packed kitchen, his hand in the small of her back. He leaned over her shoulder to shout 'The Law's here – you're all BUSTED!'

The house was rammed with people in every room and lining the stairs. Kitty pushed through the crowd. She found Orla by the back door, her blonde hair tumbling free as she struggled to open a bottle of champagne. She was wearing a peach-coloured silk dress, the front slashed almost to her waist. Orla wrapped her arms around Kitty's shoulders and hugged her.

'I love you, Kitty Lockwood. Love you.'

When she was finally released, Kitty handed over her present, a Day-glo dustpan and brush.

'I LOVE it!' Orla squealed. 'That's gorgeous!' She wrapped her arms around Kitty again. 'You NEED a drink, Kitty!' She poured a dark, syrupy goo into a champagne glass.

CHAPTER EIGHT

'Look at that! It's a present from Des. Chocolate vodka! Get that down your neck!'

Orla watched Kitty sip the gloop. It tasted like alcoholic baby food. 'Isn't that beautiful? There's people you need to meet. Follow me!'

She pulled Kitty into the sitting room: it was dark, packed with dancing bodies. The bass notes shook the walls. Kitty wondered how the neighbours would take to the new tenant. But after a while the chocolate vodka started to work. To her surprise, she started to enjoy herself.

Towards midnight Kitty was cornered by Des Tucker. She was dancing among the girls when he moved in, arms above his head, snaking between them. Des bumped up against her. The others laughed, rolling their eyes as they edged aside. Des manoeuvred her into a corner. She found herself pinned between a widescreen telly and the stereo. Des leaned in.

'Where's your dad tonight?'

'My dad?...' She was about to say that her father was dead when she realised he meant Bryson Prudhoe. Des leaned closer.

'Bryson the Bison?'

Kitty nodded, smiling so he knew she'd got the joke. She shrugged. 'Haven't a clue! At home, I would expect.'

'Tucked up with his cocoa. And Maureen...' Des whirled around, pursing his lips and nodding to the beat.

'I expect.'

'Tucked up with Mrs P!'

Des dipped down and leaned in, his lips close to her ear. 'Lets you out on your own then, does he?'

'Bryson's not...' Kitty searched for the right word. 'Bryson's not my bloke, Des. He's a friend of my mum. They worked together. At Etal Lane. Years back.'

Des nodded, twisting around, bumping his crotch against her thigh. When she accidentally bumped back, he thought this was the green light. He touched her wrists then slid his hands slowly up her arms until he held her shoulders. Raising his eyebrows he pushed his mouth close. Wet lips touched her ears.

'I'd love to fuck you...'

She stiffened and moved back. 'I'm flattered, Des.' She danced on for a few seconds then held up a finger. 'Need to make a call.'

She ducked around him, escaping to the kitchen, where she filled a plastic cup with cool tap water. Des appeared at her side, his face covered in a sheen of sweat. He leaned against her as he poured a drink.

'What's your problem, Locky?'

'I don't have a problem.' She poured another glass of water and sipped it.

'You're not bad looking. People must have said that to you before!'

She swallowed a mouthful of cold water.

'But you're a bit up yourself, aren't you."

'Is that what you think?'

'That's what everyone thinks!'

'Right.' Kitty sipped her water. 'Well, if that's what they say...'

He leaned against the sink and looked through the window. 'You know, there's a sweep going around the station.'

'Is there?' Kitty braced herself, suddenly finding a piece of lint on her dress.

Don't cry.

CHAPTER EIGHT

'The betting is you won't last 'til Christmas.'

'Is that right, Des?'

He shook his head sadly. 'It's terrible! People can be so cruel. The way they pile on when you're down.'

'I'll just have to prove them wrong, won't I?' Kitty shouted over the music.

'I'm sure you will, Locky.' He shook his head again. 'But if you're struggling ... if it all gets too much, try to hang on.'

'I will.'

'Thanks.' He turned to face her. 'Cos I said you wouldn't fuck off 'til February!'

* * *

Kitty wobbled towards home, swaying a little as she walked through the dark, silent streets of Belfordham. The bells of St Mary's rang through the still night air, chiming midnight.

Perhaps Tucker was right. If all of her colleagues believed there was something between her and Bryson Prudhoe, perhaps it was true. But it wasn't sexual; at least, not on her part. Bryson was a family friend. He was her mentor.

When Kitty joined the force Bryson promised her mother he would keep an eye on her. In the end it was Bryson who cried on Kitty's shoulder. So did she still see him as a father figure, an older man to replace her dear, dead dad? If that was true, the balance was shifting. Now she felt protective towards Bryson, looking out for his well being as she would have done with her father.

And if they all thought she was "up herself," what could she do about that? She peeled off her heels and walked barefoot, the road still warm from the day's sun. She stood on the bridge, watching the river flow. She could just make out flecks of foam, pushed here and there by the current. Even shallow water held mysteries.

Her mother was right. Coppers were a hard bunch. She would never fit in.

* * *

The next morning her hangover was crushing. Every time she thought of chocolate vodka she gagged. Yet she struggled through the shift without any disasters. When it was finished she considered going straight home to bed, though her conscience would not allow it. So Kitty heaved her sports bag onto her shoulder and slammed her locker door. Kickboxing started at six and Master Rafael did not approve of lateness. Exercise might be the perfect cure; a two-hour session would sweat the alcohol from her body.

As she walked along the corridor she noticed Bryson Prudhoe's door was open. He sat at his desk, shirtsleeves rolled up, head in hands. His face was flushed, his scalp shining through thinning hair. Kitty leaned on the doorframe and knocked. Bryson jumped. She waved goodbye, but it was too late.

'Time for a cuppa?' He was already out of his chair and filling the kettle.

'I'm on my way to my class. And I need to pick up Molly. She slept at Jacqui's last night, so I feel guilty. Dunno why – she couldn't give a toss – but it makes me feel like Bad Mother.'

'Just a quick one then.'

CHAPTER EIGHT

Bryson Prudhoe had told her that he had never wanted to be anything other than a policeman. At the start of his own career he had been a bright, fit, dedicated officer. While his mates teased him for his eagerness, they respected his bravery and commitment. Bryson was always at the front when things turned nasty. His rise to the rank of Detective Sergeant was rapid. Somewhere along the line something went wrong. The story ran that Maureen Prudhoe hated being left alone night after night with two young kids. When the chance for promotion came along he wrote the application, but never delivered it. Now he had held the same job and used the same office for so long that he was regarded as a fixture.

His appetite for work became an addiction to food. Now his most impressive clear-up rate was the canteen puddings. Kitty knew that colleagues laughed at him, called him 'Bison' behind his back. She suspected that Bryson knew it too. He wasn't "one of the lads" any more. Like Kitty Lockwood, he was an outsider.

Bryson shovelled sugar into his tea and slit open a packet of Abbey Crunch. The biscuits tumbled across the desk, scattering crumbs over his paperwork. Kitty dropped her bag on the floor and helped him clear up.

'How's it going, Locky?'

'Good. It's all good.'

Bryson tidied his papers, then traced patterns on the desk as they listened to the hiss of the kettle.

'How's Maureen?'

'Good! She's fine, thanks. A lot better.' Bryson pursed his lips. Everyone knew that his marriage was shaky. The kettle clicked and Bryson jumped up to make the drinks. He spoke with his back to her.

'It seems to me, Kitty, that you're bored.'

'I'm not bored Bryson. I have a spectacular headache.'

'You shouldn't be faffing about, chasing producers. Any Clothes Hanger around here can do that!'

Kitty nodded, biting her tongue. Bryson Prudhoe was hardly the man to lecture others about under achievement.

'You should do your OSPRE exams. You'd swan through, with your brain!'

'My brain hurts, Bryson. Got a paracetemol?'

'You should take more water with it...'

'You sound like my mother.' He looked hurt. Bryson plonked Kitty's mug on the desk, his hand trembling as he tried to avoid a spill. Bryson didn't bother with coasters. The top of his desk was pitted with rings, Kitty noted, like a map of the moon; the Sea of Tranquility.

'I had a strange one yesterday. You heard of a couple called the Kanes?' Kitty told him all about her encounter with Dorian and Richard Kane. 'He slammed the door in my face.'

Bryson licked droplets of coffee from his moustache with the tip of his tongue.

'Some people don't like the police. We make them nervous.'

'But it's so strange. They seem loaded. All that money and he behaves like a thug.'

'Embarrassment, perhaps. Wife hauled in by the bobbies. A little domestic spilling into the outside world. Shame and guilt. Gets to everyone.'

'This guy's no shrinking violet, Bryson! He was getting off on it, pitting himself against me. It was a challenge. A game.' She put the mug to her lips, but didn't drink. There was always a faint whiff of antiseptic about Bryson's coffee.

'You're the psychologist...'

'No. I'm not ... I started a degree in Psychology. I never finished it.'

Bryson looked out of the window, stroking his 'tache. 'So where's the crime?'

'What do you mean?'

'You're telling me about these people because...?'

'There isn't a crime. Not that I know of. Unless being an arrogant sod is a crime. Which it should be! I just think it's odd – he has everything.'

'And money makes people nice, of course?'

'Of course not!'

'So ... this is what, exactly? Feminine intuition?'

Kitty didn't bite. 'They're just a strange couple. She seems bright but ... there's something weird about her. And there's something scary about him. What do they see in each other?'

'Odd. Strange. Scary.' Bryson smiled. 'If we nicked people on that basis there wouldn't be many on the out.' He leaned back, putting his hands behind his head.

'I get a bad feeling off them.'

'It's the general public, Kitty! Most are fine. Some are strange. And a few are stark, bollocking bonkers!' Bryson narrowed his eyes, as if catching sight of the madness of the world outside. 'Nothing shocks me any more.'

'Ordinary people ... innocent people do odd things, don't they? Sometimes?'

'We've all done something strange.'

She reached for her bag. 'Really? You must tell me about that – sometime.'

A pink flush crept up Bryson's neck. Kitty watched him try to hide it by taking a swig of coffee. Then he placed his mug carefully, lining it up with the edge of the desk. 'Passion makes fools of the wise.'

The clock on the wall ticked softly. Her kickboxing class started in twenty minutes. He walked to the window, squinting in the hard light slanting through the glass. 'We're all Mother Nature's toys.' Bryson's voice faded to a whisper. Kitty studied the side of his face. She had always thought he seemed such a decent man. On Saturdays he washed the car and played football with the boys. The neighbours would hear the *snick, snick,* of his shears as he trimmed the hedge. But we never know what goes on inside another mind.

Even shallow water holds mysteries.

'Thanks for the tea, Bryson. And the moan. Now I'm off to kick the slats out of an imaginary assailant.' Kitty pretended to finish her drink. Bryson was staring out of the window.

'Kane. The name's familiar. Kane?'

'With a K.'

'There's something...'

Bryson tapped his forehead. Kitty raised an eyebrow.

'Feminine intuition kicking in, Bryson?'

She grabbed her bag and ran, leaving him alone, staring through the window.

CHAPTER NINE

A swatch of long black hair, twisted into a braid, is draped across her shoulder. Her fingers are slender – though the nails are chipped and bitten. High cheekbones, misty green eyes. She dresses in black jeans and a black mohair jumper. Her eyes are lined with thick, creamy kohl. This is Dorian Kane, née Dorian Eloise Frost. She's thirty one years old.

He's tall, wiry; almost thin. A prominent Adam's apple juts from the slender neck. His skin is pale and faint shadows circle his eyes, a cold blue grey. His hair is dark brown, cut short, standing straight up from the scalp, as if shocked.

He dresses to suit the occasion. In the country, it's a Barbour jacket and Hunter wellies. In town, he wears a business suit – a Pal Zileri in pale grey or a two-piece by William Hunt. His shoes are by John Lobb of St James's. There is a Tag Heuer on his wrist. He signs cheques with a Mont Blanc Meisterstück 149 in black and gold, a gift from his mother. He shades his eyes behind vintage Ray-Bans. He has beautiful white teeth – seventeen grands worth of dental work. His teeth are immaculate, so white that they gleam in the dark.

Richard Sharington Kane is methodical, neat – particular.

He's thirty four and he's on top of the world — or that's the way it seems. In the village they call him 'The Millionaire.'

So that's Richard and Dorian. Such lovely people. A beautiful couple. So devoted. Dorian and Richard. Richard and Dorian.

* * *

The VW Transporter trundled down the road below Hott, heading for Belfordham. Nathan hated the bitching van. The steering was slack and the boxy fucker weaved around every time there was a puff of wind. Rust was creeping around the doorframe. There was no poke in the engine and the gearbox was notchy as fuck. He rattled the stick, grinding it home between squealing gears.

Sweat pearled on his brow. He licked his top lip, tasted salt. He had snorted a rail of black cocaine and his heart was in his throat — bam b-bam b-bam! He was worried about money — the usual. They had sold the shit from the bed and breakfast and swapped their Ford for this van.

'Piece of crap!' Nathan slapped the wheel. Tanya said nothing; any words would have been petrol on the flame. They pulled into a lay-by and Nathan jabbed his foot on the throttle, revving the motor until it screamed. Every nerve was jangling — he just could not be still. The motor whined while Tanya hunted for the map Richard had given them. The loopy weirdo had worn gloves when he handled it, 'in case of prints,' he said.

'Where is it?' said Nathan.

A nerve pulsed in his cheek and he wheezed when he took a breath. He peered through the fly-speckled windscreen.

CHAPTER NINE

'Is this the place?' Unfolding the OS Explorer she pointed the tip of her perfect nail at a circle drawn in red marker. The nail scratched the surface of the map. Nathan could almost feel it, as if the paper were his own skin.

Nathan puffed on his inhaler, grabbed the map and battered it flat across his knees. His eyes darted back and forth over the page. Everything seemed a little too sharp, a little too close. The brown contour lines shimmied; the carmine thread of the A roads pulsing like veins.

Jabbing his finger at a clutch of star shapes, he searched the map's key to see what they meant. The symbols fluttered, like pages in a flicker book. He tossed the map aside and trained his binoculars on West Neuk Farm. A wall of honeystone swayed across the lens. His heart fluttered like a trapped bird. Bam b-bam...

Nathan scanned the house and outbuildings, searching for some clue which would confirm that this was their target. When he was satisfied they had the right place he folded the glasses and tossed them into the footwell.

'It's just a farm!' he said.

'The clue's in the name, Nathan. West Neuk Farm...'

'The way he talked, it was a fucking palace!'

'It's big enough.'

At least they were in the right place. His tension seeped away. Tanya was peering at the surrounding hills.

'How do they stand it?' she sighed. 'All this green would drive me crazy!' Nathan didn't reply. He had seen movement at the window.

'I need to think about this,' said Nathan. 'This needs thought.'

'Where are we sleeping?' Tanya yawned. Watching over

Nathan was exhausting. She needed to get her head down. Loved her bed, did Tanya. Loved her zeds.

'Edinburgh,' said Nathan, as he let out the clutch. 'Head-in-burger. Back to Scotty Land!'

Nathan jammed his foot down again, tickling up the revs until the motor whined. The van slithered along the verge, the wheels spinning an arc of mud and dust as they hit the road.

CHAPTER TEN

'Hunhhh!' Kitty's kick flew high, an inch shy of his shoulder.

'Move in, move out!' said Rafael, an edge to his voice as he spurred on the fighters. Kitty's bare feet danced across the mat as she circled her opponent. As the adrenaline ran through her veins it was as if she was waking from a deep sleep. The sensations were heightened, colours more vivid, all the edges hard and sharp and newly cut.

Though in his late fifties, her teacher was lean and fit. Rafael's brown hair was greying at the temples, his body taut and compact. He paced back and forwards in front of the class, looking each one in the eye. Kitty envied his self possession.

'Shoulder fake!'

Kitty dipped to the left, then rose to throw a flurry of punches towards Rafael's head, shrugging off her headache, kicking away her anger and frustration.

'Good! Now vary the fake!'

A smile spread across her face as he backed away, raising his eyebrows.

There were ten fighters, a good turnout on a fine summer's evening. Rafael threw open the windows and the sounds of combat mingled with the chatter of starlings in the trees around the cricket pitch.

The class had begun with five minutes of stretching exercises. Now their muscles were loose, Rafael demonstrated some new punches and kicks then showed different ways of combining the moves. Now the fighters were enjoying the pay-off, twenty minutes of airwork, sparring with different partners.

'OK!' Rafael clapped his hands. 'New partners everyone.' He bowed at Kitty. She mirrored his bow. He held her gaze, nodding and smiling. Was there a glint in his eye, she wondered?

It took a while for everyone to find a new partner, recover their breath and square up to fight again. In pairs they circled each other. All were dressed in black, the colour of the belt indicating the level of prowess.

Each fighter was soon lost in the intricate dance of punches, kicks and jumps. Rafael wandered between them, taking in every move, guaging their strengths and weaknesses.

'Stop!' He put his hand on the shoulder of the boy who was sparring with Kitty. 'What did I tell you, Stephen? *Never* turn your back!' He took both of them by the wrist and drew them close. 'You must *never* turn your back on your opponent. It is the biggest mistake you can make. Do you understand?' His voice was soft, but full of authority. '*Never* look away when you are fighting. A lion tamer would never turn away from a lion. Turning your back triggers a response in the animal. Even human animals! They know you have given up. Even a poodle would chase you if you run away.'

The boy nodded. Kitty felt the warmth in the fingers that circled her wrist.

'So hold the gaze of your opponent. Look them in the eye.

Hold that gaze, OK? Turn your back, and you're dead. Do you understand?'

Rafael released them and stood back to watch. Kitty circled her partner, her eyes fixed on his. Stephen was little more than a child. It was clear he felt unsettled by the intensity of her gaze. He looked down for a moment and Kitty kicked, brushing his shoulder with the edge of her foot. Rafael clapped his hands and beamed at her. Once more he took her by the wrist. The class stopped sparring and turned to listen.

'You see? When you spar, it's like you're soaring into the sky, seeing everything below so clearly! Like an eagle. Everything is so sharp. Sometimes we think too much. Kitty saw her opponent look away – just for a moment. A heartbeat. That was all. And she knew *that* was the moment to strike. It's instinctive.'

He smiled at her and leaned close to whisper, 'But next time, don't touch him. We don't want any broken bones, here...' He winked and Kitty shivered, a glimmer of desire.

Before the last bout Rafael asked them to sit. 'Some of you have heard me talk about this before. The style of fighting we're exploring in these classes comes from the traditional karate of Wado-Ryu. Wa means 'harmony'. Harmony doesn't mean softness, or weakness. It just means that – *sometimes* – yielding is more effective than brute strength.'

Rafael's warm eyes swept over his class. 'So you're learning a system that combines martial arts from the East *and* the West. The best of both worlds!'

Kitty had joined the class only weeks before. She had stumbled upon Rafael's class when searching for a yoga session. Kitty was a white belt, a beginner. Whether she would rise any higher she didn't know, though she did feel more flexible, more dextrous and more powerful than ever before. There was no contact in this class, no danger of being hurt or humiliated.

'Your exercises advance your body, your mind, your spirit.' Rafael's voice was like balm. 'This class is not just about fighting. Here, we're trying to make ourselves fit for life.' The rhythm of the words was hypnotic. 'It's symbiotic. Zen and life come together. As one.' He padded across the floor. It seemed his feet barely touched the ground. 'We don't see objects, we see the connections between them. Between people.'

The class stood, shaking loose their limbs, ready for their final sparring session.

'And remember, guys – *never* turn your back!' He circled the class once more, watching them fight, making suggestions, encouraging his pupils. He clapped his hands. 'Thank you, everyone.'

After a class Kitty felt calm, as if her mind and body had been shriven. All her cares, all the chocolate vodka, had been washed clean away. As she walked through the village to Jacqui's house she felt blessed. The sun was still high, dipping over the tops of the lime trees. Swallows skimmed the grass in the Recreation Field, where a game of cricket was in progress. Men in white. The pock of the ball, scudding across the turf, the sound of ragged applause. As she crossed the bridge she looked down at the water. The river was lower still, long plumes of weed drifted above the sandy bed, feathered by the current. She looked up, seeing the evening sunlight gleam on the slate roofs of houses across the water. The Voice whispered in her mind, "Enjoy it while it lasts!'

CHAPTER TEN

Kitty walked around Jacqui's house and knocked on the window that overlooked the back garden. Molly, sitting at the kitchen table, jumped at the sound. She glanced up, the ghost of a smile crossing her face as she kicked her legs beneath the table. Jacqui, wiping her hands on a tea towel, beckoned Kitty inside.

'Just in time! We're having fish fingers. Can you be tempted?'

'By fish fingers...?'

'Don't be such a snob!'

Kitty was all set to say no. But one glance from Molly changed her mind. In any case,

the exercise had made her very hungry.

'If you're sure you have enough?'

Jacqui nodded. Kitty hung up her jacket and draped an arm over her daughter's shoulders.

'What have you got there, kiddo?'

Molly flinched a little.

'It's French.'

'Need any help?'

Molly shook her head. 'I'm fine.'

Above Molly's head, Jacqui raised her eyebrows at Kitty.

'That's not what you said two minutes ago, Molly Lockwood...'

'Let's have a goosy at it, Moll,' said Kitty. 'French is one of the one's where I can help. You should be good at it.'

'Because dad was French...?'

The two women exchanged another look.

'No,' said Kitty. 'Because you're a bright girl.'

'I'm not.'

'I wouldn't say it otherwise, Molly.'

Molly dipped her head and began to write. Jacqui shot a glance at her friend.

'She's right, your mum.' She leaned close and pretended to whisper into Molly's ear.. 'And one day, you'll appreciate that...but not till you're a little, wrinkly old lady, probably.'

Molly nodded again. Her hair fell forward, brushing the page of her notebook as she wrote. There was a pop and a glooping sound. Jacqui plonked a glass of wine in front of Kitty.

'There you go. It's wine o'clock. Syrah. From the Vendee. Two glasses of that and you'll be talking French like a native...'

* * *

They reached Edinburgh in the late afternoon. Nathan signed the register as 'Mr and Mrs Neville Tyler' from Bolton. The Holiday Inn was perfect – an anonymous hotel in the middle of an industrial estate on Ocean Drive, right by the Leith docks. The only people who chose to stay there were reps, adulterers and suicides looking for somewhere clean and quiet to end it all.

They went to bed for a couple of hours. Nathan twitched as he dropped off, muttering to himself. When she was sure he had settled, Tanya allowed herself to sleep. When they woke they had dinner together then Tanya swam in the pool while Nathan went out to do a little business.

As the sun went down Nathan strolled along the waterfront. A thick mist drifted off the Firth of Forth. He walked along Salamander Street until he found a pub called *The Pond*. Nathan bought a pint of Heavy but left it, untouched, on the

CHAPTER TEN

table. He flicked through the Evening News, tapping his foot to a Johnny Cash tune on the sound system. Every time the door opened he glanced up, appraised the newcomer then returned to his paper.

After twenty minutes a short, thick-set man with sandy hair entered. He carried a black bin bag, scrunched up in his stubby fingers. He clocked Nathan, just once – then looked away. The man brought his whisky to Nathan's table. They sat in silence for a minute or so.

The man leaned forward and laid the bin bag on the bench seat. Nathan reached inside his jacket and passed a brown paper sack beneath the table. The man picked it up, finished his whisky in one gulp and left. Nathan took the bin bag to the Gents and locked himself in a cubicle. He emptied the contents on the floor: a battered little Makarov, a Russian army automatic, wrapped in an oil-drenched cloth. He dried the gun on a paper towel. There was a dent on the muzzle and the paintwork on the grip was scratched to the silver. He rooted in the bin bag until he found a cardboard box. He opened it to reveal fifty rounds of 9.3mm ammunition, the brass and lead glinting in the striplight.

The mist thickened as Nathan walked back to the hotel. On Ocean Drive a young woman was standing by the water, her mobile to her ear. She glanced at Nathan, and dabbed her eyes with a tissue. She turned away and dropped her tissue in the Leith. Nathan walked on. Tanya was waiting.

CHAPTER ELEVEN

Kitty slumped forward, her chest rising and falling as she sucked air. Her eyes were scrunched tight against the sunlight glittering on the water. She had paddled upstream for three miles, pulling herself against the current.

When she reached the weir at Chollerford she peeled off her fleece, enjoying the cool air on her skin. Her canoe turned slowly in the pool below the weir.

It was a perfect June evening. The sun dipped behind the edge of the hills, the last rays slanting across the valley. Water gurgled over the lip of the weir.

Last September, when she and Molly had paddled here, a wall of cold, fresh water had poured over the rim. Back then the river had been full of life, columns of silver bubbles streaming from the depths. Now the river crawled along the bed. Dry rocks studded the surface and trails of green weed fringed the weir.

The canoe twisted in the current, the slender hull bumping stones just beneath the surface. A moorhen hooted, scudding away from the reeds to her nest on the far bank. Kitty closed her eyes, listening to the sound of the water. The sun warmed her face. It was a perfect moment. She brushed a tear from her cheek.

She dipped the paddle into the current and started to glide downstream. For a while, she drifted along, in perfect balance. It seemed that the canoe and the water were one. She too was liquid, part of the water that surrounded her. Then he cut in.

'Left,' hissed the Voice. 'Go left.' She ignored him, dipping the paddle into the water on the other side.

'How do you feel, when you hear the voices?' Her first session with the shrink had been a week after her father's funeral.

'It's not voices. It's 'A Voice'. Just one.'

Kitty knew why the doctor was silent, waiting to see if she would elaborate. She used the same tactic in her own job. At last, the doctor surrendered and spoke.

'So...how do you feel when you hear this voice?'

'Anxious. I don't like it.' The woman made a note.

'There's no need to worry about this.'

'I don't.' Kitty dabbed her cheek with a tissue.

Don't cry.

The doctor played with her pen, clicking the top, easing it free. 'Were you close to your father?'

'Were you close to yours?'

The doctor's face was impassive. A blank space.

'We didn't live in each other's pockets, if that's what you mean.' Kitty dabbed again. 'I *know* that nobody lives forever! But...' Kitty clicked her fingers. 'Like that ... and he was gone. He'd always ... always!' Kitty shook her head. The tears welled again, but she froze when she saw the Stupid Bitch peeling tissues from the box. She dabbed her eyes, smoothed her skirt.

'Are you OK to continue?'

Kitty looked down at her fingers, twisting the crumpled, sodden tissue. She nodded, fixing on the tissue, examining the folds and creases.

'It's not an uncommon experience to hear the voice of a recently deceased person.' Her smile was thin, professional. 'It's what we call an auditory hallucination. It's often triggered by a traumatic event. Many people say they first hear their voices after a life event; the loss of a close relative, a partner … what have you …'

Kitty realised she was spouting the text of some research paper. 'You've had a traumatic experience, Miss Lockwood .'

The sun was going down. The canoe slid through the tail of the pool and slipped into another rapid. She moved through the shadows of the trees. Kitty shivered, laying the paddle across the gunwale while she donned her fleece.

The face of Dorian Kane drifted into her mind. Then Richard Kane: a strange, disturbing vision, his pupils as tight as pinpricks in the cold blue-grey iris.

Don't waste your life thinking about them. You're not paid to think about them…

'*There's sex. And there's money,*' hissed the Voice.

'What does he see in her? Why would a City slicker throw in his lot with a flaky Bohemian?

'*All sorts of people fall in lust.*'

'You really think that? Maybe she's got money. Or her family has…'

'*It's sex. We're all Mother Nature's Toys.*'

'Oh, sod off!' snarled Kitty, stabbing the paddle into the current.

* * *

CHAPTER ELEVEN

The next morning Kitty was at a desk in Belfordham nick, preparing for a meeting of DAAT: the Drugs and Alcohol Advisory Team.

Orla Harrington leaned over her desk. 'Campbell wants to see you.'

'Now?'

'This bloody minute,' was what he said.'

As an officer in the Rural West Neighbourhood Team, Kitty was answerable to Inspector Gordon Campbell. Twice a week Campbell dropped into the Belfordham office to visit them, setting up camp in an office at the end of the corridor. Kitty knocked on his door. Campbell was leaning back in his chair.

'Ah, Lockwood! ' Campbell made the words sound like a threat. 'Need to mark your card.'

There was something about Campbell which brought out the surly teenager in Kitty Lockwood. 'I have a DAAT meeting, sir.'

'What's that?'

'Drugs and Alcohol.'

'Of course.' Campbell's voice was soft as Highland rain. He beckoned with one finger, pointed to a chair. 'Pull up a pew.'

Kitty trudged to the desk.

Gordon Campbell served ten in the Black Watch before quitting the regiment to marry. His taut, pocked face was topped by a thatch of silver hair. The tanned skin was pitted, like the gleaming surface of a shiny planet. Gordon Campbell might present a jovial, cheery face to the world, but it was a lie. Behind the mask he was an angry man. All he had ever wanted to do was to spend his life in the army and his wife wouldn't let him.

Campbell opened his top drawer and flipped an iPhone onto

the desk. With the tip of a stubby finger he prodded it across the surface. He stretched his neck and squared his shoulders. Everything snapped to attention around Gordon Campbell. The world bent to his will. He tapped the mobile. 'What's this?'

'It's a mobile phone, sir. They're very popular.'

His smile was as cold as sleet. Kitty knew that Gordon Campbell disapproved of her. She suspected that he would have preferred all his workmates to be male. It was cleaner; quieter. She had overheard him in the canteen, complaining that the job was all about teamwork now; gender equality, building bridges.

'PC Harrington found it beneath the seat of your car. If it's yours, take better care of it. If it belongs to someone else, find out who. Then return it.'

Kitty nodded. 'Have you had a look at the numbers?'

'I have not. I have better things to do. I wanted a longer time with you. There are issues. But if you're booked, you're booked. Now trot along to your meeting.'

'Sir.'

Campbell was already tapping at his laptop, his beady eyes fixed on the screen.

Kitty sat in her car, turning the phone between her fingers. It was a box-fresh, silver-grey iPhone. A green tassel was attached to the corner and from this dangled a tiny spirit-level, a shiny green bar floating inside a capsule of clear oil. An inscription was etched into the back of the phone. It read 'You and I. Forever.'

She switched on the phone, noting that the battery was low. She clicked Menu, then searched 'Names' to find a clue to the owner. There were a dozen or so entries. She flicked through the names – *Bea, Dad, Dentist, George C, K-Dog.* There was no-one she recognised. But as she reached the entry for '*Richard,*' Kitty knew the owner must be Dorian Kane. She was the only civilian who had been in her car in the last couple of days. 'Correct procedure' would be to contact the woman and let her know when her mobile would be returned. But she hesitated. She twirled the phone between her fingers, feeling the heft, the silky finish. With a guilty glance around the car park, Kitty opened her notebook and started to scribble down the stored names and numbers.

'*Messages?*' murmured the Voice.

As she peeked at Messages – just to confirm ownership, she told herself – there was a hard, urgent rap on her window. She looked up to see Campbell's face, inches from her own. She opened the window. He leaned in, his hands gripping the sill.

'We need a longer chat. See me in the morning. After the team meeting.' Without waiting for a reply, Campbell marched towards his car. Kitty waited until he drove off before she returned to the phone.

There was one message in the Inbox – '*where r u? hope u feeln OK. XXXXX.*'

The number of kisses was intriguing. The text had been sent by K-Dog at 16:10 the day before. An hour after Kitty had dropped Dorian off at her home, West Neuk Farm.

In the SEND bar Kitty found a fragment of text. Dorian Kane had started to write a reply, though she had not sent it. It read: 'That was wrong. Can't happen. Sorry. x'

'OK...' Kitty murmured, jotting the words in her pad.

'Is a kiss so bad?' Dorian had said. 'One kiss ...'

CHAPTER TWELVE

The first time Dorian saw Richard Kane he was on the screen of a security camera. At the time, she was living on a diet of apples, tinned soup and cigarettes. Every day was spent watching television. Her business had collapsed and her studio was padlocked. The building was up for sale. Her career was finished.

Dorian's only visitors were close friends or medics. Her psychiatric nurse called every day to check on her. The CPN insisted that she must avoid anything that reminded her of her work. For a while, even her sketchbook and pencils were forbidden.

Mummy flew in from Switzerland to take care of her, but she was keen to make a rapid return to Geneva. 'Staying here isn't really an option, darling! Daddy needs me. I worry about his health. In any case, you're looking so much better.'

When her mother left, Dorian was alone. With rest, medication and counselling, she began to heal. Within a few weeks of the breakdown she returned to her flat where she found a small mountain of unopened bills and final demands. Her mother sent a cheque to cover the personal debts while Dorian's backers, Amschels Bank, appointed a team to go through the wreckage of the business. Going to Amschels had been Daddy's idea.

'The secret of successful business is OPM, darling. Always use Other People's Money.'

Daddy knew someone on the board at Amschels; and the bank loaned the start-up costs, raising all of her 'early stage growth finance.' As Dorian's profile grew, they invested more. They provided follow-on finance and stepped in with equity finance when she couldn't handle the interest. Her label bloomed like a fungus, outgrowing her bedroom within a few months. She set up a studio in Fonthill Road, just behind Finsbury Park train station. It all moved so quickly. In weeks she was handling thousands, instead of hundreds. To keep up with demand she began working through the night, when at least she could escape the phone and find time to think. Then Dorian had her breakdown. The whole enterprise collapsed in weeks, failing just as quickly as it had grown. Now the bank was faced with the task of picking up the pieces. The crash team arranged to sell Dorian's assets, negotiate with creditors and recover a little of their money. The team was headed by their best man, Richard Kane. That was when 'he' arrived in her life.

The first time he knocked at her door she was having one of her bad days. Feeling fragile, she tiptoed into the hall to see who had knocked. The spycam revealed the back view of a tall, well-dressed man who looked away, down the corridor. Then he turned and she saw his face for the first time. He was slim, his suit was well cut. He stared straight into the lens and smiled, catching her off guard.

'Ms Frost?' His voice was deep. He raised his eyebrows and leaned towards the security camera. She made no reply, but his smile did not falter. He had lovely teeth. Even, white and perfect. He looked directly into the camera, straightened his tie, brushed a hand over his hair, then winked – straight into the lens.

She jumped back, clamping her hand over her mouth so that he wouldn't hear her giggle.

'My name is Richard. Richard Kane. I'm from Amschels. '

He waited for a response. There was none. 'I don't know if you remember. I was on the panel that approved your loan.' His voice was reassuring. There was no threat in his manner. 'Your mother has told me all about your situation, Dorian. I'm here to do what I can to help.' He leaned forward, smiling into the camera. He knew she was there. He knew that he had her attention. 'I wonder if you might let me in? If we can sit down and have a chat, I'm certain we can find a way out of this pickle.'

Dorian pressed the buzzer. As he passed her, it seemed that the air was scented. She was struck by the way he moved, the confidence with which he glided into her world.

They drank coffee at her kitchen table. His eyes were blue-grey, his gaze intense. Richard sipped his drink then set it aside. He was like a friend – a warm, caring friend she had known for years. 'It's only money, Dorian! It doesn't actually exist, you know...'

His smile was beautiful. 'We can make this better.' Although she had known him less than an hour, this was a man she would trust with her life. He explained her options. She was a bankrupt with no real assets, other than her original designs. The studio was leased. There were sewing machines, unsold stock, raw materials. Some of these had been liberated by her workers when their wages dried up, but what remained might be sold and used to settle part of her debt. He would arrange

CHAPTER TWELVE

for all of that. 'If you would like me to, that is?'

She nodded. 'Of course. Thank you. This has been just so ... horrible.'

'This is the hard part.' He handed her a clean silk handkerchief. 'Which is why I'm here.'

He would handle all of the arrangements. She felt as if the weight had lifted.

'The bank gambled – we lost.' He shrugged. 'Investment in private companies is always risky. Someone in the research section screwed up. They didn't do their homework. Not your fault. You were the chief asset of your company. They thought your label had long-term potential. They didn't think about what would happen if you became ill.'

'I've failed. I'm a failure.'

'This isn't a personal matter, Dorian. It's just business. Look – forty per cent of angel investments fail. Investing in early stage companies – like yours – offers great opportunities. But it's very risky. Private companies are illiquid, if you'll forgive me using a bit of jargon! They tend to run out of cash easily. They need very long investing time frames.'

She didn't understand a word, but she liked the way his mouth moved when he said it. He had a slight stammer, which only added to his charm.

'These things happen, Dorian. It's not the end of the world. It's not personal. It's just business.'

That was the first of many meetings. Richard cut Dorian from the wreckage of her failed label. Even when the debts were cleared he continued to call, sitting at her table, drinking coffee. He smiled. He made her laugh. This was very personal banking. And he worked *way* beyond the money.

CHAPTER THIRTEEN

The mobile lay on the kitchen surface while Kitty cooked the tea. She was aware of its shiny presence at the edge of her vision. It seemed to accuse her. The right thing was to return it. 'Correct procedure.' She hated 'correct procedure.' She resisted the logical, methodical way of working. That was why she would never fit in, she realised.

Kitty tipped potato wedges and baked beans onto the plates and called for Molly. Looking down at the steaming mound of food, Kitty felt discouraged. Since Molly had declared herself vegetarian it was easier to cook one meal for both of them. She pushed her food around the plate as she watched Molly eat.

'How was school?'

'OK.'

'Why don't you ask someone over for tea? One of your friends?'

'I don't want to put you to any trouble.'

Kitty started to laugh, biting her lip when she saw Molly glare. She could be such a solemn, correct child. 'It's no trouble! I'd love to meet your friends.'

Molly nodded.

'So who's your best friend at the moment?'

'I don't know.' Molly sipped her juice. 'Who's yours?'

'Jacqui, I suppose.'

'Not that fat policeman?'

'Who? ' Kitty was wrong-footed for a moment. 'Bryson? No. Bryson's more granny's friend.'

Molly nodded.

'I like Emily Chan.'

'Emily?' Kitty's voice was shrill. Having gleaned a morsel of information she seized it. 'She's lovely, isn't she?' But Molly slapped her down with a long pause.

'... probably, my best friend.'

'Shall we do that then? Get Emily over? How about Friday?'

Molly swallowed a mouthful of juice then played with her glass, twisting it round and round. 'You're working on Friday.'

'No! Am I? '

'You're on a Late Turn.'

'Damn it! You're right. I am!'

'Your shift starts at two. I'm supposed to go to Jacqui's after school.'

'Of course you are! Sorry. Clean forgotten.'

Molly nodded. She finished her juice, slid down from the table and skipped into the front room. Kitty sat at the table, watching her daughter flick through the channels on the remote until she found 'The Simpsons'.

Molly tucked her ankles beneath her legs and settled down to watch the hilarious antics of a dysfunctional family.

CHAPTER FOURTEEN

Their first date was lunch at *Il Portico,* on Kensington High Street. It was quiet, the lighting subdued. Over Tuscan bean soup and tagliatelle, Dorian discovered what she could about her saviour. It was a slow process. He smiled easily. He was charming, yet he carried a certain remoteness. Something in his past haunted him, she suspected. Richard Kane was open, up to a point, but a part of him remained private. Somewhere along the line he had been hurt, she was sure. Whenever she prised out anything about his past, he would switch the question around to ask about her own family.

He lived alone. There had been a long relationship when he was younger, but now he concentrated on his career. His parents were dead. Dorian felt that wound must still be raw since he fell silent on the rare occasions they came up in conversation. They were 'lovely people' who had adopted him when he was seven. He did not know his 'real parents.' He claimed to have no curiosity about them. For the last few years he had lived alone. When his parents died the family farm was too full of memories. He moved to London and rented out the farm in Northumberland. 'For pennies, actually,' he said. 'I don't make a bean. Though I'd like to return, one day.' Now he lived in a rather large apartment in St John's Wood.

She told him everything about herself: the itinerant childhood, the parents who were loving but distant. The Frosts lived in Lausanne and were very wealthy. They cared deeply, but they wanted her to stand on her own feet.

Richard's certainty was attractive. It was such a contrast to the way she drifted through her career. He told her that before he was twenty he had mapped out his life. 'Married by thirty five – at the latest! I'll work in funds for seven years then get out with a pile of cash which I'll put into land. That's one thing they can't make more of: land. And property. I should have been an architect. My one regret.'

He knew where he would live, knew what he would be earning and when he would retire. It was all charted and costed; each stage marked as clearly as signs on a motorway.

'This country is changing, Dorian. In the future there will be very poor people...' He placed his hands on the tablecloth. '... and there will be very rich people.' He moved his hands apart. 'That's the way it will be. Like India. Like China. Given the choice, I'd rather be one of the very rich!'

When they were apart, she couldn't get him out of her head. They were a perfect fit. They complemented each other: yin and yang, head and heart, art and commerce. He made her complete, a whole person. Though she had known him for only a few weeks, Dorian trusted Richard completely.

About a month after their first date, he dropped around without calling ahead. He seemed distracted, pacing the floor. She was used to his occasional silences, but he seemed changed. Restless. As he stood up to leave, he touched her cheek and they kissed. It started as a gentle peck on the cheek.

Then their lips met; the kiss a tangle of tongues and teeth. Everything seemed to meld, to slip and blur. He moved his hands to hold her head. She had forgotten what strong magic a kiss could be. One kiss can change a life.

CHAPTER FIFTEEN

The mobile lay by the kettle as Kitty loaded the dishwasher. She lifted it as she wiped the surface then put it down again. She knew it was a bad idea to hang on to it. The longer it stayed in her charge, the trickier everything would become. Dorian Kane might call the station to report the loss. Then Campbell would discover that Kitty had not returned it. The damn thing lay there, mutely accusing her.

By seven she could take it no longer. She grabbed the phone, bundled Molly into the car and set off. She would drive it around to West Neuk Farm and rid herself of the temptation. No more fishing in the lives of the Kanes. Whatever they got up to was none of her business, as he had so firmly pointed out.

Kitty discovered her mother was out at choir, so she dropped Molly at Jacqui Speed's house. 'Fancy a drink when you get back?' said Jacqui.

Kitty remembered that she had to face Campbell next morning for their 'little chat.' She would need a clear head for that.

'Go on! Trev can give you a ride home. Can't have you losing your licence, can we, petal?'

'You're on! Till half nine anyway. Her ladyship needs sleep.

But I'll take a cab home. I don't want to spoil Trev's night. '

Molly drifted to the sofa to watch Jacqui's widescreen.

'I won't be long, Mollusc.' Kitty waited a moment, but her daughter didn't turn, her eyes fixed on the screen.

Jacqui shrugged, touched her arm. 'You get off, petal. The sooner you go, the sooner you can be back and get some anaesthetic down your neck!'

* * *

The road to West Neuk Farm followed the course of the river. The sun rode low over the hilltops as she drove up the valley. It was a warm evening and young rabbits grazed the fresh grass by the side of the road. Kitty swerved to avoid them when they hopped across her path. Beyond the hedges, the cattle flicked their tails, swishing away clouds of midges. The road was empty. If her destination had been anywhere other than West Neuk, she would have enjoyed the drive.

After ten miles she left the road, the car rocking and rolling up the quarter mile of gravel drive that led to the farm at West Neuk. She swept around the turning circle, killed the engine and pushed back her sunglasses. As she approached the house Kitty twirled Dorian's phone between her fingers. The surface felt smooth, the texture soothing; like a worry bead. The gravel was deep and new and crunched beneath her feet. In the paddock a pair of horses was grazing; chestnut coats gleaming in the evening sun. A flock of woodpigeons flew over the trees behind the farm, winging their way down the valley to their evening roost. The muffled crack of a shotgun echoed along the wooded ridge above the house.

She raised the knocker and let it fall on the sun-bleached wood. A martin dropped from her nest beneath the eves, swooping low over the grass. Kitty looked up at the windows. There was no sign of life. She was tempted to wrap the phone in a note and push it through the letter box. She knocked again. The sound echoed through the house. No curtain twitched, no footsteps sounded. Taking out her pad she scribbled a brief note explaining that a mobile had been found and that it could be reclaimed at the station in Belfordham.

As she pushed the note beneath the door it creaked and slid back a few inches. It was open. Kitty peered inside. She glimpsed a convex mirror on the wall. The reflection revealed a fisheye view of the darkened hallway beyond. A figure watched her from the shadows.

'Hi there! Sorry!' Kitty grinned, masking her surprise. 'I didn't think there was anyone in.'

There was a beat before Dorian responded. Her voice was thick, bubbling up from some deep lagoon. 'But you decided to come in anyway?'

Kitty waved the note she had written. 'I just wanted to leave this where you'd see it.'

Dorian looked her up and down. She seemed comfortable with the silence. Kitty crumpled the note, stuffing it into her pocket. Then, with a magician's flourish, she produced the mobile. Dorian Kane glanced at the phone then padded into the darkness, holding a glass of wine to the side.

Kitty took this as an invitation and followed her down a winding passage, glimpsing rooms stocked with antique furniture and walls lined with paintings – originals, not the prints and film posters that hung in her own home. The Kanes lived up to their reputation as millionaires.

The kitchen lay at the back of the house. As soon as they entered Dorian poured the wine into the sink and rinsed the glass with water. She laid it on the drainer, turned and beckoned Kitty to sit.

'Would you like a drink? Tea – or a glass of something?'

'Thanks. I have to get back. If you could just sign this to say I've returned your phone I'll leave you in peace. On your own?'

'No,' said Dorian. 'You're here.'

'Right...Of course.'

When Dorian left the room to find a pen, Kitty glanced around the kitchen. A cream-coloured Aga took up most of one wall. A huge dishwasher thrummed softly beside the Belfast sink. The cooker hood was brushed steel, the plumbing Italian, the floor tiled in antique terra cotta. On the wall a station clock from the Great Central Railway ticked away the hours.

Whenever Kitty attended a crime scene she played the same game. She imagined that she was able to hear what had taken place in a room, as if events left some sort of imprint on the fabric of a place. She closed her eyes, listening to the house. It was quiet, apart from the sound of the wind in the chimney. It was an unlikely setting for any kind of mischief.

Kitty ran a finger along the marble top. Her fingertip was smudged in dust. While West Neuk appeared to be a beautiful home, the perfection was only surface deep. A Maling bowl, piled with apples, lay on the centre of the table. Dorian returned and they sat while she signed the receipt. As Dorian scrawled her signature, a barbed wire fence of inky loops, she pushed the tip of her tongue into the corner of her mouth. Her face was feline, her almond-shaped eyes lidless and deep set.

'This is a beautiful house. Must be murder to keep on top of it!'

'I used to have a cleaner...' Dorian's voice trailed off.

As Kitty waited she looked around for details, the little clues that suggested the Kane's image of wealthy, luxurious living might not be the whole picture. The window frames had been stripped down and the wood left naked, ready for priming. A pane in one of the kitchen windows was cracked. A switch box behind the fridge dangled from bare wires. The kitchen seemed unfinished, as if the Kanes had moved in only weeks earlier.

'You having some work done? I was thinking of a new kitchen myself.'

'We'll get round to finishing it, I expect. One day...' Dorian's green eyes were on the receipt, her lips moving as she read.

'Who's doing the work?'

'Work?'

'Just that I know a couple of people. If you needed someone.'

'We had builders. Richard didn't like the standard of their work.' She waved her hand. 'It's a long-term project, this place.'

'It's finding the time, isn't it? Your husband must work long hours?' Dorian seemed not to hear. Kitty tried another tack. 'It's lovely and quiet up here! That drive into town must be a pain!'

Dorian shrugged. 'Richard drives everywhere. He works all over the country.'

'Right ...When does he get back?'

Dorian's feline eyes flicked up, fixing Kitty with a steady, cool gaze. 'Why?' She lowered the pen onto the table.

Kitty shrugged. 'I'm nosy. It goes with the job.' She smiled, holding out her hand to take the receipt. Dorian folded her arms.

'Does Richard scare you?'

'Scare me? No. Why would he?' Kitty heard the catch in her own voice.

Dorian smiled. 'You fancy him, don't you?'

Kitty half laughed, feeling her confidence slipping away.

'I can always tell when women ... when they're attracted to my husband.'

Kitty felt the floor was shifting beneath her feet. She smiled and shook her head; words failed her. This was not a safe place.

'It's OK. I'm used to it. A lot of women find Richard attractive. He won't do anything about it.'

'Well, I'm sure you're right, but...'

'Oh, I am...'

Kitty forced herself to hold Dorian's gaze. She held out her hand. 'Well. If you're done I'll take that and add it to the pile on my desk.' As Kitty pushed back her chair the legs screeched across the tiled floor, the sound ringing through the house. Dorian put a hand across her face, shielding her eyes. For a moment they were frozen – Kitty looking down at Dorian. Then she saw that Dorian was shaking, as if laughing. Tears falling through her fingers, Dorian slumped over the table. The fruit bowl tumbled to the floor and shattered. Apples bumped and rolled across the floor. Dorian laid her head down, her shoulders trembling.

Kitty gathered the scattered fruit. She found a dustpan by the Aga and swept up the fragments of china. All the while Dorian was still, her eyes closed. Laughter and tears seemed to come easily to Dorian Kane, as if her nerves lay exposed on the surface of her skin. Kitty tore a sheet of kitchen tissue from the roll and handed it to Dorian.

She wiped away a tear and opened her eyes. She stared at her hands, knotting her fingers together. Kitty saw the bitten nails, the torn skin. Dorian seemed embarrassed by her outburst. 'I'm fine. I'm sorry. It all gets a bit much sometimes, that's all. I feel like a dandelion. You know? When it's blown on.'

'Right...' Kitty pushed a fresh tissue across the table. Dorian dabbed her nose. She rocked back and forth. 'Look, Dorian. It's none of my business.'

Don't say it!

She was only a few years older than Dorian, but there was something about the woman which invited protectiveness.

You'll regret it.

'If you're in trouble you can call me.'

Too late.

She pulled a card from her purse and laid it on the table. 'I know what it's like when you're feeling a bit...' She looked away, searching for the words.

'When I'm crazy?'

Don't say it.

'I've had problems, too. In the past. I'm OK now, glad to say.'

'What problems?'

Kitty breathed deeply. She was furious with herself. 'Where I work they call it 'issues of mental health.'

Dorian straightened, widening her eyes.

Kitty reached across the table and picked up Dorian's mobile. She tapped the keypad then turned it for Dorian to see.

'That's my number. I've put it in your Favourites. On your

speed dial. See? All you do is press two.' Kitty pushed the mobile across the table. 'You're very isolated up here. If you just need to talk, call me.'

Kitty shrugged. Dorian picked up the phone and jabbed the keypad. After a moment, Kitty's mobile rang. She ended the call. 'Keep it on for a while. Or take it off. Whatever you like. If you need me, I'm there. On two.' Kitty sat back.

Idiot! You should NEVER give a civilian your personal number. You IDIOT!

Dorian stared at the phone then picked it up. Her face was impassive, though her head tilted, as if she was listening to a distant sound.

'Now, if we're all done, I'll scoot.' Kitty held out her hand to take the receipt. But Dorian Kane was looking over Kitty's shoulder. Richard Kane stood in the doorway, his shotgun cradled in the crook of his arm.

CHAPTER SIXTEEN

'You must love it here,' murmured Richard. He pulled a canvas game bag from his shoulder and dropped it on the table. Downy feathers puffed into the air. The bodies of two wood pigeons bulged through the netting, their plump breasts cut into a diamonds by the mesh. A drop of blood gathered on the tip of one beak then splashed onto the tiled floor. Kitty realised that it was Richard Kane's gun she heard as she arrived at the farm.

'What's your problem *this* time?'

'There isn't one! Your wife dropped her mobile in my car the other day, Mr Kane. I'm just returning it. We're finishing the paperwork.'

He shook his head. 'The sooner you lot are privatised the better!'

He laid the shotgun on the table and peeled off his Barbour. Dorian hung it on a peg behind the door. Then she slipped out of the room. Kane sat at the kitchen table, kicked off his boots and began to clean his shotgun. He unfurled a canvas wallet and laid out his tools: lint rags, a phial of gun oil and a weighted cord. He cracked the gun open and squinted down the barrel. The tang of cordite caught in Kitty's nostrils.

Slipping a scrap of rag through a looped cord he dropped the weight through the barrel, catching it in the palm of his hand. She watched as he smeared gun oil on the rag then pulled it through the barrel. He peered at the rag, sniffing it, rolling it between finger and thumb as if it were a fine cigar.

Kitty recalled a second year criminology lecture. *'The gun is a cock,'* said the lecturer. They had smirked as they scribbled their notes. *'Hard, powerful; the thing that defines a male. Guns are the fetishised symbols of potent masculinity.'* As she watched Richard Kane polish his cherished shotgun, it no longer seemed like a joke.

'Don't let us keep you from your good works, constable.'

'I'm waiting for the receipt, Mr Kane. Your wife seems to have disappeared with it.'

'Dorian disappears all the time.' He returned to the gun. 'As you've discovered.'

Kitty remained in her seat, determined to show she was not intimidated. 'Was it difficult? Getting a shotgun certificate, Mr Kane?'

He paused. He put down the rag and stared at her. 'What do you think?'

'I don't know.' Kitty fixed her gaze on the point between his eyes.

Never turn your back.

'That's why I'm asking.'

He picked up the rag, looked down at his gun. 'It wasn't a problem. No.'

His voice was softer now. He smoothed the oiled cloth over the barrel, holding it up to squint down the length of it, watching the metal gleam. 'I have a shotgun certificate. I have a secure cabinet. I keep the guns in one place and I store the cartridges in another.' His tone was almost jovial. 'I have everything the law requires. Everything's in order, constable. Everything is just ticketty boo. Thank you for asking.'

'I'm sure it is.' She would check, but she was certain he would be covered. Most things around Richard Kane seemed to be ordered and organised.

'Believe it.' Now he raised the gun so that it was pointed at Kitty. He peered down the barrel. She leaned forward and turned the gun aside.

'You have a problem with authority, Mr Kane.'

'Are you asking me a question?'

'No. I'm telling you. You have a problem.'

'Sent you on a weekend psychology course, did they?'

'They send me on a lot of courses.'

'Good to know our taxes are well spent.'

'I have a degree in Psychology. There was no need for a weekend course.' Inside, Kitty winced. It was a lie and sounded pompous. Yet it had an interesting effect: he rolled his eyes.

'A degree?' The idea seemed to amuse him.

She nodded. 'Would you like to see my certificate?' She was smiling now.

'No.' He shook his head. 'I was being facetious.'

'So was I, Mister Kane.'

'All those qualifications....' He lifted the barrel to his eye and blew down it, looked again. '...but you're still on the lowest rank.'

She made no reply, holding her gaze on his face. She was starting to enjoy this.

'You're schooled in psychology, but they send you to fetch bits of paper. That rather proves my point, does it not?'

'Every job has dull moments.'

He ran a cloth over the barrel, rubbing until the metal shone. 'If a gun's not kept clean there's always the risk it may blow up in someone's face.' Once more he pointed it at her and squinted down the barrel. 'N – not a pretty sight...' For all the smiles, he was furious about something. The air around him seemed to crackle, to be charged with anger.

'Mister Kane, just like you, I wish I was somewhere else. Just as soon as I have that receipt, I'll be out of here.' She held his gaze.

Richard Kane nodded and placed the shotgun on the table. Tearing off a clean sheet of lint, he wiped the oil from his fingers. 'I apologise.' The arrogance seemed to have left him, for a moment. He folded the cloth and laid it down, precisely, the edge parallel with the rim of the table. He stared at the cloth. 'I think we got off on the wrong foot. My name's Richard. Since you seem to be spending so much time around here, perhaps you might use it.' He held out his hand.

Kitty was wrong footed once more. She found herself shaking Richard Kane's hand.

'I'm s – so sorry,' he said. 'I really should not have taken out my frustration on you. Things are a little fraught at the moment. It was very ill-mannered.' He looked her straight in the eye. It was a moment before she realised that he was still holding her hand. He called his wife's name, but there was no reply. He allowed her hand to slip through his fingers. For a moment neither moved. The only sound in the kitchen was the wind, sighing in the chimney.

He began to tidy up. Kitty watched him, fascinated by the ritual. He wrapped the barrel of his gun in cloth; a tender, almost loving movement. Each step in the ritual was controlled, considered; part of a pattern. For a moment she was a child again, watching her father at his work bench. His head bent to the task; performing an adult mystery she could barely understand.

Richard Kane's soft purr brought her back to reality. 'Would you tell me your own name?'

'Katherine. Katherine Lockwood. Kitty is what everyone calls me.'

He nodded, as if he approved. As if she had met his exacting standards. 'I do hope you won't hold my boorish behaviour against me, Kitty. It's not my usual way. Believe me. Things have been a little fraught around here, lately.'

Dorian had not responded to Richard's call. They were alone in the kitchen. Richard folded the corners of the cloth over the gun. 'I wonder if I could ask you a great favour?'

Kitty knew the sensible thing would be to refuse. All she had to do was get the paperwork and leave. She owed him nothing.

'Could we talk?' Moments earlier he had been hostile; now he wanted a cosy chat. 'I really need to talk to someone.'

Kitty glanced at her watch. She should be picking up Molly by now. Jacqui would be understanding if she was late. Molly couldn't care less. But she felt guilty. Richard Kane glanced towards the door.

'It might be better if we slipped outside?' Without waiting for a reply, he rose from the table. He opened the back door and stepped into the garden. After a moment Kitty followed.

A terrace had been cut from the side of the hill behind the house. The flagstone yard was bounded by a low wall. They climbed stone steps that led to a higher level, a lawn sheltered by low bushes of lavender and rosemary. Beyond the wall lay the open moorland. In the distance, the ridge of the hill was topped by a plantation; a dense band of conifers which shielded the farm from the worst of the wind.

They stepped onto the lawn. Kitty caught the buttery scent of flowering gorse. The sun dipped behind the hill and in the fading light it was difficult to read Richard Kane's expression.

'It's about Dorian. As you probably guessed ... she's always been fragile. She's very clever; very gifted. Though ...' His voice trailed away. 'There's a price that goes with that, isn't there?'

Kitty knew her silence would lead him to say more.

'Living with someone is a journey, isn't it? A voyage of discovery, I suppose. Don't you think, Kitty?'

What Kitty thought was that this was a speech he'd given before.

'We've been together almost three years. We lived in London for a while. I was working in the City. At Amschels. The investment bank?'

Kitty nodded, though the name was not familiar.

'I needed a change. I'd always wanted to move back here. When my tenants moved out, I knew it was time to come home. This was my mother's home.'

He was leading Kitty further into the garden, away from the house. The light was fading. A soft breeze pushed columns of midges through the air. His voice dropped to a whisper and Kitty was obliged to move closer to catch the words.

'Just before we met, Dorian had a bit of a wobble. Her company folded and the bank appointed me to sort out her affairs. That's how we met. Amschels loaned her quite a lot of money, as it happens. So she's been through the mill. She's very fragile. Very precious.' He seemed to be talking to himself. 'So I knew the way she was. From the start.'

'It must be difficult.'

'It can be. It's just that sometimes she says things she doesn't mean. Does things...'

Kitty nodded, but said nothing. She was on her guard again. Something told her she was being manipulated.

'What happened the other day? When I brought her home?' Richard Kane ran the tip of his finger along his lips. 'It was something and nothing. She gets wound up. She's getting better, I'm sure but ... there are days when she's not so good. She imagines things. Has panic attacks.'

They walked in silence for a few moments.

'I work away and I do worry about leaving her. Whenever I return I'm just so relieved to see her safe!'

'What? You think she might ... get lost, or something?'

'I worry about her being alone,' he shrugged. They walked across the lawn, soft beneath their feet, the scent rising.

'She's on medication?'

'Beta blockers to control her anxiety. Seroxat. To lift the black clouds a little.'

They reached the low wall at the farthest edge of the lawn. House martins skimmed the grass, heading for their nest under the eves. The sun dipped beneath the ridge on the far side of the valley. They stood beneath the canopy of a Scots pine, the branches a hood beneath the clear, darkening sky. Kitty wanted to be on the road. It was cool in the shadows and she crossed her arms. He moved closer.

'Thank you so much. For listening,' he murmured, his voice falling to a whisper. He ran a fingertip along her forearm. The downy hairs rose beneath his touch, a charge rippling her skin. He looked into her eyes, his gaze steady. He leaned closer as something shifted in the gloom at the edge of her vision. Kitty turned to see Dorian Kane walking towards them.

'I wondered where you two had sneaked off to!' In one hand she held the receipt, in the other an empty glass.

CHAPTER SEVENTEEN

'It's the uniform!'

Kitty shook her head, hiding her face behind the rim of her glass.

'I wasn't *in* uniform!'

Jacqui filled Kitty's glass. 'The crisp white blouse. The click of the handcuffs!'

'It's never happened before!'

'Must have done!' They were in Jacqui's kitchen, sharing a bottle of rosé.

'I couldn't, anyway! Not with him! He's too tall. Too married. Too scary! And it's bad scary!'

'You're in the police. Who else are you going to meet? One of those spotty kids at your box kicking class?'

'*Kick* boxing! And it's not kick boxing, it's … what the hell is it? I've forgotten!'

Realising Molly was on the computer in the next room, Kitty clamped hand across her mouth.

'It would never happen! That would be … unprofessional! And as you well know, Jacqui, I'm nothing less than totally professional at all times.'

'Maybe you should grab a bit of fun if it comes your way!' Jacqui whispered.

Kitty wrinkled her nose. 'There wouldn't be any fun with *him*!' She found the thought of Richard Kane was very sobering. 'He's odd. There's something very strange going on there ...' She stopped. It was a bad idea to talk about work to people outside the job, though she would trust Jacqui with her life. Kitty peeped at her daughter; saw the blue glow of the screen on Molly's face.

'You can't make rules about it,' said Jacqui. 'Men and women. Sex. Love. Anything can happen ...'

'Bryson says the same.'

'He's right, the old sod! The papers are full of it. *Vicar runs off with organist. Teacher runs off with schoolgirl. Policewoman disappears with ...*'

'Psycho?' I don't think so, Jacqui. Really. I don't think so...'

* * *

Molly rested her head in Kitty's lap. Kitty stroked her daughter's brow and stared through the window. The taxi hummed along the bypass, moving through pools of peach-coloured street light as it neared the town. A shape emerged from the hedge by the side of the road; a rusty ghost, tumbling across the road ahead. The driver dabbed the brake and the car shimmied into the inside lane.

'Bloody fox!'

Molly stirred, then fell back into dreams. The fox disappeared into the fields. The taxi driver ran a finger beneath his collar, knowing he had been driving too fast.

'Bring back hunting, eh?' He glanced in his mirror, looking

CHAPTER SEVENTEEN

for agreement.

'Get a lot of bother with foxes, in your line of business?'

The driver frowned. Kitty looked away.

'Didn't think so...' She ran over the events of the day. Richard Kane had played her with such skill. Looking back, the sequence of moves was clear. Opening with a display of aggression he had unsettled her. Then his unexpected apology disarmed her. Before she had time to take breath she was in the garden, listening to his sob story of a fragile, talented wife. Kitty was not naive. How had she allowed him to manipulate her in that way?

His final move came when he made a pass at her. Was that spontaneous or calculated? Was it a human response, an understandable reaction from a stressed and lonely man? Or something more calculated? Kitty had a realistic opinion of her looks. When Molly told her she looked 'pretty,' she smiled and kissed her, though she didn't believe it for a moment. 'I'm OK,' was as far as she would go. 'Not too bad.'

Had his desire for her been genuine or just another gambit? Running over the sequence of events, she suspected it was both. He had moved from hostility to charm because it worked. He had drawn her in with a shared confidence: 'Poor Dorian, she's so fragile. Poor me, I knew about her 'weakness,' yet I was big hearted enough to marry her.' He played at seduction then believed his own lie.

He drew you in. He uses tricks – his box of tools. Aggression doesn't work, so try vulnerability. Then charm.

They were tools that he used to get whatever he wanted.

And what is that?

She wondered if it might be the pleasure of knowing he had outwitted her; the brilliant mind that duped the stupid cop.

He seemed able to change emotional gear within a heartbeat. Either he was sincere or he was psychopathic. With a gun in the house that was a dangerous mix. Richard Kane certainly seemed to tick some of the boxes that defined a psychopath. He had the charm, the grandiosity, the callous lack of empathy. Yet being a psychopath was not a criminal offence. If he was, there was little she was able to do. Except, perhaps, try to prevent harm to his wife.

Some shadow flickered in her mind, a scrap of memory. It was a paper she had read at uni, something about male rage. *Monick. Male Rage, The Phallic Wound...? Or was it Jung?* She was too wasted to remember. She'd look it up in the morning.

Kitty stared into the darkness. Beyond the edge of the light lay the wild wood. Molly stirred beneath her, troubled by a dream. Kitty stroked her brow, soothing away the fear. At least she could make some things better. Molly was the reason she went to work each day.

We start out trying to do good. We end up doing the best we can.

She closed her eyes, suddenly aware that she was drunk. She started to hum a tune. She had forgotten that she was not alone.

'That's nice – what's that?' The driver was smiling again.

'Dunno. Sorry. Just a tune in my head.'

'I like music, me!' he said. He flicked on the radio. The tinny whine of a commercial station filled the silence. *'This going out to Sandra and all her crew in Ryton!'*

Distracted, Kitty lost her own tune, just as she was recalling the title. Looking at her reflection in the darkened window, she saw Richard Kane's face; felt the warmth of his fingers on her arm. For a moment she had enjoyed his touch. She shuddered with guilt. Was she so desperate? One of 'Mother

Nature's toys,' as Bryson had it?

Much later, as she lay in bed, the elusive tune returned. *'There's always some killing you got to do around the farm...'*

* * *

The VW Transporter moved through the night, inching up the valley, crossing the Cheviot Hills like a tick crawling over folds of skin. Nathan blinked; his eyes scratchy from peering into the gloom. Now and then he saw a dim gleam of animal eyes reflected in the headlights. He was buzzing after snorting yet another line. He was hearing every sound, feeling every movement around the bubble of the van. Tanya dozed beside him, her head lolling with the twists and turns in the road.

The van crept through tiny hamlets and the scattered farms. The trees petered out after a line of wind-bent rowans and they crossed open moorland lit by the moon: pearly-grey, like the ocean floor. Nathan pushed on towards the Border.

* * *

Dorian stands in front of the full length mirror; a silhouette in the moonlight. Her skin is white, almost translucent; her hair falling to her shoulders. Silk evening gloves dangle from her fingers. She eases the gloves onto her fingers, smoothing them tight, covering the cracked skin, the chipped nails. Richard watches from the bed.

The beam from passing headlights sweeps across the wall.

For a moment the spell is broken: they are no longer alone, no longer the only people in the world. But she cannot stop. She must make things right. She tips her head, listening to the car climbing the valley road. Now she sees herself and feels self-conscious, as if caught playing a game. She turns towards the bed, sees the gleam as Richard smiles. Such perfect teeth. He dabs a fingertip in the last few grains and rubs them into his gum.

She walks to the bed and kisses him. 'Am I forgiven? '

'Perhaps.'

'It meant nothing. You *know* that!'

He is silent. She senses a flicker of his jealousy, the embers not quite dead. She kisses him again, strokes his brow. 'It's you and I, Richard. *Only* you. Forever.'

* * *

CHAPTER EIGHTEEN

'That you, Locky?'

She could sense that Bryson was excited, though he was trying to keep his voice to a whisper. Maureen snored softly by his side.

'Sorry. I know it's late.'

'It's fine.'

Kitty passed the back of her hand across her lips. She had been sleeping with her mouth open. Was it two in the afternoon or two in the morning? The television burbled softly in the corner of the room. It seemed that she had not made it to bed, since she was lying on the sofa with a blanket. The corner of a hardback book dug into her side. She dropped it on the carpet – '*Male Rage, The Phallic Wound.*' She had no idea why the book was open, then flashed a memory. She had tucked Molly into bed then pulled it from the bookshelf. She had tried to read but had been too drunk to make sense of the words. Bryson's voice buzzed in her ear.

'You know I said there was something about that name? Kane?'

'Yup.' Kitty stifled a yawn. She heard Bryson breathe heavily as he stumped along his landing, out of earshot of Maureen.

She found the remote and killed the television. She slumped

onto the sofa, her eyes tight. Sweet darkness. This was the early stage of a hangover, the false dawn before the full horror kicked in.

'His parents are dead.'

'He's in his thirties, Bryson. That's not unusual.'

Bryson cut in. 'No. But his father was killed. An accident at home. His car fell off the jack, crushed him.'

'Nice...' The image almost made her retch. But car smashes, tractor spills and shotgun suicides were hardly rare in the countryside.

'It was a sudden death, so there was an inquest. Your best mate was called as a witness, strangely enough.'

'My best mate?'

'Gordon Campbell. PC Campbell, as he was then. He must have been pretty green at the time. He and his partner were first on the scene.'

'They were suspicious?'

'You'd have to ask him. But CID went in and asked questions. The investigating officers asked for reports.'

'About what?'

'About him – Kane. The lad, as he was then.'

Kitty's eyes opened wide.

'They thought he was involved?'

'There was a whiff of something. He was there when it happened.'

'Why did they start asking questions?'

'He was a young lad at the time. The Kanes adopted him when he was a nipper. Seems he loved his mum but never got on with the dad. He claimed they hated each other.'

'That's not so weird, is it?'

'There were "incidents." This was before the accident that

killed the old man.'

'What kind of incidents?'

'Violence, disturbing the peace.'

'The law was involved?'

'Once or twice. On one occasion the father started beating the lad. His mam panicked and called 999. The second time was worse. The father called, claiming his son was drunk and threatening him with a shotgun.'

'Wow. ..'

She lay still. The room was whirling, tilting as if she was balanced on the back legs of a chair. 'There must have been charges?'

'They had a black Lab. That's the crucial word: *had*. The father loved the dog. Doted on it. It seems the lad *did* fire the gun. He only did it out of frustration, he said. Just fired across the fields, at random, he claimed. But the dog ran into the line of fire ...'

'Sounds a little ...'

'Doesn't it just! But he said it was an accident, he didn't mean it. He was distraught. Tears all round.'

'He shot the family dog?'

'It was all smoothed over. No charges. The mother didn't want him to get into trouble. The father wanted everything hushed up.'

'And that was OK?'

'The Kanes were a "respectable family." Well liked. That was the end of it.'

'What were they fighting over?'

'No idea. I've only got what it says here.'

'Right ...' Kitty closed her eyes again. She was definitely going to throw up.

'This was a long time ago. Almost before my time.'

'How did you find this out?'

'The file was at Shaftoe Leazes. I *knew* there was something! Didn't I say?'

He sounded elated, as if he'd had a win on the horses. Kitty rolled off her couch and tottered towards the bedroom.

'Tell you what. Sleep's where I'm heading right now.' Her bed seemed miles away. 'Nighty night.'

'Have a goosey at the file next time you're in. But Kitty? We never had this chat, OK?'

Kitty flopped onto the bed and closed her eyes. She was asleep before Bryson realised that she had gone.

CHAPTER NINETEEN

The Frosts left Wales when Dorian was three months old. Peter Frost was a geologist working in the oil industry and over the next fifteen years his work took the family around the world.

They made homes in Australia, Nigeria, Japan and Venezuela. They never stayed anywhere for long. By the time she was ten years old, Dorian had lived in more than a dozen houses. 'Home' meant her parents and the few treasures she brought to each new house.

She was a solitary child, able to amuse herself for hours, twisting fragments of paper or cloth into animals or people. She created her own set of imaginary friends; a family called the Nesbitts which she crafted from felt and buttons. They travelled around the world with Dorian. She would sit on the bed, talking to her 'family', weaving the story of their lives: a saga of romance, birth and death.

Every few months, Dorian's real family would move to a different country and she would be sent to a new school. Although she made new friends in each place, she learnt that these friendships would be broken when her father moved to the next posting. So she held herself back. It was easier, safer, to keep her distance. The Nesbitts were Dorian's only lasting friends. She was reluctant to trust her love to anyone else. When she grew up she vowed she would find someone and make a family and they would be so close, so devoted to each other. Nothing would tear them apart.

Dorian was sixteen when her mother inherited the family house in Barnet, north London. It was the first time that they settled in one place for more than a year. Dorian earned a place at the art college, Central St. Martins. Great things were expected of her there. Her designs were original and distinctive, though at times quite bizarre. She spun confections of antique lace and feather into hats and masks. She wove scraps of fur and bone and fabric to make gloves and bags, belts and buckles. While her tutors recognised her talent, they hinted that some of her stuff might just be a little too macabre for the wider public. Her friends teased her for making "cash from corpses," but Dorian had no doubts: she believed in magic, in passion, in danger.

Often she worked through the night, sewing beads onto the skull of a crow or stitching animal teeth onto a belt made from the glistening, limpid skin of an eel. While friends worked in bars to fund their studies, Dorian was lucky to have wealthy parents who supported her.

During her final year, the fashion editor of the Observer predicted that Dorian Frost was a big name for the future. She set up a label called *'Goldeneye.'* She had acquired a list of devoted clients. She was headed for success. Then life took a different direction.

* * *

CHAPTER NINETEEN

Whenever Richard left for a business trip, the Kanes followed the same routine. Rising early, Richard laid his clothes on the bed, choosing from a swatch of ties and shirts arranged in a neat row. Dorian left him to dress, slipping downstairs to make his coffee and scrambled eggs.

She felt her way down the staircase, her fingers tracing the rough surface of the wall. It was two years since they had moved into the farm, yet they hadn't got around to fitting a new banister. The staircase was the place where their money had run out. Upstairs, the plaster was still the original mix of horse hair, lathes and horse manure. Over the centuries the owners of West Neuk had buried the walls beneath fifty coats of distemper. Richard and Dorian chose to have it decorated in Oxford Stone, a shade mixed by Farrow and Ball. It was one of their traditional colours and they both thought it beautiful.

Renovating the farmhouse had been a difficult process. Richard was a very demanding customer. There had been a series of rows with the decorators that had slowed progress to a crawl. Now the ground floor at West Neuk was almost finished. The terracotta floor was laid and the walls skimmed and decorated. New doors and windows were fitted: oak, in keeping with the rest of the farm.

Dorian's collection of paintings lined the walls. Drawings by Gwen and Augustus John hung on each side of the fireplace in the sitting room. On a table by the stairs was a bronze of the River God Tyne by David Wynne. The piece Dorian loved was an 18th century Venetian girandole – a convex, fish eye mirror which hung in the hall, near the front door. The gilt- framed mirror was designed to reflect an entire room. Dorian would look at her own reflection, wondering about all those who had gone before, peering into that same, misty glass. Who were they? What had become of them?

In the village Richard was known as "the millionaire." The Kanes had lived in the valley for generations and had always been regarded as "comfortable". The rumour was that Richard's time in the City of London had earned him a fortune. So the Kanes poured money into the house. Richard always wanted the best; nothing less was good enough.

The banister was the tipping point. He had insisted it should be carved from pear wood to fit the contour of the stairs. The carpenter did as he was told and Richard seemed pleased with the result. The man presented his bill. That was the moment Richard began to find fault in his work. He pointed out all the flaws in the man's work: the faults in the wood, the shoddy finish. To Dorian, the banister was perfect. For the sake of peace she asked her mother to pay the bill and told Richard that the carpenter had made the changes. That was the way Richard was; a perfectionist. He required total commitment. But they had spent all of Richard's settlement from Amschels on the house. Their savings were almost gone.

Richard insisted that their cash flow problem was temporary. When Dorian hinted she might get a job, Richard was against it. She suggested she might help out at the school in Belfordham.

'Absolutely not! You have more than enough to do here. This is temporary; a matter of weeks. It's certainly not worth you catching head lice for fifty quid a week!'

When she hinted they might ask her mother for a loan, Richard cut her short. 'When Cutler's Wharf is completed we'll have more than we can spend! I've explained all this, Dorian. This is a temporary situation. It would be a help if you could try to understand that. There's no need to panic. And I certainly draw the line at asking your mother for help. We're not children. I have this covered.'

He was a proud man; too proud to ask for help. He would take care of things. Dorian liked that; it made her feel safe.

She had only visited Cutler's Wharf on one occasion. They drove down to Liverpool and spent the afternoon wandering through an abandoned Victorian warehouse on the waterfront. There were holes in the roof and pigeons fluttered around in the gloom, high above them. Richard was certain it could be transformed into beautiful apartments. While she loved the idea, she wondered if his timing was right. He teased her about her lack of business sense. Since then she had avoided the subject. Richard was the expert. Dorian trusted him. Her role was to make him happy. That was something she knew how to do.

* * *

She poured oil into the pan, slooshed it around. This morning Richard was leaving on a trip that would solve their money problems. He would be away for a week: Leeds, Liverpool, Bristol, London; then home. During that time, Dorian knew that she would be alone. She had Facebook and Twitter, of course, and her mobile. Richard would call her at least twice a day. She hated the isolation, but knew they needed to earn money.

As she cooked breakfast Dorian wondered if "he" might drop by. He was sweet, in his way, and she was fond of him. But he was only a boy. He called himself K-Dog, which was laughable: a lad from the English countryside giving himself a gangster name. But he knew that it was ridiculous too, which was part of his charm. She hoped that he would not turn up. She had made the situation clear. Though she had known he liked her, it was a surprise when he pounced that drunken afternoon. It was exciting, yet she was pushing him away at the very instant Richard walked in and found them. To see him so hurt, so angry, had been the worst moment of her life. There was no-one but Richard. There never would be.

The boy had called around to see Richard and, as usual, they disappeared up to the office. Richard had never explained why he was such a regular visitor. She knew he was Richard's dealer, delivering a little something for the weekend. Yet she suspected there was more to it. Foolishly, she had asked him to stay for lunch. She could see that Richard was appalled. But it was too late. She had made the offer for the best of intentions. Richard had so few friends.

They had all been drinking. Richard was lying in the sitting room, stretched out on one of the leather sofas. She had gone to fix another drink and "he" had followed her into the kitchen. As she stood at the sink he put his hands on her shoulders and kissed her neck. Soft, butterfly kisses, dapping along the nape of her neck. When he turned her around, she started to laugh.

'Don't be silly!' she said. She hugged him, wanting to save his feelings. That was the moment Richard came into the room and found them. Before she had a chance to explain he was screaming at her. For a while she was worried that something truly awful might happen. In the end he threw the boy out, shoving him through the front door. Then the row began. When he became angry, Richard was relentless. She covered her ears and walked out of the front door and kept on walking.

By the time that policewoman brought her home the heat

CHAPTER NINETEEN

had gone. Richard was sullen. She could tell he was hurt. In bed that night she explained what had happened. They laughed about it. The idea that she might be interested in the boy was ridiculous. Richard was her husband. He was her closest friend. He could be sure of her love.

After the way that terrible afternoon had gone, she thought it unlikely they would ever see "him" again. And that was for the best.

She flipped the fork through the eggs, beating air into the mixture. The chink of steel on china echoed on the stone walls of the kitchen. She leaned over the hob, teasing the mixture away from the edge as it caught. She was getting "the feeling"; that odd sensation of foreboding that she felt whenever Richard left for one of his trips. She dismissed it. It was loneliness; as simple as that. She had few friends in the village. They would nod and smile at her in the shop but her real friends were in London. For the first time in years she remembered the Nesbitts. The memory made her smile. Then she heard Richard, coming down the stairs.

CHAPTER TWENTY

Kitty rolled over in bed. Her eyes flicked open. A cobweb drifted through the air, swaying back and forth. The ceiling was cracking and needed a new coat of paint. Only another twelve hours until she could flop back into bed. The dawn chorus raged on. She hurled back the covers, yawning until her jaw cracked.

'Molly? What d'you want for your breakfast?'

In the next room, her daughter stood at the mirror, fully dressed. Molly threaded her dark hair into a scrunchy.

'Porridge?'

'Please...'

'Porridge. *Please* ...'

* * *

A blast of cold north wind rocked Nathan's van. They were parked in the lay-by on the top of Carter Bar, the hill that straddled the English and Scottish border. Tanya queued for tea and bacon butties beneath the awning of a battered caravan. A veil of low cloud drifted across the road. She teetered back to the van, carrying styrofoam cups. Nathan closed the window against the scent of fried bacon. The windscreen misted as Tanya blew on her coffee. Nathan took money from his wallet and handed it over.

'How much is left, Nathe?'

'Hundred and fifty, maybe?' Nathan leaned forward and wiped a porthole in the steamy window.

'We'll need more,' said Tanya.

They sipped their coffee and gazed over the bleak hillside.

'Let's have a chat with your good friend Richard.'

* * *

Kitty stirred the breakfast, pushing the spoon through the porridge while Molly watched from the kitchen table. Kitty had slept badly. She ran through her schedule. She had to drop Molly at school, speak at a meeting of the Rural Drugs Initiative. After that she had her one-to-one with Gordon Campbell about her "career path." The meeting loomed; a dark cloud in her day. After that she would go for a run. Exercise helped her sleep. She closed her eyes. As if the hangover weren't enough, she had come on that morning, the pain like an old bruise. Kitty yawned and closed her eyes. She swayed gently then sat down, just for a moment.

'Mum!' There was alarm in Molly's voice. 'Something's burning!'

* * *

Dorian sipped coffee as she watched Richard. They didn't say much on these mornings. Richard was thinking of the day ahead and Dorian was anxious not to spoil his mood. He must have nothing to worry about. Dorian wanted him to think of home as his sanctuary.

He finished his breakfast, placing his knife and fork in perfect alignment. He sat quietly. She could see his mind was elsewhere, running over the route he would take, the meetings he would make. This was a difficult time for him. She had never known anyone who was so driven. But in the last few weeks things had changed. Now his workday stretched into the evening and she had sensed him become more distant. She rose as she saw him push back his chair.

'So... I'll be back on Saturday evening. Late.' They stood at the door. She kissed him.

'Good luck!'

She stood on the doorstep, clutching her dressing gown. He turned the Porsche across the gravel and mimed 'I'll call.'

She bit her lip. The car rolled down the long drive, lurching over the potholes. Richard turned onto the main road and the car picked up speed. Dorian waited until he disappeared behind the trees. Cloud shadows scudded across the high pasture on the far side of the valley. She stood on the doorstep, the wind whipping her hair across her face. The clouds broke and sunlight flooded over Cross Fell, the hillside a cushion of green and gold velvet. The land was greening up now as new heather and cotton grass pushed through.

It would be another fine day. Dorian shivered, pulled her dressing gown tight and hurried indoors.

CHAPTER TWENTY ONE

'I don't have a lot to say...' Campbell held a sheet of A4 between his fingertips, glancing down to remind himself of the bullet points. The Neighbourhood Beat team were gathered around the table, sipping machine coffee. Notepads flipped open and rollerballs clicked as the team gazed up at their dear leader. He paced back and forth, swaying from foot to foot, an Aberdeen Angus bull strutting into a field of heifers. It thrilled him, Kitty knew, having them hang on to every word.

She sat at the end of the table, as far away as possible, cradling her coffee. To her right sat her friend, Elayne Hawes. Elayne was the same age as Kitty, though she had been in the job twice as long. She had no illusions about their boss.

'Thinks he's God's gift! It's all blether,' she told Kitty when they were first assigned to Campbell's team. 'He loves the sound of his own voice. Just play the game. Look into his eyes, pretend to listen, think about anything you want. I mean, I tune in for the essential stuff, but otherwise I just let it wash over me! He likes to crack the whip now and then. He's a bitter man. Whatever you do, don't take it to heart!

To Kitty's left sat two PCSOs, the Community Support Officers Gemma Smiles and Orla Harrington. The PCSOs were younger, just out of their probationary year. Gemma's pen hovered over a blank page in her notepad. Whenever Campbell opened his mouth Gemma's nib scratched the paper. She would scribble a note if Campbell cleared his throat. While Gemma was dedicated, Orla Harrington faked it. She put on a good impression of someone who cared as she stared up at Campbell. Her panda eyes glistening with mascara, blonde hair gathered in a chignon, she seemed eager to take in every word. Both were eager to succeed. When she first joined, Kitty had shared their enthusiasm. These days she knew they were all running on the spot, riding the treadmill, watching the same faces making the same stupid mistakes. Perhaps her mother was right. She had made the wrong choice. Campbell tapped the edge of his paper on the table.

'PC Hawes.' Elayne straightened, raised her eyebrows and tapped her pen against her lip.

'Some joker's spraying his tag on the church wall. St Mary's. It's silver paint. The vicar's peed off, so ... what do we do?'

His eyes ranged over the group. 'Why are we here? Anyone tell me? What's the function and purpose of the Neighbourhood Team?' His brows met, fusing like two black caterpillars. 'Elly?'

'We provide a highly visible contact for local residents and businesses.'

'Excellent!' Campbell bellowed, as if addressing a parade ground. 'So *do* that! Show your faces! Give the vicar a thrill!' He looked over his team, happy to see his broad smile reflected by all, except for one. 'What's up Lockwood? A smile costs nothing.'

'Headache, sarge.'

'Take more water with it...'

CHAPTER TWENTY ONE

Kitty played the game, smiling her lop-sided smile. Elayne Hawes made a careful note in her pad, winking at Kitty as Campbell turned away.

'Our aim is Total Policing. That's making life better for those who uphold the law and making it tough for those who break it. Now then...' He glanced at his notes. 'Next item: courts! Who's involved?'

Kitty raised her hand. 'I'm in two cases coming up.'

'Don't keep us in suspense, Locky ...'

'There's a preliminary hearing for Kevin Robb. Careless driving. Straightforward. That's with Des Tucker and Andy er, PC Banforth. I'm only on the edge of that. I was in the pursuit car. And next week there's the Lumley case, possession of a controlled substance, Class A, with intent to supply. He's pleading not guilty...'

'That's DS Prudhoe's case, is it not?'

Kitty nodded. His smile had gone. He did not approve of the friendship between Bryson and Kitty. Campbell had watched them together in the canteen, the intense discussions, the way they seemed at ease in each other's company. They were not the same rank, nor the same department. There was a difference in age and experience. Friendship between a man and a woman could mean only one thing.

'We all know Clive Lumley is a "major domo", a big player, as it were. We don't want any slip ups, do we? '

Kitty nodded. It would be a day of hanging around, of wondering if she might be called, though there were compensations: a good book to read and a whiz around the city shops, when the criminal justice system had finished with her.

Campbell's gaze ranged over his team. 'If you have a court appearance be clean, sober, smart. Be punctual. Most of all – be *prepared.* That's all I have to say on that.' He worked through the rest of his list. There were initiatives on public drinking, targets on speeding and strategies for graffiti. Kitty's mind wandered. She watched Orla tucking away a strand of blonde hair. Orla fixed her eyes on Campbell's face, tilted her head, slowly tapping her pen against her lip. While Gemma made notes, Orla's pen moved languidly, covering the page with a flowery doodle. She laughed at Campbell's jokes. She knew how to play the game.

After half an hour they were dismissed. Elayne leaned over. 'Can I borrow your notes, Orla?' The younger woman quickly closed her notepad.

Campbell loomed over Kitty. 'We're having a chat, aren't we, Locky?'

Kitty nodded and sank back in her seat, waiting for the room to empty. Elayne Hawes mouthed: 'Play the game.' The door closed. They were alone.

Campbell pulled up a chair and faced Kitty across the table. He swigged a mouthful of coffee, though it must have been clay cold.

He's nervous. That's bad...

Opening a folder, Campbell clicked his pen. His eyes ran back and forth over her notes. Finally he looked up, rubbed a thumb across his chin, skin rasping bristle.

Play the game.

Kitty gazed up at him. If this was going to be painful she would make the best of it.

' Mary...'

'...Hetherington?' offered Kitty.

'That's it. The Great Television Robbery. Anything?'

'A couple of con artists passing through, I suspect. I passed the report to DS Prudhoe. There's nothing to add, as far as I know.'

'That wouldn't be very far, would it?' Campbell looked up then winked. 'Joke! Don't be so sensitive. Locky! Lighten up, eh?'

She held his gaze for a moment, waiting for the next dig. They didn't like each other. It was an instinctive thing. There was no hatred. They simply did not enjoy being in the same room.

'You've followed it up?' Campbell tilted his head.

'Bryson – DS Prudhoe, I should say – went down and spoke to her. And I arranged a visit from Crime Prevention.'

'But you made a follow-up visit?'

'It's on my list. I will get round to it.'

'While we're on about things you might "get round to", did you manage to sort that phone business?'

'I returned it to the owner. Mrs Kane.'

'Next up ...' Campbell tapped his list.

'I wanted to ask you about her husband, sarge...'

Campbell looked up, his brow creased. 'The millionaire?'

'Is he?' asked Kitty.

'Tragic, that family.' Campbell shook his head. 'Just shows that money isn't everything.'

'Why do you say "tragic"?'

'The accident!'

'Accident?' Kitty put her fingers to her lips.

Playing the game...

Campbell dropped his list on the desk and looked away. He was silent for a moment, as if searching for the right words. 'This was way back. I was straight out of Hendon. This was my first job. Been up here a week. I was paired up with Peter

Flint. Lovely bloke, Pete! We were heading for home, along the 69, when we got a call. So we go up to the farm...'

'The Kanes' place'?'

'Bloody miles away! What's it called? East Neuk? West Neuk? Anyway ... seems the lad – Richard – he'd called the ambulance. We get there. The kid's waiting on the doorstep. We can hear this wailing! Howling, like an animal, or something! So we go in, just to see if there's anything we can do. Seems the father had been working underneath the car and it slid off the jack.'

The sun touched his face and she saw a tear at the corner of his eye.

'It was as nasty as that sounds. Thought I was going to throw up. His mother was beside herself. Screaming, wailing! After a while she gets up and she starts on the boy.'

'What do you mean?'

Campbell shook his head. His eyes were troubled, as if seeing it all over again. 'She starts screaming at the lad! Hitting him, her fists balled up, braying him on the chest!'

'What was she saying?'

Campbell shook his head. 'It wasn't words, as such. Or if it was, I couldn't understand them! Horrible! Just one of those horrible scenes you get. Every now and then.'

'So what happened?'

'Pete gets hold of her. Pete Flint. He holds her hands, wraps his arms around her and holds her. He was a big lad, Peter. So I take the lad, steer him through the front door, out of harm's way.'

'And what was he doing. The boy?'

Campbell shrugged. 'Nothing. He just looked blank. Shock, I suppose. Then, when I got him outside in the fresh air, he just fell apart.'

He tapped his finger on the desk. 'Some things stay with you.'

'But there was nothing suspicious about the death?'

'What do you mean?'

She shrugged. 'I heard they didn't get on.'

'Where did you hear that?'

'I think it was something he said the other night.' It was a lie, but it seemed to work.

'Lots of fathers and sons squabble. Doesn't mean a thing. As I say, the lad was in pieces when I saw him. '

'But he was questioned?'

'It was a sudden death.'

'But they *had* squabbled?'

'There was a bit of history. The lad wanted to borrow the car. Wanted money. Wanted his father to set him up in business. Blah blah. So what? Just your normal, average teenager stuff. They would quarrel over the weather! I did with *my* father. Didn't mean I didn't greet like a bairn when he passed away!'

'But there was suspicion of *something?*'

This question seemed to bring him back to the present. 'What? You think he might have picked up the car and dropped it on his dad...'

'No. But...'

'It was an accident! The father was meticulous about safety, so ... yes, that was unusual, I suppose ...'

Campbell shook his head. She could see he was in two minds about saying more. She waited, watching him. 'OK. Someone discovered there had been earlier calls to the farm, true enough. The business with the dog. But that was all explained.'

'Explained as?'

'As an accident.'

'*Another* accident ...'

'Yes – *another* accident! You've been doing this long enough, Lockwood. The countryside might look pretty, but it's bloody lethal. You know this! Farms are dangerous places. Death traps!'

'Yet somebody thought there was something not quite right ...'

He prodded the desk, jabbing his finger against the surface. '*Nobody* would think that boy could have had anything to do with his father's death. He was distraught! Torn apart!'

'And you were convinced that was genuine?'

'Of course I was!'

Kitty pretended to sip from her empty cup. She placed it on the desk. 'Richard Kane was adopted. Maybe his adoptive father resented him.'

Campbell rolled his eyes. 'Oh, *here* we go!'

'Sarge?'

'My dad looked at me funny – so I killed him.'

'Some offenders start by carrying out violence on animals. It's a pathway to violence against people. Men who commit acts of cruelty towards animals rarely stop there. It can develop into ...'

'Bollocks! Utter bollocks is what it can develop into!'

Kitty cleared her throat, composing her reply. Before she could speak, he was at her.

'We have plenty of real villains without inventing more! Richard's a smashing bloke! When you consider what he's been through ...'

'I just think ...'

CHAPTER TWENTY ONE

'You like the job, Locky?' He unscrewed the top of his pen, screwed it tight again. 'You enjoy it? Or did you just fancy the uniform?'

'Of course I like the job!' She was startled by the force of her own response.

Campbell slowly shook his head. He leaned back in his chair, clasped his hands behind his head and arched his spine until the joints cracked. He held the pose, like a stretching cat. She caught the whiff of stale sweat.

'You don't like me, do you?' The words came out of nowhere.

'That's an unusual statement.' He passed a finger tip beneath his collar. 'Let me think about that for a moment.' He looked away, gathering his thoughts. 'As it happens, you're wrong. I don't dislike you, Lockwood.'

'So what's the problem?'

'My only problem is making this team work. It's routine police work. It may seem mundane. But it requires a certain ... strength.'

'And you think I'm a weak link?'

'Somewhere down the line, I think you'll let someone down.'

'In what way?'

'Make the wrong decision. Just as you've done over this. All you have to do is return a phone, Locky. It's not difficult! Do yourself a favour – there's enough crime without inventing more.' He had wounded her, which gave him pleasure. He leaned forward, resting his elbows on the desk. Linking his fingers, he assumed his caring smile. 'This is never easy to say, Kitty.' His voice was now a growl. 'But I don't think you're suited for this job. Just my opinion.' He spread his hands and smiled. 'You're too ... *cerebral* to be on the front line. Is that the word? *Cerebral?* You think too much.'

He tapped the side of his head. Kitty bit her cheek and tasted blood. He smiled, tilting his head, waiting for her to agree. 'You would be perfect for many careers. Teaching. Social work. Something where you help people. Empathy. Understanding. Imagination. These are all good qualities.'

'*This* job needs empathy.' She glared at him.

Campbell pushed out his chin, stretching his neck. He nodded, encouraging her to expand on the notion. Kitty took a deep breath. 'The job of a Neighbourhood Team is to look at the community as a whole. To reassure the public. To ...' She tried to recall the exact words. '... to identify problems as experienced by all members of the public, including vulnerable groups.''

Campbell smiled. Her fight back entertained him. He sat back and spread his hands on the table.

'Don't waste your life, eh?' Neither spoke for a while. 'I have a meeting.'

She saw an expression of grudging admiration on his face. No doubt he had expected her to fall apart. 'Best get cracking then, Locky!'

Kitty folded her pad, put away her pen then gathered her papers, tapping the edges on the table to straighten them. 'Whatever you say, sarge. You're the boss.'

CHAPTER TWENTY TWO

The road was steep, the corners tight, yet the Porsche needed only a touch on the wheel to hold the road. Richard was glad to be on the move at last. One way or another, this week should see everything change for the better.

He stopped at the Texaco garage. For a moment he considered paying with cash. His credit card had been a bit iffy of late.

'You off again, Mr Kane?' Tommy Pearson wiped his hands on the rag he kept by the register.

'I'm everywhere the next few days!' Richard sighed. 'I'll be away until the end of the week at least. Home on Saturday night, I hope!'

'That lady of yours will find herself a fancy man!'

'Yes. Saturday night...'

Richard stressed the day, trying to fix his alibi in Tommy's mind. He dropped a packet of mints and a Telegraph onto the counter. As Tommy struggled to swipe the card, Richard studied the man's face: the oil and grime that etched the lines around his eyes. Perhaps he could find a job like that, working with his hands? Was it too late to start again? A new career in a new town? A new country, perhaps?

The till chattered and Tommy held out the machine for Richard's pin number. 'Shot four last night!'

'Did you, Tommy?'

'Aye! Four of the little buggers!'

'You'll have to give me a lesson.'

Richard folded his VAT receipt and tucked it into his wallet. 'I can't hit a barn door!'

Tommy chuckled, glad to feel superior to the 'millionaire' in one respect, at least.

'It's your breathing, isn't it? That's the secret.'

Tommy mimed raising a shotgun, swinging it around to follow the flight of his prey. 'Breathe out...That's when you're still, see? Then you squeeze the trigger, your lungs is empty, your head is still, and .... pock!' He popped his mouth, jerked with the recoil and lowered his 'gun.'

Richard shook his head, as if lost in admiration. He slipped the wallet into his pocket. As he reached the door, Tommy spoke. 'She's got a spot of rust.'

Richard turned, his hand on the door. 'Say again?'

'Wheel arch, Mr Kane. Driver's side. About the size of a five pence piece.'

'Really?'

'Fetch it in, Mr Kane. I'll have a look, if you like. When you get back.'

'Early next week?'

'Aye. Just pop in.'

'I will.'

The car was serviced in town, by specialists. There was no way Richard would let a clown like Tommy look at it.

'Thanks for that.'

'No bother. Cars, isn't it? Buggers! They fall apart. Just like everything else.'

'Have a good week, Tommy.'

* * *

Richard threaded the Porsche through the village before turning onto the A689, climbing the valley to cross the Pennines. As he cruised over the hilltops he felt a surge of elation. His car might lift into the air at any moment. He could see for a hundred miles along the blue spine of the Pennines. The Solway Firth glittered on the horizon. He was the king of the world, the car his throne, soaring above his kingdom. The motor thrummed, the road rose to meet him. He loved that machine. A 911 Turbo, a hundred in eight seconds, black inside and out, with leather seats in Carrera Red. The dash glowed like a flight deck. Perfection, order, efficiency. These were the qualities which made him feel secure. The walnut fascia gleamed. The scent of the leather filled his nostrils. He cruised across the moor, taking curves one-handed.

This was his chance to make things right. If it all went to plan he would soon have the money he needed. He would be free, though he was not without qualm. Dorian would suffer; that was inevitable. The thought tainted his happiness, yet there seemed no way around it. He imagined her being held down, bundled into the cellar, tied and gagged. He pushed those images to the back of his mind and put his foot to the floor.

The Porsche leaped forward, mounted a rise and for a moment, seemed to take flight. Bright sunshine flooded into the car, warming his face, glinting on his Ray-Bans, gleaming on his perfect teeth.

* * *

Kitty walked Molly to school then jogged home through Riverside Park. She paused by the picnic tables to practise a few kicks and stretches. Standing in the fighting stance, *Zenkutsu Dachi,* her feet apart, she imagined a sequence of moves. In her mind she was sparring with Rafael, his brown eyes fixed on her as they circled each other.

Kitty rocked on the balls of her feet, throwing kicks at the head of her invisible attacker. The sinews in her thighs stretched as her blood warmed. When she had worked up a sweat, she sat at a picnic table and watched the river flow.

The water was flat and low, the oak trees on the far bank mirrored in the surface. She decided to run home before her muscles cooled. As she pounded the path beside the river, flurries of May blossom fell through the air, gathering in drifts at the edge of the path.

She heard a whistle and a rush of air on her cheek. The stone passed an inch from her eye before splashing into the river. She watched the circles widening in the water. It took that moment for her to understand. Peering into the trees along the bank, her pulse quickened as she looked for the stone thrower. Shadows shifted in the bushes, becoming a pack of three or four young men. They broke through the undergrowth, cackling and yelling as they ran away. One stood his ground, grinning and nodding at her.

Kitty scrambled up the steep bank, grabbing roots to pull

herself up. At the summit the slope was almost vertical and she scrabbled on all fours. She pushed through the bushes and stood upright, panting for breath. The sound of footsteps and braying laughter faded into the distance.

But Kevin Robb stood in clear view. He turned towards her then skipped backwards, taunting her, daring her to follow. Dusting her hands, she walked then jogged towards him. His grin faltered for a moment as he realised she was coming for him. He turned and broke into a run. She upped her pace. Kevin glanced over his shoulder, his eyes wide as he saw she was gaining on him. He had a solid frame but he was no athlete. As they ran along a cobbled lane Kitty closed the gap.

Kevin's face was crimson, his arms and legs flailing. She jogged behind him, feeling easy, running within herself. With a spurt she drew level. For a while they ran side by side, Kevin seemingly oblivious to the fact she was there. After a while she leaned closer. 'Giving up Kevin?'

He glanced at her. 'Fuck off!' he wheezed.

Sweat ran down his face, gathering in cloudy drops at the end of his nose. They were almost at walking pace now, though Kevin's arms and legs flapped as if he was running. He glanced over and saw she was smiling. He stopped and bent double, wheezing and dripping sweat on the cobbles. She stood beside him and rested her hand on his back.

'You want to stop, Kevin? 'Cos I can go on all day.'

* * *

They sat at one of the picnic tables beside the river. 'Some people would say, Kevin, that you threw the stone because you *wanted* to be caught...'

'That's bollocks!' He was tugging a thread at the knee of his trousers, twisting it tight, then letting it go.

'Have it your way.' She watched the way his chest moved as he struggled to catch his breath. 'Maybe we should talk to your mother?'

He glared at her, but there was fear in his eyes, mixed with anger.

'OK. So talk to me instead. It's your choice.'

'Talk about what?'

'Home?'

'What you want me to say, like?'

Kitty looked over the river. A heron flew upstream, the steady beat of her wings reflected in the water. They watched the bird land in the shallows, her feet skating the surface. Within moments the creature was invisible, the grey and white plumage blending into the parched stones along the far bank.

'It must be hard. Just you and your mother, trying to make that place work.'

Kevin's leg began to bounce, bobbing in a tight rhythm. 'No money, is there? In farming.'

'I know. I know. Feed. Vets' bills. And that car of yours must cost a fortune.'

'Yeah! 'Specially when people like you run me into the ditch...'

'I feel a little guilty about that, Kevin. I've been wondering if there was anything I could do. Would you like me to ask the lads from the Drug Squad to go over your car?'

'What are you on about now?'

'They could give it a proper valet? They do a lovely job! Carpets, seats...everywhere. Very thorough. They've got all the kit, haven't they? They can give it a proper going over.

They Hoover the lot. They find every speck.'

'You charging me?'

'We could go over there now?' she lied. 'Get them to have a look.'

'What's the fucking idea, like?'

'We're just having a chat, Kevin. Just two people, sitting by the river on a summer's day. Having a chat.'

'Yeah?'

'If it *was* to go any further, that would be your choice. If anyone gets charged with threatening behaviour, say, or assaulting a police officer, or whatever ... that would be down to you ...'

A flush ran up Kevin's neck, pinking his cheeks, reaching the roots of his ginger curls. His leg bobbed around like the gear stick on a tractor.

'It's just you and me, OK, Kevin?'

He nodded, twisted the thread again. 'Just chatting.' He swallowed, his Adam's apple sliding up and down his freckled throat.

'I tell you what I think. It must be hard being the man of the house. Hard to earn enough to keep you and your mother. '

She waited.

'Aye...'

'And I think there's only one way a person could pay for a car like yours.' She watched the side of his face, waiting. After a few moments of silence, he could bear it no more. He nodded. She touched his shoulder, a gentle, slow motion punch. 'There's someone I'd like you to speak to.'

* * *

'Would you like a drink, Kevin?'

He shook his head. Kitty, still wearing her running kit, stood in the doorway of Interview Room 3. Bryson moved behind her and she stood aside to let him through. 'Kevin, this is DS Prudhoe.'

'I know who he is.'

'Thanks for coming in Kevin.' Bryson placed a mug of tea on the table. His chair squeaked as he shuffled into a comfortable position. 'This is an informal chat, OK, Kevin? We can do you a favour. I think you can do one for us'

The boy's gaze was fixed on the table top. 'I did it.'

Bryson glanced at Kitty. 'Did what, Kevin?' she said.

Kevin's shoulders began to shake. He held his fingers to his eyes, as if that might staunch the tears. He hated a woman seeing him cry. 'Ask me.'

She cleared her throat, leaned forward. 'Kevin? Just tell DS Prudhoe what you told me.'

He nodded, still hiding his eyes. 'I was buying from this lad in the Five Wands.'

'Buying what?'

'Tack. Speed. Special K.'

Bryson swallowed a mouthful of tea. 'For yourself?'

Kevin nodded. He thumbed a tear from his eye and stared through the window. Kitty leaned closer.

'And?'

'He asked me if I was interested in a deal. I'd get it free. And a bit extra.'

'And how would that work?'

'He needed someone to deliver the gear. Didn't want to get his hands dirty, I guess. I had to keep me phone switched on – all the time. I'd get a call, go somewhere and pick up the stuff.'

'Go where?'

'Different places. The park. He'd leave the gear behind a wall. Under a stone. All kinds of places.'

'What about the money you collected?'

'I left it in the same place. Wrapped in a placky bag. Every night. I just had to text, say it was there.'

'And someone would collect the money?'

Kevin shrugged. 'Must have. I never saw him after that.'

'Who did you deliver to?'

'All over. This was my patch.'

Kitty noticed a swagger, an echo of the way it had made him feel. 'Kevin? Do you have a nickname?'

Kevin shot a glance at her. He looked wary.

'I think you have. I think you're K-Dog.' For a moment he met her eyes. At that moment, something fell into place. On some level she had known the answer before she asked the question. Dorian Kane knew Kevin. He was the Kanes' delivery boy. He was the one kiss. She was the one who 'had not been a girl' for a long time.

'Bingo!' said the Voice in her head. Kitty sat back.

'Can you give me any names?' asked Bryson.

Kevin began to pick at the knee of his trousers, twisting the thread. They waited, letting the silence stretch. The boy breathed in, lifted his head and closed his eyes. He didn't want to see their faces as he spoke the words.

'Some, mebbe. Some I won't say. They're mates. There was all sorts. I was Deals on Wheels, me!'

Bryson's eyes never left his face. Tears fell through Kevin's fingers. His voice dropped to a whisper, all the bravado gone.

'That bloke. He was one.'

Bryson stole a glance at Kitty.

'Who's that?'

'You know.' This to Kitty. 'That twat. The one that's fucking loaded.'

She leaned in. 'You mean Richard Kane? At West Neuk?'

Kevin was still for a moment. Then he nodded.

'You hate him, don't you, Kevin?'

Kevin Robb said nothing, though his knee bobbed up and down. His lips might be sealed, but the body language was clear.

'And what did Kane want?'

'Something for the weekend. Charlie, mostly.'

Kitty felt her pulse quicken. On their ride from the riverside Kevin had confessed his money came from dealing. He had given no names.

For the next hour they teased the details from Kevin Robb. Days and times, weights and payments, phone numbers and hiding places. Bryson made notes, letting Kitty do the talking. All the while she knew that, although this was valuable intel, it could not be used in court, since Kevin had not agreed to make a statement. Finally, Bryson asked who ran the whole line. Tears gathered in Kevin's eyes. He shook his head.

'Nope.'

'Nope, can't? Or nope won't?'

Kevin glared at Bryson, then at Kitty. She laid her hand on Bryson's arm. 'Kevin can't say.'

'Why not?'

'Because he'd fucking kill me!' Kevin shouted.

'*You* know who it is, Mr Prudhoe. He'll kill me. Everyone knows that. And if he couldn't find me, he'd find me mam and do her!'

* * *

Kitty played the *Clarinet Concerto* by Finzi, turning it up loud so that it would carry to the bathroom. She peeled off her running kit. Resting her book on the edge of the bath, she slid beneath the surface. The warm, scented water performed the daily miracle. She lay in the warmth and tried to imagine what Molly would be doing at that moment. A hazy image appeared – a schoolroom, a teacher drawing on a whiteboard – then the picture floated away. If it was so hard to discover the truth about her own daughter; what were the chances of entering the mind of strangers?

She had always been curious about people, their infinite variety; their predictable sameness. At uni they explored the role of nature and nurture in creating personality. For Kitty, the study was not academic – it was an everyday obsession. The ways that human beings lived, loved and died were a mystery. Life was a struggle for everyone. The different ways people fought that battle fascinated her.

Her eyes closed and she thought of Gerard. He had joined the course as an overseas student. He mocked her prim, Anglo Saxon rectitude, yet it was impossible to stay angry with him. Though he was the most self-centred man she had ever met, it was never his wish to hurt. A month before her finals Kitty fell pregnant with Molly. Gerard was the father, but he had gone before she had a chance to tell him. He left a note on her pillow. 'Forgive me.'

She both hated him and missed him. For a while she felt lost in the wide open spaces of the bed. Now she was used to sleeping alone.

We all need someone, whispered the Voice.

Someone to dry while we wash, someone to fold the sheet, someone to hold at the end of the day. But she cherished her privacy, her independence. She had known other lovers since Gerard, but she could no longer trust anyone in that way.

She opened her eyes and reached for her book. She was in the middle of *'The Creative Muse* by an Indian psychologist, Madhukar Shukla. His argument was that knowledge leaped forward in unexpected ways, rather than in a logical progression. Einstein discovered the Theory of Relativity through intuition, rather than cold logic. 'There are no logical paths to such natural laws', Einstein claimed. 'Only intuition can reach them.'

The warmth crept into her limbs. Kitty felt her muscles soften, the tension flowing away. She forced her eyes open. 'Science cannot solve the ultimate mystery of nature,' she read. 'We are part of nature and part of the mystery.'

Her eyelids grew heavy. The words slid off the page. She dangled the book on the edge of the bath and it slipped through her fingers, thudding to the floor.

Sunlight streamed through the leaves outside the bathroom window, a pattern of honeyed light rippling across her toes. Dust motes turned and fell, twisting in the light. She dozed, for a moment. The face of Richard Kane drifted across her mind, his smile too close, too cocky. She felt a glimmer of desire, then disgust.

She saw Dorian Kane walking up the road towards her. What had happened on that day? She was damaged and Kitty felt protective. Yet she regretted putting her number in Dorian's phone. Why had she done that? Kitty closed her eyes. Rafael was circling, his eyes fixed on her. They moved closer. Curling her toes, she sank into the warmth, listening to the lush

CHAPTER TWENTY TWO

textures of Finzi. Sunlight wandered across her skin.

CHAPTER TWENTY THREE

'I'm on my way to *The Swan*, if you ...' Bryson Prudhoe looked awkward. 'If you fancy it? A bite, I mean. Lunch. So we can have a chat?'

Kitty glanced at her watch, giving herself a moment. 'I'll take my car. I've a meeting at one.'

The Swan was decked out in red and gold flock wallpaper. Horse brasses hung behind the bar. The scent of gravy and disinfectant hung in the air. Like so many other country pubs, it was slowly dying. Kitty found a window seat in the *Carvery*. They were the only customers. Bryson carried his pint to the table then pulled up a chair facing the window. He looked more worried than usual. Kitty guessed what was on his mind.

'He'll go down, Bryson.'

'Who?'

'Clive Lumley.' Bryson sipped his pint.

'Your boy Kevin won't give evidence. He's terrified. People who cross Clive get hurt.'

Bryson had spent months building the case, lacing together the pattern of Clive Lumley's network. The information from Kevin Robb was gold – though it would never be heard in court. Kevin Robb had been talking off the record.

CHAPTER TWENTY THREE

'Why did Kevin confide in you?'

Kitty shrugged. 'You'd have to ask him. For all the bluster, he's just a kid, isn't he? I half expected his voice to break in there. But I suspect part of it was revenge.'

'For what?'

'He hates Richard Kane.'

'Why?'

'Because he's in love with Kane's wife.'

'He's just a kid!'

'We're all 'Mother Nature's toys', aren't we? I can't remember who told me that...'

She expected Bryson would smile. But it was clear he was distracted. It was the impending court, she was sure. 'Can't you work any of that stuff into the case?'

Bryson shrugged. 'He wouldn't sign anything. We didn't tape it. In any case, it's too late to wedge in new evidence'

Bryson picked up the menu and studied it. Mention of the trial unsettled him.

'At least you've got that coke,' said Kitty. 'From the piano? You'll get him on possession, if nothing else.'

Bryson tossed the menu aside. 'When you're called, just say what happened, OK? Don't embroider, don't exaggerate.'

'Of course.' Something was eating him up. She sipped her mineral water. Her voice was low. 'I'll say it as I saw it.'

'D'you want me to pick you up? I can give you a lift to court?'

Kitty shook her head.

'I'll see you there, Bryson.' She wanted to change the subject, to move the conversation on. 'Who'd have guessed, eh? The 'Millionaire.' A coke head?'

Bryson took a mouthful of beer. It was as if he had not heard her. He glanced around the empty pub, then squared his glass on the beer mat. 'Estate agents use coke these days.'

Kitty felt as if she had been slapped down.

'It's dealers I want – not their punters. A bit of white powder won't bring down civilisation. People like your friends the Kanes have more money than sense.'

It was clear that the Lumley case had become a vendetta. Kitty wondered how far he would go to make it stick. Perhaps the gossip in Shaftoe Leazes was true – she had got too close to Bryson. She was starting to think like him.

'You said you had some information.'

He looked blank.

'When you called? The other night?'

'Right!' Bryson rooted in his leather briefcase and produced a yellow folder. 'Kane's father was under the car. A Jag. Changing the oil.' Bryson seemed his old self again. 'Car was jacked up – they had an inspection pit but weren't using it, for some reason. So the motor's chocked up with wooden blocks. The chocks give way, we're told. Car goes over – whop!' Bryson slammed his fist on the table.

'Yes. Campbell told me about this.'

'Did he? So anyway – the old man's killed outright. Kane's mother is in a state, as you'd expect. A few days later she has a stroke, though she hangs on for a while, in a wheelchair.'

'So the accident does for both of them?'

Bryson nodded.

'Kane's seventeen, an only child. He doesn't like his father; who does, when you're seventeen?'

'I did,' said Kitty.

'It's different for blokes.'

'It must have been a shock – seeing your dad killed in front of your eyes.'

'Yes. But it gets a little strange at this point. You'd think the inquest would be a formality, wouldn't you?'

Kitty nodded.

'But questions start being asked. The lad's pulled in a couple of times, just to try to find out what happened. They start to look into the father-son relationship.' Bryson slid the yellow folder across the table. Kitty pulled out a sheaf of photocopies, stapled at the corner. She sipped her drink and flipped through the papers.

'So you've got an incident report. Coroner's report on the death. And notes from the previous incident – the dog. The inquest transcripts.' This was more than an old case file that Bryson had stumbled across. This was a dossier he'd spent time putting together.

Kitty nodded. 'This is very kind, Bryson.'

'I know nothing about it, do I? Just make sure it "gets home" safely.'

'I owe you,' she murmured, slipping the papers into her bag.

'What makes you think there's something there?'

'There's just something wrong about that couple. I just can't work out what it is.'

Bryson twisted his glass. She sensed he needed convincing. 'OK. One.' She held up her index finger. Why are they together? He's fussy, picky, controlling. Everything has to be just so. You can see it in his clothes, the furniture, the car. While she's not exactly a tramp, she's a bit ...'

'Scruffy?'

'Bohemian, you might say. Bit of a drink problem. Drugs too, we know *now*. And he's screwed up tight, while she's as loose as a wizard's sleeve. He's controlled; she's spinning out of control ...'

'Opposites attract,' said Bryson. 'That's not a crime.'

'He ticks a lot of the psychopath boxes.'

'So did Tony Blair. It's also not a crime. In any case, some women put up with all sorts, don't they?' said Bryson. '"*I love him, officer. But he's got this strange little hobby.*" There's another answer, of course, why they're together. They love each other!'

'OK. Maybe. But he's a banker, or was. Top of the tree. Annual bonus of gazillions. Golden boy. Now he's a property developer. He's going down.'

'Hardly living in a cardboard box, is he? He's loaded already. Wants the quiet life. To return to his roots. His farmhouse in the hills.'

'Where he saw his father crushed to death? Where his mother died?'

'Lots of people live where their parents died.' Bryson was grinning. He was enjoying himself.

'OK!' said Kitty, counting on her fingers. '*Three.* If they're so in love, so happy, why does he hit on me?'

'You're an attractive woman. He thought he was in. Next question?'

'*Four.* He's good looking. Rich. Family farm. Beautiful, talented wife. A bit bonkers but her family are loaded. Why is he so angry? He has *everything* he wants!'

This seemed to stop Bryson's flow. He swallowed a mouthful of bitter.

'It's his personality type.'

Kitty sat back, deflated.

'In the end, Kitty, it's just a feeling you have, isn't it?'

'Don't take the piss, Bryson!'

'I'm not, I'm not!' He finished his beer. 'Something doesn't smell right. I understand that. I know that feeling.' He twisted his glass, turning it round and around. 'Used to get it myself.'

'Kane was adopted,' said Kitty. 'Not as a baby – as a child. Who knows what he might have gone through before then, poor little bugger! He might have good reason to be angry.'

Bryson waggled his empty glass. 'Want another?'

Kitty shook her head. Bryson sauntered to the bar. In the next room a fruit machine was paying out; the jackpot chiming, the coins clattering down.

Kitty allowed her mind to drift through the Kanes' house. Her 'third eye' entered the front door, passed the ornate mirror and drifted down the corridor, glimpsing the paintings, the furniture in the rooms she passed. She arrived at the kitchen, then out into the terraced garden. There was an oddness about that house, a disconnect between Richard's obsessive neatness and the way the place seemed unfinished. Kane was a perfectionist, yet the details were revealing. She recalled the bare wires, the broken window, the chipped tiles in the kitchen.

The sound of Bryson chugging his ale brought her back to the real world. He lowered the glass then wiped his lips.

'Maybe the Kanes enjoy 'a bit of strange'?''

'Could be,' said Kitty. 'There's definitely a power thing between them. The way he pushes her around.'

'Any sign of violence? Bruising? '

'Nope.'

'Paraphernalia?'

She bit her lip. 'I saw some cling film in the kitchen, that count?'

He smiled, turned his glass.

'Maybe she enjoys it – that he's so scary. So dominant.'

'You have no evidence, do you? Not a morsel! This is all guesswork!'

Kitty nodded. 'That's me! Cheap psychology. From the cheap psychologist.'

He nodded at the file. 'Well, that's an interesting read. But that's probably all it is. Sometimes you have to accept there's just nothing you can do.'

Her hand rested on the table.

'Kitty....'

She half closed her eyes, bracing herself. The surface of the table became fascinating. She felt protective towards Bryson and dreaded what he might say. The last thing she wanted was to hurt his feelings.

'I enjoy these chats.' He lifted his pint and drained the glass. As he put his glass down their fingers touched. The contact was accidental, but his hand remained by hers, his fingers warm. At that moment the barmaid teetered towards their table, balancing a tray on her hip. Kitty looked up, smiled, and eased her hand free.

Faced with his lunch, Bryson puffed his cheeks, rubbing his hands together. The menu claimed that his trout had been 'plucked fresh from the stream and enrobed in a piquant mustard sauce.' The fish bobbed, dead eyed, in a puddle of yellow oil. Bryson prodded the carcass with the tip of his fork. Steam sighed through the punctured skin.

'Well,' he said, 'would you look at that.'

CHAPTER TWENTY FOUR

Back at her desk in Shaftoe Leazes, Kitty pulled Bryson's stapled sheets from the yellow file. She read them as she sipped a mug of tea. The coroner's report stated Peter Kane's death had been a routine accident. The cause of death was respiratory failure caused by crushing injuries. Peter Kane had been working on his car when the jack failed. The Jaguar, weighing 1.3 tonnes, fell on his body. He died from multiple injuries due to blunt trauma, consistent with being crushed against a hard surface. The autopsy revealed that he had suffered fractured ribs, breast and backbones, internal bleeding in the chest, lungs and abdominal cavity. There were two five centimetre gashes on the back of his head.

Richard Kane's parents had intended to go to the theatre that evening and their son had been working on the car. Peter Kane told his adopted son to finish up then got down to help. Richard stood up. The car went over and Peter was killed outright – a traumatic event for the seventeen year old. While there was no indication of foul play, the witness statements were intriguing.

The Coroner asked Joanna Kane about her husband's death.

CORONER: Can you tell me, Mrs Kane, about the sequence of events that afternoon?

JOANNA KANE: Peter and I were going to the theatre. Richard had an argument with his father. My son said Peter promised him the use of the car that evening. Peter always broke his promises, he said.

CORONER: Did you intervene in this argument?

JOANNA KANE: They were both too stubborn to listen to me. Richard was tinkering with the car. Peter grew impatient so he went to hurry Richard along.

Kitty sensed the toxic atmosphere in the Kanes' house. An overbearing father, keen to see that things were done his way; a son who shared many of his adopted father's traits – impatience, a quick temper, the need to control and dominate. And a mother, worn out by conflicting loyalties, who felt powerless as she stood between her men.

The report of the incident in which Richard Kane shot the family Labrador was sketchy. Joanna had called the vet but the dog was dead by the time he arrived. The vet reported the incident to the police, as he was bound to do. Officers questioned the boy, yet no charges were made. His father seemed to confirm the boy's story that the shooting was accidental.

A medical report, dated soon after the hearing, indicated that Joanna Kane had suffered a stroke.

Kitty glanced around the office. It was a quiet afternoon. Orla sat at a screen, drinking coffee as she typed a report. Keying into the national database, Kitty checked Richard Kane's criminal record. There was nothing. There were no previous convictions, not even a speeding ticket.

She tapped Kane's name into Google. There were thirty-nine million entries. Refining her search, she added 'Northumberland' and cut it to two and a quarter million.

On the fifth page was an article on the web page of a magazine called *Border Living*. She opened a story about the problems of renovating an old house. There were shots of Richard and Dorian inside "their dream home," along with some guff about Richard returning to his roots, his family home. The "before" and "after" pictures suggested they had poured money into the place.

'With a job like this,' Richard said, 'you start off writing cheques for huge amounts, without even thinking about it. If cash gets tight, it starts to mean more. Nine hundred for roof tiles and you think: that's a week's wages for someone...' Not for him, it was clear. The quote nestled beneath a photo of the laughing couple outside the front door of studded oak. She recalled how bleached and chipped that door looked now.

Internet activity at Shaftoe Leazes was monitored. To search further into Richard Kane's life could be regarded as stalking. Kitty glanced around the office. Richard Kane wasn't worth five minutes of her time, yet her intuition would not quit.

'Forget it,' said the Voice. She clicked *Images*. The first few thumbnails were of smiling Californians. Then Richard Kane was there, holding a glass of wine, staring straight back at the camera. His face was tanned, his grin tight. Kitty downloaded the jpeg and zoomed in.

The text read 'Richard Kane shares a joke with Conrad Sereys, CEO at Amschels. Richard is leaving the bank to set up a freelance consultancy. All at Amschels wish Richard every good fortune for the future.'

The other man in the picture, Conrad Sereys, was an Alpha male in his early sixties. He had the profile of a hawk and a hairstyle which looked like it was moulded from platinum. His clothes were immaculate: a suit of armour in light grey wool, a Garrick Club tie. Whatever the joke they were sharing, it was not on Conrad Sereys.

Kitty found another image: Richard Kane and another older man, both wearing hard hats. This caption read 'George Cunliffe and Richard Kane at Cutler's Wharf, their exciting new waterfront development.'

Cunliffe was an older, fatter version of Sereys – his jowls were heavy, his teeth stained with nicotine. Cunliffe's suit looked like it came from Burtons. Judging by the company he was keeping, Richard Kane was going down in the world. But the most striking difference between the pictures was in Kane's appearance. Beside Sereys, Kane looked imposing – fit, tanned, brimming with self confidence – a corporate warrior at the top of his game. Next to George Cunliffe he was a shadow of that earlier man – his face gaunt, the eyes haunted. He seemed diminished. Had his drug habit taken a toll; or was Kitty reading more into the pictures than they warranted?

She printed both images then logged off. She laid the pictures on her desk, side by side. Richard Kane stared back at her. Bryson was right. The details might be intriguing, but apart from a little weekend drug use, there was no crime. Everything she had learned seemed to suggest that Kane's career was fading, yet that was hardly unusual. Perhaps she had wanted to find something because she was worried about Dorian Kane and disliked her husband.

'Having fun?'

Kitty jumped. Elayne Hawes was standing in the doorway. She wandered to Kitty's desk and picked up one of the pictures.

'This your boyfriend? *Dreamy* ...' she laughed.

'That's a good one!' Kitty reached for the photo but Elayne danced clear of her hands.

'He's familiar ...' said Elayne.

'Not my type.'

Kitty had the picture now. She scrunched up the photos and tossed them in the bin. She slipped the coroner's report into her desk drawer and locked it. They walked out together.

'Got any plans for the Bank Holiday?'

'Nothing special,' said Kitty.

'You should come over! We're having a barbecue.'

* * *

As Kitty drove home she recalled an afternoon lecture from her time at university. It must have been the summertime: she saw herself sitting on the steeply-raked benches of the lecture hall. Gerard's fingers were entwined with hers as they made notes, she with her left hand, he with his right, a mirror image. Professor Mayhew was delivering his notes on 'Folie a deux,' – a syndrome in which delusional symptoms are transmitted from one individual to another. Couples who drive each other crazy.

'They affirm each other's madness,' droned the professor. 'Typically, they will be isolated – because of geography, or their social situation. They often live in a tight, closed world in which each reinforces the delusions of the other. The most bizarre behaviour goes unquestioned.'

Was that a description of the Kanes? A control freak and a fragile woman, stoking each other's craziness until it caught fire? Now she realised why those pictures of Richard had been so unsettling. While Richard Kane's smile seemed sincere, no warmth ever reached those blue-grey eyes.

CHAPTER TWENTY FIVE

Dorian's eyes flicked open. Something had woken her. She lay in the darkness, listening to the steady tick of the grandfather clock on the landing. Her eyes slowly became used to the gloom. She could hear a scratching sound. She hoped it was mice, scrabbling in the loft. An old house is never really still. The first night after Richard left was often the worst. To steady her nerves she went downstairs and poured herself a glass of wine.

The tiles were cold beneath her bare feet. The Aga ran the length of the stone fireplace in the kitchen at West Neuk and wind whistled across the chimney; a mournful note, even in the height of summer.

Though Dorian thought of the farm as her sanctuary, there were times it felt more like gaol. She was used to the permanent glare of the city: the darkness of the countryside unsettled her. She sipped her wine. She heard the scratching again. She went into the next room, the place she and Richard had set aside as a nursery. White muslin curtains shifted in the draught. A herd of paper horses turned above the cot. The rocking horse stood by the window, halfway through a leap. She realised the sound was the breeze shifting the pines, scratching their needles across the window pane.

She returned to the bedroom and sat by the window, tucking her feet beneath her. Sparks of light were visible down the valley, other souls who could not sleep. That was reassuring. She drank until the fear was dulled. She felt drowsy. As she moved towards the bed the phone rang. She ran downstairs to the kitchen and picked up.

'Hello?' There was no reply. She could hear a wheezing, the sound of a man, breathing in and breathing out.

'*Richard*? Is that you?'

'Hello, darling,' said the caller. A man's voice. A click and the line went dead. Dorian stood in the kitchen, feeling the warmth in her feet bleed into the floor tiles. Outside, the wind rose and the bushes shifted in the darkness. She clattered the phone on to the receiver and ran upstairs. She pulled the covers over her head and lay awake till dawn, listening to the house creak and sigh as it settled into the earth. Even after six hundred years, West Neuk was bedding down, the stones huddling ever closer to the hillside.

CHAPTER TWENTY SIX

The stone arch of the gateway was filled with a single pane of bullet-proof plexiglass. Beyond the arch lay the gatehouse, an open plan control room furnished with banks of computers, scanners and closed-circuit monitors. The duty officers watched every step of Bryson's self-conscious shuffle from the car park to the intercom beside the door. He pressed the buzzer. 'I'm here to see Clive Arthur Lumley. On D Wing.'

Bryson's ID and visitor pass were scrutinised. He heard the wind keening through the razor wire that topped the walls. A prison officer with a Zapata moustache inspected Bryson. He leaned to speak into the mic. 'Is this a personal visit, DS Prudhoe?'

'What do *you* think?'

The officer looked at him, waiting.

'I'm here to interview Clive Arthur Lumley.' Bryson sighed. 'It's all been cleared with the deputy governor.'

There was a loud buzz and the outer gate slid back. Zapata waved him though, unsmiling. Another buzz, another sliding door; then Bryson held up his hands for the body search. He emptied his pockets and fed everything through the scanner.

The officer nodded towards the slim Manila file that Bryson carried.

'Papers relevant to the case,' said Bryson. The officer nodded towards the conveyor belt and they both watched the file disappear into the scanner.

Bryson was led through a narrow maze of towers and fences that twisted between the wings of the prison. The buildings loomed above him, blocking out the sunlight. Prisoners stood at the windows of their cells, stripped to the waist.

'Ay, Fatty Bum Bum!' one of the cons yelled.

'Got a head on him like a sheep,' said another. They laughed, staring hard as he passed.

'Show us your arse, Fatty Boy!'

Bryson stared straight ahead. He knew better than to respond to the taunts of the Window Warriors.

The Family Visits Area had been a chapel in Victorian times, when the prison was built. The sun shone through stained-glass windows, throwing coloured shadows across the worn carpet. Toys littered the floor in one corner – teddy bears and tractors, red and yellow plastic streaked with grime. Bryson sat at a table, placed the Manila file on the surface and closed his eyes.

He dozed in the sun. The chink of keys woke him. A young prison officer ushered Clive Lumley into the room. Lumley had grown thinner in the months since his arrest, but his smile was broad as he saw Bryson. His newly-grown goatee was peppered with grey. His blue and white shirt and faded denims were immaculate.

'Mr Prudhoe!' he beamed. 'What a treat!'

The PO slumped into a chair with a coffee and a copy of the *Sun*. Lumley and Bryson faced each other across the table.

CHAPTER TWENTY SIX

'You're working hard, Mr P. Coming to see me on a Bank Holiday...'

'How are they treating you, Clive?'

'The facilities are top class! Looking fit, aren't I?' He flexed the muscles in his arms. 'Shame I won't be here much longer.'

'I don't know about that, Clive...'

'I'm touched, Mr P. Really! You could have spent the Bank Holiday with your wife. Maureen, isn't it? And the boys? But you decided to spend it with me.'

Bryson held his gaze. If he was intimidated by this, he had no intention of showing it. 'I'm here to ask a favour, Clive.'

Lumley flicked lint from his cuff. 'You only have to ask, Mr Prudhoe...'

'You could save everyone a lot of trouble.'

'How would that be?'

'Change your plea.'

Lumley rocked back in mock surprise. He shook his head, as if stunned. 'Mr Prudhoe! Why would I do *that*?'

'I'd put a word in, Clive. Explain how co-operative you've been.'

A slow smile spread across Clive Lumley's face. 'But I haven't, Mr Prudhoe. Have I?'

'Not yet, Clive. But you should.'

Bryson saw a glimmer of doubt in Lumley's eyes. For such a long time, he had been behind the game, watching Lumley skip clear. It felt good to watch him start to squirm. Yet he knew there was a risk in taunting the man. Lumley enjoyed seeing fear in the eyes of others.

'It was a farce, that raid! I don't supply drugs and I don't use drugs, Mr Prudhoe. Never have. Never will. I prefer wine. Or a nice malt.'

Bryson nodded. The silence lengthened. The PO glanced up from his paper. Bryson held the gaze until Lumley could stand it no longer.

'There's only you and your girlfriend to say you found gear in my house.'

'We have other witnesses.'

Lumley stared at him. He glanced at the prison officer, who had returned to his reading.

'Witnesses?'

Bryson grinned. He knew Lumley's fear: that Greta had turned on him. He leaned closer, savouring the moment. 'I know how you do it, Clive.'

Lumley blinked.

'You're not making sense, Mr P. You work too hard.'

'I know how you shift the gear.'

'Sod off!'

'I've found one of your runners.' The PO glanced up again, aware of the tension. 'Very chatty. Very helpful. Times. Dates. Names.' Bryson tapped the manila file.

'You're talking bollocks, Mr Prudhoe.' snapped Lumley. He looked away, shaking his head.

Bryson smiled, knowing he had won the point. 'Well, you'll just have to trust me on that, Clive.'

'You should write for the telly! That's a powerful imagination, you've got.'

Clive Lumley folded his arms and looked at the wall. Bryson felt all the frustration of the last months flood back. It was tempting, to float the name of Kevin Robb, to hint at what he knew.

'Well. This has been a pleasure, Clive.' Bryson stood. He nodded to the PO and slid his chair beneath the table.

'Come over and I'll do what I can, Clive. Otherwise you're on your own.'

'Well, that's very kind. But I think I'll stick, not twist, Mr Prudhoe.'

Lumley stood, nodding to his escort. He tapped his head, as if suddenly remembering. 'Your little friend? She lives in Belfordham, doesn't she?'

Bryson said nothing.

'On Cloud Street. With her kid? What's she called?' He clicked a finger and thumb together. 'Lovely little kid. Don't tell me!' Clive Lumley rolled towards the door. He stopped, turned, clicked his fingers. 'Molly! Knew I'd get her. Molly. Isn't it?'

Bryson looked at him. Lumley went on. 'Nice looking woman. Bit skinny, but...I would, eh?' He opened his mouth and fluttered his tongue.

That was the moment. 'Cheerio, Clive.' Bryson couldn't stop himself. 'I'll give your regards to Kevin.'

He watched Lumley's face change. But in a moment the smile was back in place. Lumley winked and turned to walk back to D Wing, rolling his shoulders as he sauntered through the door.

Bryson stood with his hands on the back of the chair. He closed his eyes and his head fell to his chest.

* * *

Kitty parked in the lane and walked up the farm drive. As she entered the yard, a skinny collie hurled itself from the tractor shed and ran at her. She saw the whites of the creature's eyes but the dog was dragged up by a chain. It fell back in the mud, snarling. Kitty knocked on the door. When there was no answer she shouted through the letterbox.

'Carole? It's Kitty Lockwood. From Shaftoe Leazes.'

The door opened and Carole Robb appeared, wiping her hands on her pinny. 'I'm busy.'

'OK. Has Kevin told you the date of his court hearing? He's summoned to appear a week on Thursday. Careless driving.'

'He said.'

Kitty imagined there would not be a lot of secrets Kevin could keep from his mother. 'So, he'll be there?'

'Better ask him, pet. You're as likely to see him.'

'It's at the magistrates' court, in town. You know where that is?'

'Give me a clue...' Carole looked over Kitty's shoulder, reluctant to meet her gaze.

'Did Kevin mention that we'd had a word with him? The other day?'

'What about?'

'I'm sorry. I can't say. It was about another matter.'

'He told me all about it.'

'You know you mentioned that Kevin had a girlfriend?' said Kitty.

'Like I said. I'm very busy. Some of us have work to do.' Carole stared into the distance.

Kitty knew she would get no further. 'If you want to talk about it, give me a call.'

Carole Robb closed the door.

Kitty had got the reception she had expected. She felt a glimmer of pity for Carole Robb. One by one, everyone she loved was leaving her.

CHAPTER TWENTY SEVEN

As long as Dorian kept moving she was able to fend off the gloom. The way to stay positive was to fill the empty hours with work. There must be no drop in standards. Richard found that sort of thing very upsetting.

She emptied the dishwasher and stacked the dishes. She dusted and hoovered the rooms on the ground floor. Every now and then she thought about the call that had woken her in the early hours. It was not Richard's voice. It was not Kevin either. There was something about the sound of that voice that troubled her. She made a mug of coffee and carried it through to the stables. She stroked Halloween's muzzle, gazing into his soft, dark eyes.

'Beautiful boy.'

Dorian turned the horses out into the paddock. She watched them kick their heels as they cantered across the hillside.

At eleven she sat in the kitchen, reading *Elle*. The washing machine chugged and gurgled as she sipped her coffee. The radio burbled in the corner of the room. The sound of a human voice was comforting. She wondered about Richard, seeing him at the wheel of his car, the image so vivid, it was as if she was sitting by his side. It was unusual not to have a call from him.

When her housework was done, she filled a flask and climbed the stairs. She paused at the top, tilting her head to one side. The house seemed silent, yet she could hear a noise – a faint susurration, like the whisper of a baby breathing. She screwed her eyes shut, shaking that idea from her head. Today there would be no visits to the 'nursery,' no glass of red to go with her lunch. She had cut down, a little, since that awful afternoon. It was fortunate that the cellar was such a dark, unsettling place. The fear of it helped her fight temptation.

She climbed the staircase to her studio, tucked beneath the eaves. The floor was stripped pine and the room was filled with the scent of new wood. The window gave her a view all the way down the valley. The room was a clutter; her desk buried beneath cards of buttons, fabric swatches and scraps of material. Drawings and sketches were tacked to the walls and a dressmaker's dummy stood in one corner of the room.

Dorian kicked off her shoes, took a pencil from the jar and opened her sketch pad. She slid her bare feet onto the table. The pencil point hovered over the paper. She was ready.

* * *

They rode in silence, the van bucking and rolling along the road down from the Border. The hills rose on both sides, their peaks hidden by the morning mist. As they descended, the open moorland gave way to a dense forest of pine and spruce. As the road reached the valley floor it became a dark ribbon that stretched to the horizon. They passed a reservoir, the surface an oily ripple.

CHAPTER TWENTY SEVEN

'Where are we?' said Tanya.

Nathan rolled his head around to ease the stiffness in his neck, the joints cracking and popping. Sleeping in the car made him tetchy. 'Almost there,' he growled, pressing his foot to the floor.

* * *

Dorian wondered where Richard was at that moment – somewhere near Liverpool, she guessed. She pictured him drinking coffee in a service station, his pupils pinpoints, his hands shaking from gripping the wheel. She blew him a kiss; touched her fingers to his cheek. Dorian dropped her sketchbook on the desk. Pulling a history book from the shelf, she flicked through the pages, looking for inspiration. She studied a woodcut of a woman being burned at the stake, wincing at the image, wondering how it would feel.

She fired up the Mac and answered a couple of emails from friends, composing long, rambling replies to their brief messages. She was desperate to keep links to her past. But her London friends had careers, kids, proper jobs. She had all the time in the world, while they had none.

She picked at the skin on her hands, noticing it was less supple, more lined than before. She sketched a couple of shapes but the lines dwindled into nothing. She threw the pages into the bin. Music would inspire her. She needed sound! She found Fela Kuti on iTunes, *International Thief Thief*.

'Them bring sorrow, tears an' blood...' The bass pulsed in her chest, the sax soaring into the heavens. She returned to her

desk, a wide table by the window overlooking the valley.

'*Them bring sorrow, tears and blood! Them regular trademark!*' Her reedy voice rang through the house, echoing through the empty rooms along the hallway, the kitchen, the dining room.

She began to draw again – a bleeding hand raised in a fist. Soon she was lost in her work, coaxing the sketches into more intricate designs. It was all going well.

The sound of the motor had hovered near the edge of her hearing for some time. Glancing through the window she saw a van astride the verge at the end of the drive. It reversed a few yards, then crept forward. Dorian's view was blocked by one of the pine trees.

A woman jumped from the van and strode along the side of the track; blonde hair whipping like a flag in the wind. She peered up and down the road then climbed back into the passenger seat. Rain splattered the window and Dorian could no longer see clearly. She yawned, stretched, and dropped her pad on the desk. Something was happening, ideas were taking shape, but she was reluctant to force it.

She wandered down to the kitchen to brew a pot of tea. As she waited for the kettle to boil her eyes lifted towards the trees on the ridge. Cloud shadows flickered across the edge of the plantation. A goldfinch landed on the sill, inches from her face. She could see the soft, downy feathers shifting and rippling in the breeze. Dorian imagined cupping the bird in her hand. She connected with the mind behind the black jewel of the bird's eye.

There was a rap at the door and the finch was gone. For a moment she thought it might be the boy. If it *was* him she had no intention of allowing him inside. Creeping down the hallway, Dorian put her eye to the door. A woman was framed in the spyhole, her figure distorted by the lens. It was the woman from the van. Dorian felt a moment of disappointment, then guilt. The stranger wore a tan leather jacket and silver jewellery, earrings and bangles. Her blonde hair fluttered across her face as she turned to look down the drive.

Dorian was about to creep away when the stranger turned her head. The woman stood on the tips of her toes and pressed her eye to the spyhole. It seemed that she was looking straight into Dorian's eyes.

Dorian flinched, biting her lip to stifle a giggle. The woman called out.

'Hello? I know you're in there. It's OK – I'm not selling anything!'

Dorian opened the door as far as the chain would allow. She peered through the crack.

'Wow! Great!' said the stranger. 'You *are* in!'

Dorian heard a trace of a scouse accent. The woman edged closer.

'Look, I'm really, *really* sorry to bother you!'

Definitely Liverpool.

'I've got a problem. With the van?'

Dorian peered over her shoulder towards the road. The van stood on the grass verge, close by the entrance to the drive.

'I skidded into the ditch! I can't shift it! Now the sodding thing won't start!'

Though smiling, she seemed on the edge of tears.

'Sorry. I don't know anything about cars.'

'Me neither! But I was just wondering ...' She held a mobile phone in her fingers and waggled it. 'My moby's on the blink. I was hoping I could use your phone? To call the AA?'

The stranger furrowed her brow. 'I'll pay for the call, of

course.'

Dorian slipped the chain and opened the door. As the woman darted through the door Dorian caught her perfume: the tang of lemons and mimosa. The stranger leaned forward and shook raindrops from her hair, her heels clicking on the tiles. Straightening, she looked at Dorian and laughed. Dorian was wrong-footed. The laughter seemed odd. Was it relief at escaping the rain, or triumph at gaining entry? The woman continued to smile, then turned and closed the door.

'So ...'

Dorian backed away a step or two.

'... your phone?' The visitor raised her eyebrows. Dorian blinked.

'Sorry! Yes!' She put a hand to her brow. 'It's in the kitchen. The landline.' Dorian pointed down the hall, towards the back of the house.

She followed the stranger to the kitchen where she pointed to the phone on the wall. The woman picked up the phone and began to dial. She smiled at Dorian while she waited for her connection. Dorian appraised her guest, running her eyes from top to toe. Older than herself by a year or two. Her hair was clean and well cut. The nails were manicured and varnished. The clothes were stylish – a Nicole Farhi jacket, a Missoni top.

Dorian tugged at the cuffs of her jumper, pulling them over her palms. She felt shabby beside her guest. The stranger pointed over her shoulder, towards the stove. Dorian realised the kettle had been whistling for some time. She yanked it from the hob and filled the pot. She set it down while her guest finished her call.

'Thanks for that! You're a star.'

CHAPTER TWENTY SEVEN

'What's happened to your mobile?'

'Bloody battery! Isn't it always the way?'

There was an awkward pause. 'Would you like something to drink?'

'I'd love one! I'm wet through. It's not properly raining; it's just sort of – *damp* – out there.'

'Misty. It gets like that sometimes. The clouds just drift over the hill.'

The visitor peeled off her jacket and draped it over the back of a chair. 'I love this house!'

'Thanks ...'

'I keep telling my feller we should get a place like this. Get out of the city! It must be dead quiet, is it?'

Dorian nodded. 'Sometimes!' She felt guilty. She would never have said that had Richard been there. Dorian pulled a towel from the Sheila Maid and gave it to her visitor. The woman dabbed her neck and hair. Dorian was fascinated by her guest, her eyes wide, as if a panther had appeared in her kitchen.

They sat at the table, waiting for the tea to brew.

'Who did you call? Your ...your chap, was it?'

For a moment, less than a heartbeat, the woman's smile faltered. 'Thank you so much for this! I've got a cheek, haven't I?' Tanya held out her hand. 'I'm Ginny.'

Dorian took her hand. The skin was smooth, caramel; warmer than her own.

'It's short for Virginia.'

Dorian tugged the threads of her cuffs over her own chapped hands. 'Dorian.'

'That's unusual!' Tanya held on to her hand. Her gaze was direct.

'It's Greek – my father's idea. He wasn't Greek, it's just that he liked the country. We lived there for a while.'

Tanya was still holding Dorian's hand, holding her pale fingers in warm, golden skin. The woman's eyes were green, flecked with gold. Smiling yes. Something was amusing 'Ginny'.

'They said an hour and a half.'

'Who did?'

'The AA!'

'Really? I thought …?'

'What? What did you think?'

Dorian felt a flicker of unease. 'Just that they would be here sooner. I suppose. A bit sooner than that.'

'Thing is, you're a long way from everywhere, up here. Aren't you?

Dorian was daunted by the idea that she had would be obliged to entertain her guest until the AA arrived. Ginny was polite and charming. Her clothes were immaculate. Yet Dorian was anxious; a little intimidated. Perhaps it was simply that she was unused to company. In her old life she would not have been worried by this. She blurted the first words that came into her head, to fill the silence.

'Where are you from?'

The woman sipped her tea, her eyes never leaving Dorian's face. 'Does your husband enjoy living here?'

It was clear she preferred asking the questions.

'He loves it! This was Richard's home when he was a child! We were lucky. It fell vacant just as we were leaving London.'

Ginny looked around. 'You must have spent a fortune renovating the place.'

Dorian talked about her work and asked Ginny about the

clothes she was wearing, hoping her visitor would reveal more of herself. But every question slid off Ginny's shiny surface.

'I'd love to see your work, Dorian! It fascinates me the way people like you come up with ideas,' she purred.

Dorian sensed her guest was stroking her, just passing the time while she waited for the AA. But she dashed upstairs to find some drawings that were good enough to show. In the studio she grabbed a few sheets and notebooks, making sure she selected her best work.

'These are just rough,' she called as she trotted downstairs, her arms full. 'But they give you some ...'

Halfway down the stairs she froze. A tall, elegant man was standing in her hallway.

'Sweet!' Nathan pulled a fob watch from his waistcoat. 'Right on time.'

CHAPTER TWENTY EIGHT

The first thing Dorian noticed was the shaven head: the sleek, dome of coffee-coloured skin. His presence seemed to fill the room. He was tall, well-built; his shoulders broad. He stood perfectly still, looking up, appraising her. His gaze was intense, his eyes dark. He held his head perfectly still, like a cat. The collar of his black cashmere overcoat was turned up, the edge brushing the lobes of his ears. He put an inhaler to his mouth, puffed it twice then slipped it back into the pocket of his waistcoat.

Dorian was halfway down the stairs. Her free hand reached out to the wall. The sketches fell from her grasp, tumbling down the steps. Her legs were trembling and she feared they would give way. Her fingertips grazed the whitewashed plaster as she steadied herself.

The man walked to the foot of the stairs. He stooped, picking up one of the drawings between his fingertips. 'Sweet...you're a talented lady.'

His voice was deep, with a Liverpool lilt – just like 'Ginny', who now stood at his side. He held out the sheet, offering it to Dorian. She could not move. Her heart thumped as the adrenaline hit. Her eyes locked on the man's face. Then he shrugged, laying the sketch on the hall table. He shook off his coat and the one who called herself Ginny pulled it from his shoulders.

'Don't get comfortable,' she murmured. 'Just do it and go.'

He held a finger to his lips.

She hung his coat on a rack on the wall. He turned to admire himself in the convex mirror by the door. He tugged at the wings of his waistcoat. He seemed utterly calm.

'How did you get in?' Dorian's throat was tight, her voice skirring like the wings of a bird. 'Tell me what's going on? Why are you here? Who are you looking for?'

The man turned from his own reflection, his gaze flicking between Dorian and the doorways which opened onto the hallway. 'We're alone?'

'Let's just do it and go.'

'You've checked?'

A beat, as his partner looked at him.

'I haven't checked all the ....'

'Check them now!'

Dorian watched her open her lips to reply. But 'Ginny' said nothing and began her tour of the house.

'It's bigger than I thought,' said the stranger, looking around. 'The house looks pokey from the outside, but, no. It's sweet.' He lifted the fob watch from his waistcoat, studied it, tucked it away.

'Look. Who are you?' said Dorian, her voice a whisper. 'My husband will be back at any moment.'

He chuckled. Dorian felt blood rush to her face. He leaned against the wall, running his fingertip along the grain of the panelling, before returning his gaze to Dorian. She heard Ginny's heels click clack over the tiles as she returned to the hallway.

'Clear?'

The woman nodded. Despite her fear, Dorian noted the change in the dynamic. Now they both deferred to the man.

'Can I wait in the car?'

Her voice was low. She tapped the point of her shoe against the floor.

The man sighed, lowered his chin onto his chest.

'You know? I don't feel like ...'

He held up a finger, taking a moment before he continued. 'My feeling is there's no rush here.' He lingered over 'rush', allowing it to escape slowly. He yawned, stretching his arms. 'No need to hurry. There's time.' He turned to Dorian. 'You can cook?'

'I'd like you to leave.'

'See? There's no way my good friend here can cook. She prefers to eat out.' He smiled at the woman, who stared at the floor. 'Isn't that right, babe?' He chuckled. 'She's not a provider. What do I mean, Dorian? What's the word I'm looking for? A homemaker!' He clicked his fingers and grinned. 'My good friend here is not a 'homemaker!'

Dorian moved back a step, no longer paralysed. The shock was fading and her instinct was to run. But the man blocked her way to the front door. She might run upstairs and lock herself in the office. Perhaps she could climb up to her studio before they caught her? Would she have time to dial 999 before the door was kicked down? Was that even the number? The police station in the village was manned just one day a week. Would anyone be there? It would take them half an hour to reach her from Belfordham, nine miles down the valley. By then ...

CHAPTER TWENTY EIGHT

A weapon?

She had scissors upstairs. Upstairs, where the gun cabinet lay. Richard was meticulous in the way he cared for his shotguns. They were stashed in his office, at the top of the house. But the gun cabinet would be locked. She recalled he had told that policewoman.

The mobile...

'Do it,' said the woman.

He reached into is pocket. Dorian moved back, up one stair, taking herself deeper into the house, towards her studio, her nest beneath the eves. As long as they were talking, nothing bad would happen. Dorian pushed her hands in the pockets of her cardigan, drawing it close for comfort. Her fingertips touched her mobile, the cool, rounded surface. She would need a distraction, something to cover the movement. She blurted the first thing that came into her head.

'If I make you something to eat, will you go?'

Another step backwards. The man pulled his hand from his pocket. 'We can talk about that. Later.' As he turned away to talk to the woman, Dorian opened the phone. She kept her hand in her pocket, as she slid her thumb across the screen she heard the soft click as it unlocked. At that moment the man was looking at 'Ginny'. He seemed to be gauging her mood. Dorian glanced down at her phone as she touched the screen, her fingertips darting across the keys, searching for the right app, the right button, top row, middle. It had to be right: if she pressed the wrong key there would be no second chance. The man put his inhaler to his mouth, puffed it twice. Dorian glanced down, her fingertips sliding across the glass. She found 2, pressed it.

The man put away his inhaler. He beckoned her downstairs.

'Here,' he said.

She took her hands from her pockets and tucked them beneath her arms. Dorian had no way of knowing if her phone was making the connection. She walked down the stairs. The tiles in the hallway felt like ice beneath her feet.

CHAPTER TWENTY NINE

The Rural Drugs Initiative met on the first Tuesday of each month. In the upstairs room of Belfordham Health Centre, a group of youth workers and GPs gathered to discuss 'the drug problem' in the countryside. The Initiative moved like a glacier, the members edging into a world they did not quite understand.

Kitty's role was to supply figures for arrests and prosecutions and to tell sexy anecdotes about dealers and crack dens. She hurried through the numbers of arrests, cautions and prosecutions, explaining how the drugs profile of the area was changing. Some of the panel glanced at their watches. Now and then she fantasised about slipping in something just to see if they were listening. She was thanked for her contribution. She sat back. There were no questions.

They shared a feeling of impotence. The young of Belfordham enjoyed 'getting gakked' on ketamine and cheap cider. Kitty wanted to suggest that if drugs were legalised they would lose their glamour. Legal drugs would be as dull as a pint of bitter, which would put dealers like Clive Lumley out of business. But this was not the time, nor the place, to raise it.

The atmosphere was drowsy, the room warmed by the afternoon sun slanting through the blinds. The air conditioning hummed softly and dust drifted through the beam of the overhead projector. 'Half my patients are self medicating on alcohol,' said a local GP. 'If it wasn't for booze my drugs bill would rocket!' It was a familiar dance in which everyone knew their steps. '*Everyone's* at it! If kids know their parents are experimenting with cocaine, why can't they?'

As Kitty stifled a yawn her mobile shuddered across the table. Muttering apologies, she crept from the room. The caller ID read *Dorian Kane*. Putting the phone to her ear, she moved up the corridor. She could hear a woman's breathing. 'Hello? Mrs Kane?'

There was no reply, though she could hear distant voices. Kitty paced the floor as she strained to hear. 'Dorian?' Kitty was about to end the call when the sound cleared.

'*Tell me what you'd like?*' It was Dorian's voice, sounding edgy. A man's voice replied, indistinct, though Kitty caught a few words.

'*What have you got?*' The man's voice, deep and booming, as if they were in a bathroom. More breathing, then an echoing pulse, as if Dorian was walking through a tunnel. Suddenly the sound cleared, though it was still faint. Kitty heard the ambience of a kitchen – the clatter of pans, the hiss of a tap: familiar, domestic sounds.

There was nothing to worry about. The stupid woman had sat on her phone. Yet Kitty kept the connection open. Perhaps it was the thought of returning to a dull meeting. She could hear nothing out of the ordinary, yet some instinct compelled her to keep the call live.

Listen. Just a feeling; a premonition of danger. She spoke Dorian's name again, this time in a whisper. She heard the sound of approaching footsteps, then silence. Kitty leaned against the wall. The doctor was droning on about young farmers skulled on pig tranquillisers. Her plan had been to leave the meeting, pick up Molly, feed her, drop her at Jacqui's and get to her kickboxing class at six. She made the calculations. There was not enough time to do everything. Diving back into the meeting room, she grabbed her jacket, pointed at her mobile and mimed apologies.

She ran down the corridor and sprinted down Main Street towards the station in Shaftoe Leazes. Orla was behind the desk. Kitty signed off her shift. 'You're always in a rush, Kit,' said Orla, without looking up. 'Always running. Run, run, run! We should call you the Running Policewoman.'

'Needs a little work, does that, Orla. Sorry – gotta run!'

She thought about telling Orla where she was going, but that would take too long.

'Big mistake!' said the Voice. Kitty's finger hovered over the button that would speed dial her mother. Heather Lockwood loved to see her grandchild, but Kitty would have to explain why Molly needed sitting and why; yet again, she was putting work before parenting. So she sprinted to the car.

Belfordham Middle School smelled of afternoon drowsiness, gravy and children. She plucked Molly from class before the child had a chance to say goodbye to her friends. Molly yawned. 'Are we going to Jacqui's?'

'Not yet, Mollusc. We have to do something else first.'

* * *

Dorian slipped the phone from her pocket and slid it behind a jar of macaroni. The connection was live, though the screen had dimmed. The longer she took to cook the meal, the more time there would be to think of something. She would not panic. Richard would never panic. The woman leaned against the surface, arms folded, tapping her foot. The man sat at the table, popping his joints as he stretched. She could feel him watching her every move. He smoothed his hands over his waistcoat. He looked as if he was starting to feel at home. 'Maybe if you tell me what you want?' said Dorian. 'Richard will be back very soon,' she lied. 'Was it my husband you came to see?'

He frowned, a crease furrowing the smooth skin between his eyes. The silence grew. She wondered if he had not heard. 'If it's money, you've come to the wrong house. We're broke at the moment. I know it may not look that way ...'

He scooped the watch from his waistcoat pocket and ran his thumb across the glass. He glanced up at the kitchen clock. 'Is that clock right?'

'It's five minutes fast.'

Dorian shook her head – that they were holding such a banal conversation defied belief. The man nodded, slipped the watch into his pocket. As Dorian sliced the onions, a tear fell on her hands. 'Please! Just tell me!'

He sighed. Then he took a silver box from his waistcoat, clicked it open. He began to roll a spliff. He pulled cigarette papers from the packet. 'You have potatoes, darling?'

That was the moment she recognised his voice. He had been the mystery caller. The thought made her shiver. She watched him lick the edge of the papers and stick them together, running his thumb along the join.

'I just love mash! With butter. And chicken and onion gravy! Can you make gravy, Dorian?'

Dorian was holding the kitchen knife. It was a chef's knife, a Wusthof, the edge as sharp as a cut-throat razor. She felt the heft of the wooden handle, the way it balanced the blade. If she walked around the table she could hold the knife to his throat.

'Yes. Of course. Gravy. Whatever you say.'

She rubbed her eye with the back of her hand.

'The chicken pieces will take a while.'

'How long?'

She glanced at the clock. 'Forty minutes?'

'We can wait an hour, can't we?' He turned to his partner. 'I think we can.' He jabbed his finger towards Dorian. 'See? A homemaker!' He turned back to Dorian. 'Make enough for three. We'll all eat together.' He rolled the papers into a tube. 'That'll be sweet.'

She watched him crumble hash along the line of tobacco. Then she turned back to the Aga, needing to look at something that was real, something that made sense. He rolled the joint between his fingers, then held it up, admiring his work.

Dorian filled her mind with the task – chopping onions, boiling water – anything but the strangers who had crashed her world. She crumbled a stock cube into the pot, stirring the flakes, watching them melt away. Her hands were trembling. A tear rolled down her cheek and fell into the pan. She stirred it all together. Why wasn't Richard here, to take care of this?

Stop whining!

Boiling water – that might be a weapon. What if she missed? She didn't care to think how he might take his revenge. She closed her eyes, knowing she would do none of these things. If the man threatened her she would plead with him. She was a coward. She would beg. She would do anything to survive.

Dorian took the chicken pieces from the fridge and peeled

off the plastic wrapper. Without pausing in her work, she stole a glance at the mobile. The screen was black. The man was busy building his joint, while 'Ginny' had turned to look through the window. Perhaps she had enough courage for this. Dorian tapped the mobile, bringing the screen to life. Her fingers were claws, knuckles gleaming white through the sheath of skin. Nothing had ever scared her so much. The screen glowed – the connection was still live.

'Dorian?' said the stranger. 'Come here.'

CHAPTER THIRTY

Richard found that navigating his way through Leeds was a nightmare, as ever. He missed his turning and found himself orbiting the one way system. As he hurtled along in the stream of cars he glimpsed the familiar landmarks passing by. He flew past the West Yorkshire Playhouse and the Henry Moore Institute. His rage, never far beneath the surface, began to simmer.

* * *

They drove up the valley in silence, Kitty drumming her fingers on the wheel. Molly sensed her mother's anxiety.

'Where are we going?'

'A place called West Neuk. Just a little further,' said Kitty.

'You're driving fast.'

Molly was right. A half-baked hunch was no reason to have an accident.

'Are you going to kickboxing tonight?'

'Might give it a miss, Molly. I really don't know.'

'I'm hungry.'

Kitty nodded. The guilt kicked in. The Bad Mother, putting

work ahead of her daughter. What on earth was she doing, running around after Dorian Kane? She didn't even like the woman.

* * *

Dorian was aware that they were fighting. It was a low key skirmish, conducted in stony silence, but she could feel the tension. While the woman wanted to get out of the place, he seemed to be excited about being inside a stranger's house. For Dorian, the adrenaline shock of the first minutes had faded. She went through the familiar rituals, kidding herself she was cooking for a couple of friends who had dropped by. She bustled around the kitchen, easing the woman aside to open the pan drawer.

She laid the table, working her way around him. He sat in silence, taking a draw on another spliff, resting his arm on the edge of the table. His hand trembled, the smoke hovering as it rose into the air. Perhaps, she thought, he was readying himself, gathering courage.

No word had passed between the strangers for some time. She stood by the door, tapping her phone, while he blew rings, squinting as the smoke drifted across his eyes. Dorian wondered how this might turn out. They would eat, they would talk, perhaps get to know each other a little. She would tease out personal details from the pair, perhaps find some common ground. They would relax, start to laugh and share secrets. Perhaps they would be so entertained by Dorian's company that the idea of hurting her would seem impossible. But that hardly seemed likely.

They could take whatever they wanted. She would even help

CHAPTER THIRTY

load the car, as long as they didn't hurt her. If they tied and gagged her, she could handle that; for a little while, at least.

As long as they're talking to you, they're not killing you.

She stole a glance at the woman she knew as 'Ginny.' It would help if she knew their real names. Dorian carried the food to the table. How she wanted a drink, a huge glass of wine, something to take away the sharp edges! She spread her hands wide.

'Dinner is served...'

CHAPTER THIRTY ONE

The satnav led Richard to the slip road near Tetley Wharf. He cruised down the slope and into the city, found a slot in the multi-storey and switched off the motor. The engine pinged and ticked as it cooled. Richard dabbed his brow and glanced at his watch. There was no hurry – Abid Mirza was always late. Richard had a few minutes to reach the curry house, the *Shikara,* on Crown Point Road.

Abid Mirza ran a clothing warehouse on Firth Street. He was keen to take three apartments at Cutler's Wharf and Richard's research revealed that he was wealthy – just the sort of buyer that they needed. He was buying off-plan and would pay a deposit, by cheque, that day. A quarter of a million should stuff the mouths of Paitons. The money would keep George Cunliffe quiet too.

It was an irony that if Mirza came through and Richard closed the deal, there would be no need to go through with his other plan. But it was too late to stop. By now they would be inside the house.

He slipped his mobile into his pocket and checked he was carrying business cards, brochures and notebook. Richard knew Mirza would try some last minute haggling. He couldn't pick and choose his buyers, the way things were. He slipped a mint beneath his tongue, passed a fingertip along his eyebrow and bleeped the car. Car parks were not his favourite places. Richard always thought of himself as the hunter, not the prey. Yet car parks made him uneasy. He glanced around, worried as always that thieves might jump him. But he was alone. He jogged up the ramp to street level, where he emerged to blinding sunlight. The city centre was as busy as ever, crawling with shoppers and students. He strode down the centre of the pavement and found the *Shikara* with five minutes to spare.

* * *

Dorian stole a glance at the faces of her guests. The stranger had placed himself at the head of the table. She heaped his plate with grilled chicken breast, mashed potato and bobby beans. As he poured the onion gravy, he inhaled the steam, grinning like the Bisto Kid.

'You see? Happiness lies in simple things.' He scooped mash onto his fork and sighed with pleasure. 'Good food. Good company.'

The woman rested her fork on the side of the plate. 'I've been saying that,' she murmured.

'Hey! You *know* what would go well with this?' Dorian stole a glance at 'Ginny'. 'A glass of white. Or bubbly.' The man's voice was a soft plaint of regret. 'A Perrier-Jouet. Or a chilled Piper Heidsieck! He rested his knife and fork and looked at Dorian, a wide-eyed boy who knows dreams can't come true, but who asks anyway. The woman looked down, fluffing the mash with the tip of her fork. It was clear to Dorian that she wanted to be out of there. And though the man was smiling, his mood seemed brittle. There was an edge in his voice.

'We have wine,' said Dorian, her voice bright as tin. 'In the cellar.'

The man leaned back in his chair.

'A wine cellar?'

'Richard has a few bottles put by. I don't know about champagne, but we've bottles of white. About five hundred, actually.'

The smile on his face grew wider still. 'Five hundred?' He whistled, though he knew everything about the wine cellar.

'If you like, I could have a look.'

'Sweet! We *do* like!'

Dorian got up and headed for the hall. She paused, at the kitchen door, waiting for permission to leave. The man nodded then he winked at his partner. 'Perhaps you could give Dorian a hand?'

A beat, as 'Ginny' seemed to be considering her reply. Dorian saw something in her eyes – fear perhaps, or anger. Then her chair scraped across the flags as she rose to follow.

Dorian loathed the cellar. She hated anything that scuttled or rustled. There were mice and rats on every farm. She could hear them at night, scrabbling in the walls. So she always made a lot of noise before she entered the cellar – just to let them know she was coming.

The door was a slab of white oak, cut to fit the gap beneath the staircase and secured by a stout bolt. As Dorian walked towards it she suffered a moment of panic. Perhaps this was their plan, to trick her, to get her down there without a struggle. If she went down the stairs, what might they do? She lifted the latch and the door swung open.

CHAPTER THIRTY ONE

* * *

A Bhangra tune crackled through the speakers. Richard walked through the gloom and took the table at the rear of the restaurant, facing the door. It was cooler here and he liked to see the enemy coming.

Clients were his prey. He felt that way when he worked at Amschels, though it had been so different then. In those days he was a magician, an alchemist. His clients had been in awe of him. He knew all the tricks that turned their nest eggs into mountains of gold. Outside the bank, he felt diminished, somehow. He had swapped a career at the top of the mountain for one in the foothills, where he scratched around, scrabbling for points, hoarding petrol chitties like some rep. This job reeked of petty cash, VAT returns and luncheon vouchers. These days, clients needed to be coaxed and flattered before they were fleeced. His punters were the general public. They were teachers, newsagents and elderly widows. Fat middle-aged men living on disability benefits; builders and bookies and bums.

The world changed when he lost his job. In the village they might call him 'Mr Kane, the millionaire,' but he knew the truth. There was no longer a performance bonus or company car. There were no weekends at Amschels' villa near Menton. Now he spent his days trawling a database or phoning friends of friends. He could no longer lure his prey to the boardroom with a bottle of fizz. Now he was obliged to drive to semis in Cheadle and Chorley and Wenlock Edge. His clients had Stag Minstrel bathrooms and synthetic tigerskin rugs. They had to be charmed and seduced before he prised the cash from their fingers. They were the enemy.

He dreaded the moment when they looked him in the eye and said, 'So ... what's this going to cost me?' That was the moment when the bluff and the bonhomie fell away; the moment he saw the greed in their eyes.

The twang of a sitar floated through the sound system. In other circumstances the ambiance might be soothing. But Richard had psyched himself up. He was ready to sell. Within minutes he would have to go over the top, selling property in a dead market. He glanced at his watch. Abid Mirza was late.

Richard leafed through the prospectus once more. The brochure was slick, the colours bright, the Mersey a Mediterranean blue beneath a dazzling sun. Pencil and wash drawings showed young couples walking beside his waterfront apartments. The figures in the pictures looked so happy. He looked towards the door.

There had always been a blankness whenever he imagined this meeting. On some level, Richard knew from the start that Mirza would never arrive. The door was not about to open. His client would not run in from the street, gasping apologies. It was never going to happen. Richard had put the hours in, making the calls and setting up meetings. He worked his balls off chasing the deal but Mirza always needed reassurance, the lure of discounts and special rates. Richard stabbed the point of his knife into the tablecloth. A waiter crept from the gloom.

'Would sir like a drink?'

Richard gouged the cotton into loops. The waiter kept his distance, sensing his customer's mood. He noticed the ragged hole Richard was opening in the tablecloth. The waiter studied the face of his guest, a man who repaid hospitality with fury.

'Fuck off!' said Richard.

The waiter retreated to the kitchen, leaving the strange man

CHAPTER THIRTY ONE

alone with his rage.

CHAPTER THIRTY TWO

Chastened by Molly's disapproval, Kitty drove towards West Neuk as slowly as she could bear. She wanted this to be over. Whatever fascination the Kanes once held, it was fading. She knew this journey was a mistake. Molly was fidgeting, hungry and bored. She kicked the button on the glove compartment, which fell open, spilling CDs into the footwell.

'Oh, for Heaven's sake, Molly!'

Kitty stopped the car, shoved the CDs back and slammed the glove compartment shut. They travelled on at speed.

Kitty wondered what might be waiting for her when she arrived at West Neuk. The Kanes might be eating. Her sudden appearance would seem odd and she did not want to reveal that her number was on Dorian's speed dial. Her plan was to check Dorian was safe then make an excuse and leave. She would pretend that she happened to be passing and that this was a standard follow-up visit. It was lame, but it was the only story that came to mind. And she would block calls from Dorian and she would never, *ever* give her personal number to a citizen again.

They rounded a bend and the house was there, perched on

the hillside.

'Are we there yet, mum? I'm *really* hungry!'

* * *

For his first birthday in their new home, Dorian wanted to give her husband something special. Searching the web, she discovered the racks at a farm sale in Provence. She had them shipped to England. She and Richard spent two days knocking them together in the cellar at West Neuk. When they were done they stood in the dim light, grimy and out of breath, admiring their work. Richard opened a bottle of Syrah, a Burgaud Cote Rotie, to celebrate. They clinked glasses to their usual toast: 'You and I. Forever...'

He smudged a cobweb from her cheek. She lifted her face and kissed him, allowing him to steer her against the rack. She giggled at the sound of chinking bottles. That afternoon flashed into Dorian's mind as she and 'Ginny' moved between the racks, searching for the right bottle.

Richard had filled one rack with vintage and organic wines. A hundred and twenty bottles of Marchesi de Frescobaldi Montesodi, dark as squid ink, lay in neat rows, their labels turned to the vaulted ceiling. Bottles of Masi Campofiorin Ripasso 97 filled another rack. Rows of Chateau Mazeris, Canon Fronsac and Clos de l'Escandil stretched into the darkness.

The whites were at the far end of the cellar, where cobwebs hung in sooty swags. Dorian ran her finger across the labels, rimed with dust. Her lips moved as she read the names. She reached for a bottle and felt the weight of it in her hand. As she glanced at 'Ginny', waiting at the end of the row, she knew this was her chance. When they reached the top of the stairs she would use it as a club. Whack her once and run for the door. At the very moment she formed this thought, a fat spider crawled across the label. Dorian felt the legs creeping across her fingers. She screamed and the bottle slipped from her grasp, smashing on the stone floor. The crash echoed around the cellar. There was a noise by the far wall, the click of claw on stone as something ran along the floor. Dorian grabbed two bottles of La Baume and turned to find 'Ginny' at her side. The woman seized the bottles and marched to the stairs.

'Wait!' said Dorian.

'Ginny' turned.

'Sorry! I hate it down here.' Dorian looked up at the woman. 'Your name isn't Ginny, is it?'

'Don't play games,' said 'Ginny', her face an inch from Dorian. 'You'd lose.'

Without waiting for a reply, she walked up the stairs. As she reached the top she switched off the light. Dorian scuttled after her.

* * *

'I've changed my mind.' The waiter emerged from the gloom, tilting his head like a bird. 'Bring me the wine list,' said Richard.

He checked his watch. They would be working now, inside the house. They should have left by three, if all had gone to plan. That he could not be certain about this made him anxious. There was no way he could control what happened. And that was one thing he disliked above all.

CHAPTER THIRTY TWO

The waiter laid the folder on the table. Richard scanned the list, looking for something that would take away the edge. That was all. He must be calm, not drunk. 'I'll try the burgundy – the Chevalier-Montrachet.'

It was a white, but this didn't really count – it was medicinal. The waiter opened the bottle and poured a few drops into Richard's glass. He took the bottle, filled the glass and drank. His mouth puckered. His appetite had gone. He felt a sick, nervous excitement. Mirza had screwed him, but at least he had a Plan B. He needed an alibi for Plan B. So the idea was that he would be away on business when it all kicked off. He would love to know what was happening a home. But he had always found it difficult to delegate. He would never admit to a weakness but, if pressed, he would allow that this was an area that needed attention.

The waiter stood against the wall, eyeing him nervously. Richard dropped a twenty on the table and left. In the end, he would win. Because he was a winner.

CHAPTER THIRTY THREE

Dorian watched as the stranger fussed over the wine, his lips moving as he read the label. The liquid rolled around the glass as he held it to the light. The *gloop gloop* as he poured was the only sound in the room. Dorian sipped her drink, forcing a smile.

'This is nice!' The man smacked his lips and sighed his appreciation. 'Civilised. Don't you think, 'Virginia,' darling?'

Dorian bit her lip.

'What I think is: we should be finished here,' replied the woman. The clock ticked away the seconds. 'We should be fifty miles away,' she murmured, sounding less certain now. The man's gaze was fixed, his head perfectly still. The silence lengthened. His eyelids flickered, the edges meeting and parting. In the past week he had gone without sleep, fuelling himself on coke and adrenaline. Now he was coming down, his body forcing him to stop.

Dorian saw his eyelids flutter, then close. 'Where's home?' she said. He blinked, chuckled, and was awake once more.

'I don't think we should answer that, Dorian.' His voice was soft. He took her hand, folding her slim, pale fingers in his and stared into her eyes. It was as if they were alone in the room. 'He didn't say how...' Then he stopped. He blinked and shook his head. Then he started again. 'What will be, will be, Dorian.'

She watched as he traced his fingertips across her skin. This was beyond her understanding, but she managed to smile in spite of the fear.

'What will happen here, will happen,' said the stranger. 'It's all been planned. All been worked out before.'

'I don't understand. Planned?'

He stroked her hand and looked deep into her eyes. 'Planned. Mapped out. By a higher power, Dorian.'

She shook her head, closing her eyes. The woman lay her hand on his arm. 'It's time we were gone. You're tired. We should go. Before you ... before we make a mistake. Do what you need to do.'

The man inched his chair closer to Dorian. 'This was before we were born, sweetness. We don't make things happen. We just live it out! We play the roles we're given.' His pupils were dark jewels.

'Nothing like this has happened to me before,' said Dorian.

'No shit!' he wheezed. His shoulders shook with laughter. 'No shit!'

He threw back his head and laughed. He slapped his thigh and shook his head. 'You're a funny lady!'

She could hear a wheeze in his breathing. 'Is this a robbery? Are you kidnapping me?'

Dorian's voice trailed away. 'What is this? What is it you *want*?'

He stopped laughing. The only sound that faint hiss from his lungs. Dorian stared at her plate. The hand holding her fork started to shake, the tines chinking against the plate. 'Please don't hurt me. Please.'

The man looked at 'Ginny'. He winked. He slid a forkful of mash into his mouth, dropped his fork and swayed back in his chair. 'Dorian, don't. You're spoiling the moment. We were having such a sweet time.' He shook his head, disappointed in her. 'I know this is hard. You're minding your own business, milking the sheep, whatever it is you fuckers do out here, then – *blam*!' He slapped his hand on the table. 'We crash your world!' He dabbed his mouth with a napkin. 'This is hard for *all* of us, sweetness!' His fingers smoothed the back of her hand. He teased the ragged strands of mohair from her skin. His fingers curled around hers, trapping them in a soft, warm cage. He put her hand to his mouth and kissed it.

Dorian searched his face, desperate to understand. Perhaps this was an elaborate joke? Maybe her husband worked with these people. Perhaps they were old friends from the bank? But Richard, more than anyone, must know what this would do to her. Whatever the truth, she could not find it in the stranger's expression. She could read nothing there. Her hand nestled in his fingers like a small bird. Again he kissed her fingers. He held Dorian's hand in his lap. She found it hard to look at him, so she looked down at their hands, fixing her gaze on the line where their skin touched.

'Hard for all of us...'

* * *

In the gloom and echo of the multi-storey, Richard closed his eyes. One glass of wine on an empty stomach; he felt the rush ripple up his spine and swoosh over the top of his head, a cool wave breaking in slow motion. He listened to his breathing.

CHAPTER THIRTY THREE

'In ... steady ... out through the mouth ...'

Dorian's voice was in his head. She had taught him this as a way to cool his rage. He saw Dorian's face, felt the guilt. He needed to sleep. His mobile bleeped, the phone slipping through clammy fingers, scuttering across the seat.

'Is that Richard?'

'Speaking.'

'Good day to you! It's Abid Mirza.'

'Abid!' Richard swallowed, changing gear: a shot of sincerity, a spoonful of honey. 'Good to hear from you.' He imagined Mirza's plump, well-fed face.

'You know, I was certain we said one, one fifteen?'

'I am so sorry, Richard! Please forgive me – I seem to have a touch of food poisoning.'

'Oh dear! I *am* sorry!' *Hope it's fatal*. 'How are you feeling?'

'I'm so sorry I wasn't able to make it.'

'Yes.'

'I would have called earlier but I just couldn't find your number.'

'Listen. No problem, no problem. Let's reschedule. I'll be back down here ...' He was due back in Leeds next month, but if there was a chance they might still meet – a cheque from Mirza would solve everything. 'I could be down next week, Abid. Or ...' he juggled days and times '...we could meet on my way back up the country. Is this Friday any good?'

'I don't want to put you to any trouble.'

'No trouble, Abid! Why don't we meet in Liverpool? I'd love to show you around the site. It's looking beautiful! We're selling apartments hand over fist! The bottom of the market is the smart time to buy. I'd hate for you to miss out.'

'Things have changed, Richard.' The silence hung there.

Don't taunt me. Have some respect. 'Abid. Look. It would be a shame to miss making a killing because of a tummy bug.' *Play the guilt.*

But Abid Mirza had set his face against the deal. Richard suspected he knew about his troubles. He was not about to be hustled into buying when the price was falling by the hour. The silence lengthened.

'I won't be around for the next few weeks, actually, Richard.' He sounded almost bored. 'We're going to Hyderabad. Family business. And to watch a little cricket.'

'Lovely!'

'Isn't it? The first time my wife and I have been back together, so we're making a holiday of it! A few months actually.'

'Lucky old you!'

'Perhaps I will get in touch when we get back? See how the market is then?'

Richard's cheque was in shreds, the pieces fluttering away, melting like snowflakes falling into the sea. The cheque he needed for the bank; that would allow him to keep face with Cunliffe. All gone. He turned the key. The Porsche trundled down the ramp. How fortunate that he had shown foresight, the kind of strategic thinking only the strongest show. The sun bounced off the pavement, searing his eyes. He reached for his sunglasses.

* * *

Kitty turned into the drive at West Neuk. Molly opened the window to see the horses, who were turned out in the paddock. They turned their heads up, eyeing the car.

'Aah, mum! Can I feed them?'

'Not now, Molly. I'll only be a minute.' The gravel crunched as Kitty turned a circle, ready for a quick exit. She killed the motor. 'Doesn't look like there's anyone at home.'

Molly only had eyes for the horses. There were no messages, no missed calls on Kitty's mobile. She climbed out of the car. 'Wait here. I'll be two minutes. OK?'

Molly said nothing, her eyes on the horses as they trotted towards the fence. Kitty walked to the Kanes' front door, knocked and waited.

* * *

Richard's briefcase closed with a crisp click. The guys from Amschels bought it as his leaving gift – Smythson's of Bond Street, the leather sleek and handsome. He ran his fingers over the spotless surface – perfection was so pleasing.

'All set?' George Cunliffe nodded at the kit arrayed on the table. Richard's BlackBerry, notepad and pen lay in a tight, tidy wall. His line of defence. Cunliffe had no papers, gadgets, no props. He didn't need them.

'All set.' Richard's mind was elsewhere. He stole a peek at his watch. *Why didn't they call? They should be clear by now.*

'Am I keeping you from something, son?' Cunliffe's voice dripped sarcasm. 'Only, if there's somewhere you'd rather be ...'

'I'm tired, George. That's all. I have trouble sleeping at the moment.'

'I'm not surprised.'

The atmosphere in the lobby of the Adelphi Hotel was subdued. Cool light filtered through muslin curtains. The air was scented with coffee and Danish pastry. An endless piano tune tinkled from speakers behind the potted palms. George Cunliffe flagged a passing waiter, drawing a circle in the air over the empties on their table.

'Same again.' The waiter swished away. 'You're working too hard, son.'

'I enjoy hard work, George.'

'You look shagged out! Got another woman?'

Richard forced a smile. Never let the enemy know you're down. Business is all about confidence.

'Are you still up for this, Dickie?'

Richard nodded. Air whistled through George Cunliffe's nose, each breath a tight wheeze. His cheeks were mottled with broken veins. Richard turned away to avoid his breath, which reeked of whisky and cigar smoke. 'I went to the site yesterday. I've been there most days.'

'How's it all looking? I've not had a moment to call by.'

Richard's last visit had been three weeks earlier. He had left after an awkward discussion over money with one of the contractors. 'Bloody marvellous!'

Cunliffe leaned back, allowing the waiter to set their drinks on the table. As the man left, he leaned forward. 'That's not the problem, is it? When blokes don't get paid, they tend to shove off ...'

Richard picked up his pen, laid it down again, moving it to fit a gap in his wall. Cunliffe prodded a fat finger on the glass-topped table.

'The big stuff's done. Wiring. Plumbing. Fixings. It's plastered and skimmed to the fourth floor. But the painters are sitting on their arses. No fucker works for fresh AIR! '

Cunliffe had a habit of barking the last word. Richard bobbed his head in agreement.

'I see that.'

'We have a cracking property. But we won't sell any units till the FUCKER is FINISHED!' Across the lobby, heads turned. 'I've done MY bit. Put up my share of the dosh. You, on the other hand, are seventy K shy!'

Richard was silent.

'Ha'porth of tar. Know that one?' Richard shook his head. 'Thought not ...'

'I'm sure you're right, George.' Richard turned his pen, nudged the Blackberry. 'It's not that I can't find the rest of the capital. It's just that my side ...'

'There are no "sides", Richard! It's a partnership. We work as one. Split everything.'

'Of course.'

'That's the thing about you sods. Bankers. You know DAMN ALL about real business. That was the deal that you SIGNED. Don't play the slippery sod, Richard!'

'Of course! What I was going to say was that one of us was bound to reach their budget target before the other. It happened to be you.'

Richard's face was pale, his thin smile tacked on. 'You must see that!' *Lectured! By a pygmy!*

'I'm not pulling your plonker, Richard. You need to shell out!'

Cunliffe drained his glass, set it down with a click. Richard bobbed his head. He was humiliated. For a moment he had the oddest feeling. It was as if his father had returned from the dead. His heart kicked a beat. He felt a brief, overwhelming flurry of rage. He breathed through pursed lips, counting. But Cunliffe seemed not to notice. He sighed, leaned back, shaking his head.

'If there's a problem, let's talk about it! We all have lean years. Pharaoh's oxen, yes?'

Richard nodded. He had no idea what the old bastard meant, but he wanted to end this.

'You know Richard – I'm not short of cash.' Cunliffe glanced around the lobby. 'If you want, I can cover this. I can find a little here and there so we can pay these guys. Then we can get to the fun part, which is selling the buggers and banking the dough.'

Another nod from Richard. He was back in control of himself.

'But if I do that, Richard – then we have to take another look at the points.' Cunliffe spread his spade-like hands. 'The more I put more in, Dickie, the more I take out. Fair's fair!'

Cutler's Wharf was Richard's project. He had found the original building, came up with the concept, found the architect. He brought Cunliffe in for his financial muscle – the man had no ideas, no flair, no imagination. Now the creep wanted Richard to roll over and let him take over.

'It's make your mind up time, Dickie.'

Richard needed a moment to think. What was happening at home? If all went to plan he would claim on his insurance. That might take weeks to process. Another week for the cheque to clear. The cavalry were coming, but they were nowhere close.

'You're very perceptive, George.' *Grovel. Take your lumps.* 'I should have known that I'd never bluff the Master. I've got the money! No problem about the amount. None at all. But ...' Richard jabbed a thumb over his shoulder '... everything's tied up in trusts, in other projects. I just need a little time to work it through the system. So ...' He ran a finger along his brow. 'If you were able to cover me? Up to the seventy K? I'll have my own funds by...mid August. The twentieth, at the outside.'

Cunliffe peered at him from beneath his dark eyebrows. He made a wheezing sound, his toxic breath whistling around his sinus. His tongue flicked across his lower lip. He scratched his cheek, looked away. Richard recognised the little play, designed to make him sweat.

'It'll cost you!'

Cunliffe looked down. Richard watched him counting on his stubby fingers as he calculated the numbers, lips moving as he did the sums.

'Shall we say another two per cent?'

Richard met his gaze. This was better than he could have hoped for. He pursed his lips, blew air. He ran his tongue along his immaculate teeth. Richard stretched out his hand, slowly, and Cunliffe took it.

'Agreed. I'll pay the lads what they're owed and you settle up with me in August?'

Richard smiled.

'Top man! Excellent! Onward and upwards, eh? I'll get the office to do us a bit of paper on this,' said Cunliffe. He mimed writing. 'But listen ...' He leaned forward, speaking softly, the wise uncle. 'If you have difficulties, TELL ME!' His bullet eyes glinted. Richard scooped up his Blackberry and slid the rest of the wall into his case.

'So. That deserves a drink!'

Sooner drink my own piss. 'I'd love one!'

'Good man! A proper drink!'

Richard thumbed a bead of sweat from his brow. The drinks arrived and the older man raised his glass. Richard raised his

glass, chinked it with Cunliffe's.
'Here's to crime!'

CHAPTER THIRTY FOUR

'*Nathan!* There's a car!'

Dorian was sitting at the kitchen table when she heard Ginny cry. She followed Nathan into the front room, where they found her staring through the window. They watched the car circle and came to a halt by the paddock fence.

'Come here,' murmured Nathan.

Dorian stood beside them, peeking through the window. *His name is Nathan.* This '*Nathan*' seized her arm, pulling her close. They saw the door of the car open. They watched Kitty climb out and look up at the house.

'Who is it?' he hissed. Dorian shivered. She had pressed the speed dial and the woman had arrived. But the sight only made her more anxious. One woman, on her own: what difference could she make? And now Nathan and 'Ginny' were trapped in the house.

As Kitty glanced at the window, all three inside pulled back.

'She's seen us,' said 'Ginny'. 'Do you know her?'

Dorian havered, unsure of the safest answer. 'Yes. She's just a ... friend.' They heard the gravel crunch as Kitty walked towards the door.

'Into the kitchen, Tanya.' Nathan pulled the gun from his

pocket. 'You stay with me,' he said to Dorian. He took hold of her arm and moved her into the hall. They reached the front door as Kitty's knock echoed through the house.

'Don't answer. Just leave it!' Nathan pulled Dorian closer, putting his lips to her ear. 'Don't let her in. You're busy. You'll call her later!' Another knock, the sound ringing through the hall. She felt his warm breath in her ear. 'Do what I say and everything's sweet.' He shook her, his face in her hair. 'I'm watching. I'm listening. All the time. OK?'

Dorian nodded.

Tanya stood in the door to the kitchen. Nathan gestured, moving her back, deeper into the house. When she was out of sight he pushed Dorian towards the front door. She took a deep breath and turned the handle.

* * *

The idea was to raise cash – just enough to buy a little time. The bank had turned him down, which was ironic since Richard had sat on the other side of that desk. He had to refuse funding so often. Dorian had hinted her mother might help, but he would never ask the old witch for a loan. The Frosts could have funded a dozen Cutler's Wharves without dinting the family chest. But Richard was too proud to beg.

They were short of cash, yet rich in possessions. Though he had drawn as much as he could against the house, the contents were untouched. Relatives had left them such gorgeous things. Though most of them had come from Dorian's side, there were others that Richard had earned by the sweat of his own brow. So many beautiful pieces – the Lalique mirrors, the Louis XVI armoire, the sketches by Augustus John – glorious, beautiful objects. But you can't spend things, can you? They had to be parlayed into cash. Dorian suggested they sell one or two items, just to tide them over. Richard refused; he didn't want to part with a thing. That would have been going backwards. But it gave him the idea.

Liquidity. He needed liquidity to pay the contractors. His idea was to exchange those precious things for cash, on a temporary basis. Just for a month or two. Insurance companies have money to burn and Richard had no qualms about taking them for every penny. 'Insurance is an organised con, a legal scam,' he told himself. He was stealing from no-one but himself. Everyone claimed on their insurance! All Richard was doing was taking that everyday, suburban 'crime' a little further; giving it a little twist. Turning *objets d'art* into cash was another form of alchemy. He knew all about that. He was a magician, after all. He flew above the crowd. They would see that, one day – the little people, the pygmies. Mental midgets like George Cunliffe, like his old boss, Conrad Sereys. Like his father ... the King of the Midgets; the smallest of the Little People.

The idea was to strip West Neuk of everything of value. Over recent months he had upped the insurance. It was unlikely to raise suspicion – they had been under insured for years. He drew up an inventory of the targets. The smaller, more delicate pieces had been spirited away months ago. Richard smuggled them out over several weeks and stored them in a warehouse on an industrial estate. Since he was always making changes to the way the house looked, Dorian had not noticed.

Richard knew where he was going. Like a sailor guiding his craft through a storm, he never lost sight of the harbour. He was merely tacking a little, jinking to the side before resuming his course.

Finding Nathan had been the hard part. But that was down to his connections. For all his gangster front, Nathan was a lazy, venal thug. He would take a few thousand and keep his mouth zipped. Nathan wasn't complicated: scary, but biddable; a thug with predictable habits. Richard had discovered that Nathan was a man he could manipulate.

Nathan's role was to con his way in, take the stuff and go. Dorian's jewels - the Pavel Bure wristwatch, the Guilloche enamel and amethyst pendant, the platinum – that was where the value was. These were family pieces, left to her by Dorian's grandmother. He could never ask her to part with any of that. Selling them was unthinkable. It would have been cheap. This was the best way to do it. There was another thirty K covering the AV kit and the computers.

Then there was the art. The Augustus John painting, 'A Study of Dorelia', was a beautiful piece – such simplicity, such clarity of line! It was on loan from Dorian's mother. The old witch said it was valued at thirty five K.

There were his shotguns, the antique Purdey and the Freemantle and Sons with the open choke Damascus barrels. The .22 rifle was a cheap Czech job, not worth bothering about, but some Yank had offered him $90K for the Purdey shotgun and the Freemantle had to be worth seven thou, easy. It all added up.

There was cash in the safe, a few stocks and shares, which Nathan would leave alone. He had "disappeared" a few of his better bottles of wine to the warehouse – they were easy to hide and very expensive. It added authenticity, that sort of detail. He might claim for malicious damage to the furniture.

There was even cover for the "sanitary ware and the ceramic hob", but he'd drawn the line there. There was no need for this to get messy.

The beauty of this idea was that his insurers would pay up quickly. He had contacts through Amschels. When he worked for the bank Richard had been a "high end customer." Over the years he had steered a bundle of business their way. Numbers counted.

Connections again, you see? Connections.

The settlement would be swift and painless. It was such a pity he had to go through this. But the plan ticked like a Swiss watch, because:

A) Richard would not be there. He would have a perfect alibi.

B) Dorian *would* be there. No-one would believe a man would put his own wife through that sort of ordeal.

C) They would not lose a thing.

That was the best part of all! Nathan would deliver everything to the storage facility. All the bawbees would be stored in one container: discreet, secure, and surprisingly economical. Three hundred quid for a year. Nathan had set it up under one of his many aliases. *Bish, bash, bosh.*

When the insurance came through Richard would arrange for the paintings and the jewels to be 'found' again. Anonymous tip off to the police – Nathan again. If the insurance company wanted to adjust their settlement, that was not a problem – Richard would be rolling in it by then.

He would have saved the project. They would be out of the swamp. There was risk, of course, but wasn't he a risk taker? Richard Kane was a buccaneer. Nothing could stop a strong man with courage and ingenuity. He'd been far sighted, setting this emergency plan in train. Richard Kane was a man with vision. He was not one of the little people. Strong – but compassionate too. No-one would be hurt. No-one would suffer. This wasn't personal. This was just business.

CHAPTER THIRTY FIVE

Carole Robb sat at the kitchen table, watching her son eat. Kevin had the same breakfast every day – bacon and two eggs, fried bread, mushrooms, coffee, toast and marmalade. She sipped her tea, leaving her toast untouched.

'The latch on the farm gate needs seeing to. When you've got a minute, son.'

Kevin nodded and gulped another mouthful of coffee.

'What have you got on today?'

'This and that.'

She watched his face. He was a quiet young man, but today there was more to his silence; he was avoiding her eyes and she knew he was hiding something. If only he knew how easily she read him. He pushed his plate aside and reached for his jacket on the back of the chair.

'Where will you be? If anyone asks?'

'Going through to Kyloe. The big house. About a bit of work.'

Carole shivered. She knew the house, knew what they said about the people who owned the place. As her son walked past her chair she reached out, taking his wrist between her bony fingers. 'You know, son, you can tell me anything.'

He kissed the top of her head and went out. She sat alone, listening to the roar of his car as he drove down the lane.

* * *

Dorian's face peered around the front door of West Neuk. Kitty saw the white skin above the black cardigan. A sheen of perspiration covered her face. In an odd way Dorian's appearance reassured her. Seeing the woman like this justified her hunch that all was not well. 'How are you, Mrs Kane?'

'Good, thanks.'

'You don't look it!'

Dorian drummed her fingers on the door frame.

'I got your call..?'

'I didn't call.' Dorian swallowed.

'My number's in your speed dial. You called me,' said Kitty.

Dorian's mouth fell open. She stared at Kitty, her eyes wide, as if pleading. She seemed to shake her head. Nathan twisted the gun and Dorian winced. 'Maybe you sat on the phone? Pressed it by accident?' Even as she said the words, Kitty knew there was something very wrong. Her mind was racing as she tried to understand what was happening. 'So ... just thought I'd drop by,' she said. 'Check you're OK.' Dorian's whole body was shaking. Kitty looked down to see a dark stain spread across the fabric between her legs. Kitty moved forward, her hand on the door, easing it open. It was an instinctive move. 'Shall we go inside?'

As Dorian edged back, she stumbled. Kitty moved with her, hands on her shoulders.

'Is your husband here?' Dorian backed away, shaking her

head as she allowed Kitty to cross the threshold. 'Are you are on your own?'

At that moment Kitty glimpsed movement in the fish eye mirror on the wall. Her brain tried to turn the reflection into Richard Kane, but the shape was all wrong, the shoulders too broad. Kitty's next movement was pure instinct. She pushed hard, ramming the oak door against the unseen figure. The door caught Nathan's cheekbone and he toppled back. As he fell he squeezed the trigger. The blast filled the air. The walls pealed like a bell as the shot echoed down the hall, ringing through the house. The 9mm bullet smashed into the ceiling, showering plaster dust. Smoke and dust puffed through the air. As Dorian crawled towards the kitchen, screaming, Kitty tumbled forwards, landing on all fours. Tasting blood, she panicked, thinking the bullet had caught her. Nathan lay sprawled on his back, blinded by falling dust.

The Makarov was a semi automatic, the blowback pushing another round into the chamber. It would fire as fast as the shooter could pull the trigger. Though dazed, Nathan levelled the gun at Kitty. She imagined the bullet tearing through her flesh, splintering bone. A drop of blood ran along her lip, splashing onto the tiles. Blood on blood. Cardinal red.

Nathan climbed to his feet and dusted plaster from his shoulder. He aimed the gun at Kitty's face.

CHAPTER THIRTY SIX

Molly unclicked her seatbelt, opened the car door and tiptoed across the gravel to the paddock fence. 'You're lovely, aren't you, boy?' She glanced over her shoulder, wary that her mother might hear. But Kitty was standing on the doorstep, waiting for the door to open. Molly could not resist the horses, their tails swishing in the evening sun. Glancing back to make sure the car was between her and her mother, she leaned on the fence and fluttered her fingers.

The horses edged closer, heads nodding as they moved across the paddock. The darker one, Halloween, reached the fence, snickering as she lowered her head.

'Are you hungry? asked Molly. She picked some fresh grass, holding it out on her open palm. She climbed the first rung of the fence to make herself taller. Halloween nuzzled her, then munched the grass, as if doing a favour. Molly stroked her muzzle, fingertips pushing through warm brown velvet. She glanced again at her mother, who was chatting to the lady in the doorway. Molly scratched Halloween's cheeks. The other horse drew close. Molly plucked another handful of grass and hitched herself up a rung so that she was level with Halloween's dark eyes.

CHAPTER THIRTY SIX

The crack of a gunshot. Molly tumbled from the fence onto the gravel. The horses scattered, wild eyed as they galloped up the hill. Molly turned to see blue smoke puff through the open doorway. She heard women screaming, a man shouting. Her mother lay on the ground, half inside the house. Molly picked herself up and ran towards the door, her footsteps crackling on the gravel. As she neared the door her mother pushed herself to all fours. The man twisted around and pointed something at her mother's face.

'Mum?'

Her mother had raised herself to her knees. Her face was creased, as if she was about to cry. 'RUN!' she screamed. Her mother waved her hands, shooing Molly away. She froze then started to run down the drive. She looked over her shoulder, willing her mother to follow. The man had grabbed her mother by the hair and was dragging her into the house. Another figure appeared in the doorway: a woman, running, chasing her, calling for her to stop.

Molly ran towards the main road. Footsteps pounded the gravel behind her, moving closer as the woman gained ground. Molly's lungs burned and a stitch cramped her side. Chips of gravel bounced off her bare legs as the woman ran closer. Molly saw her shadow merge with hers and felt fingers at her throat.

* * *

The Porsche swooped down to the motorway. Richard soared through the early morning traffic. He slipped a Neil Young CD into the player. He was singing *'The king is gone but he's not forgotten'* as he cut through the little people to take his place in the fast lane.

* * *

Nathan struggled to hold the woman still. He was twice her size but she was wiry and her strength surprised him. He sat astride her and grabbed a fistful of hair, banging her skull against the tiles, but she bucked, arching her back. He fell sideways and lost his grip. She jabbed her elbow into his groin and he gasped, doubling over with pain. She broke free and scrabbled to the door. He lay on all fours, waves of pain rushing between his legs and into his stomach. Then he heard her shouting. He turned to see some kid, a girl, standing on the gravel outside the house. The kid began to run. Nathan whipped the pistol across the side of the woman's head. She went down, crumpling onto the tiles. He stood; his foot on her neck, pointing the gun at her head. She lay still.

Tanya rushed past him and chased the kid down the drive. Nathan felt sick. He could see that Tanya was gaining on the kid. Every few seconds he glanced down, just to check the woman was where he wanted her. Blood flecked the tiles beneath her head. Her eyes flickered then closed. He looked towards the kitchen where the other one, Dorian, was crouching in the doorway. Her body was shaking as she peered at him through her fingers.

'Bitch!' Nathan's teeth chattered, his gun hand shook. He bent over as a wave of pain surged through his stomach. Sweat poured down his face. He was in shock. People died from shock. He looked up to see that Tanya had the kid by her neck. They whirled around, as if playing a game; a blur of hair and legs, then fell on the grass beside the road. The girl broke free then dropped as Tanya grabbed her ankle. They lay still. Nathan looked down at the woman under his foot, fascinated by the blood on the tiles, red on red. She was still. He looked out to see Tanya pulling the girl to her feet. She stooped, putting her mouth close to the girl's face, then steered Molly back to the house. Nathan cocked his ear, listening for a car along the main road. There was nothing but the sound of the wind. He wiped his brow and lifted his foot from Kitty's neck.

They were close to the front door when the kid saw her mother lying on the ground. She howled and tried to pull free. Tanya held her, clamping her hand across the kid's mouth.

'Inside!' Nathan said. Tanya steered the kid into the house and Nathan slammed the door. The woman lay still, blood oozing from the wound. He took hold of the kid's hair. 'Shut UP! SHUT THE FUCK UP or ...!' He waved the pistol in the kid's face. She froze, glaring at him.

'For Gods sake, Nathan! Put it away.' Tanya turned the child around, away from the sight of her mother. She kneeled, whispering and stroking her hair. Nathan stepped away. Tanya rarely raised her voice. When she did, he listened. He paced around the hall.

'Knew it! I fucking *knew* it! All the way!' He sat on the stairs, watching as Tanya calmed the girl.

'Listen, listen...'

Nathan tucked the gun into his belt. He pulled a handkerchief from his pocket and mopped his brow. He hated the sound of the kid bleating. Tanya was stroking the kid's hair. Somehow, this afternoon had turned into a nightmare. This job had always been a mistake. He'd known it was jinxed from the start; from the instant he'd set eyes on that plummy-voiced cocksucker.

'Listen girl, it's OK. It's OK.' He reached out to the kid but she flinched, as if scalded. He tried to sound gentle. 'Your mother's fine! She's had a little accident but that's all! She's going to be fine.' Nathan waited for the kid to look at him, but she was staring at her mother. She was shaking like a whipped puppy. 'Tanya? Can you explain?'

Nathan stood. He leaned against the wall, shaking his head. He walked to the doorway. He stood over the woman's body, looking for any movement. The gun was digging into his back. He reached round to shift it and his finger curled around the trigger. That had been so close. He had almost ruined everything. The gun was for safety – he never intended to use it. He'd promised Tanya.

Sweat poured down his face. Kids scared him. Kids and animals. He knew men, understood men. Women were easy. But kids – he never knew what to do with them. What the fuck did they talk about? What did you say to a kid? He watched Tanya working on the girl. She smoothed the hair from the kid's brow, pulled a tissue from her pocket and dabbed away the tears. All the time she was talking, talking, talking.

'It's going to be OK. We're good friends of your mummy. Nobody is going to let anything bad happen. Alright, sweetheart?'

Nathan rolled his head around, easing the tension. Tanya used to say she wanted a daughter. That was when they first got together. The house was quiet now. His pulse was slowing, all the tension flowing away. The woman on the floor lay still. Nathan started to relax. His shoulders softened. His eyes lost focus as he listened to Tanya.

'Really! It's OK, honey. It's like Nathan said. Your mum had a little accident. She's having a sleep. She's hurt her head, but I promise she's going to be OK. There's no need to cry! Alright?' Tanya held the kid's shoulders, turned the child to face her. 'You and I will make her better, OK? What's your name, darling?'

In a small voice she told the lady her name. Tanya stroked her face, told her again that everything would be fine. Her crying faded to a sniffle. 'Tell you what, darling! While we're waiting for your mummy to get better, why don't we get ourselves a drink? I'm thirsty, aren't you?' Tanya held out her hand. Molly glared at her. Tanya put a hand on her shoulder and guided her towards the kitchen. 'It's all going to be OK, honey.'

Tanya's glance at Nathan was loaded. 'Isn't it, Nathe? Everything's going to be just fine.'

CHAPTER THIRTY SEVEN

The white peacock stalked across the newly-mown lawn. As Kevin Robb slammed the door of his precious Citroen, the bird reared and flashed his tail feathers. Kevin screwed up his eyes at the sunlight reflected in the windows of Kyloe House. The wooden front door, shattered during the dawn raid, had been replaced with a sheet of steel, sheathed in cedar cypress.

Kevin tugged the bell pull, which set off the dogs inside the house. He could hear claws scratching the tiles as they fussed in the hall. After a minute Greta Lumley opened the door, holding the security chain in place. One of the dogs, a Rhodesian Ridgeback, pushed its broad snout through the crack and growled, drooling onto the chequered tiles. Greta tucked a lock of ash blonde hair behind her ear as she struggled to control the beast.

'You won't know me, Mrs Lumley. I'm a friend of Clive's.'

The dog lunged at him, trying to squeeze his sleek, muscled body through the slit. Greta pushed the animal back with her thigh.

'I know you,' she said. Her beautiful face was a mask. Kevin was unsettled.

'I need to get a message to Clive?'

'He told you never to come here, didn't he?'

'I need to tell you something.'

'He was perfectly clear. You never come here.'

'I only need a minute.' Her eyes flashed and for a moment he backed away, fearing she was about to open the door and set the dogs on him. 'I know something that can help.'

'Clive said you'd grassed. You've done enough to 'help' already!'

Kevin looked down. He had come too far to be turned away. 'One minute ...?'

* * *

Thursday was Chicken Korma in the canteen at Shaftoe Leazes. Bryson heaped pickles onto his plate and balanced a bowl of mint yoghurt on the side of his tray. He sat in his favourite seat, at the corner of the farthest table, facing the door. A man needs to see his enemies coming. He sat alone, crumbling his poppadom, slipping the fragments between his lips. It was late afternoon and the canteen was almost empty. All was as it should be – the freshly- wiped melamine tables, the creaky plastic seats and the striplights casting their pale blue glow.

Des Tucker and Andy 'Pandy' Banforth sat at a table by the door. Their shift had finished and they were winding down, bickering about last night's match. Gemma Smiles sat at the window table, on her own, scribbling notes in a ring binder. Bryson listened to the clatter beyond the kitchen doors as they prepared for the evening rush.

The basmati rice was too watery. Bryson pushed it to the side of the plate where it lay, oozing moisture, like a heap of drowned maggots. But the korma was immaculate – the hint of ginger, the tang of coriander working against the sweetness of the carrot. Steam rose from his plate as he scooped another forkful from the mound. The texture of the chicken was perfect. As his belly filled he started to feel better about the world. It struck him that Kitty would often join him on a Thursday; then he remembered that she was on an early turn. By now she would be at home. He would be eating alone. Bryson munched his curry, moving across the plate like a buffalo grazing the prairie. The chicken glowed in his mouth, blushing warmly as it settled in his stomach.

His mood sank as he saw Gordon Campbell arrive. Campbell made a big entrance, joshing the lads in the corner, clapping hands on shoulders as he leaned in to whisper a joke. They cackled at the punchline as Campbell moved to the counter. Everyone loved Gordon Campbell, it seemed. He placed a banana and a bottle of still water on his tray, joking with Irene behind the counter, tossing and catching his banana like a juggler. He left her laughing as he turned to find a seat. When he clocked Bryson in the corner, Campbell picked his way through the tables and headed over.

Gordon Campbell was the shape a man should be. He was a silver bullet; his upper body an inverted triangle of muscle. As ever, his uniform was impeccable. Not one speck of lint or flake of dandruff had been allowed to mark the blue serge. His shoes gleamed like dark mirrors. Each strand in his silver thatch fell into its allotted place.

As he watched Campbell approach, Bryson felt fat. Very fat. It was as if his body flowed outwards in every direction from his neck. He sucked in his stomach as Campbell raised his bushy eyebrows and spoke.

'Room for a little one, Bry?'

Bryson nodded, dabbing the corner of his mouth.

'Just when you thought you had the place to yourself, eh, Bryson?' Campbell placed his elbows on the table, rested his chin on his hands and watched his companion slide another forkful into his mouth.

'Enjoying that?'

Bryson nodded. Campbell shook his head.

'You're one of a kind, Bry.'

Bryson swallowed and ran his tongue around his teeth. 'How should I take that, Gordon?' Bryson swigged his tea.

'It's a compliment, Bry. I'm sure I couldn't manage it!' Campbell peeled his banana and folded the skin, as if it were a favourite shirt. He sliced the fruit into six equal portions. He slipped one section into his mouth, chewing quickly; sharp teeth shredding the pulp. His neck rippled and it was gone in one smooth movement. Bryson was reminded of a snake swallowing a mouse.

'Where's your protégé today?' said Campbell.

'Don't go all cuntinental on me, Gordon.' Bryson rummaged through his curry. 'Who d'you mean?' He skewered a chunk of chicken.

'Locky. Katherine Lockwood. She's your protégé, is she not? The Sorcerer's Apprentice. She's usually found somewhere nearby. Worshipping at your feet.'

'I haven't a clue where she is, I'm afraid.' Bryson slotted the piece of chicken in his mouth. 'I don't expect to see her until tomorrow morning. We've a court. '

'That ... that Lumley thing?'

Bryson nodded. He stabbed his fork into meat.

'You're still in then ...'

Bryson's fork was almost between his lips. He paused then set it down with care on the side of the plate. He levelled his gaze at Campbell. 'What does that mean?'

The uniforms by the door fell silent. Gemma Smiles stopped writing and watched them, over the rim of her mug.

Gordon Campbell smiled. He looked down as he selected another slice of banana. 'People talk, Bry.'

'Do they?'

Bryson pushed away his plate. It had been such a beautiful curry – now it was ashes. Campbell popped the banana between his lips. Bryson stood. He pulled his fleece from the back of the chair, took a mouthful of tea then slowly poured the dregs over Campbell's plate. Chunks of banana bobbed in the liquid; pale logs in a muddy stream.

'Well, Gordon ...' Bryson pushed his arms into his fleece. 'They'll certainly talk about *that* ...' Bryson Prudhoe ambled from the canteen, swaying between the tables without a sideways glance.

* * *

Nathan heard a noise, like hoofbeats galloping towards the house. He paused, his head on one side. It was music, coming from somewhere close by. The tinny drumbeat became the first few bars of '*I Fought the Law.*'

'What the ...?'

He ran to Kitty, tearing the pockets of her jacket as he searched for her mobile. She moaned, popping a bubble of blood between her lips. Nathan found her phone. The caller ID read *Bryson*, which meant nothing to him. He opened the front door, walked onto the drive and hurled the phone as far as he could. It bounced on the gravel, turning end over end before landing in a clump of nettles at the edge of the paddock. He wiped his brow as pain burned into his balls. He bent over to spit, a long thread of silver trailing from his lips to the ground.

* * *

Bryson was buzzing as he drove home. The clash with Campbell had been brewing for months and it felt so sweet to release his anger. Yet he had a sense of unease, which he put down to anxiety over the Lumley hearing. He needed to talk to Kitty about it, just to set his mind at rest.

Bryson pulled over and made the call. Kitty's phone rang then went dead. He turned his mobile in his hand, tapped it against his lip. He tried her land line. Her home phone went straight to answer machine. He rang off. For a while he watched the traffic streaming along Leazes Lane, parents making the school run or heading for the supermarket.

Bryson called Kitty's mother. Heather Lockwood sounded breathless. 'Hello. That Heather, is it? Look, I'm sorry to bother you but I'm after Kitty. She has court in the morning and I just wanted a quick chat. I wondered if she was with you.'

'She's not here Mr Prudhoe. I haven't seen her since Tuesday.'

'Have you any idea where she might be?'

'She never phones me, but that's the way she is. I tried her phone this morning and couldn't get through.'

'If she calls can you tell her I just need a chat? '

'Will do. I hope Molly's OK. You've got *me* worried now!' Heather laughed.

Bryson rang off. It was curious that Kitty was unreachable. Odd perhaps, but no more than that.

* * *

Kitty stirred, her eyes flickering as the man hobbled into the house. He seemed to fill the doorway, blocking out the light. She looked up at him then closed her eyes. A drop of blood slid from the corner of her mouth, staining her top. She lay against the wall. The side of her face felt tender. Her flesh was bruised and swollen, her hair matted with drying blood. Her eyes were soft, as she tried to focus. Someone was dabbing her mouth with a tissue. She could hear them talking.

'Downstairs,' he said. Kitty opened her eyes and saw he was pointing to a door beneath the stairs. The blonde woman pulled the door wide and pushed Dorian into the darkness.

'Move!'

The walls trembled when he raised his voice. The woman helped Kitty to her feet and guided her into the cellar. Molly took her mother's hand. They trooped down the narrow wooden staircase, feeling their way between the racks of wine.

'Any grief and this will be the last thing you hear.' He brandished the gun, looking each of them in the eye. Kitty could see that Molly was scared, yet there was a glint of defiance in her daughter's eyes. With a nod the man gestured his partner should leave. He followed her up the stairs. The door clashed shut; someone dropped the bolt and killed the light.

In the darkness Kitty slumped to the floor. The side of her

face burned with pain. She prodded her wounds with her fingertip. Her cheekbone felt raw and she tasted blood as she touched it. The skin was split at the corner of her eye and her gum felt tender. But the damage seemed to be on the surface. As far as she could tell, nothing was broken. She dabbed her mouth with a tissue.

'I hate the dark,' whispered Dorian. 'As long as I can see something it's not too bad. '

The only light in the room was a sliver of white beneath the door.

Kitty rested her back against the wall. She wrapped her arms around Molly and pulled her close. 'What have we got ourselves into, kiddo?' Her instinct had been correct, though that was little consolation. She had acted on impulse – without thought and with no plan. She had put Molly in danger without letting another soul know where she was going. This was a disaster and it was all her fault.

* * *

Nathan leaned against the cellar door; his eyes squeezed shut, his chest tight. He puffed his inhaler until it became easier to breathe. Tanya put her hand on his shoulder.

'Let's just go, babe.' She touched his face. 'Let's get in the car and drive away from here!'

He shook his head. 'I can't leave with nothing.'

'But you were right! It was always a bad idea. Listen – no-one's dead! We can just go home.'

'Maybe. Maybe ...' Nathan checked the bolt on the cellar, picked up the bronze statuette from the hall table and wedged it beneath the door. He went back to the door again and again, checking it was closed, testing the bolt, prodding and pulling, just to make sure. His brow gleamed. Sweat dripped into his eyes. Finally, he was satisfied the door was secure. His mind slowed to a crawl. His skin was cotton wool, his head a sack of feathers. He walked into the kitchen where he pulled a wrap from his top pocket. He opened the paper and tapped out a line on the surface. He chopped the grains, cutting it fine. Tanya watched as he skulled it. He rubbed his nose as he snorted the powder deep into his head. He dabbed a fingertip over the last grains and rubbed them into his gum. Nathan filled his lungs with air, holding it then let it go. The fog in his head cleared. He sat for a moment as he thought about what to do.

'OK. We take everything he asked for. Then we grab a little more – for all our trouble; a little extra insurance. What's he going to do – call the feds?' He laughed, stretching his arms wide. Nathan howled like a dog, spanked Tanya and strode through to the hall. He was a happy man again. He had a plan.

CHAPTER THIRTY EIGHT

For the next four hours they worked their way through the house. They found the loot, packed it, then stashed it in the van. The Augustus John sketches were wrapped in sheets and stacked against the sides. Tanya rifled Dorian's jewellery box, wrapping the trinkets in tissue before Nathan tucked them into the spare wheel compartment. They stripped the house clean.

Around half one in the morning, Nathan moved into the upstairs office. He packed the computers, drives and printers, wrapping the leads in tight bundles. With each load the van sunk lower on the axles. Nathan returned to strip the office. Kane wanted him to take the guns – the Purdey and the Freemantle – so he rooted through the drawers, searching for the key to the gun cupboard. Richard had promised it would be in the desk drawer.

He rummaged through the pens and paperclips but there was no key. His eyes scanned the junk in the drawer but the shapes made no sense. It was a tangle of pens and paperclips, their edges shaking and blending. He closed his eyes. They had worked for hours without a break, with only a line of charlie to keep him sharp. All his energy drained away in a heartbeat.

Nathan slumped onto Richard Kane's office chair. Soft, orange light glowed through his eyelids, the blood flowing through the skin. Golden light washed over him. His mouth opened, his head fell forward and he was gone.

* * *

Tanya wandered around the house, opening drawers and rooting in cupboards. She carried Richard's inventory of everything that was to be stolen. Finding a small bronze figure of a woman, she turned it over, feeling the dimples in the metal, running her fingertips over the face. She rested the bronze on the table as she searched the inventory. She ticked her list, the nib skating across the page. This was the kind of thing other people did every day – making lists, ticking them off, making lists again. In that moment she saw herself from the outside. It was a moment of pure clarity. This was Tanya as she might have been.

If she had not met Nathan that night in the *Zanzi*, life might have been so different. She saw herself as someone else – confident, self-possessed, independent. This other woman would have her own house. A child, perhaps. Tanya sat down for a moment, allowing herself to explore her unlived life. She saw herself running her own business, in antiques, or clothing, or furniture. She was buying stock and meeting clients. Everything seemed possible. She and Nathan would live a quiet life, instead of waking up each day feeling hunted. She was tired of it. She was thirty years old and still running around like a kid.

She had no friends because Nathan didn't trust anyone. They lived in a caretaker's flat in a warehouse because the

CHAPTER THIRTY EIGHT

address wasn't listed. They had to keep moving, keep looking for the next score. At that moment she realised that the life that once seemed glamorous had become a trap. She had shackled herself to Nathan, who hated straight people and their tidy lives. She knew that the truth was that real life scared him. If she wanted a different kind of existence she would have to find it on her own. She could have a better life, or she could have Nathan. That was the choice.

The house was silent. Tanya always knew where Nathan was. Day and night, she knew how he was feeling. Was he hungry, horny, or high? Nathan needed watching. There were always other women circling, with their fuck-me eyes, smiling sugar at Nathan and daggers at her.

She knew he was upstairs, but could no longer hear him. There was no sound from the cellar. Tanya hoped they were sleeping. They would call out if they needed anything. That new woman, the one with the kid, had been hurt. Perhaps the cow had concussion. What if she was bleeding, inside her head? Nathan had whacked her pretty hard. What would happen if she died? If they were caught, they could be looking at manslaughter. Murder, perhaps. And they had heard their names.

She closed her eyes, took a deep breath. Outside the wind was rising, rushing through the leaves. But inside the house, all was still. Nathan was so sweet, sometimes – when they were alone. No-one else saw that; no-one else knew the real Nathan Turner. She listened for him.

Tanya put her ear to the cellar door. There was no sound from there, so she climbed the stairs, peeping around the doors into the empty rooms. The Kanes' master bedroom looked so beautiful. The carpet was knotted blue silk, the bed linen crisp and white. Tanya would love to sleep in a room like that. The bitch had taste. Dorian might look like a tramp, but her house was a palace.

Tanya walked to the mirror. Her skin was puffy, while her hair stood in spikes. It was stress. She had warned Nathan that this job was beyond him. He would never admit it was out of his league. Violence wasn't their thing. They didn't do guns – they were good at the small stuff. They had that down. Nathan lacked the skills for this kind of thing. 'He lacks people skills,' she said aloud, as if she were a manager, appraising a junior. She said it again, watching the way her mouth moved as she spoke. She imagined herself in that business suit as she teased her hair into shape. She turned side on, flattening her stomach with the palm of her hand. She pushed it in, let it out, watching the way the flesh moved. She turned away and trailed her fingers over the bed: the crisp sheets, the billowing duvet, the pillows as soft as clouds.

Tanya sat on the bed. This was where the Kanes lay their heads. This was the pillow where creepy Richard laid his scrawny neck. And here, next to him, the place where Dorian snuggled down. She was dippy, that bitch. *Mad as a hedge!* But at least she slept in the same bed every night and lived in her own house. She had everything that bitch. A huge house, beautiful clothes, a walk-in wardrobe with floor-length mirrors. Tanya could never stick it, living out here in the wilds, but this room was pretty. The bed was huge, the frame antique French walnut, the linen crisp and white and even. That delicious, soft, scented bed; it looked so sweet, so tempting.

But first, she had to find Nathan.

CHAPTER THIRTY NINE

The cellar was icy cold, the air dank, even on a warm summer evening. The stone walls sucked the heat from the air and dampness oozed through ancient mortar. Kitty felt her ankle being squeezed.

'Are you awake?'

Kitty pushed herself upright, leaning back against the wall. The cellar was in total darkness. 'How long have we been here?'

'I don't know,' said Dorian. 'Three hours? Five?'

'I hurt …' The flesh around Kitty's eye was tender. Her lip was swollen and she could taste blood. It was ironic that Kitty had come to the house to check on Dorian's safety. She shivered. 'I feel damaged. But it's too dark to see.'

'Wine needs total darkness. Ultra violet light destroys it, Richard says. That's why it's in coloured bottles. It's for the flavour.'

'But there's a light down here?'

'The switch is outside the door.' Dorian moved away and clambered up the stairs. 'Which is locked. It won't shift. Richard had a bolt and padlock fitted when we had builders here. He was worried they might help themselves.'

Kitty squeezed Molly. 'Are "they" still in the house?' Kitty whispered.

Molly lifted her head. 'I heard them moving around, mum. Talking. I don't like them!'

'Are you OK, petal?'

'I'm a bit cold.'

Kitty squeezed her again. She was furious with herself for putting her child in danger. But she pushed that from her mind. She could do nothing about the past but she could make the right choices now. If they got out of this, Molly would remember how she had behaved.

'I'm fine,' murmured Dorian. 'Thanks for asking.'

The house was still. The footsteps overhead had stopped. Kitty wondered if they had left. She reached for her phone, patting her pockets as she tried to recall when last she had seen it.

'He threw your phone away, mum.'

'When?'

'He heard it ringing and chucked it through the door,' said Dorian.

'You keep losing phones, mum,' said Molly.

She kissed the top of her daughter's head. Most of the kids in Molly's class had phones, but Kitty had resisted Molly's begging. *You were strong. Brilliant. Now you're stuck here without a phone.*

'Where's your phone, Dorian?'

'It's behind a jar in the kitchen. I hid it. But the battery's probably flat by now.'

'Where's your husband?'

'He's away. On business.'

'Where, exactly?'

'I don't know! Leeds? Liverpool. Back to Leeds, I think. Then home.'

'When's he due back? '

'Saturday. Late Saturday, he said.'

'Right. So we could be down here for another twenty four hours.'

'I guess...'

Dorian irritated her. There was something about the woman that bothered her. The thought of spending another day with her, in this dark, cold pit, was oppressive. Closing her eyes, Kitty willed herself elsewhere. Perhaps, if she was very quiet, very, very still, she might disappear. She and Molly would slip through a crack in the floor and be somewhere else, in another room, in another time.

'But that isn't going to happen, is it?' said the Voice.

Other than the man upstairs, no-one had ever landed a blow on Kitty. When it came to violence, she knew that she had been lucky. Most weekends she handled drunks – young men who called her a cunt and swore they would cut her face. She blunted their anger with icy calm. Reality was so skewed for them that, at that moment, they barely recognised her as human. Her mother had warned her of the dangers.

'You have to deflect the hatred, never reflect it. At the end of the day, Katherine, *you* go home to your *own* bed, in your *own* home. They won't.'

She prodded the skin on her face. Her lower lip was swollen, the flesh puffed like a wasp sting. Her cheek was bruised where her head had cracked into the tiles. With her fingertip she traced the cut that zigzagged her left temple, where the Makarov sight had raked her scalp.

'Dorian? Do you know the pair upstairs?'

'Of course I don't!'

'So you've never seen them before?'

'Of course not!'

'When did they get here?'

'A couple of hours before you arrived, I suppose. I don't know!'

'How did they get in?'

'She knocked at the door. Said her car had broken down. Like a fool, I fell for it!'

'Tell me what happened.'

'She asked to use the phone. I thought she was calling the AA. She was probably calling him. I gave her some coffee. She found out what I do, what I used to do, and she asked to see some of my stuff. So I went upstairs to get some sketches and when I came down, he was *there*! In the bloody hall!'

'Then what?'

'They wanted to eat. Well, he did. So I cooked a meal. I know it sounds odd but ... I would have done whatever they asked to be honest. I was terrified...'

'Did you hear their names?'

'She says her name's Ginny, but it's not! He calls her Tanya. He's called Nathan.'

Nathan and Tanya. The names were familiar. '*Nathan, he called himself ...*'. The pair who robbed Mary Hetherington. So was this a chance encounter? They had been in the area for at least ten days. Where had they been holed up? She wondered.

'Do they know about me?' said Kitty. 'What I do?'

'I just said you were a friend. I can't believe I let her in! I was so stupid!'

Kitty laid a hand on her arm. She felt guilty about Dorian. Though she stirred her protective instinct, she inspired no warmth. Dorian seemed such a lonely figure, separate from the rest of the world. If she could relive the last few days, there were many things Kitty would have done differently. But Dorian Kane had been in trouble and she had done the right thing in checking it out. She had trusted her instinct and it had been correct. She might be a lousy parent but maybe she wasn't such a disaster at her job.

With luck, Nathan and Tanya would take what they needed and go. But he might want to make certain that no-one would follow. She put herself in his place. If caught, he would be charged with aggravated burglary, assaulting a police officer and using a firearm. He would do time. She, Molly and Dorian were the only witnesses.

One day you will die.

'Dorian? If you get the chance, let's get your phone back. We need all the help we can get.'

* * *

Tanya gazed down at her man. For days Nathan had fended off sleep with another line of cocaine. Now he had crashed. He lay in the office chair, his long legs sprawled across the desk. Sleep softened his face, smoothing away the care lines. He looked so innocent when he was dreaming. His head tilted back, his mouth open, his lips curled in a smile. His eyelids parted, revealing a sliver of eyeball. He snored, each breath a gentle susurration, a wave breaking on a distant beach.

If only he could be like this all the time. She reached out to touch his shoulder then hesitated. It was always a bad idea to rouse Nathan. When he woke he would be in a filthy mood, his head sore from all the blow. He needed to wake gently, at his own pace. It was a prison thing.

Tanya found a blanket in a cupboard on the landing and laid it over the sleeping giant. His eyes flickered then closed. She stood over him until his breathing was even then crept along the landing to the master bedroom. Pulling off her shoes, she laid them beside the bed. She pulled the duvet back and crawled beneath it.

The house was quiet. She listened to the sound of the wind through the trees. Her eyeballs felt as if they had been scratched with sandpaper. She turned off the bedside lamp. She would not sleep – she would close her eyes, just for a moment. Well, perhaps just a catnap. If Nathan awoke, she would know. Tanya yawned, lowered her head and inhaled the scent of clean, white sheets.

* * *

Richard plunged into the water, kicking towards the depths, pushing himself down until his feet grazed the bottom of the pool. In the warmth of the evening the water was icy. He kicked again, broke the surface and paused, listening. The only sound he heard was lapping water. His phone lay on a towel at the edge of the pool.

They had agreed that Richard would not make contact while they were in the house. The police had software that could pinpoint the place and time of a call from a mobile. If he called home, that would show up in the records. So Richard swam his lengths, waiting for Nathan to ring.

The plan was that they would leave by six in the evening. When they were safely on the road they would make contact. Now it was three minutes to seven. The job should be finished.

CHAPTER THIRTY NINE

Each time Richard swam by the towel he stared at his phone, willing it to ring.

Another three lengths and I can check.

He reached for the phone, checked the battery and signal – both were fine. He began to swim. As he cut through the water he pushed aside his feeling of guilt: no-one would come to harm. After thirty lengths he rolled onto his back and watched light ripple across the ceiling.

No-one will get caught.

* * *

There was no escape from the old goat. An hour later, Richard and George Cunliffe sat facing each other in the hotel dining room. Cunliffe devoured the daub of beef, a drop of gravy running down his chin. Richard pushed his halibut around, eating only an occasional morsel. His appetite had gone. Though the meal was a test of endurance, at least it would confirm his alibi. As he listened to another of Cunliffe's stories, he imagined George being questioned by the police.

'*How did Richard Kane seem to you that evening Mister Cunliffe?*'

'*Fine*,' said the fantasy George Cunliffe. '*We enjoyed a very pleasant evening. He loves listening to my yarns …*'

Richard placed his phone on the table, beside his cutlery. Every few minutes he turned it over to check that he had not missed a call. It was impossible to forget what was happening at home. As he watched Cunliffe's lips flapping, he wondered if something had gone wrong. Perhaps there had been a struggle and it had got out of hand.

Cunliffe was wittering about some deal in Abu Dhabi.

Richard glanced at his watch. They must be done by now? 'I'll call when I'm clear, Mister K,' Nathan had said. 'Just keep your phone switched on.' Richard realised that Cunliffe had fallen silent. He looked up. Cunliffe was dabbing his chin with a napkin.

'Think I'll try the poached pears. What you having?'

Richard ordered a black coffee. Outside the hotel it was getting dark. The cars on Paradise Street were showing lights now, the city filling with kids as the weekend began.

They had to be clear by now!

'What's up, son?' Cunliffe waggled his spoon. 'Lost your appetite?'

'It's been a long day, George. I'm for an early night.'

Cunliffe looked piqued but guessed Richard would not be swayed. 'At least we're sorted now, eh? We've earned our corn today!' Cunliffe sat back. Richard smiled at the old man.

I'd love to kill you.

'The future,' said Cunliffe, raising his glass.

Back in his room, Richard paced the floor then lay on the bed, flicking through the television channels. Every ten seconds he looked at his watch. The air conditioning had dried his sinus, giving him a headache. In the alley beneath his open window he heard the cooks, their shift finished, smoking and cackling at each other's jokes. The hiss and rumble of city traffic filled the air. Richard placed his mobile on the pillow, by his head. Around two in the morning he fell asleep, his shirt stuck to his skin.

CHAPTER FORTY

As he drove home, Bryson replayed his encounter with Campbell over and over again. At first he was exhilarated. Yet each time he thought about it, he came out feeling more foolish. By the time he reached home the doubt was eating into him. When he told Maureen what had happened, she said nothing.

He woke at four, his heart rattling. For a while he listened to his stomach gurgle then rolled his tongue around his teeth, taking an inventory. Something was going on with that molar, upstairs left. He rooted with the tip of his tongue, searching for a cavity. Bryson heaved himself out of bed and stumped along the landing to piss. He had been dreaming of Campbell. He sat on the side of the bath with his head in his hands, groaning at his own stupidity. The story would run around the station. He would not seem like the hero, facing down the bully; he would come across as just a little bit mad.

'He's finally cracking up,' they would laugh. 'Poor old Bison.'

He went down to the sitting room and turned on the television. He kept thinking about what he'd done. Campbell couldn't harm Bryson's promotion chances – not directly. He might make a complaint, but the 'Silver Fox' liked to pretend he got on well with everyone. But there would be talk.

Bryson crept upstairs and toppled into bed. Maureen snuffled, turned over and was still again. He watched the morning light creep around the edge of the curtains. His court appearance was less than six hours away. It was the biggest case of his career. He wondered how Clive Lumley was sleeping, in his prison bunk.

Bryson ran over what might happen in court. However hard he tried to think about the rest of the evidence, his mind drew him back to one moment in the months it took to build the case. He was back in Lumley's bedroom, teasing that bag of coke from the strings of the piano. He saw Lumley's look of shock turn to derision. He saw Kitty staring, wide eyed at the bag of cocaine. He heard her whisper, 'That was lucky!' as they walked down Lumley's stairs at Kyloe House. He groaned, shaking his head. Had he done all of that to impress her? Or was it because he needed to win? He had spent a year of his life on that case and he needed a result. He was tired of being the butt of jokes. Clive Lumley was a villain. Had it been so wrong to load the dice? Bryson closed his eyes as he tried to push guilt from his mind. It was vital he was sharp on the witness stand. He needed sleep. He allowed his mind to drift, to float at will.

She was swimming towards him. She stood up in the surf, the waves breaking over her skin, droplets glistening in the sunlight. He cradled her head in his hands, pulled her close. The moment before their lips met she dangled a small plastic bag in his face. 'That was lucky,' whispered Kitty.

Bryson groaned again then dived beneath the duvet.

CHAPTER FORTY

* * *

Nathan thrashed his body like a drowning man. The blanket was tangled around his neck and he jerked upright, coughing as he fought to free himself. In panic he kicked away the swivel chair, crashing it against the wall. He fell across the desk, gasping for air. He sat up and flailed around, searching for his inhaler. The Ventolin he puffed into his lungs eased his breathing and calmed him. *Only a dream*, he told himself. *Only a dream ...*

The tightness in his chest eased. It took a moment to realise that he was at the farm, not in his pad at Strangeways. *Only a dream ...*

He tucked the inhaler into his waistcoat and patted his jacket, feeling the pistol through the fabric. He righted the chair and looked across the moorland. His heart slowed, ticking down. The sun had risen over the ridge at the top of the valley.

'Tanya?' he shouted. 'TANYA!'

She lay in the next room, wrapped in white linen. She jerked awake and hurried into the office, rubbing her eyes, smearing her make up. 'What time is it?'

Nathan pulled the fob watch from his waistcoat pocket. 'Nearly seven.' He scratched sleep dust from the corners of his eyes.

'Got to go,' said Tanya. 'We *have* to go.'

In the bathroom Nathan splashed water on his face. He looked at his reflection, watching the drops roll down his cheeks. In his dream the walls of the cell had been sliding closer. The ceiling had been creeping down towards the floor. It was his usual prison nightmare.

Only a dream...

He was alive and free. That was worth a smile. Using one of Richard's razors he shaved, taking his time. In the bedroom he riffled through Richard's clothes and selected a shirt in dark blue silk. It was soft, like another skin. He admired himself in the floor-length mirror, shooting the cuffs and smoothing the collar. On him, it was tighter than on that skanky beanpole, but it felt sweet.

Tanya ran round, tight lipped, her face drawn. Nathan stretched out on the bed, watching her rush her make up. 'It's cool, Tan. If the feds knew we were here, it would have happened already.'

'We need to go, Nathe.'

'Want to join me?' He patted the bed.

She paused, lipstick in hand. She looked at his reflection. He lay on the bed, one hand behind his head. 'Really, Nathan. We *need* to go...'

'We finish up.' He spoke softly. 'We'll go in our own time.'

'What about them?'

He looked at the ceiling. Sex was off the menu. Next ... 'Tell them to make us some breakfast.'

'Nathan! We can eat later, for heaven's sake!'

It was a matter of pride to appear calm at all times. 'Tanya. Tell them – to make me – some breakfast.'

She hurried down the stairs.

* * *

The clatter of the bolt woke Kitty. The sudden light was dazzling. Kitty pulled Molly to her feet. Dorian shielded her eyes with her hand.

'You have two minutes to use the bathroom. Then make toast and coffee. We're leaving in twenty minutes. Move!'

'All of us?' said Dorian.

'NOW!' screamed Tanya, as they scuttled towards the bathroom.

* * *

Nathan cruised the Kanes' bedroom, searching for treasure. He stuffed Richard's shirts into an overnight bag. He picked up a dress watch and a pair of silver cufflinks, slipping them into his waistcoat pocket. He emptied the drawers, starting at the bottom, tossing the contents across the bed. As a kid he broke into houses just for this – the buzz. It was exciting to "do a creep", wandering through darkened rooms while the owners lay asleep. He felt that old, familiar rush as he rifled cabinets and drawers.

He padded along the landing to the office. Standing at the window, he gazed across the moors as he punched Kane's number. Clouds scudded towards the house, their shadows rippling across the hillside.

'Good morning to you, Mister K!'

'Where the *hell* have you been?'

Nathan realised he had woken Kane, who sounded furious.

'It's all good. The van's packed. The ladies are cooking breakfast. Then we're gone!'

'Breakfast? You're still in the house?'

'There was a blip, OK? We're cool now. One thing ... you know the key to the cabinet?'

'Key?' Kane's yell was a crackle. 'What fucking key?'

'We discussed this,' Nathan sighed. 'When last we met?'

'Which key?'

'It's not where you said it would be.'

'It's taped beneath the top right hand drawer on the desk.'

'Beneath? You said 'inside', Mr K ...'

'Never mind what I said! Forget the guns. Forget your fucking breakfast! Just get OUT of there – NOW!'

In reply, Nathan whistled. It was a slow release of air, indicating his disappointment, his shock at Richard's lack of decorum. 'Don't upset me, you long streak of piss. That would be a big mistake. Show some respect.'

Nathan slid open the drawer and tipped the contents onto the floor. He turned the drawer over. 'She's here!' he said. 'Here she is.' He peeled off the tape and slipped the key into his waistcoat.

'How is ...?'

'Your wife? Or our guests?'

For a moment, Nathan heard only the crackle of the static.

'Guests? What guests?'

Nathan rolled the square of gaffer tape into a tight ball and flicked it across the room.

'Her friend. And the kid.'

He picked up the key to the gun cabinet and turned it in his fingers.

'I don't know what you mean.'

'Your wife's fine, Mr K. She's a little shaken, but sweet. But I was obliged to give the other lady a little tap.'

'What "other lady"?' Kane's voice sounded tight.

Nathan tapped the key on the desk, pushed it between closed fingers, turned it, pushed it again. His words were paced like steps in a slow march. 'How – the hell – would I – know?'

CHAPTER FORTY

He had never liked Kane, now he was getting seriously vexed.

'She's some friend of your wife. Cute face. Brown hair – short, tied back. Reddy brown, I'd say.'

'How old?'

'Thirty, maybe,' said Nathan. 'Bit scrawny. Nice arse! She has a kid with her.'

Nathan sensed that he was delivering bad news. He peered at his nails. He held the gun cabinet key and turned it in the sunlight. He picked fluff from the cuff of his new silk shirt. The only sound was Richard Kane's breathing, whistling like the wind across the chimney.

'You got a touch of asthma there, Mister K?' There was no reply. 'I'm a sufferer myself. We should have a chat sometime. Dust is your trigger. There was plenty of dust here yesterday!'

'I don't care about your asthma. Shut up. Let me think.'

'Everything is sweet here! The ladies are downstairs; they're quiet. It's all good.'

'She's police.'

Nathan felt cold fingers around his throat.

'She's a cop,' he heard Kane say. 'She came to ...' Richard sighed. 'It doesn't matter why she came. She's a policewoman. But you "gave her a little tap," you fucking moron!' Kane sounded resigned now, rather than angry.

Nathan's lips formed a perfect O. '... that's interesting news, 'Mister K.' Nathan's mouth was dry. He scraped the gun cabinet key along the edge of the desk, back and forth. 'A cop?' He laughed. 'No shit?' Sweat pricked his forehead. Fear was useful. It made enemies more pliable, friends more respectful. Sometimes Nathan allowed himself to be hurt, to taste fear. Just to motivate himself. But showing it was a different matter.

'A cop ...'

Nathan had spent his childhood in a string of homes. He was in a Young Offenders' Institution at seventeen. After that he'd run with a gang for three years before a two stretch in Strangeways. Then Durham for four. He swore that Durham would be the last time.

Tapping a cop was a four stretch by itself, but with his record it might be seven to ten. Or Her Majesty's Pleasure? And the cop had seen his face. She had heard his name. He would go down for a long time. He would rather die. 'That's a pity, Mister K...'

'A pity? It's more than that ...'

'I should sort this out.' Dorian Kane was flaky. If this ever came to court she would be an unreliable witness. She would never remember enough detail to have them caught in the first place. And if she did, Kane would see that it came to nothing – he had promised that at the start. But this other woman was different. She would remember everything. She was a threat, especially after the way he had treated her.

'D – do nothing. D'you hear me? Don't do a thing! Nathan? What are you going to do?'

'Right now?'

Nathan watched the clouds rushing towards the house. If the feds took him, this would be the last day he would feel the sun on his back. Though he dreaded prison, life inside fitted him like an old coat. He understood the code, the rituals: the protocol. There was a structure to prison life that was lacking on the out. But he would be an old man, in his eyes, when he saw the outside world again. He would sooner die.

Outside the window, open moorland stretched to the horizon, but Nathan felt the walls of his cell closing in on him.

CHAPTER FORTY

They were getting closer. He could almost touch them. In Durham, the walls were covered with yellow gloss so the screws could hose them down. Wash away the blood and the piss and the shit. He saw the grille at the window, the bars framing the same piece of sky day after day, year after year. The stink of prison: the bad food, the showers, shit parcels tossed from barred windows. The stench of men steeped in their own madness. But fear should be used – never revealed.

'Right now, Mister K? I am going downstairs to enjoy some breakfast!'

Nathan broke the connection. The wind whipped clouds over the ridge on the far side of the valley. He pulled out the Makarov, checked the magazine was full then tucked the gun into his belt. He slipped the key to the gun cupboard into his waistcoat pocket and walked towards the stairs.

* * *

In his room at the Adelphi Hotel, Richard sat on the bed. From the alley below came the clatter of breakfast dishes. The description Nathan had given could fit a million women, but Richard saw only one. He knew it was that meddling Lockwood bitch. Fear welled up, choking him, swelling in his throat. The moment he met that woman he knew she was trouble. He lay back, staring at the ceiling.

CHAPTER FORTY ONE

Kitty blocked out the kitchen clatter and the scent of the food. She hugged Molly, kissing her brow. A kiss of guilt – she had to think of a way to get them out of this. Under Tanya's watchful gaze, Dorian bustled around, toasting bread and pulling cups and plates from the dishwasher.

'What would everyone like?'

'To go home,' whispered Molly.

Kitty ruffled Molly's hair. Nathan appeared in the kitchen. He looked around the room, avoiding Kitty's eyes. She sensed danger. Looking at Dorian, he waved his hand over Kitty's head.

'Don't worry about these two.' Nathan opened the back door with a tilt of his head to indicate that Kitty and Molly should leave. He stood by the open door, drumming his fingers on the frame. Kitty knew what was coming. She knew Molly would be listening.

'See you later, Dorian. Don't worry! I'm sure he's just taking us home.'

As she walked to the door she realised she was shaking and feared her legs might buckle. At the last moment she wrapped

CHAPTER FORTY ONE

her arms around Dorian.

'Call me!' she said, loud enough for all to hear. 'When this is all over.'

She kissed Dorian, pulling her into a tight embrace. In the tangle of arms and hair she put her lips to Dorian's ear and hissed 'Do it *now*!'

As they separated their eyes met for an instant. Then Kitty took Molly's hand and walked out. Nathan slammed the door as they left.

They filed across the yard, climbing the stone steps into the garden behind the house. The tiny spears of grass glistened with dew. As they trooped across the lawn Kitty rested her hand on Molly's shoulder, ready to pull her close. Nathan avoided her eyes.

'Where are you taking us?'

Sliding the Makarov from his jacket pocket, Nathan pointed towards the plantation, a wall of firs that stretched along the brow of the hill. 'Just a walk in the woods.'

'A walk before breakfast,' said Kitty, squeezing Molly's shoulder. She tried to keep her eyes on Nathan's face. She had no intention of making this easy for him. He looked away as he steered them towards the edge of the pasture. Kitty helped Molly over the fence that marked the edge of the garden. They climbed the hill, stumbling over tussocks of reeds that studded the hillside. The horses followed, shadowing their little group, walking to the side, as if sensing the fear.

Kitty saw Nathan glance at the horses, then look away. It seemed the animals made him edgy. She heard him wheeze and saw him rubbing his eyes. He pulled out his inhaler and puffed it. From the corner of her eye she saw him shifting the gun in his hand. She guessed that if the animals came any closer he might fire at them.

Kitty tripped over a tangle of ragwort and fell. Nathan took her wrist and pulled her up. Then he jabbed the gun into her back, pushing her towards the trees. They reached the stone wall that surrounded the plantation.

'Why not Dorian too?' she said as she watched him climb the stile.

He ignored her. They moved into the wood. Sunshine gave way to a cool, grey gloom. Above their heads a mesh of branches and needles blocked out the sun. With every step the light faded, the wood growing more silent. There was no birdsong in here. The only sound was the breeze singing through the tops of the trees. The mat of fallen needles deadened their footsteps. The scent of leaf mould hung in the still air. The earth was barren, as dead as the ocean floor.

'Dorian heard your name,' she said. He was silent. It was like a dream in which Kitty walked along the sea bed, following her daughter into the darkness. As she touched Molly's shoulder, Kitty could feel the slender bones moving beneath her daughter's skin.

* * *

Dorian fussed around the kitchen, wiping surfaces, tucking chairs beneath the table. Something bad was happening – she could sense it. She glanced at Tanya, who was standing by the window, looking up the hill, towards the plantation.

'Where's he taken them?'

Tanya said nothing.

As Dorian dabbed the marble top she glimpsed her mobile through the curve of the glass jars. She looked over her

CHAPTER FORTY ONE

shoulder. Tanya was staring through the window, clicking her thumbnail against her teeth.

With her left hand, Dorian scrubbed the surface, pushing invisible crumbs around the tiles. She watched Tanya's reflection in the surface of the toaster. She had not moved from the window. Dorian's hand darted towards the phone. The battery was dead, she was sure, but there was a click and the phone came to life. Dorian screwed her eyes tight. When she opened them Tanya had not moved. She was looking down, running her fingertip along her arm.

Her heart in her throat, Dorian touched 'Favourites.' She pressed 2. The screen read 'Kitty Lockwood: calling mobile.' She had done as Kitty had asked, yet there seemed little point. She knew Kitty's phone lay in the paddock, where it had landed.

* * *

They were forced to bend low, ducking beneath spiked branches which tore their clothes and scratched their skin. Nathan was soon out of breath, panting as he blundered through the tangle. Too broad-shouldered to walk upright between the pines, he stooped, crouching as he squeezed through the mesh of dead wood.

Kitty glanced back at him. He was caught on a branch which had spiked the lapel of his coat. Nathan freed himself, dusting the splinters from the cloth. Maddened, he thrashed at the branches with his free hand.

This was her moment. The maze of pine trunks extended in every direction. Kitty gauged the angles, seeking a route into darkness and safety. To the left she glimpsed a path, running along a narrow ridge. If they were held up for a moment

Nathan would have time to aim and shoot. She squeezed her daughter's shoulder, leaning forward to whisper her plan. Molly half turned, her eyes wide.

'Stop!' shouted Nathan. 'Just wait there.'

In that moment the choices spun through Kitty's mind. Run and risk being shot – or wait and be killed. Kitty hesitated and the moment passed. Nathan caught up with them, wiping his brow with his gun hand. He pointed the gun towards the centre of the wood.

'Stay close. No wandering ahead.'

* * *

Bryson spat on his shoe and rubbed the leather until it gleamed. Then he stumped along to the bedroom to choose a tie. Maureen rolled over, opened her eyes and stared at the ceiling. Bryson chose the green one she had bought for his birthday. His face turned pink as he struggled with the knot. Squeezing into his grey tweed jacket, he looked in the mirror then flicked dandruff from the shoulders. He dabbed cologne on his newly-shaven cheeks. He raked his fingertips through his moustache then patted pockets for keys, wallet and pen. He reached into his trouser pocket and jingled the column of £2 coins he always carried.

He unpacked his attaché case, making sure he had all of the papers: Lumley's statement, witness statements and his own notebooks. The case file was an inch thick. He should have time to skim read it before the case was called.

In the kitchen, Maureen was cooking breakfast for the boys. They squabbled over some game they were playing on their mobile phones. The atmosphere was cool. Maureen could signal her wrath merely by the way she opened a cupboard or rattled the frying pan.

'Do you want anything?' she said.

'Eaten already,' he said, patting his stomach. 'OK. Well. That's me, then. All set!'

She nodded as he pecked her on the cheek.

'Back by seven. A bit later, if all goes well!' He winked at the boys, who stared straight ahead, as if he were invisible.

It was the biggest day of Bryson Prudhoe's career. He turned the key in the Galaxy and set off for the city. The traffic was light and he went into autopilot, letting his mind drift. Lumley would go down for five to seven, he predicted. Supply of Class A; second conviction. He had declared his innocence and given them nothing, which would not help his chances.

Whatever the result, the trial was a huge event for both men. It marked the end of one stage of Bryson's life. Eleven months of graft; two hundred days spent tickling up informers as he grubbed around, searching for a way into the network. There was a mountain of intel, most of which was circumstantial. Thirty-seven nights of surveillance; twelve hundred hours of meetings and report writing – today would see the end of all that, whatever the result. Bryson was nervous – excited too. But as he drove towards the town, Bryson felt his sense of foreboding growing. He alone knew the little flaw, the rotten prop that might bring the roof crashing around his ears. He knew, because he had put it there.

Bryson checked his mirror, temperature and fuel gauge. He stayed inside the speed limit. He flicked the radio on, then off. He stretched his neck, rolling his head, pushing out his chin.

Think it through. Just follow the logic. Bryson knew that he would spend most of the day waiting to be called. When he took the stand, he would try to remain calm. Take his time, pause then compose himself before each answer. He would stick to the story.

Stick to the facts.

It would be an ordeal, of that he was certain. Lumley's money bought the best legal advice. The lawyers would pick away at the case until they found a flaw then tear it apart. In the past, Bryson had let his anger get the better of him in court. He would not let it happen this time. There was a slim chance that Lumley might crack and plead guilty, hoping for shorter time. It was unlikely. But Bryson found some comfort as he thought about the day ahead. And, at the very least, he would see Kitty.

Some connections are more than friendships, though less than love affairs. That was the attachment between Bryson and Kitty. He cared about her, but he expected nothing in return. He knew that it would never "go anywhere". He was too old and too fat, and in any case, he loved Maureen and the lads. Yet the link with Kitty meant so much.

He remembered her, as they left Clive Lumley's bedroom that morning, the plastic bag of cocaine in the palm of her hand. He recalled the look on her face, the way she glanced up at him. He saw her lips form the words.

'That was lucky!'

* * *

They walked until they reached a clearing, a circle twenty yards wide, deep inside the plantation. 'Stop,' said Nathan. 'This is the place.'

A column of sunlight shone through the gap in the canopy.

CHAPTER FORTY ONE

They stood ankle-deep in leaf litter, the ground a bed of tawny pink needles. All three were out of breath. If they ran now, Kitty knew they would not reach the edge before he shot them. She put her hand on Molly's shoulder. Nathan pointed towards the centre of the circle.

'There,' he said. 'Stand there.'

He waved the gun, shooing them into position. Then he stretched his neck and yawned. 'This will do,' he murmured.

'What's happening?' asked Molly. Kitty squeezed her shoulder. Nathan started to pace around the clearing, walking along the edge, trailing his fingers over each tree he passed. As he walked he started to slap his free hand against the bark. She guessed he needed to hurt himself, to cut his flesh, to feel pain so that he could work up the rage to do it. The Makarov dangled from the index finger of his other hand. Kitty turned with him as he moved around the circle, her eyes locked on his.

'You don't have to do this, Nathan.'

He glanced at her then looked away. 'I do. I have to do this.'

Molly looked up. 'What's he *doing*?' she whispered.

Nathan was talking to himself, muttering under his breath as he psyched himself to point the gun and pull the trigger.

'Nathan? If anything happens to us, you know they'll come after you.' Her grip on Molly's shoulder was tight. *If I break down now, that will be her last memory. Fear.* 'Nathan. If you touch us, they'll find you. They won't stop.'

He circled her, tearing the green tips from the branches, twisting them and hurling them away. She watched his lips move. She guessed he would walk until he had steeled himself. When he stopped, he would turn and shoot. 'They'll come after you, Nathan. If you hurt me they'll never give up. They'll come for you and they'll come for Tanya. You know that! *Think* about it. Think about what they'll do to her.'

Kitty pushed her fingers through Molly's hair. She listened to his footsteps brush through the dead needles, waiting for the rhythm to change. He kicked the pine litter with the toe of his shoe, spraying waves of it in the air. Beneath the pink crust the needles were darkened and rotten. Kitty kissed the top of Molly's head.

This, the last thing you will see.

The *shoosh shoosh* of his footsteps slowed. He was going to kill them. That knowledge set her free. Now she could say anything, try anything.

'Whatever you're getting for this, I'll give you more.'

He snorted, shaking his head. Nathan stopped. 'You think I'm doing this for *money*?'

'I don't know why you're doing it, Nathan. I have no idea why anyone would do something as cruel as this.'

'You know my name.' He waved the gun at her.

'*Dorian* heard your name! Why take us but leave Dorian?'

'Want me to fetch her? Do you?'

'Of course not ...' At that moment the links fell into place, like tumblers in a lock.

'Dorian's different.' He was pacing again, his eyes fixed on the ground beneath his feet. 'She's different. Isn't she, Nathan?' Her voice had an edge now. 'You've mustn't hurt her! Isn't that right, Nathan? You've been told not to hurt her? '

Nathan laughed, shaking his head.

'Obeying the Boss, aren't you? Just doing what you're told!'

He shook his head again, but it was too late. She had seen through him. He should have finished this sooner, when he

CHAPTER FORTY ONE

had his foot on her neck. 'Richard Kane hired you to do this. To steal his own stuff. Isn't that the truth, Nathan? You're just his "Joey"...'

Nathan looked into the trees. His smile had gone. He couldn't meet her gaze. But her pleasure in solving the mystery was short-lived. Now that she knew the truth, Nathan had no choice but to kill them both.

CHAPTER FORTY TWO

Bryson licked his lips, tasting the tang of salt. He walked along the riverside, hunched against the breeze that blew from the sea. Above him the slender span of the Redheugh Bridge, framing the High Level: a skeleton of dun-coloured iron. Further down the river the eyelid of the Millennium Bridge winked open to allow a pleasure boat to sail upstream.

Bryson thrust his hands into his pockets and strode along the riverside walk, chinking his stack of £2 coins. The heft of them soothed him, the comfort others might find in a rosary or prayer beads. He looked troubled as he struggled with the premonition that today would not go well. He called Kitty's phone. As he waited for a connection, he watched a plastic carton, yellowed with turmeric, bob along the surface of the river. It floated towards the sea as he held the mobile to his ear. No answer.

Bryson was not blessed with empathy. He found the idea of precognition ridiculous and telepathy was "airy-fairy bollocks." Yet he knew Kitty Lockwood was not at the wheel of her car. He knew she was not stuck in traffic. He was certain she would never arrive for the trial. He flipped his collar against the breeze and trudged towards the Crown Court.

The front of the court house was a cliff of red granite. It was the full weight of the law, manifest in stone. The columns planted at each corner of the building seemed about to topple, to crush the puny figures who bustled through the doors, hoping for justice. Sunlight glinted on the glass-walled lifts that skittered up and down the outside of the building. Another day at the factory of justice. Barristers swooped from their chambers in Broad Chare, gowns flapping like dark wings. Film crews hovered on the pavement, trying to snatch pictures of the guilty and the grieving. As they saw Bryson walk towards the court they turned their cameras on him, just in case he had an important role in any of the day's trials. As Bryson walked through the entrance he glanced again at his watch.

She's not coming.

He flipped through the names on his phone and found her number. His thumb hovered over the call button. It was just a feeling. He was overwrought. Maureen always told him he was being neurotic. He would give it ten minutes. He closed his phone and got into the lift.

* * *

Kitty floated above the trees, looking down on the woman and her child below. She was familiar – the slender neck, the reddy-brown hair. A man circled the pair, the tails of his coat swirling as he walked. Now he moved closer, raising his arm, pointing at the woman. His tread quickened, feet swishing through leaves as he rushed towards her.

Nathan grabbed Molly, tearing her from Kitty's arms and

hurling her aside. Kitty watched Molly try to stand and saw her legs buckle. She screamed as Nathan pressed the muzzle of the gun to her daughter's head.

Kitty forced herself to look into Nathan's eyes. She held his gaze, her eyes locked on his. 'What do you want? I'll do anything you want. Just let her go.' Waves of fear swept over her, each higher than the last.

Nathan was perfectly still. He held Molly with one hand, the muzzle of the gun pressed against the child's head.

* * *

The doors closed as the woman slipped into the lift. Her ash blonde hair was immaculate; her tailored suit a perfect choice for her big day in court. It was a moment before Bryson recognised Greta Lumley. She moved beside him, her arm touching his.

'Can we talk?'

The lift rose.

'I'm listening.'

Greta leaned closer. 'It's about a man called Kane. I hear you're interested in him. Richard Kane.'

* * *

Kitty fell to her knees. She watched the scene from above – weightless, drifting above the treetops, looking down on the figures in the clearing. Three people: the man, the woman, the child. They were still.

Nathan's hand trembled. He loosened the grip on the gun,

stretching the muscle then curled his index finger around the trigger. 'Turn around.'

She breathed in, breathed out. The only sound was the air moving through the pine needles.

'When you fight, you're an eagle...' Master Rafaele, talking to her, his fingertips on her wrist. *'... an eagle, soaring into the sky, seeing everything below with clarity.'*

'Turn around,' said Nathan, an edge in his voice.

All is sharp. All is clear.

'Turn away.'

Hold his gaze.

'Close your eyes!'

Don't turn your back.

Her head was still, her eyes unblinking.

Never turn your back.

He passed his free hand across his face. His mouth was dry. His skin prickled, his eyes scratchy, scoured by sand. His finger slithered over the trigger, feeling the tension of the spring, the heft of the metal.

'Close your fucking eyes!'

She would not turn away from him. It was obstinacy as much as courage. This man was threatening her child. She could not allow that. *How will she remember me, if I break down now?* Kitty had nothing further to fear. She was as good as dead. The condemned are set free. She could do whatever she wanted.

'You don't want to do this Nathan. You know it's not right.'

She would never look away. Her eyes were open wide, fixed on his. She would never look away. When he pulled the trigger she would be looking into his eyes. He passed his hand across his brow. He raised the gun, pointing it at her face. She saw his hand was shaking as he squinted along the barrel.

Then he blinked, rubbed his eye and lowered the gun. He looked down. For a moment, all three were frozen. Then his grip loosened and Molly walked free. She stumbled across the clearing and fell into her mother's arms. Nathan tucked the gun into his belt and dusted his hands. He would not look at her. They stood in silence for a time.

'Who knows you're here?' he said.

For a moment Kitty was tempted to lie, to pretend that the cavalry were just over the hill.

'We live alone.' She found Molly's hand, squeezed it. 'But I expect someone will be looking.'

Nathan turned his face to the sky. The buzzard wheeled above the wood. His shoulders fell. 'This never happened.'

Kitty shrugged.

'None of it. OK? This never happened.'

She nodded. In return for her life she could give him that, at least.

They started back through the plantation. The breeze blew through the tree tops, sighing through the needles.

* * *

'Why are you telling me this?'

Greta smiled and tapped her nails on the table. 'Why do you think, Mr Prudhoe?'

Bryson watched her fingers. He found the click as they danced across the polished wood oddly arousing.

'I have an idea...'

'You've always been an intelligent man. It's a very attractive quality.'

Bryson laughed. He knew when he was being stroked.

CHAPTER FORTY TWO

'Is this your idea? Or hubby's?'

'It was suggested to me. By a friend.'

'Right.'

He guessed that Kevin Robb was involved. Bryson wondered if the Lumleys knew the whole truth about the information Kevin had given him. Perhaps the uncertainty had scared them. Kevin could count himself a lucky lad to be still living.

'How does your husband know Richard Kane?'

'I've really no idea, inspector. You'd have to ask him that.'

'Clive supplies him with drugs?'

Greta shook her head, as if disappointed in him.

'Come on Greta. Someone gives Kane a little bump for the weekend. If it's not Clive, I'd love to know who.'

She watched him, a smile on her lips.

'OK. So, Kane asked your husband if he knew anyone who might break into his house? This was an insurance job. In and out, *bish bash bosh*?'

'Clive, of course, wanted nothing to do with it.'

'No doubt he was appalled ...' said Bryson.

Greta's smile was steady. Bryson wondered where Clive had found her. He had punched above his weight. There was no doubt that Greta Lumley had class. At that moment Bryson realised he'd been looking in the wrong direction all the time. Rather than being the trophy wife, Greta Lumley was the brains behind the whole enterprise.

'In business you meet all kinds of people, Inspector. Clive didn't approve, but he felt he had no choice. He gave him the number of someone he vaguely knew. And that was that.'

'And now ...'

'Now, he realizes what he's done. He wants, *we* want, to do anything we can to help.'

'And, of course, to save his own neck. Do you have any idea when this all might be taking place?'

Greta tapped her nails on the surface of the table, click, click, click...

* * *

Nathan trudged down the hill. The witch had hexed him. Perhaps it was for the best. Killing the fed and her kid would have brought all kinds of grief on his head. He watched them walk ahead, the woman resting her hand on her daughter's shoulder. What was it with women? The way they talked to each other? The way they touched each other?

He thought about the moment he had given in. Something inside him had given way. His will. It was as if his steel had melted, tearing and dissolving like gauze. He was getting soft. He hadn't the stomach for it any more. The moment he looked into her eyes he knew she would never look away. She would watch him do it. If he pulled the trigger, he would never be able to wash that image from his eyes. He knew he would have seen Kitty's face until his dying day. He had hesitated and in that moment, he lost. But in a way, it felt good to let go.

Find Tan. Leave this hole and never come back.

Linking his fingers, Nathan pushed his hands away, stretching his arms, popping the joints. He would keep all the stuff, he decided. Kane could go screw himself. That way they'd have something to show for all of this.

* * *

The drinks machine gurgled, splattering hot brown liquid

over Bryson's fingers. He wiped them with his handkerchief, picked up his plastic cup and flopped onto the bench.

The witness waiting room was empty. Through the open window came the sound of traffic from the street below, yet all he heard were the words Greta had whispered. All he could see was that plastic bag in Kitty's fingers as they stood in Clive Lumley's bedroom. For the twentieth time he called Kitty's mobile.

Her recorded message told him to leave a message. He called her landline, letting it ring twenty times. He stared at the river for a moment then called Shaftoe Leazes. Orla Harrington answered.

'It's Bryson. I need a number.' Orla gave him the number of the middle school. The sun sparkled on the river. A weary voice answered.

'Wanless Lane Middle School?'

'Is Molly Lockwood in school this morning?'

'Are you her father?'

'No ...'

'Then I'm sorry, I can't give you that information. It's not school policy.'

'It's Detective Sergeant Bryson Prudhoe. I work with her mum, Kitty Lockwood.'

'I'm sorry. It's not policy.'

'You know Molly's mother is a police officer?'

'Hold the line ...'

Bryson heard a muffled conversation. He watched a thin man swill a bucket of water over the deck of a cruiser moored on the quay. The man tossed the bucket into the river, hauled fresh water then swabbed the deck. The muffled voices droned on. The line cleared.

'Molly isn't in school this morning.'

'Did her mother call in?'

More whispering. 'The absence was unreported.'

'That means 'no,' does it?'

'Yes.' The voice dripped poison. 'That means no.'

Bryson rang off. In his mind he replayed his conversation with Greta Lumley. Richard Kane had met Clive and asked for someone to burgle his house.

'He wanted someone who could help him out. Someone from outside the city ...' Bryson called directory inquiries, got the number of Kitty's friend, Jacqui Speed. He called Jacqui and explained who he was.

'Have you any idea where she is, Jacqui? She has a court appearance this morning.'

'You know what the traffic's like. If there's been an accident on the A69 ...'

'If she was late, she'd call. Her mobile's switched off.'

'There you are then!' Jacqui sounded relieved.

Bryson watched the man on the deck of the boat. Now the man leaned against the rail, lighting a cigarette, looking up the river.

'Do you want me to give her a knock?'

'Call me back, would you?'

* * *

They trooped into the house. Tanya touched Nathan's arm as he passed. He glanced at her and whispered. 'We're out of here.'

He walked into the hallway and leaned against the wall. Tanya followed, leaving the others in the kitchen.

CHAPTER FORTY TWO

'Hey! You're back!' Dorian clapped her hands. She raised an eyebrow at Kitty, who now sat at the table, her arms around Molly. Kitty shook her head.

'Tea?' said Dorian, to fill the silence. She put the kettle on the hob.

Kitty knew that Molly was shivering. Her face was pale, her eyes glazed.

She wrapped her arms around her daughter and pulled her close.

'Was he really going to hurt us?' said Molly. She buried her face in her mother's top.

Kitty looked around the kitchen as she tried to find the right thing to say.

'I don't know exactly, Mollusc.' She kissed her daughter's head. 'He was confused. Scared, I think.'

'Not as scared as I was!'

'No. It was a scary moment. But we survived. We got out of it. We're still here, OK?'

Molly nodded. The trembling stopped, but Kitty felt tears soaking through her top. She squeezed Molly tight.

'Listen, kiddo. We're going to get us out of this. Very soon we'll be home and you'll be wondering why you couldn't have been born to some sensible, intelligent woman who works in a shop. Or teaches mixed infants. This will pass. We'll soon be back home, squabbling over the telly. We'll be fighting like cats and dogs, I promise! But just now...just for now, I need you to be tough. Just for a little while. This is horrible but it will pass. We're going to get out of this.'

Kitty tilted Molly's head until she could look her daughter in the eye. She peeled a strand of hair from Molly's tear-stained face. She forced herself to smile, then pulled Molly close and kissed her before her own tears arrived.

Molly was still. Kitty had persuaded her this would end well. All she had to do now was convince herself.

Dorian rattled a box of biscuits in front of Molly. 'Thought we might not see you for a while,' she whispered to Kitty. 'It crossed my mind …'

Kitty mouthed the word 'Phone?'

Dorian nodded, glancing towards the doorway. Kitty moved her chair so that she could watch the couple in the hall. They were deep in whispered conversation.

'So what do we do?' She heard Tanya say. Nathan was staring at the floor. Tanya coaxed him, running her fingertips down his arm. When he did not meet her eyes, she glanced towards the kitchen. She saw she was being watched and was back in the room before Kitty could warn Dorian. Caught with her phone in one hand and the mug of tea in the other, Dorian spun around. The phone slipped from her grasp, clattering onto the floor in front of Tanya. Dorian looked up, wide-eyed with terror.

Tanya picked up the phone, turning it between her fingers. She glanced at the door, as if about to call out to Nathan, then looked at Kitty, meeting her eyes. Tanya slipped the phone into her pocket.

'Go downstairs. Now.'

Kitty rubbed Molly's shoulder as they entered the cellar. She was halfway down the stairs when she heard Nathan speak. She turned to listen. Tanya was framed in the doorway. Nathan touched her face.

'Keep them together. OK?' he said, as he kissed her. He reached for his phone.

'We'll soon be gone.'

CHAPTER FORTY THREE

At that moment Richard was walking through the hotel's underground car park. He had checked out of the Adelphi, leaving a message for George Cunliffe to say he'd been called away. '*Home*' flashed up on his caller ID. Richard was expecting to hear Dorian's voice.

'Are you alright?'

'Sweet, Mr K. It's all good, ' said Nathan.

'You're calling from the house? Are you completely stupid?'

Richard bleeped the Porsche and tossed his case in the boot.

'The price just went up, Mr K.'

'Look. It is what it is. The price is fixed.'

'Things change Mister K. We've been put to a lot of trouble by your guests. I've been thinking about things since your call. So I'm "retaining" certain items. In lieu of payment.'

'Listen ...'

'It's not personal. It's business. End of.'

'Listen you fucker! Just do it as we agreed. I'm on my way back NOW.'

Nathan sighed. This was not turning out to be a good day. 'You think you're the business, Mister K. Think you're *dee - luxe*, don't you? You're SCUM! Like the rest of us!'

Richard powered the car up the slope and onto the street. It would take over an hour to get home. Nathan might cause a lot of damage in that time. He had to regain control. 'Nathan, Nathan... Listen. We can work this out!'

'Don't grovel, Mister K. Have some fucking self-respect! If I want to talk to you, I'll call. Until then – go fuck yourself.'

Richard Kane hit the motorway at eighty five, cutting through the morning traffic like a blade. At least two people inside the house knew the whole sordid story. That was a problem he needed to solve.

* * *

John Stafford QC, the prosecuting counsel in the Lumley case, strutted like a bantam cock down the corridor outside court number two.

'Can I have a word, Mr Stafford?' said Bryson.

'Can this wait, Mr Prudhoe?' Stafford sighed. 'Perhaps you could speak to my clerk? Unless it's urgent...'

Bryson laid his hand on the barrister's chest. Stafford froze. He looked down at Bryson's hand, appalled, as if it was a dead bird that had landed there.

'I wouldn't ask if it wasn't,' said Bryson.

Stafford glared at the policeman then nodded; one brief dip of the head. As he led Bryson down the corridor Stafford's voice dropped to a whisper.

'Then let's make this a little more private, shall we?'

He crooked his finger and beckoned Bryson along the corridor. Stafford found an empty conference room and perched on the corner of the table.

'Make it quick, would you? We have a busy day.'

CHAPTER FORTY THREE

'Kitty Lockwood. She's missing.'

'Missing? But she *is* en route, is she not?'

'There's no answer on her mobile.' Bryson's cheeks wobbled as he shook his head. 'Nor at her house.'

'So you have no idea where she is?' Stafford peeled off his wig and dropped it on the table. 'This is not good, DS Prudhoe.' He passed his hand across his scalp. The skin was shaved and it gleamed in the dim light. 'You're not making me happy. Say something to cheer me up. Please.'

'Kitty Lockwood would never let me down.'

'Self evidently, she *has* let you down!' Stafford shook his head in disbelief.

'She knows what this case means. If she's not here, there has to be a good reason.'

'And what do you suppose I can do about it?'

'Perhaps you could delay things while I find her?' said Bryson.

'*Delay* things?' Stafford flapped his gown. 'I'm not cooking a bloody chicken! How long will it take you to find out where she's hiding?'

Bryson guessed it would take him forty minutes to reach Kitty's home in Cloud Street. That would be the first place to check. After talking to Greta he had a good idea where to go next, if that proved fruitless. 'An hour and a half?'

Stafford spent his working life sifting the true from the false. Bryson could tell Stafford knew he was being lied to. But there was little Stafford could do. He glanced at his watch, shaking his head. 'We have to select the jury. Swear them in. Opening remarks. It may go smoothly, but the Law of Sod operates. You stay here. Send someone else to find her. If she's ill, or there's a problem, let me know and I'll ask for an adjournment.'

It was clear there was to be no further discussion. Stafford walked to the mirror that hung by the door. He looked at his reflection and seemed pleased with what he saw. He donned his wig and straightened his collar. 'You've put a lot into this case, Mr Prudhoe. We all have. Let's not piss it all away at this late stage, eh?'

He turned, clapped Bryson on the shoulder and swept from the room.

* * *

Kitty watched Tanya file, buff and polish each nail before holding it up for inspection. She wondered how much time Tanya spent on her appearance. That level of perfection was not achieved without putting in hours of work.

Tanya's face was a mask, her armour against the world. She sat on the cellar stair, the tools in her nail kit arrayed at her side. Kitty saw that Molly was watching her from beneath her fringe. Aware that she had gathered an audience, Tanya looked up.

'Come here,' she ordered Dorian. 'Sit.' Dorian shuffled to the lower step. 'Show me.'

Dorian held up her hands. Tanya took them and spread the fingers, which peeped out from the frayed cuffs of her jumper. Beside Tanya's hands they seemed rough and neglected. .

Tanya curled the fingers around her own, turning them to inspect the torn and chipped nails. Dorian flinched so Tanya tightened her grip, holding them up to the glare of the strip light.

'I spend a lot of time with the horses. You know?' said Dorian. 'Mucking out the stables.'

'Try using a shovel,' said Tanya. 'These are a disgrace.'

Dorian laughed and surrendered, allowing Tanya to work. She filed Dorian's nails into shape, pushing back the cuticles, working them into smooth ovals. For a few minutes they had a chance to forget their fear.

Kitty studied Tanya's face as she worked. Her skin was bronzed, the corners of her eyes etched with faint lines. The flaws in the mask were touching – a hint of vulnerability. But Tanya's mouth was determined, her lips set in a tight line. A strand of tawny hair fell across her eyes and she tucked it behind her ear as she bent to her work. She gently blew away the flakes, a frown creasing her forehead as she peered at the result.

Kitty edged closer, leaning against the wall, resting her hand on Molly's shoulder. She wondered how Tanya had ended up with such a clown, a cartoon gangster like Nathan Turner. 'You're good! Where did you learn to do that?'

'College,' said Tanya, without raising her head.

'Really?'

Tanya paused, lifting her face to look directly at Kitty.

'Yes, Mrs Policewoman. Really.'

She bent her head again to blow over Dorian's nails. Kitty felt she had found a chink in the armour. 'Why'd you give it up?' Her voice was soft, little more than a whisper.

Tanya paused again. 'I chose a life of crime. The pay's crap but the hours aren't bad.'

'Thanks for not telling your guy about the mobile,' said Kitty. 'Why did you decide to do that?'

'Questions, questions ... maybe I thought this had gone far enough.'

'Thanks.'

Ignoring Kitty, Tanya spoke to Dorian. 'I don't see you as the farmer's wife type.'

'Richard wanted to move back here. His family come from the village.'

'His parents still live here?' said Kitty, her voice as casual as she could make it. Dorian shook her head.

'Richard's parents are dead,' said Dorian.

Kitty nodded, as if hearing this for the first time. 'What happened?'

'It was when Richard was younger. It was horrible. An accident with the car.

'A crash?' asked Kitty.

'I don't really know what happened. Richard hates talking about it.'

I bet he does.

'Richard's daddy was working under his car. The jack gave way. His father was killed instantly. Then Richard's mother died soon afterwards. She never got over the shock.'

'It must have been terrible for him,' said Kitty.

A shadow flickered over Dorian's face. Something about the incident troubled her. She looked at her hands as Tanya searched for a suitable bottle of nail varnish. Tanya held up the bottle to the light.

'That's lush!' sighed Molly. Kitty was relieved to hear her voice. It seemed that Molly felt safe enough to speak to her captor.

Shaking the vial, Tanya smiled at her. 'You've got good taste, kid!'

Tanya brushed varnish in thick, even strokes onto Dorian's nails. They all watched, their heads huddled together.

'You're done,' she said at last. Dorian rippled her fingers, admiring the gleam of the light on the plummy sheen of the varnish.

'That's gorge!' said Molly. Kitty kissed the top of her daughter's head.

'You next?' smiled Tanya. Molly shook her head, smiling shyly as she wriggled deeper into her mother's arms.

'Do mine?' Kitty spoke softly. Dorian moved aside, clearing a space for Kitty who was waiting for a sign that Tanya gave her permission.

'If you like,' shrugged Tanya. She raised her eyebrows. 'Special rate for the feds.'

Kitty sat on the stair at her feet. Her hands were steady as she laid them on Tanya's knees. 'It's been a while,' said Kitty.

Tanya avoided her eyes, all business as she examined the nails. From above came a loud crash and the sound of breaking glass.

'Where'd you meet him?' asked Kitty. There was another crash from above, shaking dust from the striplight. 'Your fella?'

'A club,' sighed Tanya.

'I used to go to clubs,' murmured Dorian. 'In another life.'

'Which club?' asked Kitty.

Tanya paused. She raised her head. 'Why do feds ask so many questions?'

'It's what we do,' smiled Kitty.

'The Zanzi,' said Tanya. 'I met him in The Zanzibar.'

'Sounds exotic!'

'It's a hole!'

'What did you think? The first time you saw him?'

Tanya passed the file over Kitty's fingertip, back and forth, rasping away the nail, the dust falling on her lap. 'He looked like trouble!' Tanya's frown had gone. She smiled at the memory. 'I can remember it now, see it now, the way he smiled.' She shrugged, opening the bottle of varnish. 'Some things you don't forget, do you? Some moments. They're like photos, aren't they?' She glanced up at Kitty. 'Little pictures. In your head.'

She stroked a line of varnish onto the first nail, then held it up. Kitty nodded, willing Tanya to keep talking. Tanya parted the fingers so as not to smudge the varnish. Her tongue peeped between her lips as she smoothed it over Kitty's blind, pink nails.

'You got anyone? A man?'

' I *had* one. He ran away! Years ago.'

'No-one at the moment?'

'Nope.'

'Where'd he run to?'

'Back to France. He was Molly's dad.'

'Your daddy?' Tanya said to Molly, who nodded.

Tanya smoothed a line of varnish down Kitty's nail.

'Break your heart, did he?'

'No!' said Kitty.

Kitty was uncomfortable talking about Molly's father. She hated the thought that any of that pain might pass on to her child. 'Well ... I don't know. Maybe a little.' Some wounds are so deep they never heal.

'Just get another one, darling. Really. It's easy! They're all over the bloody place!'

'For you, maybe!'

Smooth, creamy varnish, spread across the nail. Tanya glanced up. 'Easy to pick up, hard to lose. Like shit on your shoe!' She looked at Molly. ''Scuse my French.'

CHAPTER FORTY THREE

'You get used to your own ways of doing things,' said Kitty. 'Why would we want someone to come in and mess that up? It's getting a *good* one. That's the tricky part.' As she looked into Tanya's eyes, Kitty saw the shutters fall once more. She had got too close. For a moment they were silent, Tanya working, Kitty watching her face. It was Dorian who spoke next.

'Why did you ask?'

'Ask?' said Kitty. 'About what?'

'Before. When you asked about Richard? About the accident?' Dorian tugged at the cuffs of her jumper.

Kitty might have sidestepped and moved on, but she sensed that this was the moment. 'It wasn't an accident.'

'What?' Dorian's voice was tight. 'What does that mean?'

'Your husband has been lying to you, Dorian.'

Tanya paused for a moment, without looking up. As Kitty withdrew her hand, Tanya held it firmly. Then she started again, smoothing varnish over the nails.

'Why?' Dorian reared back, fury in her eyes. 'Why do you say such awful things?'

'Because all of this didn't just happen. Your husband arranged all of this. These two have been in this area for a while. Isn't that so?' She looked at Tanya, who worked on, as if she had not heard. Kitty turned to Dorian again. 'Richard planned for these two to get into your home. He told them what to look for. He paid them to come here, to tie you up, to steal your property. The reason we're stuck down here is because your loving husband planned it.'

Dorian shook her head but Kitty pressed on. 'This is all his idea, Dorian.' She turned to Tanya. 'Isn't that so?'

Tanya glanced up, meeting Kitty's eyes for a moment.

'Right! she said, her voice notched hard. 'That's you done.' Tanya looked away and busied herself packing away her kit.

'I'm sorry, Dorian,' said Kitty. 'It's better you know the truth. But this doesn't have to end badly,' said Kitty.

As Dorian looked at her, wide-eyed, a deafening crash shook the ceiling. Dust showered down, falling on their heads. From above came the crunch of splintering wood and breaking glass. It sounded like a Chieftain tank was ploughing through the house. They stared at the ceiling, following Nathan's progress as he smashed his way through the rooms above.

'Sounds like someone's having fun,' said Kitty.

'Nathan always enjoys himself,' murmured Tanya. She slotted the brush back into the bottle, packed her files and Emery strips back into the leather pouch, snapped the catch and dropped it into her bag.

'We can work this out,' said Kitty.

'It's too late for that,' said Tanya.

Dorian stared at the floor, her fingers pressed against her lips. The truce was over.

* * *

As Richard hit the road, all the tension left him. Anger drained away, the charge earthing from his body, leaving him serene. The muscles in his neck softened, his grip on the wheel eased. His mind floated free. For a while he drove as if hypnotised, turning the wheel without any conscious thought. The tears took him by surprise, waking him from the trance. As he rubbed his eyes he realised that he loved Dorian. He could not live without her. At that moment he experienced a glimmer of deeper understanding – he loved her and he had been foolish

CHAPTER FORTY THREE

to put her at risk. This 'plan,' he realised, was punishment. Punishment for kissing that stupid lout. This was all so stupid. But in the next moment he dismissed that thought. To hesitate now, to lose his nerve, that would be a mistake.

His anger welled from an older, deeper wound. He was a freak. A reject. He was shop-soiled. He was secondhand goods.

CHAPTER FORTY FOUR

Nathan tapped his mobile against the kitchen surface. His other hand curled into a fist which drummed on the marble. He recalled the many ways he had been disrespected by Richard Kane. He grabbed a bottle and hurled it at the far wall, spattering sauce across the kitchen. Nathan grinned as the jagged arc of goo slithered down the wall.

'Sweet,' he murmured. He giggled as he picked up a bottle of organic tomato pesto and tossed it from hand to hand. He smashed the bottle onto the Aga. Splinters of glass skidded across the work surface. Nathan yanked a drawer from the unit, ran across the kitchen and hurled it through the kitchen window. He pulled the phone from its socket and swung it by the cord until it shattered against the cooker. He stamped on the handset until it was splinters. Knives and forks clattered across work surfaces, bouncing off the sink and skittering across the tiles. Sliding a carving knife from the wooden block, he wandered through the house, searching for something to cut.

Sunlight slanted through the sitting room windows, gleaming on the leather sofas. Nathan paced the room as he chose his next target. He paused, bounced on the balls of his feet then moaned as he lunged at the sofa, pushing the blade deep into the body, shredding the leather. Nathan circled the chairs, enjoying the feeling as the blade slit the taut hide. He slashed the skin again and again, slicing it into long ribbons. Clouds of stuffing bled from the wounds, spilling across the floor and puffing into the air. In less than a minute the suite was in shreds, the wooden skeletons inside exposed to the sunlight.

Nathan stood for a moment to admire his work. Fibres caught in his throat and tears ran down his cheeks. His chest felt tight so he sucked on his inhaler as he wandered into the hall. There he picked up the bronze figure he had used to wedge the cellar door. He tossed it up and down, weighing it in his hand. Using it as a hammer, he bludgeoned the Venetian mirror that hung by the door, smashing the glass and the frame into fragments. Returning to the sitting room, he sprinted across the floor and hurled the bronze through the window. The pane shattered, spraying glass across the gravel outside. The bronze bounced across the drive, coming to rest in the centre of the turning circle.

For the next fifteen minutes Nathan ricocheted from room to room, breaking whatever he could. He swept through the house like a dark angel, chopping and cutting and slashing everything in his path. Kane had insulted him. That witch of a cop had faced him down. He had been humiliated and angry with himself. But this felt good. It redressed the balance. He felt cleansed, his power restored.

At last he was done. His chest felt tight from the dust and feathers in his throat and lungs. Each time he breathed his throat whistled like a kettle. Nathan sat on the front step of the house and puffed his inhaler. He looked across the valley, across the folds of wide open heather. Not another human was in sight. The sun had disappeared now. He patted plaster from the knees of his trousers. Behind him dust and feathers swirled in the breeze.

Nathan closed his eyes and sucked cool, clean air into his mouth. He filled his lungs then let it go, slowly, softly, out through his nose. His pulse slowed. It was all going to be fine. Everything was sweet. He had taken his revenge. Now it was time to go home.

***

Bryson Prudhoe sat in the witness room, skimming an article about slug pellets. He tossed the mag onto the table and wandered over to the window. He reached for his phone. 'Gordon? It's Bryson.'

At his desk in Shaftoe Leazes, Gordon Campbell opened his desk diary at a clean page. He ran his hand up the seam, pressing the pages flat. He pulled the top from a Fineliner and wrote Bryson's name.

'I'm listening.'

'You know I'm in court this morning? The Lumley thing?'

'Still listening.' The two men had avoided each other since the incident in the canteen.

'Locky's a witness. Kitty Lockwood.'

Campbell sighed. 'I've a pile of paper here a foot deep, Bry. Say something that I don't know?'

'She hasn't turned up. She's not at home. Her daughter never arrived at school. I've tried her mobile but it goes to answerphone. The landline's the same.'

'So? What's that got to do with me?'

'You're her bloody manager!'

CHAPTER FORTY FOUR

'If I'd heard from her, I would have said so. '

'Trace her phone, Gordon ...'

Campbell sighed. 'I would require a warrant to do that.'

'As a favour to me, Gordon.'

'And I'd need clearance from the Home Office.'

'Do it. Just do it, Gordon. Do it as her manager. Out of reasonable concern.'

'I'd need an S22.'

'Please.'

'Have you heard of the RIPA Act, Bry?'

'If anything's happened to her, Gordon, it's your face in the papers.'

Campbell drew a straight line across the page as he weighed the risks. He cleared his throat. 'So what would you suggest?'

'I suggest you get off your arse, walk down the corridor and GPS her car. It's fitted with a tracker.'

'I could do that.'

'Then will you, Gordon? Will you do that?'

'That would be a massive favour, Bryson.'

'It would, Gordon. It would be a massive favour. What would it take to get you to do this "massive fucking favour"?'

'An apology.'

'I apologise Gordon. You c –'

'Thank you, Bryson. I'll call you back.' The connection broke.

Bryson pressed his fingers into his eyeballs until he saw stars. When he opened them he looked down to the quayside. The river cruiser was casting off, chugging backwards into the current. Bryson's phone bleeped in his hand.

'Mister Prudhoe? It's Jacqui Speed. I'm round at Kitty's.

There's no sign of her. And the car's gone.'

As he stared at the river, Bryson could hear the sound of birdsong in his ear piece. 'What can you see through the front door?'

He heard Jacqui grunt as she stooped to peer through the letterbox. 'Just letters on the mat. Bills and stuff.'

So Kitty had not been home the previous night. 'Try the back door.' He heard Jacqui puffing as she ran around the house, snuffling as she peering through the windows.

'Ummm ... no sign. Merlin's going mad!'

'Who the chuff is Merlin?'

'The cat.' Bryson watched the current catch the boat as it slipped into the middle of the river. The craft picked up speed as she moved towards the sea.

'Mr Prudhoe? Bryson? Are you still there?'

Bryson Prudhoe was squeezing his bulky frame into the lift that dropped him to the street below.

* * *

Richard Kane jockeyed for position in the fast lane, pushing a hundred and ten, tailgating a dusty white van. Richard leaned on the horn and flashed his lights. The van man flicked his fingers as the Porsche roared past.

Time equals distance over speed. Ninety miles an hour, seventy miles to the farm. He'd be home in forty six minutes. What he would do then was harder to calculate. He called Nathan, breaking his own rule about calling the house. If it became a problem, he'd claim a missed call from an unknown number. He'd think of something.

'Nathan? Look, I just want to say I'm sorry.' He dabbed the

CHAPTER FORTY FOUR

brakes, dipping to a hundred as he took a long bend.

'Listen mate, what can I say? I am SO sorry! You must have thought I'd flipped!' When there was no reply Richard continued. 'I've been thinking.'

'Have you?' Nathan sounded wary.

'Yeah. I've been giving it a lot of thought.' Richard roared past a car transporter, the old cars shaking; rusty wrecks on their way to the scrappers. 'I don't think I've behaved very well. Towards you.' Richard waited, but heard only silence. 'Look. I've thought of a way I might make it up to you.'

Richard weaved into the middle lane to undertake a Lexus. 'This has been hard for you, I know.'

He eased back into the fast lane, foot to the floor, pushing her up to a hundred and fifteen.

'We're leaving, Mister K.'

'Now? You're not leaving now, surely?'

'I'm done here.'

'Hang on an hour or so.'

'We're gone.'

'But I have something for you ... I promised. Made a promise ...'I want to give you a little something. A gift. Soon as I get back.'

'What are you talking about?'

Richard grinned. Nathan was so easy to manipulate. His appetite always trumped his common sense. 'A bonus. To make up for me being such a pain in the arse!'

'Van's loaded. Motor's running. We're on our way, Mister K.'

'I'll be with you in forty minutes! Have a cup of coffee. It'll be worth it, I promise!'

'What kind of bonus?'

'It will make everything OK. Trust me.'

In the silence that followed the Porsche covered the best part of a mile. Richard glanced at the dashboard and calculated that he would reach home in thirty five minutes.

'I'll think about it,' said Nathan.

Richard gunned the car up the rise to Junction 42 as he left the motorway.

* * *

The striplight hummed above their heads. The noise of battle had ended and the house was silent. They sat on the floor, their backs to the cold stone.

Dorian sat apart, teasing threads from the cuff of her jumper and twisting them into points, brushing them over her lips. She had not spoken a word since Kitty told her about Richard. Dorian might be fragile, but she was not crazy. And while Kane had many of the traits of a psychopath, he functioned pretty well in the business world. He was aware of everything he was doing. Kane threw tantrums whenever he was thwarted. Winning was the most important thing. As Kitty watched Dorian play with the threads, she felt guilty about what she had said to her. It seemed too cruel.

'You know, I'd love a drink,' said Kitty.

Dorian waved her hand. 'Help yourself.'

Kitty glanced along the racks of wine.

'I don't know if Tanya would let us.'

Their jailor lay on the stairs. She yawned, her eyes half closed, but said nothing.

'Richard hardly drinks a drop,' said Dorian. 'This is all just an investment.' Tears welled in her eyes. Her voice sounded small. She seemed distant, distracted. Kitty guessed she was stunned by the news of Richard's betrayal.

'Where were you walking, that morning we met?'

'We'd had a fight,' said Dorian, twisting another thread, teasing it to a point.

'I don't make much money, you see. Not a penny!' She smiled, shaking her head. She traced the line of her lips with the strand of wool, moving the tip around and around, like a child. 'I used to. Then I got ill.' She tapped her head. 'I have an addictive personality, apparently. I'm not allowed to work. And Richard doesn't want me to, but we're short of cash ...'

'You had a fight about money?'

'That was behind it, I expect.' Dorian worked on another thread, teasing and twisting. 'But no. It wasn't about money.'

'Sex?' said Kitty.

'Why say that?'

'It's always one or the other, isn't it?'

Dorian nodded towards Molly. 'Are you sure we should be talking about this?'

'It's fine,' said Kitty, anxious that nothing should deter Dorian, now that she had opened up. Dorian shrugged.

'I can't remember. We had a drink, with lunch. Just a glass or two. It doesn't take much to get me drunk, these days. And then it just sort of ... carried on. It became one of those afternoons.'

'I thought you said Richard didn't drink?'

'He doesn't. I was drinking with ... we had a guest.'

Kitty knew that Dorian was hiding something. She waited, but it seemed that her secret would remain intact. 'What sparked off the quarrel?'

'It must be strange. Being a man. All that *pretending* to

be strong.' Kitty nodded. Whatever happened that drunken afternoon must have been the start of it all.

'Richard hates talking about money,' said Dorian. 'He thinks it's his job, all of that. It's this property he's renovating, in Liverpool. I think the money's run out. I mean, I *know* it has! I wanted to ask my mother for a loan and he almost gave in. He's never done that before. So I knew things were bad.'

Kitty glanced towards the stairs where Tanya lay, feigning sleep. 'He wanted you to borrow money from your family?'

Dorian nodded. 'All their money is tied up. I'd ask, if it would help. Richard has done everything for me! So I had to tell him. We had a row. Out of nowhere. '

But it was the kiss.

'There was something else, wasn't there?'

Dorian's smile was rueful. She nodded. 'He walked in the room. I was being kissed, at the time.' She looked down at her new, shiny nails. 'Which was a little awkward ...' At the memory, Dorian clenched her fingers.

'So there was a fight?'

'I've never seen him like that! He *never* loses his temper with me! I started walking down the drive. I was scared. It was fine, later. He just said that everything seemed to be spinning out of control. That's the thing, when there's just the two of us, in a place like this.'

Kitty glanced over at Tanya, who lay on the stairs, eyes closed; her chest rising and falling.

'Who were you kissing?'

Dorian laughed and shook her head, as if to wipe away the memory. 'This boy. Kevin.'

'He had a crush on you?'

Dorian shrugged. 'I guess that's what it was. It didn't

mean a *thing!*' She shook her head. 'Not to me! But Richard flipped. It just seemed to set him off. He threw Kevin out. He threatened to kill him! So he drove off. Then I had to get away. I wanted to give Richard time to calm down. When I got to the bottom of the drive I couldn't face going back. It just seemed easier to keep walking. '

Dorian twisted the threads of her sleeve into a fresh, sharp point and circled her lips. 'Then I met you! And I bet you're SO glad about that!'

CHAPTER FORTY FIVE

The phone jangled on the passenger seat of Bryson's car. He pulled over to take the call. 'We got a signal Bry,' said Gordon Campbell. 'But it's miles away, out in the wilds of Wannee.'

Bryson sensed reluctance in Campbell's tone.

'So are you going to tell me?' he said.

'I don't know what to make of it, Bry. She was talking about this to me a few days ago.'

'So where is it, Gordon?'

'Have you got a pen? It's at the top of the valley. Somewhere near that farm. That place they call West Neuk.'

* * *

'I told you to stay with them!'

'They're fine, Nathan,' said Tanya.

'But you locked them in?'

There was a beat before she replied. 'They're not going anywhere.' What difference did it make? She thought. She had not bolted the door but she and Nathan were leaving. She didn't care any more. Soon they would be gone. Nathan lay

CHAPTER FORTY FIVE

on the stairs, his inhaler in his hand. He flicked the tails of his coat to the sides. Out of the corner of her eye Tanya could see the devastation he had wrought. A breeze blew through the shattered window in the sitting room, puffing the curtains like the sails of a galleon. The air was loaded with fibre he had torn from the furniture.

'Nathan! He'll kill you if he sees this!' Her mouth fell open. 'I'd love to see his face.'

'Take a seat.' Nathan shuffled to the side, patted the stair carpet. 'He'll be here any minute.'

'No.' She shook her head. 'I really don't want to be around for that.'

Nathan rubbed the heel of his hand in his eye socket.

'Kane has something for us. I bet!'

'A bonus. For all our trouble.'

'He'll give you more than a bonus when he sees this!'

Nathan shrugged. 'I told him the fed put up a struggle. And if he doesn't like that, I'll take it anyway.'

That sounded like his final word. But Tanya knew when her man was bluffing. 'You promised we would go ...'

Nathan got to his feet and moved his face close to hers. She tensed, waiting for the blow. But he seemed relaxed, almost happy. He wrapped her in his arms and put his lips close to her ear. 'We've come this far, babes. We take what he's got. Then we'll go.'

She listened to the steady, strong beat of his heart. Something told her that their time together was coming to an end. She stroked his neck and they sat down, side by side, at the foot of Richard Kane's staircase, to wait.

* * *

The Porsche climbed the lane from the village at a steady sixty. A nerve at the corner of Richard's eye was twitching, tugging the lid. He shook his head and blinked. He was shattered, yet he had made good time. For a moment he worried that a speed camera might have picked him up, which might become a problem. He would explain that he was an innocent man dashing home, crazed with worry over a strange, threatening call from his home number. He was worried about his wife, who had a history of mental illness. He convinced himself. It was not a problem. Richard believed his own lies. If he believed them, then others would.

The Porsche rolled up the drive to West Neuk. The car bounced over the ruts, wheeled around the turning circle and crunched to a halt beside an old Saab. The rust bucket must belong to the policewoman, he figured. Nathan's van squatted by the front door, low on its axles.

The first thing Richard noticed was chips of glass scattered amongst the gravel. As he approached the house it became clear that something was badly wrong. Curtains billowed through the empty window frames, white muslin flapping in the breeze. The glass was gone, the windows like blind, empty sockets. Richard stared, open-mouthed, at the hole in the front of his house. A bronze figure lay on the gravel where it had landed. He picked up the figure and tried to make sense of what he was seeing. The front door swung open and Nathan walked onto the front step, twirling his little Makarov pistol around his finger.

'Welcome home, Mister K!' he boomed.

Nathan greeted Richard Kane with a flourish and a low, extravagant bow.

CHAPTER FORTY FIVE

* * *

Kitty crept up the cellar stairs and put her ear to the door. She could hear the sound of voices outside – Nathan was talking to another man. She pressed her ear to the wood but could only make out the odd word. She opened the door and peered through the crack. She could see Tanya, sitting on the stairs, looking towards the open front door. The voices were coming from outside the house, angry voices, too distant to hear. Instinct told her the brew was coming to the boil. She needed to be ready.

She closed her eyes. In her mind she took the stance of a boxer at the start of a bout. She visualised the moves, arms flexing for balance, calf muscles stretching as she prepared for combat. Outside, the voices of the men rumbled on, the anger building. In her own mind she replayed the speech Rafael gave at the end of every session.

'We live in this moment.' He clicked his fingers. 'And this.' *Click.* ' ... and this ... Life is layer upon layer of sounds and sights, memories and thoughts. Trying to recall them is like capturing the thread of a fading dream. Let it go – we cannot change the past. The present –that we *can* do something about.'

* * *

Nathan flexed his trigger finger as he rocked, shifting his weight from one foot to the other. 'Good to see you, Mister K,' he boomed, waving the gun in Richard's face.

'Put it away.'

Nathan levelled the gun at Richard's head. 'Everything's sweet! Sweet as a nut.' He closed one eye, squinting down the barrel, sticking out the tip of his tongue. '*Pshooo!*' Nathan popped his lips, making the sounds of gunfire. 'Pyowww!'

Richard leaned closer. The muzzle was now an inch from his eyeball. They stood in the doorway: Nathan in his overcoat, Richard in his shirtsleeves, silk tie flapping in the breeze. Their eyes were level, locked together. Richard held his bronze figure. Nathan lowered his pistol.

'Just havin' a little fun with you, Mister K.'

Richard brushed Nathan aside as he walked into the house.

Nathan followed at his shoulder, bobbing up and down. He shook his head, sadly. 'That bitch put up a struggle!'

'So I see.'

Tanya watched from the stairs.

'Still. Job done, yeah?' said Nathan.

Richard picked his way through the wreckage. He crunched through splintered wood and shattered glass. He had paid for a tidy little burglary. This was not the way he had planned things. 'What have you done?'

'I told you – bitch went crazy!' Nathan wafted his hand through a cloud of drifting fibre. 'Had to hit her. *Bop!*' Nathan tapped the barrel of the gun against his forehead. 'Look, all this shit, all this mess – it just makes it more *authentic*.'

'Authentic?' Richard's voice broke. He was giddy with fury, his head shaking as if it might spring clear from his neck. If Nathan had not been holding a gun he would have killed him right there, right then.

'Don't stress Mister K! Insurance pays for this!' Nathan picked up a splinter of broken wood and tossed it aside. 'You'll get it back. You can buy some new stuff!'

CHAPTER FORTY FIVE

Richard turned to glare at Nathan, as if seeing him for the first time.

'So. Mister K. You mentioned a little bonus? Shall we settle up now? We need to make tracks. We want to get all your shit stashed away.' He winked.

Richard felt himself swaying. He put one hand on his head, rubbing it back and forth across his spiky hair. 'Bonus?' He said the word as if he was trying it out for the first time. As he swayed he noticed that Nathan's eyes were pinking up. Tears gathered in their corners. Richard looked down at the bronze figure in is right hand. When he looked up again, Nathan was making a show of pulling his watch from his waistcoat and checking the time.

'Yeah. We really need to be on the road!'

Richard could hear that Nathan was wheezing now, as each breath squeezed tighter than the last. 'Of course,' Richard murmured. 'I have just what you need.' He swung the bronze in a flat arc. It reached full momentum as it split Nathan's skull from the eye socket to his ear. The blow knocked him off his feet and he crashed against the wall. He groaned, curled into a ball and lay still. Blood oozed from the wound and spread across the tiles. In the silence, Richard stared at the figure on the floor.

To think that I was scared of this man!

Richard rolled his shoulder. There was pain there, definitely some damage.

Behind him, Tanya began to scream.

CHAPTER FORTY SIX

Kitty opened her eyes and peeped through the door. She could make out the figure of Nathan lying on the floor, his legs twisted beneath him. His bloodied head rested against the wall. Tanya was kneeling astride him, dabbing at the gash with a tissue. There was blood on her fingers and on her clothes. Drops of blood trickled down the wall. A dark pool was gathering on the floor. Blood dripped from the point of Nathan's chin, falling across his waistcoat, sliding down the silver links of his watch chain. Tanya was whispering to her man, trying to wake him. It was plain to see that he would never hear another word she said.

* * *

The bronze figure fell from Richard's fingers and clattered across the tiles. He pushed Tanya aside and wandered up the stairs. He was trembling as he walked along the landing. He stumbled into his office and leaned his head against the wall. All he needed was a moment to think.

The plaster felt cool against his forehead. He would claim that he had acted in self defence. When he returned home

CHAPTER FORTY SIX

he found the place had been broken into by intruders. He confronted the man, who had held a gun to his head. He grabbed the first thing that came to hand as a weapon and struck out. Sadly, the man died. It was close enough to the truth, Richard convinced himself.

Then he saw the problem with that. Tanya had been there. She knew everything. She had seen him kill Nathan. Now he would have to kill Tanya. If he killed Tanya, what would the policewoman do? Then there was the child. There must be no-one left to testify, no trail to follow. He put his head in his hands. The clouds of stuffing and feathers that drifted through the house seemed to fill his mind. He had made one mistake, but the consequences were never-ending. Killing Nathan had set in motion a wall of dominoes, each one tumbling onto the next. Nathan, so Tanya, so the woman, so the child, so ... He shook his head. None of them mattered. The only person that counted here was Dorian. What would she think?

Load the guns. Then decide what to do.

The gun cupboard lay open. Nathan had taken the shotguns, as planned – doing as he was told, for once. The weapons had left faint silhouettes on the wall, white on dusty grey. But Richard's old .22 rifle still hung in the usual place. He took the rifle, loaded it then sat down, cradling the gun in his lap. He had come too far to ruin everything like this. He had too much invested in the plan to abandon it. He slotted the rifle back into its place.

* * *

Kitty eased herself through the cellar doorway. She moved to Tanya's side and felt for a pulse in Nathan's neck. There was nothing – no respiration, no flicker of movement in his eyelids. 'I'm sorry. He's gone,' said Kitty. Tanya fell across Nathan's body, reaching her arms around his broad shoulders.

Kitty turned to see Richard Kane at the top of the stairs, looking down on the little people below.

CHAPTER FORTY SEVEN

Bryson's mobile bounced around the bucket seat as he hurtled up the lanes towards West Neuk Farm. The signal in the hills was patchy. If John Stafford called, Bryson would claim he was out of range. Though he willed the phone to remain silent it chirruped as he neared the village of Hott. Gordon Campbell's voice rasped in his ear.

'Where are you? Precisely?'

'I'm three miles from the Kanes' house. Just below Hott.'

'What about your court?' Bryson looked up the valley. Clouds were stacking up in the west, trailing veils of rain across the hilltops.

'I can get back in time. I'll just check, make sure Locky's OK. Tell Stafford, would you?'

'Bollocks, Bryson! I'll send back-up!'

'I don't know what the problem is, yet! She might be fine!' Bryson tossed his mobile onto the seat and ran his finger beneath his collar, peeling it from the skin. He rolled his neck, easing his knotted shoulders as the first drops of rain spattered the windscreen. When he reached the village, Bryson coasted down the narrow street. The place seemed deserted. When he cleared the last house he put his foot down. The road glistened, slick with rain. The trees rocked in the rising wind. He reached open moorland and scanned the skyline, searching for the farmhouse on the hill.

*　*　*

'Dorian?' The catch in his voice was perfect. 'Dorian? DO-RIAN?' Louder now, giving the words an edge of real fear. 'Where are you?' Richard Kane clattered down the staircase. His wife stood in the cellar doorway, her face white. She was staring at Tanya, stretched across Nathan's body. Richard was rattled. There were no smiles of relief, no welcoming hugs for the returning hero. They were silent, watchful.

They know.

He ran to Dorian, gathering her in his arms, kissing her face, filling the silence with gasps of joy and relief. 'Thank God!' He held her at arm's length. 'Thank God you're safe!' Tears ran down his cheeks. 'I've been searching everywhere!'

Yet Dorian remained still, her body rigid in his embrace. She was staring at the body on the floor. Richard looked over her shoulder, stealing a glance at Kitty. Her eyes were dark, attentive – almost compassionate. She smiled that strange, lop-sided smile; the woman who was ruining his life.

She knows.

'Did they hurt you?'

'Who's 'they', Mister Kane?'

'These animals!' He jabbed his chin towards Tanya, who lay across the body of her man. Her face was buried in Nathan's chest, her hair matted with blood. Richard turned away, as if the sight disgusted him. He kissed Dorian, steering her towards the kitchen. If he could get them out of the way, he might be able to bustle Tanya into the van and force her to drive away. But Dorian raised her hands, her face white with shock. None of this was going to plan, he realised. Where was the breathless, grateful welcome? Where were the tears of gratitude? He'd been through so much lately. This was quite exhausting.

Dorian walked into the kitchen, where she sat at the table. Kane trailed after her. The room was gloomy now, the morning sun just a memory. A gust of wind rattled the window.

'Darling,' he said. 'I was so scared when I saw all this! I ran up to the bedroom ...' He leaned over her in a clumsy move and rained soft, fishy kisses on her brow. Dorian shuddered, shaking herself free. He stepped back, shocked. 'I can't imagine what those people have put you through.'

'Why not?' said Kitty. 'You paid for it.'

He shook his head. He needed time. Just a moment to think. He had to get his story straight; then do something about Tanya.

'I'm calling an ambulance,' said Kitty. She moved past him, searching for the phone. But Nathan had smashed the landline phone to pieces. She turned to Dorian. 'There's a phone upstairs?'

Richard rubbed his hands over his face. He could feel the walls closing in. 'Don't worry about that – I can make the calls!' He stood in the doorway to the kitchen, smiling, masking anger with concern. 'Please sit down. I'll deal with this.'

But the bitch wouldn't have it. She skipped past him and ran up the stairs, taking them two at a time. As he followed he saw that Tanya was no longer by Nathan's body. For a moment he wondered where she had gone, but there was a more pressing problem. He had to stop the policewoman. He ran up the stairs to find her by the desk in his office. She punched the buttons and waited for the call to connect. The windows were streaked with rain, the wind howling through the warped frames. Lightning flashed above the plantation and he heard thunder rumble down the valley. Storm clouds filled the sky, blooming like blood in water.

'Is it working?' he said, leaning over her. 'Those bastards must have broken everything!'

She was ignoring him, jabbing the buttons on the phone. He leaned across the desk and took the phone. For a moment he held it to his ear, as if listening. Then he laid it in the cradle.

'You know,' he said. 'I don't think that's such a good idea.'

CHAPTER FORTY EIGHT

They stood together, side by side. He was so close she could feel his breath on his face. She saw the pulse in his neck, counting down the heartbeats. 'You're hurt,' he said. He touched her cheek, running his fingertip down her scar, the thin seam of dried blood running from the cut at the corner of her eye.

She watched him. Waiting.

'Let's just think about this for a moment.'

His voice was calm. At the edge of her vision Kitty saw the door to the gun cabinet, which was hanging open. 'Are you going to kill me, Richard?'

He smiled, shaking his head. 'You have a strange idea of me. I would never hurt anyone unless it was necessary.'

'You killed your father. Was that 'necessary'?'

His smile faded. The charm switched, in a heartbeat, to fury. His lips set into a firm line as his head turned from side to side.

'M – my father died in an accident!'

'No.' Her voice was barely above a whisper. 'You killed him…'

He shook his head.

'There's just you and me here, Richard. You can say it. Go on! Confession is good. Good for the soul.'

He grabbed her throat, tightening his fingers, the nails cutting the flesh. She gasped but jabbed her fist into his Adam's apple. His grip loosened and she wriggled free. He lunged over the desk and pulled the rifle from the cabinet. He twisted around to level the gun at her head.

'You know *nothing* about me! You barge in here, poking your face into my life, into *our* private life. This is an outrage!'

She leaned against the desk and folded her arms. 'This is the second time I've had a gun pointed at me today. I'm starting to get used to it.'

'Downstairs. Now.' Sweat gathered on his forehead. He looked like a dead man.

'I'll go down. I'll go downstairs when you tell me about your father.'

Though her gaze was fixed on his face, she was aware of the barrel of the gun, that dark eye, watching her.

'We have nothing further to say to each other. Downstairs.'

She turned her back, tensing her body against the impact. As she moved to the door, she expected the shot at each step. Her hand on the frame of the door, she turned. 'You hated him.' The barrel of the gun was inches from her face, yet she held his gaze. 'Tell me, Richard. You can say it ...'

'I hated him. Happy now? Hated everything about him. His voice. The stupid things he said. The way his teeth clicked when he was eating. The way he touched her. Mauled her, running his filthy hands ...'

'He was your father.'

'No.'

'Your dad. He loved you.'

'He hated everyone! We hated each other. That was the only thing we shared! Why would he love me? Don't you get it? They *found* me! They *chose* me! They picked me, the way people choose a stray dog from the shelter.'

* * *

Life moves in circles. This room, at the top of the house, was once his father's study. It was here, one idle Saturday afternoon, he had made the discovery, all those years ago. His parents were out, trudging through the mud at some agricultural show. Richard mooched about the house, drifting from room to room. It was inevitable that he ended up in the room beneath the eves. Something about his father's study had always fascinated him. It seemed to contain the essence of what it meant to be a man. An adult, who made his own decisions, who knew how the world worked – not a fifteen year old kid, fizzing with hormones and boredom, jailed in the countryside. Somewhere up here, among the pipe racks and dusty books and fishing rods, somewhere up here lay the answer.

His father's creel hung behind the door, smelling of fish and perished rubber. He picked open the strap of cracked leather. The whicker lid creaked and swung loose. Richard rummaged through the contents; bobbins of nylon line, the fly reels, their rims damp with oil, the tin boxes of artificial flies, confections of feather and tinsel, masking the cruel barbs. He closed the basket and moved to the desk, trying the drawers, one by one. All were locked, save for the lowest. He dug through the layers of paper, the holiday magazines and brochures. There was a porn magazine, a copy of Club International. He felt disgust, shoving aside his father's guilty secret with the tips of his fingers. Beneath that lay a sheaf of papers, tied in a grey manila folder. He cocked an ear, listening for any movement in the house. His parents would be gone for hours. He untied the green ribbon that bound the folder and the papers tumbled across the carpet.

He scooped them up, trying to keep them in the order in which they had lain. As he tucked the last one into the file he noticed his own name – Richard Sheringham Kane.

He picked up the sheet and tried to make sense of the words. It had been issued by Gloucestershire Social Services Department and was dated six months after his birth. He read the letter again – 'Richard Sheringham Kane, born Richard Sheringham, Oxlynch, Gloucestershire.'

He stared at the sentence. 'Born Richard Sheringham.' It made no sense. The words would not fix in his mind. It hit like a kick to the stomach. He slumped to the floor and read the letter again. 'Richard Sheringham. Mother – Marion Sheringham. Father unknown.'

He lay on the floor, waiting for tears to fall.

And here he was in the same room, years later, holding a gun. Circles.

* * *

'I spent my school days looking down on adopted kids. Then I learned I was just like them. Damaged goods.'

'They still loved you!'

'You never love an adopted child like your own. I was a freak. Unwanted by my real parents. Lodging with people who pass you off as their own.'

CHAPTER FORTY EIGHT

'They must have loved you. I'm sure your mother...'

'Nobody loved me!' he screamed. 'Nobody! That's why I was there!'

Flecks of spittle hit her face. 'Don't you know *anything* about people?'

His eyes were slits, screwed tight, as if he was in pain. He jabbed the muzzle of the gun against her chest, pushing her towards the stairs. For a moment she thought to grab the weapon but he read her mind, moving away out of reach. She walked onto the landing and he followed, prodding her between the shoulder blades.

As she walked down the stairs, Kitty wondered if the gun was empty. Could she take that risk? She edged down, feeling for each step. Would she hear the bullet before it hit?

'I know you feel trapped, Richard.'

The blast was deafening. It filled the air, ringing through the stone walls. The bullet grazed her shoulder, tearing her shirt and smashing into the wall. The plaster cracked like eggshell, showering fragments over the stairs.

'I don't want to hear any more. I need to think. I require silence. Do everything I say or I'll kill your little girl. Do you understand?'

She heard him pull the bolt and slot another round into the chamber. The brass casing tumbled down the stairs, tinkling as it fell. A single shot weapon – he would need to reload each time he fired.

Nathan's body lay in the hall. The front door was wide open. It seemed that Tanya had taken her chance to escape. For a moment Kitty was overwhelmed by fear. It was only the thought that Molly was in the house that stopped her running through the door.

They entered the kitchen where Molly perched on Dorian's lap, wide-eyed as her glance flicked between the adults.

'I'm going to ask you to return to the cellar,' Richard said to his wife. 'I'm sorry. It will be for the last time. You won't be there for more than a moment.' He swung the barrel of the gun towards Molly. Kitty held out her hand towards her daughter, who ran into her arms. They trooped down the cellar stairs in silence.

Kitty gathered herself, ready to fight and end it there. She knew he must reload between each shot – that might give her time. But Richard remained at the top of the staircase, looking down on them.

'I'm so sorry,' he said. He closed the door and they heard the bolt slide home.

* * *

Bryson parked on the road, beside the farm gateway. While it would have made more sense to drive up to the house, something told him to wait. There had to be a reason why Kitty was out of reach. Some instinct told him not to announce his presence by rolling up to the front door.

He looked up at the house on the hill. Kitty's Saab was parked on the gravel outside the porch; beside that stood a green Porsche. From that distance nothing seemed out of the ordinary. It all seemed so peaceful. The shadows of clouds rippled across the fells, the stiffening breeze rocked the Scots Pines around the house.

The front door opened and a tall man emerged. He crossed the gravel, sauntering towards the paddock where a pair of horses were grazing. The man carried something beneath his

CHAPTER FORTY EIGHT

arm – a stick, perhaps, or a whip. As Bryson stretched to get a better look the man put his fingers to his lips and whistled. The horses trotted to the paddock fence. The man raised his gun to his shoulder and fired. One horse fell, tumbling forward and sinking to her knees. Dark blood streamed down the creature's muzzle.

'Holy shit!' said Bryson, clapping his hand to his mouth. His phone slipped through his fingers and clattered onto the road. Hearing the noise, Richard looked up. Bryson ducked behind the wall. After a moment Richard turned back to the paddock. He reloaded and fired. The stricken horse rolled onto her side and lay still. The other animal whinnied and galloped away, kicking her heels.

The man fired again. The second horse tumbled across the pasture then fell; she twisted on the ground, long legs flailing as she staggered to her feet. He reloaded. The gun cracked again and again, the tall man loading and firing until the creature stopped moving. In the silence between the shots the bullet casings clinked on the gravel. The man walked into the garage beside the house.

His fingers were trembling as Bryson picked up his mobile. He wiped it clean, then sat on the grass, his back to the stone wall. 'Gordon? How soon can you get the Armed Response Team here?'

'Twenty minutes?' said Campbell.

More like thirty, thought Bryson.

'Why? What's happening there, Bry?'

Bryson peeped over the wall to see the man emerge from the garage carrying a green petrol can. A .22 rifle in one hand, 10 litres of petrol in the other. 'The millionaire' strolled to the front door of West Neuk Farm and disappeared inside.

'It's starting to kick off. No sign of Kitty but her car's parked outside. Then some bloke comes out of the house and shoots the horses. Just like that! Now it looks like he's planning to torch the place. '

* * *

Game over. As he climbed the stairs, Richard wondered what might have happened had he got away with it. The money would have arrived. The apartments at Cutler's Wharf would have been completed. He would have skipped across the line that separates failure from success. His colleagues at Amschels would claim they always knew he was a winner – *good old Richie*! What would the papers say now? '*Mayhem of Millionaire Murderer,*' perhaps.

He had no choice. As he looked around his broken home he knew that all of this would be taken away – the house, the business, his life. He would not let it happen. No-one should take that from a man. Least of all someone like that bitch in the cellar!

In his office he poured a tumbler of whisky. There was no shame in a little Dutch at a time like this. It was a special occasion. He sipped his glass of Bowmore, liquid gold from Islay. Thirty four years old. Older than Dorian.

For a moment Richard toyed with a fantasy of going on the run. He had enough money to escape. He might do a Lucky Lucan. Leave the woman and her brat in the cellar, escape abroad and start again. But without Dorian, all of it meant nothing. And she would never forgive him.

Hearing a noise downstairs, he lurched to his feet – the

booze had gone straight to his legs. As he walked downstairs he saw Tanya, standing in the hallway. She looked up at him. He saw the blood on the front of her clothes, the dark smudge of it on her cheek. She was holding Nathan's little automatic. Her hands were shaking and it was clear that the gun might go off at any moment. He lifted his rifle and pulled the trigger, firing from the hip. The bullet caught her in the chest and she took off, tumbling backwards. He reloaded and put the gun to her head, turning away as he fired the second shot. Tanya lay still. He slipped another bullet into the breach, stepped over her and entered the sitting room. Everything he loved, everything he held close, had been in this room. The time he spent with Dorian. The beautiful view of the valley.

There was a figure at the far end of the drive, scuttling behind the stone wall. A little fat man, dressed in black, popping his head up to peek at the house. Another pygmy. No doubt the little people would soon have him surrounded. There was no way out. The dominoes were tumbling, closing in, the wave falling closer and closer. It was strange that the voice he heard was that of his father.

Time to be a man. Time to finish it.

CHAPTER FORTY NINE

Kitty paced the floor between the wine racks. Molly was singing to herself as she drew hearts in the dust that lay on the bottles of Krug and Haut Bailly. She might have been waiting for the school bus. Dorian, in contrast, seemed to be awaiting execution. She leaned against the wall at the foot of the stairs, staring at the floor. Kitty moved to her side and rested a hand on Dorian's wrist.

'Are you OK?'

'That's one thing I'm not.'

'I know it looks bad.'

'He lied. Every memory is a lie. All of them.'

'Richard will be thinking about everything that's happened. Everything he's done. He may decide that there's no escape.'

Dorian lifted her face, flicked her tongue across dry, cracked lips.

'When he realises that he's lost everything, Dorian – you, the house, his life – he might decide that no-one else can have it,' said Kitty. 'But we *can* get out of this.'

To Kitty's surprise, Dorian laughed. She looked down at the floor, chuckling as she shook her head. Kitty leaned against the wall, listening to Richard's footsteps as he moved through

CHAPTER FORTY NINE

the house above.

* * *

When Conrad Sereys collared him in the executive washroom, Richard knew it was over. For a week the rest of the floor at Amschels had treated him like a leper. Colleagues dropped their gaze and fell silent when he entered the room. The pack scented death.

Sereys stood beside him, shoulder to shoulder at the mirror. There was a thin smile on his lips as he smoothed liquid soap over his hands. 'Got a minute, Richard?' Conrad never shouted – his voice was a smoky whisper, a snake moving through dead leaves.

'Sure,' said Richard.

They rode the lift to the top floor. The older man led the way down the corridor. Richard followed, studying the cut of the Italian suit, the Russell and Bromley brogues padding over the carpet. At one time, Conrad had been his mentor. In the early days he told Richard that a sign of leadership was the ability to turn and walk away, knowing the troops would follow. Conrad Sereys never looked back.

One wall of the boardroom was glass, giving a vista of the river and the city below. Afternoon sun gleamed on the walnut table and the air was scented with beeswax polish. Sereys flipped open a manila folder and slid a sheet of A4 across the table. He rested his chin on his hands.

'Let's take the results for Q4 ...' He tapped the sheet. Richard barely glanced at the paper. He knew the figures better than anyone. 'We can't, I'm afraid, sustain losses like these.'

Richard nodded. There was nothing to say, so he remained

silent.

Sereys reached into his pocket and opened a tin of Parma Violets. He slipped a lozenge beneath his tongue. He closed the tin and set it down, aligning it with the edge of his paper. The silence stretched on. Richard was the first to crack. 'The problem we faced, Conrad, was …'

'We all know how things are.'

There was no escape, no excuse. Richard knew it too and so he leaned back, waiting. Over the years they had enjoyed many chats like this. At one time it was their Friday afternoon ritual – reading the runes of housing starts and interest rates. At one time they had been very close. Like a father and son.

'Your strategy was unbalanced.'

Richard noted the past tense – "was" not "is." He belonged to the past.

'It's easy to see that *now*, Conrad. Funny how everyone could see it coming, once it had happened …'

'This is not *our* money. It belongs to other people.'

'I know that!' Richard could not keep the edge from his voice. He tried to speak more softly, to mirror the man who had once looked out for him.

'What would you like me to do, Conrad?'

'The board has decided we need to take a defensive position. We'll reposition funds. Look long term.' Sereys nudged the little tin with his knuckle. 'As for your own situation…'

Richard gazed across the river. A haze of dust and monoxide hung over the city. As he waited he looked at a distant tower, another ant hill. The workers come and go, but the colony lives forever. Buying and selling the world.

'Perception is crucial, Richard.' Sereys raised his hand. 'People give us their money to make it grow, not to …' He

CHAPTER FORTY NINE

seemed about to slam the table. At the last moment his hand slowed, a dead leaf falling. For the first time Richard noticed the older man's face was lined with tiny, broken veins. Conrad Sereys was an old man. Just another old man. Like his own father.

'We need to write your exit music, Richie. Let's spend an hour working on a statement. We want to present this as a positive move. For everyone.' Sereys leaned forward, a look of kindly concern on his face.

'The bank will honour your contract. Bonus, relocation payment, company car. All that is set in stone.'

Richard swallowed. This was real. This was going to happen. What would he say to Dorian?

* * *

Richard propped the .22 against the wall at the bottom of the stairs and went to work. Donning the rubber gloves from the cupboard beneath the kitchen sink, he pulled them tight. He fitted a builder's mask around his mouth and nose, crimping the edge to make it snug. Then he climbed to the top floor of the house and entered Dorian's studio.

He started by the window, pouring as he crossed the room in a diagonal line. The liquid slopped over the wood and slipped between the floor boards. He soaked Dorian's desk, drenching the papers. He felt a glimmer of regret as he saw her sketches lying there, so delicate, so vulnerable.

As he picked up a drawing of a sleeping man he realised that it was a portrait of him. Dorian must have sketched it without telling him. The picture showed him lying on the couch in his office. Behind him, the open window revealed the hills, that familiar horizon suggested with a few simple lines. The sleeping man looked so innocent, so at peace with himself. Dorian had such a gift. Sensing a moment of weakness, Richard dropped the sketch and doused it with petrol, moving quickly, before he changed his mind.

He worked on, faster now, splashing it over everything, soaking the whole room. He was careful to make sure the petrol never strayed too close to the sockets. It would be such a shame if everything went up before he was ready.

The air was heavy with vapour. The stench scoured his throat and nostrils and he tightened the mask, fitting it closer to the contours of his face. He moved down the stairs, pouring as he went.

***

Behind his stone wall, Bryson Prudhoe sheltered from the rising wind. He pulled his collar up and tried to peek though the stones of the wall. It was several minutes since he had put in the call to Campbell. There was no sign of the Armed Response Team. He put his head on one side to listen – no sound of an approaching car. It might be another half hour before they arrived. There was also no sign of movement at the house. No sound, since the horses had been killed. He peered over the wall and the bodies were still there. The sun flickered through and gleamed on the flanks of the dead animals. He shook his head, trying to wipe the image from his eyes.

Kitty's car was parked outside the front of the farm house. She was inside, he was certain. And Molly? By the time the Armed Response Team arrived, it would be too late.

Bryson found himself standing. He felt his heart thump

against his ribs. A drop of rain, thick as a bullet, splashed his cheek. Then he was walking towards the gate. He walked up the drive, towards the farmhouse. He had no idea what he was going to do when he got there. He called Campbell.

'Gordon? I'm going to have a look inside the house.'

'Don't be stupid Bry! They're on their way. They'll be with you in two minutes. There's no sense in you taking that risk.'

Bryson broke the connection. He walked on, climbing up the slope, puffing a little as he reached the turning circle. The front door hung open. For a moment he was reminded of the morning they had smashed their way into Clive Lumley's place. This time he was on his own. There was no sign of movement, apart from the breeze puffing the curtains through the shattered windows. Bryson stood on the threshold. The inside of the hall looked cool and dark. The house seemed so still.

* * *

The scent of petrol filled the air. Kitty knew that Richard would return at any moment. She had to convince Dorian that her husband had made his decision. She had heard the shots. The killing had started.

'When Richard sees he can't win, he'll want to deprive his "enemies" of their prize.'

'What 'prize'?' Dorian looked blank. Her whole life was gone.

'Some men, when they feel threatened, they sort of ... cross a line. They go into fight mode. Adrenaline kicks in. It doesn't stop until the "battle" is done.'

Kitty glanced at her daughter. She knew that Molly was

listening. She had to convince Dorian but was aware that what she said might terrify her own daughter. 'They don't know what they're doing. Richard might do anything.'

'Kill himself?' said Dorian.

Kitty nodded.

'What you mean,' said Dorian, 'is that he'll kill us?'

'Afterwards, when the violence ends, they're shocked at what they've done. But while it's happening, rage blinds them.'

'Richard would never do that!'

'...they find release that way. Peace.'

Dorian put her head in her hands.

* * *

It was Tanya's body he saw first, lying across the doorway. Blood stained the front of her clothes. A smudge darkened her cheek. Bryson swallowed and stepped over the body. He kneeled down to check for signs of life, though it was clear there would be none. Unfolding his handkerchief, freshly ironed for court that morning, he picked up the gun which lay by her hand. Beyond the woman lay Nathan, slumped against the wall. He checked for a pulse. There was nothing. Bryson knew he should say something, call out, but his lips were open and his mouth was dry.

* * *

The day they moved in together Dorian's life fell into a new pattern. Richard left for Amschels before eight each morning. She tidied the house, chipped a meal from the freezer then read for a couple of hours. In the afternoon she listened to the radio while cooking. Richard returned around seven. It was an easy, gentle routine. Work was forbidden. In a while she might be permitted to pick up her sketchpad, under careful supervision. But for now she was ordered to rest. She had to recover her strength. Richard kept a close watch.

'Your job is just to get better.'

One evening in April, Richard did not appear at his usual time. Just as she was calling his mobile, Dorian heard his key in the lock. Richard stumbled through the door and fell into her arms. They stood in the hallway for a moment or two. He seemed to be sobbing, though he made no sound. After a while he kissed her then walked into the sitting room; he poured himself a whisky and asked her to sit down.

'I have some news,' he said, as he laid his head in her lap. 'I'm leaving the bank.'

She had no idea what to say. His career meant so much to him. 'Has something happened?'

'I won't let them drag me down! It's like a slow motion car crash down there. I won't be the fall guy.' He began a rant about his boss, Conrad Sereys. 'Conrad's two faced!' he said. 'Too slow. Too old. When you're making the numbers he's all over you.' He gulped his whisky. 'I am the *only* person in that building who knows how to steer a fund!' The room was in darkness now. 'It's time to go! If a plan isn't working, tear it up and start again!'

This was so unlike Richard. He always knew the way forward. His certainty was one of the reasons Dorian found him so attractive. She suspected that Sereys had questioned his judgment and Richard was hurt. To lose the confidence of his boss must have been a shock —like losing his father all over again.

'I'll build up something for us. Something magnificent. I'll show them!'

She stroked his neck. 'Whatever you want, Richard. You know that. It's you and me. Together.'

* * *

The screech of the bolt, rust against rust. 'Talk to him,' whispered Kitty. '*Lie* to him, Dorian...'

She watched Richard Kane move down the stairs. It seemed he had no reason to hurry. In one hand he held the petrol can, in the other the .22 rifle. The eye of the muzzle swept back and forth as he descended the stairs. Petrol vapour filled the air around him. His hands, in pink rubber gloves, resembled dainty, fuschia-coloured spiders. He waved the gun, indicating the women should move back.

'Come here,' he said to Molly. She shook her head, trying to bury herself in Kitty's arms. He laid the can on the ground. Kitty saw him aim the gun at Molly's head. 'What's her name?' he said.

'Molly. She's called Molly.'

'Molly?' He was trying to sound like a kindly uncle. 'I need you to do a little job for me. I want you to pour this over the bottles. Can you do that?' He went to his knees and held out the can. Molly took it. She walked along the aisles, sprinkling petrol over the wine racks. All the while he kept the gun levelled at Kitty. When it was empty Molly set it down by his feet. She returned to her mother's arms.

He shook the last drops from the can, laid it aside then pulled down his mask. Kitty was shocked by his smile. He looked beatific, as if at peace with the world. It was the first time, Kitty realised, that she had seen a genuine smile on is face. But the stench of petrol was sickening, flooding her nostrils and making her gag.

'Let her go.'

Kitty's voice was soft, but steady. She did not plead.

'That's not part of the plan, I'm afraid.' His voice was calm.

'Richard? Molly's no danger to you.'

He appeared to consider this for a moment, scratching the side of his nose. 'Too late. I'm sorry.'

'She's a child.'

He shook his head. 'What I *can* do is give you the choice. Would you like to be first?'

Kitty shook her head. 'You never fail to surprise, Mr Kane.'

He nodded, smiling as if she had paid him a compliment. 'It would be better if you faced the wall.'

He pulled back the rifle bolt to check it was loaded then slotted it home.

'Turn your back, and you're dead.'

Kitty pulled Molly to her side. 'We're fine as we are,' said Kitty. She felt Molly tremble, though she said nothing, her eyes fixed on the man with the gun.

'Turn around.'

Kitty guessed he would kill her first. *Even a lapdog will chase if you run.*

'Turn around!' His voice was hoarse. Dorian watched him, wide-eyed. Kitty wondered if she had finally realised the truth. He mouthed the words: 'It's you and me,' at Dorian. She walked to him, tilting her head, as if waiting for a kiss. As he leaned in she spat at him. Kane recoiled, wiping his face as Dorian moved to the wall and turned her face to the stone.

Since Richard entered the cellar she had been waiting for a moment to strike. He gestured with the gun and she turned to face the wall. She watched his shadow raise the gun to his shoulder. In that tight space the first shot was deafening.

Kitty was surprised to find herself still standing. She turned to see Bryson, framed in the doorway at the top of the stairs, pointing the Makarov at Richard. His shot had missed but he was aiming another when Kane fired. Bryson fell, tumbling backwards through the doorway. Kitty pushed her daughter aside and moved as Richard slid another bullet into the breach.

Kitty ran at him. As Richard raised the gun she jumped, arcing through the air. The edge of her foot caught him beneath the throat, snapping the clavicle, the bone cracking like a twig. He fell back, arms flailing. His skull crashed against a rack, knocking bottles to the floor. His gun clattered across the flagstones. Molly scrambled beneath the racks, her screams ringing around the cellar walls.

Kitty threw herself across Richard's body as he scrabbled for his rifle. He writhed beneath her as he reached for his weapon. The gun, wet with blood and wine, slithered from his fingers. Kitty straddled his chest, seizing a handful of hair and jabbing the point of her elbow into the socket of his eye. He screamed as the bone cracked and blood smeared his face.

'You bastard,' she screamed.

Stunned, Richard tried to sit up as the blood dripped onto his chest. He roared with anger. Arching his back, he threw Kitty aside and staggered to his feet, half blinded. He searched for his gun.

For a moment the only sound was the gloop of wine dripping from broken bottles. Blood-drenched, Richard's face creased as he tried to focus. The barrel of his gun glinted in the debris.

CHAPTER FORTY NINE

Kitty lunged across the floor. Realising that he would reach it first, she checked her movement and grabbed the neck of a bottle. As Richard swung the rifle to aim she broke the glass across his face. Wine and blood spattered the wall.

As Richard fell he squeezed the trigger. The bullet pinged around the arched roof, smashing the ceiling light and showering sparks through the air. There was a moment of silence as they stared at each other. Then the pressure wave whoomphed through the cellar, a dull roar sucking the oxygen from the air. The room filled with flame. Richard Kane became a shadow, his mouth wide as he clawed at the flames.

Kitty fell to the floor, her eyes tight against the heat. Seizing Molly's wrist, she ran towards the exit. They clambered up the stairs by touch. She dragged Molly through roiling flame. Above her the beams popped and cracked as the fire took hold. She pushed Molly through the door and fell across the top stair.

Kitty crouched on all fours and retched. She coughed smoke, her tears tracking through the soot that covered her face. As she pushed Molly through the front door she heard Dorian's scream. Thick black smoke billowed through the open door, flames licking the edges of the staircase. The air in the doorway shimmered. Kitty felt a searing pain in her head. Her hair was alight. She ran to the kitchen and soaked a towel under the tap. Her scalp was blistered, her hair scorched to stubble. Dorian screamed again.

Just do it.

She clamped the dripping cloth to her face and ran back into the smoke. Her eyes screwed tight, she edged down the stairs one by one, feeling the heat in her throat. Halfway down her foot touched something soft and she heard Dorian groan. All around her was the crackle of timber as it buckled and snapped in the heat. Bottles cracked and burst, the wine hissing as it turned to steam.

Kitty grabbed Dorian's clothes and dragged her upwards. She could see little but shadows. As she pushed herself towards the light, she made out shapes in the doorway. Kitty fell through the gap and was held. Arms cradled her, carrying her through the door of the house.

They laid her on a blanket, wrapping another around her shoulders. Rain fell on her face. Out here everything seemed so still. Kitty shivered. Behind her flames were rising through the building. Fire rushed up the staircase, the flames skittering along the trail of petrol laid by Richard Kane. Smoke billowed from broken windows, puffing through the open door and spiralling into the sky. A black plume rose above the house, was caught by the wind and carried, twisting and turning, over the brow of the hill.

CHAPTER FIFTY

'Should have brought grapes, shouldn't I?' Kitty perched on the far corner of Bryson's bed and handed him a bunch of filling station flowers. The arm that had been hit by the bullet from Kane's .22 was encased in a cage and dressings. Bryson took the flowers in his "good" hand.

'Thanks for these,' he said, looking awkward. 'And yes, you should have brought grapes.'

A young nurse swished into the ward. 'Sorry! We don't allow that,' she said, smiling stiffly.' They ought to have told you that at the desk.' She whisked the flowers away.

Bryson raised his eyebrows and Kitty's mouth cracked into a smile.

'I like your hair...' he said.

She touched her scalp, ruffling the charred spikes of hair. 'It wasn't what I asked for...'

'Suits you! Short. Scorched. It's a good look.'

She ran her tongue across peeling lips. Her skin was pallid, though the bruises on her face had faded to yellow. 'How's the arm, then?'

'I'll not be playing snooker for a while,' he smiled. 'So.

What's the verdict on you?'

'I won't be kickboxing any time soon.'

'How's your girl?'

'She never mentions it!' She smoothed her hand across the sheet.

'Which is weird, isn't it?'

'You'll sort her out! You're full of psychological tips and wrinkles.'

'Wrinkles, anyway ... anyhoo...you chose a good time for a lie down.'

'Did I?'

'Trust me, Bryson. You're better off where you are. It's utter chaos! They've taken every detective in the force, put them into a lucky dip and moved everyone into new jobs. Reactive DCs into Intel, Intel bods into Serious Crime. Some good staff back into uniform.' She shook her head. 'Crazy! And it's all put down to saving money!'

Kitty smoothed the sheet again, flattening invisible creases. She stood and moved to the window. She looked out at the evening traffic, a solid line on Queen Victoria Road, cars creeping along, bumper to bumper, inching ever closer to the scrap yard.

'He's gone then,' said Bryson. 'Your chum, Kane.'

'Not a lot left of him.'

'A result.'

'I suppose.'

'The wife?'

'Switzerland. Back to her family. The poor cow. You know that Clive Lumley skated free, don't you?'

'Probably for the best. I got that one wrong.'

'There'll be other chances,' said Kitty.

Bryson picked at a speck on the sheet. 'There'll be other eighteen-month investigations, costing half a million quid, involving dozens of officers and mountains of intel...' His smile was rueful. Yet Kitty could tell that the collapse of the case had been a relief. She glanced at the door. They were alone.

'That bag of coke, Bryson...'

He nodded.

'What about it?'

'It must be tempting sometimes.' She raised her eyebrows. 'To fix things?'

He turned to look at her. 'You think I'd do that?'

'I know you believe in the law.'

'I believe in justice, Kitty. It's not always quite the same thing.'

Bryson looked down, twisting his wedding ring around his finger.

* * *

Gordon Campbell slit open a pack of ginger snaps with his thumbnail. 'Help yourself, Locky.' He fanned the biscuits across the plate and waved his hand, inviting her to his banquet. 'We're all very proud of you, Lockwood. It's important to me that you know that.'

Kitty crunched her biscuit. A crumb escaped her lips and rolled across the desk. Campbell affected not to notice, though his eyes darted back to the morsel every few seconds. 'I knew, if push came to shove, you'd hack it.' Campbell rested his elbows on the arm of the chair. 'How are you feeling?'

'Now and then I can smell smoke. Apart from that, I'm good

...' She ran a hand over her scalp. 'Though I'm thinking of getting a wig.'

Campbell nodded.

'Blonde,' she said. 'Time for a change ...'

He put his fingers together and tapped them against his lip.

'I regret what happened. I hate any of my team to suffer. Human resources is two words. And the first one ...' He held up a finger. 'So, if you need more time off, just let me know!' He waved the magic hand. This was a new experience, seeing Campbell on the back foot. She enjoyed it.

'I'd rather work than hang about at home. If that's OK.'

Campbell ran his finger along the edge of the desk. 'You thought there was a problem. And you were right.'

'I stumbled into what was happening, sir. It was no great insight.'

'You showed guts. As a team, I think we can all take satisfaction from that.'

'That's very kind of you, sir.' She sipped her tea. 'And the team ...' The afternoon sun slanted across the desk. There was a change in the air, an early hint of autumn. 'While I'm in credit, I wonder if I can ask a favour?'

'If it's in my power.'

'Drop the charges against Kevin Robb.'

'Why would we want to do that?'

'I think he deserves it.'

'I'll have a word.'

'Thank you.'

'I'm glad we've had this ...' His finger moved back and forth across the arm of the chair.

'And I've decided to put in for my exams,' said Kitty.

'Is that so?' Campbell tapped his fingers on the edge of the

CHAPTER FIFTY

desk.

'I want to move out of uniform.'

'Do you?' He nodded, eyebrows raised. 'Is that so?'

* * *

Three weeks later Kitty walked into the canteen at Shaftoe Leazes. She was met by whistles and a round of ironic applause. Kitty squeezed between Orla Harrington and Des Tucker, while Elayne brought her a mug of tea and a slab of chocolate cake. No-one mentioned the blonde wig that covered the stubble on her head.

'Mad was he?' said Tucker. 'Your nutter?'

'The millionaire,' said Orla, twisting a strand of hair around her fingertip. Kitty shrugged.

'He was used to getting his own way. So if he was thwarted, someone had to pay.' She looked around the table. 'It's the 'common pattern of male rage,' Des.'

'Yeah, yeah ...' Tucker yawned.

'His world fell apart, so he got angry. In the end he knew he'd lose everything. So he smashed it up.'

'If I can't have it, then no-one will,' murmured Elayne.

'Men spray their rage outwards.' Kitty spoke softly, knowing she would be teased. 'Women direct it at themselves.'

Des Tucker nodded gravely, stroking his chin. 'Talking of spraying...'

Kitty pulled off her wig and dropped it on Tucker's head. He ran his fingers through the curls and pouted.

As the laughter died the conversation moved on to their plans for the evening. Their appetite for criminal psychology was easily sated: they faced it every working day.

Kitty sipped her tea and looked around the table. She was enjoying the banter, she realised, even the cruel jokes. This was how they coped with the job. For the first time, it all made sense.

* * *

She had an odd feeling when she thought of Richard Kane. When she accused him of killing his father, it had been 'intuition.' A lucky guess, but one she knew to be correct. Proving his guilt, however, would be another matter.

When you're dead, you're dead.

The ordeal proved that she was stronger than she knew. When death seemed inevitable, it gave her a kind of freedom. She had chosen to be brave; she had nothing to lose. It was a while, she realised, since the Voice had spoken to her. And that felt good.

Tonight she would go back to Master Rafael's class in the village hall. On Saturday, she would take Molly to town. And on Monday she would work again. *Love and work.*

In the end, all we have is other people – friends and family, those we love and those we like. Her mobile chimed. She moved away from the table to listen. The clipped tones of Carole Robb scoured her ear.

'When's Kevin's case coming up? You just piss him around! You drag him to court then you can't be arsed to turn up!'

'Mrs Robb,' said Kitty, as she walked into the corridor. The canteen door closed behind her.

'Carole. You have no idea how good it is to hear your voice…'

Exclusive

GET A FREE EXCLUSIVE KITTY LOCKWOOD STORY

Building up a readership for my books is one of best things about publishing. I occasionally send newsletters about the Kitty Lockwood Crime Mystery Series with details on new releases, special offers, competitions and insights into my writing.

When you sign up I'll send you an exclusive Kitty Lockwood short story 'Another Year.'

You can get the short story by signing up to **www.kittylockwood.com**

Reviews

Enjoy this book? You can make a huge difference.

Whilst I do everything to get readers to see my publications, it can be difficult without big advertising budgets. But I think I have something far more powerful than money can buy, and it's my readers.

Honest reviews of my books can make a big difference to whether anyone discovers my writing. If you have three to five minutes spare I would love you to give Cars Just Want To Be Rust a review, so that others can discover this book and the Kitty Lockwood series. It doesn't have to be long, just a couple of lines if possible.

Thank you very much.

Also by Tony Glover

The **Kitty Lockwood** story continues....

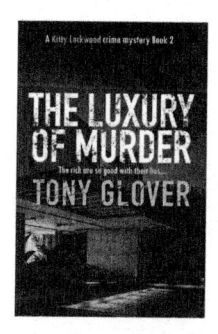

The Luxury Of Murder (Book 2)
At the same time a rich patron of the arts is attacked, a crazed assailant decapitates a businessman in a hotel. Are the two crimes connected? Newly appointed Detective Sergeant Kitty Lockwood steps in to solve a presumed case of jealousy. But as she delves into the suffocating opulence of the art elite, lips stay sealed and soon Kitty finds herself fighting to save all that is dear to her. Will she crack beneath the pressure? Someone lurking in the shadows with a samurai sword, will stop at nothing to turn the odds against her.

Footsteps Of The Hunter (Book 3)
When a school teacher finds the body of a Afghan veteran hanging in a forest, only DCI Kitty Lockwood believes it's murder. As the teacher's life spins out of control, he escapes with a schoolgirl and heads for the Italian/French border. Plagued by her own demons, Kitty goes in pursuit. But the schoolgirl's family have dark ties to the Corsican mafia. As time closes in, Kitty races to untangle the mystery of the soldier's death and save the girl. But has the hunter already become the hunted?

The Hunger Of Ravens (Book 4)

When a human jawbone is washed up on a beach, only Kitty Lockwood's persistence connects it to Spyder, a young drug dealer, who disappeared at a farm six years ago. Determined to find out why he was murdered, Kitty encounters the resistance of both criminals and the police alike. But when a close colleague tries to kill one of the suspects, Kitty has to make choices, between loyalty and the truth.

Printed in Great Britain
by Amazon